THE STRANGER'S GUIDE TO

Talliston

THE STRANGER'S GUIDE TO

Talliston

JOHN TARROW

Matador
Unit E2 Airfield Business Park,
Harrison Road, Market Harborough,
Leicestershire. LE16 7UL
Tel: 0116 2792299
Email: books@troubador.co.uk
Web: www.troubador.co.uk/matador
Twitter: @matadorbooks

ISBN 978 1805140 979

British Library Cataloguing in Publication Data.
A catalogue record for this book is available from the British Library.

Printed and bound by CPI Group (UK) Ltd, Croydon, CR0 4YY
Typeset in 12pt Bembo by Troubador Publishing Ltd, Leicester, UK

Matador is an imprint of Troubador Publishing Ltd

CONTENTS

IV

FOURTH MOON: WOLF MOON (OF BEASTS)

MANSE L'ESTRANGE

BAYOU ST JOHN, LOUISIANA, USA

MONDAY 4 JANUARY 1954 | 07:34:36

V

FIFTH MOON: STORM MOON (OF NATURE: SEA)

THE LIGHTKEEPER'S HOUSE

TRANØY, HAMARØY, NORWAY

SUNDAY 9 FEBRUARY 1986 | 08:29:06

VI

SIXTH MOON: EAGLE MOON (OF BIRDS)

TIGH SAMHRAIDH

BOYNE VALLEY, COUNTY MEATH, IRELAND

SUNDAY 26 MARCH 1933 | 11:45:21

VII

SEVENTH MOON: SNOW (OF NATURE: LAND)

WISAKEDJAK LODGE

KINGSMERE LAKE, SASKATCHEWAN, CANADA

FRIDAY 9 APRIL 1948 | 13:07:05

VIII

EIGHTH MOON: HARE MOON (OF BEASTS)

THE WAYSTATION AT TZU

D'ARKADIA, 12TH MOON, MALORIAN STARSTATION

MONDAY 8 MAY 2282 | 14:59:12

II
SECOND MOON: BLOOD MOON (OF MAN)
PALAZZO DI OMBRE
SACRO MONTE DI VARESE, LOMBARDY, ITALY
TUESDAY 24 NOVEMBER 1992 | 02:42:16

IX
NINTH MOON: THUNDER MOON (OF NATURE: SKY)
RAVNSBRAE MANOR
STONEHAVEN, SCOTLAND, UNITED KINGDOM
MONDAY 26 JUNE 1911 | 17:23:49

X
TENTH MOON: HONEY MOON (OF MAN)
EISH AL KAMAR
ALHAMBRA, GRANADA, SPAIN
SATURDAY 16 JULY 1977 | 18:56:01

XI
ELEVENTH MOON: OWL MOON (OF BIRDS)
TREVELYAN VEAN
NEW YORK, NEW YORK, USA
MONDAY 5 AUGUST 1929 | 21:18:09

II
SECOND MOON: BLOOD MOON (OF MAN)
PALAZZO DI OMBRE
SACRO MONTE DI VARESE, LOMBARDY, ITALY
TUESDAY 24 NOVEMBER 1992 | 02:42:16

XII

TWELFTH MOON: STAG MOON (OF BEASTS)

SAN PHRA PHUM

KAMPONG PHLUK, TONLÉ SAP, CAMBODIA

SATURDAY 25 SEPTEMBER 1965 | 23:17:51

XIII

THIRTEENTH MOON: OAK MOON (OF TREES)

BAH–HAS–TKIH

MONUMENT VALLEY, ARIZONA, USA

MONDAY 12 OCTOBER 2015 | 00:00:00

O

ALL GODS' DAY (MIDNIGHT)

NO. 51 NEWTON GREEN

GREAT DUNMOW, ESSEX, UNITED KINGDOM

NOW

FOR MY MOTHER, JEAN,
WHO TAUGHT ME TO BELIEVE

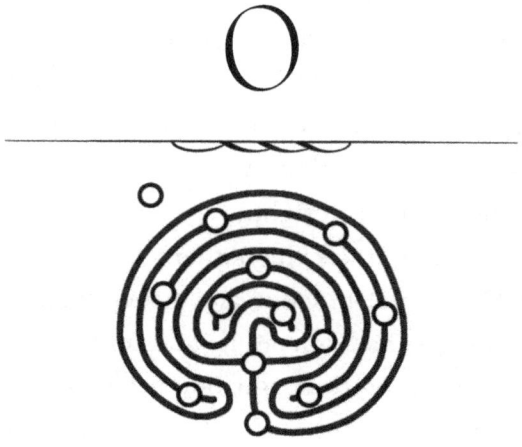

ALL GODS' DAY (MIDNIGHT)
NO. 51 NEWTON GREEN
GREAT DUNMOW, ESSEX, UNITED KINGDOM
NOW

THE BOY LIVED ALL ALONE in an old abandoned school bus in the middle of a wooded roundabout. His father had once called it the magic roundabout, but the boy didn't know why. He wanted to believe in magic, just like his mother. But if magic did exist, it certainly didn't exist anywhere around here.

The boy's name was Joseph, but everyone called him Joe. Everyone meant his father and mother – and the strangers that offered them sanctuary on the road. For as long as he could remember, Joe's parents had been on the run. Thomas and Laverna Darkin never stayed anywhere for very long, and everywhere they did, they found a safe house where they could lie low in emergencies. The bus was one of those places and where Joe had gone on the night he and his parents were attacked. The roundabout was large and densely packed with trees so tall that travellers to the motorway or the airport or the nearby villages and towns never knew the boy and the bus were there at all. Like the wood, the bus was there long before the overpass, the roads and the tarmac that surrounded it, and now both the trees and the vehicle were intertwined. His father said the bus was hiding in plain sight, and the boy knew everything there was to know about *that*. He spent every day hiding in plain sight.

On the night of the attack, his father's last words to him were, "Go, son, run! Go to the hideout and never look back. We'll get there when we can." Joe had done as he said, and he hadn't seen them since. That was a very long time ago, but as he had no electricity to power anything, he didn't know the date, and sometimes not even the day of the week. He got up when he woke and went to bed when it got too dark to see or do anything. The boy could not be certain how long he had been living rough in the bus. All summer at least. Joe spent every night fearing his parents would never come back for him.

And every day Joe spent following The Rules.

To keep him safe, his father had made his son memorise a whole heap of dos and don'ts. These weren't the usual things like 'Always Eat At The Table' and 'Don't Jump On The Sofas'. It was strange stuff, like 'Formulate Contingency Escape Routes' and 'If It Howls, Feed It'. Over time, Joe had simplified that list and now it looked like this:

RULE #1: NOWHERE IS SAFE

RULE #2: ALWAYS HAVE A WAY OUT

RULE #3: BE INVISIBLE

RULE #4: DON'T MAKE FRIENDS

RULE #5: DO NOT TALK TO DEAD PEOPLE

Then there was the most important rule of all. The One Rule To Ring Them All. The rule Joe must *never* break.

A GOOD BOY TAKES HIS MEDICINE

Joe had been born sick. He had a rare disease that had a very long name and meant that if the boy placed too much strain on his body, his heart would break and he would die. The doctors had discovered this when he was five, during hospital visits after a bad accident. To treat this condition, Joe had a bottle of medication that he had to take every thirteen hours. No matter if it was midnight or breakfast or when Joe was in the bath or taking a dump. Joe wore a clockwork timer around his neck and when the countdown reached zero, wherever he was, whatever he was doing, he had to take his medication. It was another rule on top of all the other rules. The rules that governed every day of his stupid existence. Joe lived his life by these two truths: The Rules kept him safe and The Medicine kept him alive.

Which had been all well and good until today. Because this afternoon he had drained the last mouthful of the thick, white, foul-tasting liquid. Now the ribbed brown bottle was empty and had to get some more. Automatically Joe had twisted the timer to thirteen and it began its countdown, quietly ticking away his final hours.

It was a curiously warm evening, stuck somewhere between summer and autumn, and the boy prepared to head out to the nearby town. He'd finished all the bottled water and his stores of crisps and baked beans were also dangerously low. Being a teenager and with all the normal children back at school, Joe tried not to be spotted outside during the day. He couldn't use his bike and he couldn't go scavenging. So he was waiting for that perfect time between after school and before dark, when a boy on his bike with a bag of shopping would seem like the most natural thing in the world. Though there was emergency cash at the bus, he used it sparingly, preferring instead to scavenge what he could. He had no prescription and nothing save the label on the bottle to identify The Medicine. Still, he had to try even if it meant throwing a brick through a chemist's window and braving the consequences. He knew he had to go before he got too weak or too desperate.

So now Joe sat outside beside his mountain bike and waited for dusk. While he waited, he played with his Wolverine action figure. The maverick superhero was who Joe wanted to be. With his super-strength and super-healing, Wolverine never quit. His skeleton of pure adamantium never tired or wore down. His ability to regenerate pretty much any part of himself within seconds made him invincible. Joe sighed, envious to own even a millionth of the superhero's abilities. Life wouldn't be so dark and ugly then. It would be unthinkably brilliant.

In the deepening twilight, the school bus shone bottle green, edged with a curved crown of rust. The front ended in a large snout, while the rear was one big doorway, shielded by a sagging fabric porch. Inside all the seating had been unbolted and pushed against the walls, making space for a table and for sleeping. There was a plaque by the front door that announced the bus had been manufactured by GMC Truck & Coach Division in Michigan, USA.

"This bus is American," his father had told him. "It's 1940s, judging by the shape of it. I guess it came over in the war, got parked in this wood and now it's never gonna leave."

I know how it feels, thought Joe. It's abandoned and alone, just like me.

It hadn't always been like this. When Joe was very young and they lived in Cornwall, his parents took him everywhere. But that world felt a million miles away, and the boy rarely allowed himself to think of that golden age before the wood and the bus. Yes, he was lonely and scared. He went hungry most days. But the worst feeling wasn't being lonely or scared or hungry. It was the knowledge that this was all his fault. He was to blame for being cast aside like a broken toy.

The thought of leaving the wooded roundabout filled him with dread, while in his mind his parents' voices rang like great bells of doom.

"We can't protect you, son, if you don't follow The Rules," his father said.

His mother added, "The doctors can't cure you, if you don't take The Medicine."

Joe's forehead beaded with sweat. His hands shook. In the quiet of the clearing, his fragile heart hammered. Anxiously the boy fumbled for the timer. As he held it in his slick palm he saw the marker was already well past seven. He had to go.

His mother had said that the longest a murdered person had lain unidentified was on a roundabout and this made the hideout a safe place. Even when winter came – and Joe was not looking forward to that at all – the bus would be all but invisible from the road. For now the wood was filled with crisp copper leaves, only just hinting at the scarlet and faded gold they would become. Joe concentrated on the leaves and calmed his rising panic.

With barely a sound of beating wings, the dark form of the crow appeared on the table beside where the boy was sitting. Griswald was his only friend, the solitary companion the boy allowed himself. It was easily the biggest bird he had ever seen, though where that strange name had come from he had no idea. Had he heard his father use it once? The crow was a frequent visitor to the farmhouse and had found this secret camp the first day Joe had arrived here.

"Cr–r–ruck," croaked Griswald as he landed upon the side of the table.

5

"Yes, of course I'm still here," said Joe. "No one's come back today." The crow clucked as if scolding him, tapping the table with his formidable beak. "I'm not like you. I can't just up and fly away. If I do, how will they ever find me?" This was how their conversations went, with Joe imagining the crow's cawing and chattering as questions and reprimands. "Do you think they're ever coming back? Maybe they feel they're better off without me."

The crow stood so close Joe could easily reach out and touch him, though the boy decided against it. That long scimitar beak looked far too dangerous. The bird let out a longer cry. He sounded hungry. Joe showed Griswald his empty hands.

"No food," he said, and shrugged. "Maybe later."

The bird responded by hopping backwards, then bobbing and staring at Joe as if trying to tell him something. In the creature's black eyes all of Joe's world – the bus, the wood and himself – was reflected, like a life drowned in a bottomless lake. It was all the boy could do not to shout, "I know! It's all my fault! I'm responsible for this mess. A good boy should always take his medicine." The two regarded each other for a moment more, then with a flow of dark wings, the bird was gone. As he vanished, Griswald filled the wood with another echoing croak, and this one definitely sounded nothing like a caw for food.

This one sounded like a warning.

Off through the trees, branches snapped. Something was approaching. Mum! Dad! It was them. They were back!

With a sudden burst of blue and red, a dozen sirens filled the wood from end to end with sound and light. Joe leapt to his feet in terror. Instantly the trees were alive with shadows as searchlights seared away the gathering darkness and filled it with blazing brightness. Struck cold with fear, Joe froze like a rabbit in headlights. He stifled a cry for help, knowing a trap had been sprung. It wasn't his parents. No one was coming for him. He had to do this on his own.

Just like he had on that last night with his mother and father.

With luck, he was all set to leave. Grabbing his rucksack, Joe swung the pack over his shoulder and straddled his bike, then was off. Pedalling as fast as he could, he headed away from the sirens and the searchlights, muttering, "Rule Two. Rule Two. Always Have A Way Out," under his breath. Large shapes moved between the trees, a ring of people closing in on all sides except one. The grassy escarpment that led to the overpass. Thankfully he'd spent many hours planning contingency escape routes and he was sure of his path. Taking a self-cleared dirt track, Joe dropped gears and pumped furiously as the route started to rise steeply. Suddenly he felt a sharp pain in his chest. It was his heart. Without his medication, overexerting himself could be fatal. The boy dismounted and pushed the heavy bike up the slope. Snatching glances behind him, he grabbed only glimpses of his pursuers. They all wore hooded coats, their faces just black pits. Joe didn't know how they had found the hideout, knew only that he had to escape. If only he had more medicine.

At the top of the escarpment Joe climbed back on his bike and headed down the hill. Pedalling faster and faster as he descended, he ducked torch beams and then he was freewheeling off the pavement, past the white sign that read PRIORY WOOD ROUNDABOUT and across three lanes of traffic. Cars swerved and lorry horns blared. The boy winced at the thought of being pulverised under their enormous tyres, but gravity was in control now. Somehow he wasn't crushed or hit. Instead he careered the wrong way down a littered filter lane, up another bank and into a cluster of trees.

With the bus and the roundabout hideout discovered, Joe had no idea of where he should go. Initially his only thought was of escape. Now he stopped, dismounted and dragged the mountain bike into the V-shaped channel of a disused railway line maps named the Flitch Way. The tracks were gone, leaving behind a weed-choked hollow that ran all the way from the motorway alongside the villages. Joe knew this was risky – for a kid on a bicycle this would be a fairly obvious route – but the base of the cutting was relatively flat and obstacle-free. Most importantly it kept him off the roads.

In his mind, he heard his mother yelling, "Stop snivelling! You did this. You brought this on yourself. On all of us." He knew she was right. He'd brought all this upon them.

Joe shivered as the evening turned ever colder. Where should he go? Lifting his sweaty palms off the handlebars, he focused on what he'd been taught on making critical decisions under pressure. In a crisis situation even if you were scared or hurt or people were dead and dying, doing nothing was not an option. It all boiled down to doing something. To making a decision. He needed The Medicine. He needed food and shelter, a place to hide. All those things were found in the town. He had to head for Great Dunmow.

The boy felt sick to his stomach just thinking about it, but it seemed to tick all the boxes. Before the bus and the attack, Joe and his parents had lodged in an isolated farmhouse on the edge of the market town. It was the last place he'd seen his parents. He didn't want to return there – not after what had happened – but he could think of nowhere else to go.

Passing under old Victorian railway bridges, he made his way slowly east. Joe would have killed to have Wolverine's ability to pinpoint an enemy and sense incoming danger right now. A couple of times he heard the gunning of car engines in the night and once he hid in a thicket as torch beams darted overhead in the trees, but otherwise he heard and saw nothing.

Well after dark, Joe emerged from the old railway line, wheeled his muddy bike over a wooden plank bridge and back onto the road that led into the town. The night was clear and though there were stars, there was no moon. Now was the hard part. He knew how to blend in, but the problem was that in these empty streets, at this hour – he guessed it must be approaching ten o'clock, maybe even as late as eleven – not raising suspicions would be tricky. A young boy on a bicycle would be something noteworthy. Especially to those in an official capacity.

Level head, he thought. Eyes straight. Remember The Rules.

Nowhere Is Safe. Always Have A Way Out. Do Not Talk To Dead People.

'Dead People' was what the boy called everyone else. He imagined all the people on the planet were now flesh-eating zombies and it turned the task of avoidance and evasion into a game. That way if he ended up meeting people he was trying to avoid or was trapped in an awkward situation, it gave him a way to respond.

Even when he had taken The Medicine, he rarely ran. A fast person was far more noticeable than a slow person. He had to avoid bumping into people who would ask if he was lost or where he was going. To avoid these questions, he'd been taught to slow down, look thoughtful and move with purpose.

Entering the edge of the town, Joe kept his head down and cycled on. He passed a guesthouse and saw he was heading towards a thatched pub. Outside smokers crowded the area beside the car park.

Look straight ahead, he told himself. Steady, natural pace.

Before him a sleek black car was parked half in the car park, half across the pavement. Its bonnet was stuck right across Joe's path. A bald man was standing beside the vehicle talking with the regulars. In his hand he held a large torch, and seeing this Joe's throat tightened. Without thinking he started cycling a little faster and at that exact moment the figure looked up and right at him. The boy's heart leapt and he swerved involuntarily out into the road. It was all the indication the man needed. Immediately he jumped into the car and the engine sprang to life. Joe knew he couldn't outrun a vehicle. He needed to be invisible. Now. Instantly he was furiously pedalling, making the wheels spin as fast as he could. He didn't look back. Immediately opposite the pub was a way off the main road, and he sped down it, desperately searching for a place to hide.

He wasn't far down the lane when Joe realised he'd made a big mistake. The narrow road led into a wide circle of semi-detached council houses set around a green. It was a dead end. There was no way out. At his back he heard his pursuer's engine and knew he only had seconds before he was caught. Swerving right, he mounted the kerb and tried to keep himself as close to the garden walls and hedges as he could. The car entered the cul-de-sac and thankfully turned left. Its headlights swept the entire green and Joe could see if he had chosen that way he would have been spotted. While this was some comfort, he also realised that he was far from safe. Once the car had made a full circuit of the road, Joe would be seen for sure.

It was then that he caught sight of the giant black bird.

Griswald was sitting on the pavement about ten feet away. In the light from the street lamps, Joe saw the bird was standing on a lump of something dead. What was he doing here? Had he killed some poor child's beloved pet? Skidding to a halt, Joe found the thing was a giant rat and probably once lived in the horror house that stood before him. For while the other properties on the green were in good repair, this one was wild and neglected. The front garden was surrounded by a hedge that was so overgrown it resembled an immense thorny thicket. It was so tall that nothing could be seen of the house except the very top of the chimney. Almost invisible in the dense foliage was a low iron gate, but even that was overgrown and twisted with brambles.

Hanging upon the gate was a big, rusted sign that read DANGEROUS BUILDING. KEEP OUT.

"Great place to hide, Griswald," the boy said, but there was no time for sarcasm. The car was almost upon him. Pushing his bike into the hedge, Joe pressed on the gate, but found it impossible to move. Thorns cut into his hands making him flinch away. The car turned the last curve, its stark headlights already sweeping across the next-door neighbour's fence. Desperately, the boy threw his whole body against the iron gate, and this time the branches and brambles gave way. He half-fell through the dark opening, crashing to the ground. It was not a moment too soon.

Headlights shone through the leaves, illuminating where he had just been standing but finding only empty pavement. Griswald took flight, a swift silhouette against the brightness, then was gone. Closely followed by the lights and the growl of the engine.

Danger passed and Joe allowed himself to get back to his feet. He still needed The Medicine, supplies and a new place to hide, but at least for now he'd escaped.

"Don't move a muscle," said a rough, growling voice in his ear.

I

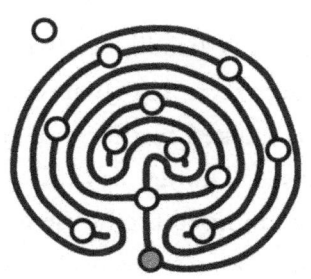

FIRST MOON: HUNTER'S MOON (OF MAN)
THE OLD RECTORY
GREAT DUNMOW, ESSEX, UNITED KINGDOM
WEDNESDAY 13 OCTOBER 1852 | 00:01:11

THE VOICE WAS LOW, GRUFF and very, very close. Joe's body went stiff, feeling the monstrous presence of the dead person behind him. Do Not Talk To Dead People, he thought, but there was nothing for it. Silence was not an option now. "Don't hurt me," Joe said to the darkness. "I didn't mean to trespass. I was—"

"Never you mind what you was doing," came the voice again. Now the boy could feel something hard pressed into the small of his back. "What are you doing *here*?"

"I was hiding from…" Joe didn't know what to say. Who was he hiding from? Twisting around, Joe looked over his shoulder into the face of his captor and was surprised to find it was only another teenager. Though his voice was very deep with a coarse London accent, he was no more than a few years older than Joe. He had a gaunt face and cropped hair, shadowed under a dark hoodie. Just like the—

"Are you… one of them?" Joe knew he sounded stupid, but that's what came out.

"Gunner's just Gunner and I ain't with no one. Who are you?"

"I'm… Joe," he said.

Above them, another car's headlights swept through the thorny hedge. Was it Joe's pursuers retracing their steps? Looking for where he'd vanished? Both boys ducked further into the darkness at the base of the wall, and Joe realised Gunner also didn't want to be found. As the silver light passed, Joe glimpsed the house for the first time. Beyond the wilderness of the garden rose a ramshackle overgrown door framed by boarded windows. He also saw that Gunner was holding a large book and guessed this was what he'd felt against his back.

What should he do now? He knew he couldn't go. Not yet. Not with the terrifying prospect of being caught. So he decided he would have to wait. Wait and talk to Gunner. But when he began speaking, the older boy cut him off.

"You here for the house?" He sounded both suspicious and threatening.

"No," said Joe. "I just got lost."

Gunner snorted. "Lost? Yeah, that's what it wants you to think. That you just stumbled in here by mistake." Joe thought of the crow and all that had happened that evening. "Come take a look."

Joe didn't trust Gunner one bit, but he needed to keep the situation quiet and contained. And, sometimes, even Dead People had their uses. Anyhow, the way he was acting, it seemed like maybe Gunner had a use for him too.

The boys headed towards the derelict building, though Joe tripped at every step. It's so dark, he thought. Within the boundaries of the tall hedge the orange street lights hardly penetrated. Fishing in his bag, he fumbled for his torch.

"Whatcha doing?" asked Gunner.

"I can't see a thing."

"No lights for now. Let your eyes adjust."

"Is there a path?"

"No. Make your own."

Walking up to the derelict house, they passed through taller plants while above large swathes of ivy crawled across the brickwork. There was an air of desolation all around, from the boarded windows to the rotted woodwork. The front door was secured by three rusty bars, each one fitted with a formidable padlock.

It's in the middle of this ordinary street, but it's like a house in the woods, he thought. Or a bus on a roundabout. Abandoned and alone.

Gunner led him to the boarded downstairs window and pointed to a rotten corner that exposed dirty glass beyond.

"Now you can look," Gunner instructed, gesturing to Joe's torch.

Joe flicked it on, almost blinding himself, and pressed it against the hole. Inside the room was a chamber of horrors. The carpet was gone, the floorboards bare and scattered with debris. The wind and rain had stripped the walls of paper and colour, and circular water stains made dark pools on the plaster ceiling. Along the window ledge beneath the shredded remains of once-orange curtains he noticed tiny animal tracks. Over by the fireplace the entire wall was hung with hundreds of cocoons, each silky chrysalis twitching in the invading brightness. The whole place was infested. Had the owners died? And if so, why was it left derelict and not sold to someone else? These and other questions lingered in the cracks and corners, along with the dusty spiderwebs and encroaching ivy. When the people moved away, the night creatures had moved in. And perhaps – Joe shivered – other things.

The house is like me, he thought bitterly. Infected with an incurable disease. But this reminded him only of the empty medicine bottle he carried and the urgent reason he was here.

Something chattered close by the boy's head, and he jumped in fright. The unseen creature skittered along the window ledge and down onto the back of a threadbare sofa.

"It's just a deserted old wreck," Joe said, flicking off his torch. "What makes this place so special?"

"This is the house that swallowed my sister."

The way Gunner said this sent chills down Joe's spine. Joe turned and saw the older boy's face. It was deadly serious. Swallowed? Joe didn't know what to say to that. What do you want from me? he thought. Why would you even be interested in telling me this?

"But it's just a house," he said.

"No, it ain't. It's haunted and it's dangerous. She came here and went in, and she never came out. The house…" Gunner searched for the right words, "…took her."

"What? That's crazy."

Instantly Gunner turned ugly. Bad move, Joe. Very bad move.

"You piece of bull spit," the older kid spat and shoved Joe hard. He fell back, tripping on hidden rubble. As he stumbled, Gunner deftly reached out and dragged Joe's rucksack off his shoulder. Landing heavily, Joe watched as Gunner pulled out his own torch. It looked much like Joe's but when he flicked it on it shone deep red. Hunting torch, thought Joe. Gunner searched through Joe's bag. He didn't seem interested in the items he found there. He just pulled them out, took one look, and tossed them into the undergrowth. Everything the boy possessed and treasured was in that bag, and it never left his side. It was painful to see Gunner casually discarding the things he held so precious. "You know what the pigs told me?" he said as he did this. "After they'd searched the place?"

Joe lay on the ground like it was thin ice. Knowing this could all get out of control very quickly. "What?" he whispered.

"Children go missing all the time."

Gunner looked down at Joe and smiled a sinister smile. And Joe knew exactly what that smile meant.

He's a lunatic, Joe thought.

"Well, well. What's this?" Joe looked up and Gunner was holding his Wolverine action figure. The yellow and blue costume looked red and black in the torchlight. The hooded boy sniggered. "Looks like Joe's a little queer who plays with dolls." Taking the figure by the legs, Gunner made the superhero dance. He watched Joe squirm for a while, then laughed and tossed the toy away. Another car crawled slowly by the hedge and Gunner ducked into a crouch. Joe glared and wondered why Gunner was hiding. Why he was keeping him around. Maybe it was simply that bullies liked to have someone to tyrannise. Joe's father spoke a lot about tyranny. Usually in the same sentence as talking about his mother.

"Get up," ordered Gunner once the danger had passed. "Let's go."

"Go where?"

"Inside."

"I'm not going in there," Joe blurted.

At this Gunner's face contorted into a scowl of anger, then suddenly he was holding a fearsome serrated knife.

Perfect, thought Joe. He had a hunting torch. Why wouldn't he have a knife to go with it?

"Like hell you're not. Came here with Shane, but some bird flew in his face and he crapped himself. Stupid prick. Now I got you."

"For what?"

"To read this dumb book." For the first time Gunner mentioned the book he was carrying. It looked like an old encyclopaedia or Bible, being bulky and bound in leather. In the middle of the cover was an engraved tree, but apart from that its use or contents were a mystery. It didn't seem like the kind of book Gunner would own or read. Joe wouldn't have been surprised to learn the thug couldn't read at all.

"What's this?"

"This is the way we're gonna get inside."

Joe glanced up at the dark shadow of the house. "I'm not going in there," Joe repeated.

"You want my beef?" Gunner snarled. Joe shook his head, never taking his eyes off the blade. In the torchlight it already looked like it had been dipped in blood. "Good. 'Cause you don't want no beef with me. My pretty little sister knows that. Now you know that."

Joe began to realise what might actually have happened to Gunner's sister. Reluctantly he took the book from Gunner, opened it and looked inside. On the first page Gunner's torch illuminated a hand-drawn tower rising from a line of green trees. On the second page was the book's title.

THE

STRANGER'S GUIDE TO

THE DARK HOUSE &

DANGEROUS GARDENS

OF

TALLISTON

INCLUDING THE KEY TO

UNLOCKING ITS

IMMORTAL LABYRINTH &

THE SECRET THAT

LIES WITHIN

Joe's eyes darted from the book back up to the ramshackle building, then all around him in the darkness. At his back the wind whistled through the boarded windows as if the house was breathing. Was this

Talliston? How could a derelict council house be a labyrinth? The only labyrinth Joe had ever heard of was the Greek one with the Minotaur. None of this made sense. In Joe's mind, the rusted sign on the gate blazed in neon: DANGEROUS BUILDING. KEEP OUT. Right here and now, these sounded like the sanest four words the boy had ever heard.

"Go on," Gunner urged, stabbing the air with the knife. "Get to the part about the labyrinth and the dead moon."

Turning the page, Joe found the illustrated contents. The first chapters covered topics about places and almanacs, but the third was titled 'III Mapping the Labyrinth of the House'. Obviously this was the one Gunner was referring to.

This is such a big mistake, Joe thought. I need my medicine. I need to get away. Even getting caught was better than this craziness. Slamming the book closed, he offered it back to the older boy.

"What you doing?" spat Gunner.

"Look, I'm sorry about your sister. I really am, but…"

"But *what*?"

"But I think you'd be better off sorting this out yourself."

The slap came out of nowhere. One moment Joe was offering over the book. The next he was on his knees, cupping his stinging cheek in both palms. Above him Gunner loomed, then his mouth was close to Joe's ear and he was hissing, "Don't mess with me. You wanna be cut? Huh, do ya?" Joe's eyes gleamed wet, but he forced himself not to cry. The pain brought back other pains. Vivid memories of the last time he hadn't taken his medicine.

IT WAS THE START OF summer and Joe's birthday, and they had been living for the past few months in the Great Dunmow farmhouse. This was owned by a couple called Aunt and Uncle B, though the boy knew from long experience they were not relatives. The five of them had been preparing a barbecue in the orchard for Joe's thirteenth birthday. It was to be a special day, one that they had all been planning for weeks, and then this morning his mother had ruined everything by announcing that this weekend on the farm would be their last.

Joe had hated not having friends and being invisible to everyone, but the news that they were moving again was unbearable. This was not just a few hours away to Exeter or Bristol or Welwyn Garden City. No, this was to another country. This was to the middle of nowhere in Scotland.

Even though the sun had just set, the evening was still warm and humid. The trees glowed in the last light of the day, while above the cloudless sky began turning an inky blue. It would have been the perfect evening for a birthday barbecue, but now the circular garden table, the floral plates and bowls, the flickering candles in red jam jars had been abandoned. The grill stood unlit, the trays of meat and vegetables forgotten. Every door to the house was open, and from inside his parents and fake relatives could be heard searching every room, in every drawer and cupboard. Searching for where he'd hidden his medication. Joe couldn't care less. He sat on the swing bench under the ancient apple trees that lined the far wall of the garden. In his lap he cradled an Uncanny X-Men comic, but he had no interest in its contents.

He'd had enough. He wasn't going.

He wanted to stay here and pretend he was one of the boys in the playing fields he saw from his window. Why had they told him on his birthday? Of all the days to pick, why choose that one? Because they were cruel and heartless – and didn't give a toss what he thought or wanted.

To Joe, the best thing about Wolverine wasn't that he was consistently awesome or that he regenerated pretty much any part of him within seconds. No, it was that Wolverine didn't follow The Rules.

Joe gritted his teeth and forced his hands under his thighs.

My only power is this, he thought over and over as he sat on the iron bench. My only power is *this*.

Last night he'd decided to get sick. Because sick boys couldn't travel. And if he died that would serve them right. They deserved it. They'd probably welcome being rid of him. If he had to take medicine to survive, then he was never meant to live. At four in the morning the clockwork countdown had reached zero, waking the boy with its fierce buzzing. And he had done nothing. Well, if you called breaking The Rules nothing. Instead he had crept to the bathroom and hidden every last bottle of The Medicine he could find.

His mother's frantic voice burst from somewhere inside the house, making Joe squirm on the bench. She sounded angrier than he'd ever heard her. "The problem with bad children is they don't listen – and they never learn." The boy scanned the open windows in fear and that's when he saw the creeping shapes crawling from between the bushes along the side of the farmhouse. They moved like dark water through the shadows and in their hands blades glinted. There was a moment where he sat up very straight, the comic falling to the ground, the grown-ups feeling so far away as to be already lost in the Highlands.

Then the evening, and all evenings after that, changed forever…

NUMBLY JOE LIFTED HIS HEAD stared into Gunner's screwed-up face. It was threatening more violence and pain. Not wanting to be hurt again, the younger boy dropped his eyes and said nothing.

"Good," said Gunner. "Now let's pick up where we left off."

Joe retrieved the book and opened it again. He turned the crackling pages, found the right chapter and by the blood-red light started reading. Whoever had written this guide had lived many years ago. The sentences were long and very formal. This section explained about how labyrinths were very old and differed from mazes by having only one path to the centre. The next page talked about entering the labyrinth and then there was the section Gunner had referred to.

The Dead Moon was the dark of the moon, a period that lasted three days between the phases of the lunar cycle.

Joe looked up at the pitch-black sky above.

"Is the dark of the moon tonight?" he asked.

"Yeah. It happens just after midnight."

"What does?"

"You'll see." Gunner pulled up his jacket to reveal a bulky watch. The face glittered in sickly green. "So now we wait."

"What for?"

"The crack in the night, you little shit."

And so the two boys – the one with the book and the one with the knife – waited for the precise moment of the crack in the night. Joe hated waiting as it felt like he was standing looking into a dark pool. Time felt still and immeasurably deep. As it got later and later, the lights in the houses turned off. Soon only the street lamps were left, and then they too faded to black. It was like the entire world was shutting down. Now the only illumination was the red torch and the distant glow of the airport reflected off the black sky.

Once it reached midnight, Gunner kept checking his watch. Counting down to the appointed moment. Joe wanted to check his timer, but dared not reveal it to the older boy. So he just sat and tried to stay calm. He was almost asleep when the older boy finally announced the time had come.

"Ten seconds," he said suddenly. "Five…"

At first the house and garden looked and felt no different, then it changed. The near night gathered and deepened, falling in waves as if the air were actually water and the entire world was sinking into the depths of a bottomless ocean. If Joe had thought it dark before, now every shred of light from the houses was extinguished. All traces of the haze from the airport and motorway were gone. Even the red hunting torch dimmed, diminishing to nothing.

All that was left was thick inky black, an oil-slick darkness that kept getting darker.

Darker.

Darker.

Blacker.

Blacker.

Black.

Joe felt he was going to suffocate, to be crushed under the weight of that impenetrable night. There was a stomach-churn feeling of falling, of missed footing on an unexpected step. Joe struggled not to cry out and then the immense tension broke. There was an audible splintering, a terrible sound like ice breaking underfoot. Joe shivered as the pitch black receded, and then he was rising out of the inky blackness back into normal night-time. Suddenly stars and planets appeared above and Joe marvelled. He had never seen so many or so clearly. Yet that was not the most startling alteration. As the torch burst back to life, the boy found himself no longer standing beside a derelict and overgrown council house. Now the ruin was replaced by a much taller building. The street was gone, and in its place spread a wide expanse of formal garden. Gone too were the weeds and rubble. Now the boy crouched upon wide flagstones. These formed a rough cross and at its centre stood a huge, rough-hewn stone. It was easily a head taller than even Gunner and reminded Joe of Stonehenge. Around it other smaller stones stood, along with beds of neatly clipped hedges packed with flowers. The scent of the blooms was overpowering. Gone was the smell of the airport. In its place the air smelled sweeter, tinged with wood smoke.

Gunner was smiling, his crooked teeth all displayed like a predatory animal about to strike. Lifting the torch, he pointed it at the stone. And there Joe saw cut deeply into the face a carved circular maze. No, not a maze, he corrected himself. It was a labyrinth. Just like the drawing in the book. Its circular design wound around and around on itself in one singular path in a pattern that looked older than Time itself.

"Yes," Gunner drawled. "It wasn't a fricking fluke. It does happen every time."

Joe looked about him, searching for one thing that his eyes or nose recognised, but there was nothing. Wherever this place was, it wasn't Great Dunmow. Perhaps it wasn't even England.

The derelict building was gone. In its place stood a house straight from a tin of fancy biscuits. The front was now a large bay window with diamond glass panels. Instead of the padlocked entrance, a rose-covered porch stood, shading a black panelled door set with an oval stained-glass window. As Gunner shone the torch into the darkness around him, Joe made out brick pathways, herbs and plants. The thicket of thorns that surrounded the abandoned house was now a neatly trimmed hedge, centred by an arched wooden gate. Whatever was beyond the hedge was invisible, as nothing broke the perfect darkness, not even a single street light.

Seeing this, his mind focused upon a line he had read in the book: 'If this house is lost, we are all lost…'

"What is this place?" he managed, stunned. Inside, his guts trembled like a frightened animal.

"It's like I told you, knobhead," said Gunner. "It's where my sister went."

Joe gazed up at the carving on the stone. Along the spiralling lines, holes had been bored, each as wide as the end of a child's finger. The boy reached out and traced his hand along the path. Was it a map? Unconsciously he counted them. There were twelve – no, thirteen.

There was one last hole set outside the labyrinth, unconnected to the rest. The associations with that number sent shivers down his spine. He was thirteen. He had to take his medicine every thirteen hours.

"No, I mean, where? What happened to the house?"

"The book says it's the 'Old Rectory'. Still eleven minutes past one. Just now it's Wednesday 13th October 1852."

Eighteen fifty-two? That wasn't possible, but it did prove Gunner could read the book. "But that's over a hundred years ago."

"So?"

"Gunner!" The older boy's lack of concern was terrifying. If true, if somehow this was 1852, the Great Dunmow chemist shop would not even exist. The Medicine would be gone. He would sicken and die and no one would ever find him.

Still, it was becoming clear to Joe what Gunner thought had happened to his sister. How she could have got lost in a three-bedroomed semi. How they could all get lost and become trapped forever in wherever this was. No wonder the writer of the guide had called it dark and dangerous. Ignoring for a moment how any of this was even remotely possible, Joe's mind burned with a far greater and more urgent question. "Gunner?" he asked quietly. "How are we going to get back?"

"Get back?" The older boy didn't appear to understand the question. "Who said anything about going back?"

Joe gaped. Not going back? What had he got himself into?

Out in the perfect night there came a long, low howl. Joe's body stiffened. Up until now this night-time garden had been eerily silent, which he realised he far preferred to hearing sounds of man-eating animals.

Gunner cursed, then pushed Joe behind the stone. "It's just like before. We ain't got much time. They'll be here soon and then things get bad. We need to get to the Hall of Mirrors."

Joe decided to skip asking what that was, and who 'they' were.

Instead he said, "Can't we hide inside?"

Gunner looked from the stone to the house, weighing up their options. "Yeah," he said at last. "We need time to work things out. And I can show you where I found the book."

The howls were getting louder now and the boy imagined a wild mob marching up to some beast's castle with pitchforks and hammers, intent on murder. With a shudder, Joe thought of the birthday barbecue and the last time he had seen his parents. Then he was following Gunner onto the porch and stepping through the front door. This opened into a hall centred by an oval table crowded with plants and flowers. To the left a carved wooden staircase rose up to the first floor.

"Come on," whispered Gunner and led him deeper into the rectory. The next room contained hampers and baskets filled with food from some harvest festival gathering. Wicker seats and armchairs crowded around a fireplace, its coals smouldering a faint glow. In that light Joe could see a floor strewn with toys and a large carpet bag spilling sketchbooks and biscuit tins. Beyond the table and around the walls every available shelf or drawer was crammed with antiques of every description. But Joe saw they were not antiques. They were new.

The whole place was welcoming and comfortable, and the boy could easily imagine a large family gathering here after church on Sundays, children playing games while servants brought them hot tea on trays. This made the boy feel sad and more lost than ever. Joe looked around, trying to get his bearings, but one thing was certain. This definitely wasn't the living room he had seen through the window of the derelict council house.

"Is this the…" Joe found it difficult to finish the sentence. "Hall of Mirrors?"

"What're you stupid? Of course it ain't. C'mere." Gunner crossed to a great iron chest. He opened it to reveal an inside filled with papers and journals. "The book was in here."

Joe read some titles and found them to be baptismal, marriage and burial registers, some of which were very old.

"No book," Gunner said.

"Does that matter?"

"It sort of proves stuff."

"Stuff?"

"It proves not everything resets back. Some things can change. The book was here, now we got it, so it's gone."

Joe let that go, keeping himself concentrated on what he should do next. Everything seemed to point back to what was contained in *The Stranger's Guide*.

Moving towards the light of the fire, Joe sat in one of the wicker chairs and laid the leather book on his lap. He opened *The Stranger's Guide* and turned to the first page of the chapter called 'Places You Will Discover'. Here was a pullout map of the world, marked with locations drawn on folded tags. The map was titled 'The Thirteen Rooms of Talliston'. Again, that number. The first room was the Old Rectory, the date 1852, but there were many others. Room #2: Palazzo di Ombre 1992. Room #5: The Lightkeeper's House 1986. Room #9: Ravnsbrae Manor 1911. On the next pages were detailed sections of each location. For the rectory there was a hand-drawn diagram of the gardens from above showing the site to be that of an ancient standing stone circle. The date on that page was Wednesday 13th October 1852. The time, 00:01:11. Just after midnight.

Was it in any way conceivable this was 1852 and that they stood inside an ancient rectory house built upon a place like Stonehenge? Were all these places part of this labyrinth the book kept mentioning? Back when Joe went to school, the kids had discussed time travel, but it was not something anyone had ever convinced him actually existed.

Obviously something had occurred, but right now Joe had no idea what. And if they truly had fallen through some black doorway of the dead moon, then...

Joe wanted to read more of the book, but Gunner was already twitching anxiously at his back. "We ain't got all day." The older boy's eyes darted around the room as if every shadow held horrors. "We gotta get to the next room. Fast."

Joe said nothing, knowing not to question Gunner. Already his heart was pounding, and that reminded him just how long it'd been since taking his medication. How weak his heart was.

The older boy grabbed the book from Joe. "It's something to do with the nursery rhyme," he said as he began flipping frantically through the pages. When he found the correct place, Gunner shoved the open book back into the hands of the younger boy.

"Just read it!"

On the page was indeed a children's poem, scribbled with notes and annotations. So Joe read to himself the rhyme of the Tallis Stone.

> STONE! STONE! THE TALLIS STONE
> RING AROUND THE TALLIS STONE.
> IMMORTAL SKY: HEAVEN'S HALLS
> ETERNAL FOREST: GUARD THESE WALLS
> INFINITE OCEAN: THE DEEP UNKNOWN
> CIRCLE ROUND THE TALLIS STONE.
>
> STONE! STONE! THE TALLIS STONE
> STAND BEFORE THE TALLIS STONE.
> ENTER THIS HOUSE THOSE WHO DARE
> WHEN THE MOON IS DARK: BUT WARE!
> TO WALK WITHIN IS TO WALK ALONE

FOR DANGERS HAUNT THE TALLIS STONE.
STONE! STONE! THE TALLIS STONE
KNEEL BEFORE THE TALLIS STONE.
HERE THE LABYRINTH PATH BEGIN
TO FIND THE SECRET THAT LIES WITHIN
KEEP THE WAYS THESE WORDS HAVE SHOWN
AND PASS BEYOND THE TALLIS STONE.

"I want to go back," Joe said.

"There's no going back." The knife was again in Gunner's hand. "We must go on. I must find her."

"Master Crowe, is that you? Tobias?"

Both boys jumped at the voice. It was coming from the hall. Gunner whirled and Joe leapt up from the chair, slamming the book and almost dropping it. Rule #1: Nowhere Is Safe, his mind scolded. How had he been so careless? It was only then that Joe realised there were no other doors from this room. Rule #2: Always Have A Way Out. Stupid. Stupid. Stupid.

"Go!" Gunner snapped.

Slipping on the rugs and polished floor, they fled back into the hall. Above on a gallery stood a man in a patterned robe holding a candle lantern. He was very old, and had just risen from sleeping.

"Who is it, Nathaniel?" asked a woman's voice from off elsewhere in the house.

"It's two boys, Mary," he said firmly. "Two *strange* boys…" The way he said 'strange' made Joe's flesh creep. He was joined by a woman in a white gown. Everyone fell into shocked silence. Nobody moved. The adults stared down at the boys and the boys stared up at the adults. "What brings you to the house of dreams and nightmares?" Nathaniel asked quietly. Before anyone had a chance to answer sudden light poured through the stained-glass door. As if someone had lit a giant bonfire. In its radiance the old man saw the leather volume in Joe's hands and his eyes opened wide.

"The book. Ghûl thieves! Stop!" The pair began descending the stairs.

"Run!" shouted Gunner, picking up one of the plants and throwing it at the approaching rector and his wife.

Fleeing outside, the boys found the entire garden surrounded by flaming torches. Each was held by a hooded figure beyond the tall hedge. Joe was reminded of the attack at the roundabout. It felt so eerily similar. At the open gate stood their leader, a tall, lean man who gripped the wooden arches with bony fingers. His face was lost in the shadows of his hood, all but his nose, which jutted out like a broken stick. Flanking him stood two hounds, almost as tall as he was. Their eyes shone blood red in the torch light.

"Grim Grotesques!" spat Gunner, drawing his knife.

"Who?" Joe's mind reeled.

"Total jerks. Shaved heads. Scar." He tapped the back of his skull. "Nasty pieces of work."

"We're trapped."

"Not if you can work out that stupid book."

Joe scanned the rhyme again, but it still made no sense. The book had been written in fragments, in no discernible order, over what appeared to be a very long period of time. It was confusing and had no real explanations. All Joe could do was approach it more like a puzzle than an enchantment. I don't have time to learn all this, the boy thought desperately.

"It says to stand before the stone," Joe said. "Then to kneel."

"Do it," hissed Gunner.

Behind them the rector and his wife emerged from the house, and as they appeared the leader of the rabble shouted, "Howdy do, Reverend Grey. I behold you have visitors this night. Strange visitors."

"Get away, Damfino. I want no violence or disorder here."

The thin man placed his hands upon the heads of the great hounds and then sniffed the air, as if smelling an invisible rose. "Hand them over, rector. Or this will go bad for you."

As the two men conversed, Joe frantically scoured the pathway. In the red light of the torch he found a bronze bumblebee inlaid into the flagstones.

"Bees?" Gunner said. "So what?"

"There's another over here," Joe said. "And another. One on each side. They mark the four directions of the paths."

North, south, east and west, he thought, but which is which? And did it matter? Did the instruction to stand before the stone mean to stand looking at the house or away from it? It had something to do with the start of the labyrinth, and it sounded like a spell, but whatever magic it contained was lost on the boy. He needed his mother. She was the one who knew magic, not him.

This is madness, he said to himself. Am I really trying to open a magical doorway?

Reverend Grey left the shadows of the porch, passed the two boys and stood on the steps between the upper and lower gardens.

"You have no business here, Damfino. I command you to leave this place and never return."

"Oh, I have every business. I am master of the Wild Hunt," the grim-faced man replied, "and these boys are wolfshead. Give me them and I will leave like lightning."

"This I will not allow. All those who enter here are protected by my sanctuary."

"Look!" Gunner pointed at the figure lurking on the threshold of the gate. "He can't step into the garden."

That's some relief, thought Joe, as it looked as if the snarling mob – Grim Grotesques, Gunner had named them – would tear them to pieces if they could.

"Mary," the rector commanded, "go inside and bar the door." Then to the boys, he muttered, "I see now you are neither Ghûl nor enemy. Go north." He said this as if compass directions were things everyone knew by heart. "To the sanctuary of Newton Hall. Take the book and run. I will meet you—"

"Grey, you were warned," shouted Damfino. "By tooth and claw, we will fall upon you, and you shall cover us red." The leader of the mob signalled to the others, and, as one, the Grims or Ghûls or whoever these wild-eyed lunatics were began chanting. The sound started whispered and deep, building slowly in volume and density.

"Time we left this place," said Gunner.

But Joe had no idea what to do next. It all seemed to be somehow his fault. It was like the day he lost his parents all over again. Except this time there was nowhere to run. No bus to escape to. No way out. Not unless he solved the message inside the cryptic nursery rhyme.

The reverend responded to the rabble's chants by pulling something from the folds of his night clothes. Joe imagined it would be a crucifix, but it turned out to be a necklace. It looked like a small piece of coal threaded on a leather cord. Ominously, Damfino laughed at the gesture.

"I threaten to gnaw the flesh from your bones, holy man," said the mob's master. "And you think to defy me with *that*?"

"I knew you before you left the righteous path, Damfino," said Grey. "Back when men called you Abram Kyle. I am not afeared of you and your huntsmen. For a praying man is as bold as a lion. My secret is simple. It is within."

"We all have our secrets, Maje," Damfino replied. And with that, he drew out his own white jewelled necklace and stepped across the threshold of the gateway. As he placed his booted foot onto the stone beyond, his face writhed in pain, but then the gemstone pulsed a sickly yellow and he continued. In response, the reverend's jewel also glowed, his a shadowy grey. Slowly the hooded man descended into the vegetable garden as his followers' shouts grew louder. Under his hood his anguished eyes shone jet black, rippling like pools of ink. The air was filled with another sound now, the howling of his great black dogs.

"Joe, move it!" shouted Gunner. His hands shone sweaty around the hunting knife. The younger boy grasped the book and tried to concentrate, but couldn't help but keep glancing up at the master and his hunters.

Fearlessly, Reverend Grey faced the oncoming man. He removed the necklace from around his neck and held the jewel before him like a holy symbol. In hard, deliberate tones, he began to pray:

"Forged in Fire. Carved in Ice.
Rooted in Rock. Wild as Wind.
Shielded in Shadow."

Damfino sneered at these words, but noticeably slowed his approach. The rector continued:

"The Walls of these Rooms ward us.
The Power of these Doors protect us.
The Magic of these Moons encloak us.
Wherever we are; whenever we are; Talliston is."

The master of the Wild Hunt took a step back.

Joe focused on a further passage that was something to do with the portals and getting them to open, but the words were swimming across the pages now as he slipped into panic. His mind boiled over with incomprehensible gibberish about moons, rooms and doors. He was shivering, his breath steaming in the coldness of the night.

Suddenly Reverend Grey let out a chilling cry and Damfino was screaming, "By fang and flame, the raven!" Joe's head shot up just in time to see Griswald swoop out of the midnight and pluck the necklace from the rector's fingers. The next moment the bird landed atop the standing stone and dropped the black stone into Joe's hand.

At once, whatever force or fear keeping the Grim Grotesques at bay was gone. Hurling their torches into the gardens, they swarmed over and through the tall hedges, looking like the dead people in Joe's zombie nightmares. As they moved their hoods were flung back, revealing diseased features and wild, bulging eyes. In three steps, Damfino reached Reverend Grey and attacked instantly. Throwing back his hood to reveal dark hair and horns, he grabbed the rector's head on both sides and forced his fanged mouth to the man's face. It was all too horrifying to take in.

Unable to watch them come, Joe looked away and into the eyes of the black raven. Amidst the chaos, Griswald waited calmly, dipping its head down towards the carved labyrinth. Joe looked at the black necklace in his palm, then to the standing stone. Then he reached up and touched one against the other.

At once there was a splintering as if the universe was being split in half, and the rectory house began to transform. As he watched, the front entrance melted from black to brown, growing into a towering set of arched double doors. The stained-glass oval vanished, the porch evaporated replaced by iron windows and stone columns. Then the arched doors split, spilling clear, cold morning light.

"Go! Go! Go!" shouted Gunner and the boys ran headlong at the doorway. The younger boy was closer and leapt through first, sliding on polished marble and skidding to a stop at the base of a set of stone stairs. There was a sound like sudden thunder and then utter silence.

"We're in!" Joe had never been so overjoyed by anything in his entire life. He pressed his sweat-drenched back against the freezing floor and breathed steam. For a moment more he lay panting on the black and white chequerboard, then turned to check on Gunner.

But Gunner was gone.

Joe sat in the stone hall alone.

II

SECOND MOON: BLOOD MOON (OF MAN)
PALAZZO DI OMBRE
SACRO MONTE DI VARESE, LOMBARDY, ITALY
TUESDAY 24 NOVEMBER 1992 | 02:42:16

"CRU-UUK," CAME A FAMILIAR SOUND. Well, not entirely alone.

Griswald stood at the very top of the stone steps beneath a magnificent chandelier and stained-glass skylight. The plasterwork was cracked and ancient, and thick tangles of roots forced their way through the ceiling as if someone had planted a forest on the roof above. Joe lifted himself up and looked around. He was sitting on the chequerboard floor between three doors; the one he had entered and two smaller wooden ones. The fourth way led to a steep staircase shielded by green and gold curtains, hung with ornate beadwork and tied onto hooks in the shape of dragons. All around him upon the marble tiles he sat in a sea of scattered pages, blown into piles at the foot of the stairs.

This was not the rectory hall he and Gunner had entered; this was the hall of a stately home. That realisation was disorientating and strange, and the boy had trouble thinking back through all the places he had travelled in the last few hours. And now he was alone. Gunner was a thug and bully, but he knew this house far better than Joe. The boy felt the icy fingers of panic begin to reach up inside him. Without help, without his medicine, without knowing how he was going to ever get back, he would die. Panicking, Joe grabbed for the clockwork timer and froze in horror when he pulled it up to check it. The marker pointed to two notches past three, but it was not ticking. The dial had stopped.

"I'm going to die," he wailed. "My heart is going to break."

He wanted to throw open the front door, to see what waited outside, but just the thought sent more ripples of cold through his gut. Instead he forced himself to his feet, leapt to the door and threw the iron bolt into place. As quickly he skidded back and returned to his place on the floor. With the way barred, Joe felt calmer, but as he tried to think of what to do next, he became aware of the immense weight of the stone pressing down around him. The hall felt like being sealed inside an Egyptian tomb. Above him the twisted roots were knotted around ironwork and through the stone blocks like giant hands that seemed intent on ripping off the roof. Just immeasurably slowly.

So much for him being some fearsome superhero.

In his hand he held still the rector's black necklace. Slipping the cord around his neck, he inspected it more closely. What outside had looked like a lump of coal was instead a highly polished gemstone. It was surprisingly heavy and its dark brown, almost black surface gleamed with star-like crystals.

Griswald cawed a second time, a little more urgently. Joe looked up.

It was because of this bird that he was here. Griswald had led him to the house and helped him reach this place. Joe didn't know whether this was a good thing or not. With all the attacks by swarming crazies, perhaps he should stop following the raven so blindly and start making decisions for himself. Still, Griswald had alerted him to the danger at the roundabout.

Joe's stomach gave a loud grumble. The kind a belly makes when you stay up well past bedtime and dinner was many hours ago. For the boy that meal had been just a few crackers washed down with the last of his milk. No wonder he was hungry.

Kneeling over his rucksack, he fished around and pulled out the box of snacks. Taking a handful, he started munching them, trying to fill the hole in his stomach.

In three hops Griswald moved from step to step until he perched on the lowest stair beneath the drapes. Tilting his head, he clicked a few times and Joe understood that the raven wanted to eat, too.

"Well, I have no idea if you're friend or foe," Joe said, "but nobody likes being hungry." The boy offered one of the small circular crackers and the bird took it in one swift movement and began destroying it with his beak. It was funny watching the bird eat, and so Joe gave it another.

So are you helping me or leading me into danger? the boy thought as the raven ate. He decided that he needed to trust the bird, because without him he really was all alone in this strange place. While Griswald was crunching on a third cracker, Joe reached out to stroke the bird's shiny back.

"Ye gods!"

Obviously shocked, Griswald let out a piercing squawk, stamping up and down in anger. He chattered and cawed, then, grabbing up the last piece of biscuit, leapt into the air, flew up the stairs and was gone. But the raven had spoken to him. Hadn't it? Or did he just imagine those two words?

It had all happened so fast, Joe couldn't be sure.

The boy's eyes fell on the leather book. *The Stranger's Guide* sat where he had dropped it by the large entrance door. Pulling out his torch, he cast its beam around the hall. He found the pages scattered by his frantic entrance were from a calendar. Collecting them together, he saw the months were marked with names like Hunter's Moon and Blood Moon. Then he noticed the years. The first one was 1852, the next 1977 and, alarmingly, another was 2282. A little shiver ran down his spine. What was this place? The guide listed pages and pages of magical gateways, and while Joe had tried and failed to manifest his mother's innate magical abilities, this was far more than reading auras, channelling spirits and casting hexes. This was in another league. Surely *actual* magic didn't exist, but what was the alternative? Was he dreaming? Delusional? Going stark staring mad? None of these questions had a reasonable answer. He had seen an ordinary derelict council house transform into a gothic rectory – and now he had entered a different building entirely. Were these all the houses built on this spot of land? Was he experiencing movement in time or space? Or – he shuddered a little at the thought – both? Well, whatever was happening, two things were certain: he was on his own now, and there was no going back. Not with that screaming pack of demented freaks on his tail.

In the hollow space of the hall there was a low cracking sound. Joe threw a worried look at the main door, thinking that any second Damfino and his Grim Grotesques would burst in and catch him. But it was the roots. The roots were moving, twisting and creeping, forcing their way further into the walls of the house. Seeing this, the boy wanted to move on from this place. He needed somewhere to hide and work out what would happen next. For if the book was right and this was a labyrinth, then there was only one path and only one way to go. Which prompted the question: what would he find at the centre?

After all that had happened, Joe felt exhausted. Driving down the fear of what monsters lurked behind closed doors, Joe opened the one to the left of the stairs and found a small stone room with an arched ceiling. The room was bare and dusty. It looked as if no one had been in there for years.

Nowhere Is Safe, he thought wearily. He was past caring. He needed to rest. He also wanted to read more from the guide.

Joe slid his back down the wall, set the book on his knees and pulled out the torch. He opened the book at a section marked 'What to Do When You Become Lost in the Woods of the House'. That seemed a good place to start reading.

He was asleep before he had finished the first page.

"*CIAO, COME HAI FATTO A entrare?*"

Joe woke with a dark shape looming over him. Framed by sunlight that spilt in through the doorway, the figure was tall with hands fixed firmly to his hips. "*Dove sono i tuoi genitori?*"

Panicking, the boy skittered back across the room shouting, "No, no, don't! I'm lost! I'm lost!"

"*Immagino che tu non parli l'italiano,*" the deep voice muttered.

The man did not move forward and, thankfully, didn't seem to be threatening him. Instead he said in heavily accented English, "I am Romano."

"I'm… Joe," said Joe.

"Hello, Joe. I am pleased to meet you. I am a photographer. Where did you get lost?"

"Photographer?" Joe replied, still disorientated and afraid.

Romano held up a rather impressive camera. "I take pictures of abandoned buildings. Just like this one. I travel all over Europe. Are you on holiday? Where are your parents?"

41

The boy ignored his direct questions. "This place doesn't look abandoned."

The man crouched down and picked up the torch and the book, then offered them back to Joe. He had a heavily tanned face and short beard. He wore working trousers, jacket and boots, as if about to set off on a brisk walk.

"It is not, my friend." Joe could see that he was trying not to scare him. "This palazzo is the home of signore Balthazard, bought recently to restore. But the village around us is… *paesi fantasma*… a ghost town."

"Ghost town?"

"Yes, abandoned to the shadows. But come, let me show you."

The photographer extended a hand and Joe stared at it uneasily. Rule #4: Don't Make Friends, he thought instantly. Seeing the boy's distrust, Romano stepped back and indicated for him to follow up the stairs.

Through the curtains the stone walls were hung with a series of enormous mirrors set in ornate frames. Each reflected the other, though not directly as giant hooks tilted them forward. When you looked into them it was like gazing down other hallways curving away into infinity. Reflecting each other and the soft morning light that now filtered down through the stained glass of the skylight, they made the narrow stairs seem much larger.

The Hall of Mirrors, Joe realised.

"Where am I?" he asked.

"These steps lead from the loggia to the upper rooms."

"No, I mean, where is this house?"

"This is Palazzo di Ombre. Once a summer palace for wealthy Italian merchants in a thriving village. Now all that is gone. Now it is the home of only signore Balthazard."

"And where is this place in England?"

Romano laughed in surprise.

"Little one, you are not in England. You are upon the Sacro Monte di Varese, the sacred mountain that rises high above the city of Varese. In Italy."

"Italy? But that's not possible!"

"Why is it not possible?"

"Because I just walked through that door from Great Dunmow."

"Great Dunmow?" The name sounded extremely foreign in Romano's mouth, as if he were speaking about Atlantis or Avalon.

"In Essex. England." Joe tried to think of other ways to describe where he had come from. "The United Kingdom?"

"That is not possible."

"That's what I said."

"Are you sure you have not fallen? Where are your parents? Are you sick?"

You have no idea, thought Joe, but what he said was: "Prove it." Romano hesitated, unsure what the boy was asking. "Prove I'm in Italy," Joe insisted.

The photographer nodded in understanding. "Come. Yes, I can prove this to you."

At the top of the stairs the man turned right and led Joe along a short corridor of doors to a room at the end. Inside was a large guest bedroom with a tiled floor and windows hung with heavy curtains. From the look of the piled equipment cases this was the photographer's room. The air was cold here too, and crossing through half-open shutters Romano led him out onto a balcony. Though it was still very early the entire scene was lit with soft dawn light.

Joe found himself looking over a magnificent vista. Below stretched an endless landscape of trees as far as his eye could see. Morning mist shrouded the shores of a vast lake in the distance, while above snow-topped mountains reached high into the clear skies. He was in a large villa set in hills among the ruins of a small village of stone houses. Below similar buildings clustered around the single spire of a church. It was too much to take in and sudden vertigo overtook him. Grasping the stone balcony, he swayed dizzily. This was impossible. Where was this place? And more importantly, how was he ever going to get back before he died?

Seeing the boy's distress, Romano asked if he was OK and if he would like to eat or drink something. "Milk? Hot tea?"

Mumbling assent, the boy followed the man back down the hall and to another set of steps. These were grander and led down into a tree-lined courtyard. Unfamiliar birds filled the sky with their swoops and cries, dipping down to drink from a circular pool. The crisp mountain air felt strange in Joe's throat, his tongue tingling with every breath. Passing between lines of columns, they crossed a tiled entrance hall and from there entered the kitchen of the villa. He tried to keep track of where he was in relation to the Hall of Mirrors, but the house was far bigger than any the boy had ever visited. Joe sat at a large refectory table while Romano filled a kettle, looking around at the stone walls and beamed ceiling. Though the gas stove and furniture looked ancient, the boy knew from the photographer's equipment that he was no longer in the distant past. He wanted to open the book to find out more about this villa and more importantly what *The Stranger's Guide* had to say about escaping.

"Do you know anything of where you are now?" asked Romano.

"No," Joe lied. "Perhaps if you talk I'll remember something."

The man looked sceptical, but started talking anyway.

"This palazzo is built upon the highest point of the sacred mountain of Varese. There are nine sacred mountains in northern Italy, and this one is the site of fourteen chapels that sit along the mountain path. For many years people have travelled through on pilgrimage to Jerusalem. This house is built on the site of an ancient shrine from before history.

In medieval times the villa was used as a safe haven from the plague. Have you heard of such things?"

"My mother taught me all about the Black Death when I was younger. If that's what you're talking about."

"Yes, the Black Death. All of Europe. It was a bad time. This place was seen as a sanctuary."

The kettle spluttered then began to whistle and Romano busied himself making the hot drinks: tea for Joe and black coffee for himself.

"I photograph lost and abandoned places. My images capture mystery. Moments. The lens is like opening a door into an unknown world. And when we do this, everything we see inside is important." He shrugged. "It is hard to translate what I do."

"I sort of understand." But Joe wasn't thinking about the house or the photographer's work. He was thinking about returning to the Hall of Mirrors and taking another look around. He needed to know why Gunner thought it was so important.

"Do you want something to eat?" asked the photographer. "I have some food from dinner."

"No, I'm fine," Joe lied, torn between his need for food and the Rules. Deep in his chest a pain was building. Is this how it starts? he wondered. Unconsciously he raised his hand to his heart, then gritted his teeth and said, "Why was the town abandoned?"

"In the Renaissance, this villa was built by Italian nobility for a second summer home. The entire village grew under the shadow of their wealth and power. When the lords and ladies moved away, so did everyone else. And once trees take the place of the people within the old stone houses, no one wants to live there."

"No one except Mr Balthazard."

"Yes," Romano said, finishing his coffee. "No one except signore Balthazard."

"Can I see him? Is he here?"

"Ah, no. The master is as much a ghost as the village." Seeing Joe's widening eyes, Romano added, "I mean, he is travelling. He is not here so much."

They sat there for a while, each lost in their own thoughts, then Romano stood and said that he needed to alert the proper authorities. "Though to whom you report finding a lost boy who appears by magic in your house, I have no idea." Joe stayed silent and tried to look as if he had no idea either. "The telephone is in the hall where I found you. Will you be OK here in this kitchen while I go to call?"

The boy nodded and sipped his tea.

"OK, stay here. I will be right back."

As soon as Romano had left, Joe reached into his bag and pulled out *The Stranger's Guide*. Flipping through the pages, he found the section on the villa. The book referred to the place as the second of thirteen locations. Here a calendar was pasted for the month of November 1992. Tuesday 24 had been circled in red and marked with a black blob that the boy assumed meant it was the dark of the moon. No surprise there. The author had also included a photograph of the abandoned town, some information about the house and its history, plus a room map. All of this was interesting but largely unhelpful. Joe's only lingering thought was that he wouldn't even be born for another ten years. The boy turned back a few pages, past the entry for the rectory, to a concertina-style world map. Upon it labels had been stuck with lines pointing all over the world. Four ended in Great Britain, marking houses in England, Scotland, Wales and Ireland. There were four more in the Americas with the rest scattered across Europe, with one in Cambodia and another in Japan. Joe wasn't the best at geography, but it was a simple task to find the label marked 'Palazzo di Ombre, Lombardy, Italy' and follow it to the area just above the Mediterranean Sea. On the opposite page was a checklist of the various locations with ticks against nine of the thirteen places. Joe had to find either the way back to England or — and he shuddered at this next thought — the path through the entire labyrinth. So many doors, he thought, but every door has a lock and every lock has a key. If the key to the Old Rectory was found in the garden, perhaps Gunner was right and the key to the next door would be found in the Hall of Mirrors.

There was the sound of shoes on tiles and Romano walked back into the kitchen. He announced that he had made a call to the *polizia*, but there was an issue. "There's been a train derailment," he explained. "They are detained, but will get here as soon as they can."

"How long will that be?" asked Joe.

"There is no knowing and, as I do not want to leave you alone here, will you join me in my photography?"

THE BOY AND PHOTOGRAPHER SPENT all afternoon until sundown photographing the ruins of the deserted village. Joe enjoyed Romano's company, hearing his tales of travels to castles in the Black Forest and derelict Scottish manors, but inside he carried the rising dread of his illness. The headaches started as he climbed a villa staircase littered with fallen rubble. Soon after he felt his fingertips numb as he sat watching Romano set up his camera to perfectly capture the bleak beauty of the ruins. Apart from a few birds, everywhere was empty and still. Everywhere except within him. They returned at dusk, and as the authorities had still not arrived, Romano showed Joe to a room and said he should stay for the night. It was just what the teenager wanted.

As soon as it was dark and the house was quiet, Joe slipped out of bed, crossed the courtyard and returned to the Hall of Mirrors. He was only half-surprised to find the raven perched upon the telephone on its ornate shelf, waiting for him. "Hello, Griswald," he said. "Do you

THE STRANGER'S GUIDE TO TALLISTON

want to tell me anything?" The bird looked back with unreadable eyes and said nothing. Joe pulled out the black necklace and slipped it over his head. "Anything about giving me this?" Silence.

Of course he's saying nothing, Joe thought. Birds don't talk.

By the light of his torch, the boy began searching. He started with the front door, drawing back the bolt and peeping outside. The rectory garden had now been replaced by a tiled avenue lined with tall trees, but thankfully there was no sign of Damfino and the Grim Grotesques. Next Joe searched the shelves that flanked the entrance door and found a variety of time-telling devices. There was a tide clock, a sundial engraved with dragons and a cuckoo clock carved with birds. The smallest timepiece was a silver and gold pocket watch, the largest an elegant wall clock with a heavy pendulum. Each one had stopped. Slowly he counted them and was not surprised to find that there were thirteen.

One clock for each room, he thought. Surely that's no coincidence. All brought here to this place. But for what purpose?

Looking up at the wall clock, he saw that the hands read eleven minutes past five. It didn't take him long to check *The Stranger's Guide* and find a time that matched it. It corresponded to the next room on the labyrinth: a medieval tower in Wales. The calendar was circled on Wednesday 14 December 1887 at 05:11:23. This was the night of the dark of the moon too. So, the clocks showed the time the doors would open for each location. But which door was which? And surely he did not have to wait until nearly Christmas for the next one?

Confused, he returned to the stairs and inspected the mirrors and their infinite reflections. Joe saw himself in the gloom for the first time in a long while. His fair hair was long and messy, his blue eyes turned dark in the bronzed glass. Around his neck Nathaniel Grey's black jewel glinted in the torchlight like a watching eye. Under the cloak of night everything ordinary had become ghostly and strange. Even his reflection seemed distorted and unfamiliar. At first he couldn't place what it was, but then he had it.

"I look older," he whispered into the darkness.

"Of course you do," said a voice in reply, making Joe jump in fright. "It is natural for one within the walls of all worlds."

At first Joe thought it might have been the raven that had spoken, but this voice was far more ancient.

"Who said that?" he asked.

"I am known by many names, little cub, most in languages now lost from mortal speech." Joe looked up and into the face of a bearded old figure in an alcove. The voice was coming from a metal mask. "I am Saturn, Kairos, Zurvan, Aeon and Old Father Time. I sleep in the grave of the Earth. I am the Reaper and the acorn's seed. I am Time itself."

Immediately images ignited in the mirrors, each showing a male figure at different ages; as a boy faun, a bearded robed man with great curved wings, and everything in between. Not one of the characters was static, but moved through many forms, becoming older or more youthful, endlessly flowing through years and centuries. As the words continued, all these figures spoke together, but there was only one voice.

"How is this happening?" asked Joe.

"Look to your throat," the voice said. "You carry a talisman of great power. It is a shadowstone, one of many relics that fell from the Immortal Sky in ages past. It was discovered in Peru by an Inca king. It is a stone of moving forward, of finding the true path and perhaps even your true self." Joe grasped the stone in his hand and held it tightly. "These tokens are rare and magical gifts. They are known to manifest our wishes," the mask continued. "Your wish is to know which door to take; thus have you summoned me to answer that question."

This isn't happening, thought Joe, stunned by Saturn's words. Am I still sleeping? Is this a dream? "What is this place?" the boy asked in a daze.

"This was once a temple dedicated to me, the site of an ancient oracle."

"What's an oracle?"

"I am." At once images poured into the mirrors like water, swirling, ebbing and flowing, showing all that the oracle spoke of. "Upon this mountain in times long past a magical spring was discovered. Its source was the Infinite Ocean and its waters connected the underworld of the Within to the Eternal Forest of the mortals. This sacred place was dedicated to me, Saturn, by a healer and prophetess. She was the White Sibyl, and many came from across the empire to ask questions of the oracle and hear its answers."

In every looking glass the shrine shone like a white beacon in the woods, filled with light and colour. As Joe watched the temple grew, stood trembling upon the mountain, and then fell into ruins.

"This palazzo stands where that temple stood, upon an unseen river of time that connects many others. The waters rise still in the deep places of the house, seeping down into the lakes and rivers that eventually flow as far as Rome itself. To conceal the nature of this place, the other hills of the Sacro Monte were named magical also, and in that way the true nature of this sacred place was preserved through the centuries."

"And how does it work, this oracle?"

"The doing is simple. One, offer up your sacrifice. Two, speak your question."

"What sacrifice?"

"One of three things must be offered. One of the three things that Time cannot kill."

"What are they? What things?"

"That is for you to discover, my little rabbit."

Joe had no idea what things were required, but looking up to the face he saw that below it on a small shelf stood three things: an hourglass, a scythe and a small cup or bowl with handles fashioned as snake heads. The three things that Time cannot kill? There was also a green branch filled with white berries that he recognised as mistletoe. Was this also something that couldn't be killed?

The raven hopped from its perch and came to see what he was doing.

"Help me," Joe asked, but the bird cocked its head in a very disapproving way as if to say, 'No, you must work this out for yourself.' Joe had an idea. He held up the shadow talisman and said, "Raven, show me the way." As soon as he said those words, Griswald shivered noticeably.

"*Tempus edax rerum*," said the raven.

"What?"

"Time devours all things. Do they not teach you Ovid?"

"Who?"

"Latin? Alchemy?"

"No."

The bird made a disparaging clucking sound in its throat.

"No wonder the Eternal Forest is all but lost."

"You have to help me."

"And where would be the instruction in that?"

Joe sighed, then said, "How can you speak?"

"All things can speak, it is just people like you who cannot understand Nature's Tongue."

"Nature's…"

"Nature's Tongue is the language of the universe. It is the reading of the sun's glinting reflections upon a summer's lake. Or the language of starlings as they flock upon the evening air. It is the glossy wake of the snail or the movement of the leaves in the crown of the oak tree. For those so versed, even the stones can share their ageless wisdom. Yet in sacred places all things are one. Through the power of this house you can understand my words and their meaning. In the waves, in the

51

wind, in the wilds – in these last magical places on the earth – we are our true selves."

"That's incredible!"

"How so? Language is essential in the evolution of all species. Surely it would be more incredible if after all these millions of millennia, the universe would *not* have adapted a common communication between all things?"

"Well, when you put it like that…"

"I think it far more incredible that *Homo sapiens* can communicate with people upon the surface of the moon, but not with the birds in their garden."

"I never thought—"

"And when you try to tell them," Griswald added curtly, "humans are just far too stupid to understand."

Joe was going to argue that point, until he realised it was true.

Neither bird nor boy spoke for a while and then the raven's head darted up suddenly, at once alert and stiff with fear.

"No, no, no," it chattered.

"What is it?" said Joe, but a moment later he heard it too. Sounds had woken in the walls. Like a thousand crawling beetles moving behind the stonework. Above, the roots tensed and flexed, twisting and tightening like ship's ropes in a storm.

"They are coming," said the bird.

Nowhere Is Safe! Find a way out!

Crossing to the entrance door, Joe opened it the tiniest of cracks. Outside the night was almost pitch black, but beyond the villa's iron gates, a single light swept erratically through the trees. It was a car, the engine sound clear in the quiet darkness.

"Is it the master of the house?" he asked.

"No, it is the authorities come to take you to Varese." The bird was so matter of fact, at first Joe couldn't take in what he meant.

"But I don't want to go."

"Then work quicker, Joe of Great Dunmow."

Even as the bird said this a black car drew into view. Written upon the side was CARABINIERI. Two uniformed figures got out and approached the gates.

Joe closed the door and began pacing. Trying to think.

"Why can't Saturn or whoever that is up there just tell me what to do?"

"You are required to offer gifts to travel through this world. Find the oracle in each room of the labyrinth."

"But I don't know—"

"And you are also required to *learn*," said the raven.

"Learn what?"

"That," said Griswald calmly, "is one of the things."

Joe boiled with frustration. He gripped his hands into fists and was just about to scream at the bird when above them a brass bell rang. The shrill sound echoed through the empty hall and off into the villa.

The doorbell! Romano!

Quickly, Joe shooed Griswald into the stone side room and followed in behind. He was not a moment too soon. Watching through a crack in the door, the boy heard the photographer walking down the stairs, then saw him pass through the curtains and cross to the front door. He was wrapped in a large dressing gown, his hair a black mess. Joe watched as he threw the switch for the electric gates, then headed out to meet the police.

Joe didn't have much time.

Slipping back into the hall, the boy and raven returned to the stairs. Helpfully Romano had left the door half open, so Joe found that if he crouched he could keep an eye on what was happening outside. Security lights now lit the front gardens, illuminating the open gates, the photographer and the two policemen.

"Come on, Joe. Think!" the raven chided. "Look and learn." But all the boy saw when he looked around was his frantic self looking back from the ancient glass. "It's right in front of you." Now it was Griswald's turn to sound frustrated.

"That's it!" Joe said, at once excited and relieved. "The mirrors. A thing that Time cannot kill." Griswald let out a strangled croak, but the boy was already continuing. "I offer my reflection."

"Done!" boomed the metal mask, and all the villa shook. "That is a worthy gift." Instantly the boy's reflection disappeared from every mirror. "Yet," the voice said in a lower tone, "that is not the correct sacrifice." Joe's heart sank.

"By Jove! Look to the book!" squawked Griswald. "Do you not think its author learned the secrets of this test?"

Outside the policemen had stopped talking to Romano. They were pointing at the house.

All the muscles in Joe's legs turned to water, and he half-sat, half-fell onto the stone steps. He pulled the guide from his bag and reread the palazzo pages from Chapter IV, 'Times You Will Visit on Your Journeying'. Now he paid more attention to the mentions of the Italian oracle. There was a drawing of the hourglass, sickle and wings of Saturn. It also said the key to its secret lay with Saturn's sons. That they were Jupiter, Pluto and Neptune.

Joe tried to concentrate, to remember where he had seen those names before. Why couldn't the book just tell him the answer? Why did it have to be so cryptic? Or was it him just being thick?

"You do not have much time, boy," reminded the raven unhelpfully.

Joe began to sweat.

He knew that Neptune was the god of the sea. Everyone knew that. But what about the others? Hadn't he seen something about the ocean? There were just too many pages to read through each and every one.

Out in the night, Romano and the *polizia* appeared to be arguing. He could hear their raised voices clearly across the gardens, but unfortunately everything they said was in Italian. Griswald left Joe's side and hopped into an open archway. Perhaps the bird could understand them.

"What are they saying? What's happening?" Joe asked.

"The man invites them in, but they want him to bring you out. They are squabbling. It is quite pathetic."

Looking out past the bird, Joe saw one of the policemen reach up and remove his cap to scratch his head. His *shaved* head. When he saw this Joe heard Gunner saying, "Total jerks. Shaved heads. Scar." They can't step into the villa, Joe realised, because it's a sacred place. They're not police. They're Grim Grotesques.

"It's the Wild Hunt. They've found me."

The raven cocked its head and would have rolled its eyes if it could.

Snatching for the amulet, Joe started frantically leafing through the book, looking for something that might help. Finally, near the guide's centre he found a diagram of a great oak tree, marked with all kinds of symbols. It was titled 'The Three Realms' and these were annotated as the 'Immortal Sky', 'Eternal Forest' and 'Infinite Ocean'. And there on the opposite page were the names of the sons of Saturn:

JUPITER • GOD OF HEAVEN AND LIGHTNING

PLUTO • GOD OF THE EARTHLY REALM AND THE DEAD

NEPTUNE • GOD OF THE SEA AND EARTHQUAKES

And beside the names were their elements:

JUPITER • SULPHUR • AIR

PLUTO • SALT • EARTH

NEPTUNE • MERCURY • WATER

Air, Earth, Water. The three things that Time cannot kill. He had it!

With a sound like thunder, a gunshot cracked the stillness of the night like a shattered mirror. Joe jumped, dropping the book and almost falling down the stairs. Outside he saw the three figures silhouetted as before against the harsh security lights, then Romano staggered back. He was grasping his stomach, then he collapsed to the ground. The policeman fired twice more at the photographer until he stopped moving.

Until he was dead.

Joe cried out, unable to stop himself, making the policemen look up. The one with the pistol did not hesitate. He raised his gun, aimed and fired. The bullet blasted a great chunk out of the stone at Joe's feet.

"Joseph Elijah Darkin," the raven said urgently, "Air, Earth or Water. Now!"

There was a second shot. This time the elegant pendulum clock exploded into pieces of wood and glass.

Joe backed up the stairs and grabbed for the pot on the shelf. Air was simple; the bowl already contained that.

More shots. Both men were firing now. In the hall below bullets blasted into walls, ricocheted off tiles and shredded curtains.

Replacing the snake-headed bowl on the shelf, he cried, "O mighty Saturn, I offer you air. One of the three things that Time cannot kill."

"What is it you wish to ask the Oracle?" boomed the mask.

"How do I open the door to the next room? To Wales. Snowdonia."

"Which room?" the Oracle asked.

Joe read from the book. "Room Three. The Mead Hall of..." The boy faltered over the next part of the name. He had no way of knowing how to pronounce 'Twr-Â-Gân'.

"Tour-Ah-Garne," finished the raven, his Welsh perfect.

"It is as you wish."

Down in the lower hall, the doorway that previously had led to the kitchen melted, and in its place appeared a stout oak door on thick black hinges. Hung upon it was a plaque bearing the sign of a bird set within a carved star. Around the painted frame a series of symbols faintly glowed an iridescent gold. At once the door began to swing open. Joe hesitated. To get through the doorway he would have to walk right through the gunfire.

All the night seemed to take a deep breath. For a heartbeat, even the Grim Grotesques' guns were silent.

"Fly, Joseph. Fly!" squawked the raven. "And remember, the only way out is in."

Stuffing the book into his bag, Joe flew. Taking two stairs at a time he rushed down the steps and faced the open door. In the eerie light, he could see an opulently furnished room beyond. Exploding into the walls and staircase, bullets filled the hallway once more. Joe felt something hit him in the shoulder, spinning him around. With a last desperate lurch, the boy hurled himself over the threshold of the new room. Griswald tried to follow, but was beaten back in the spray of masonry.

"And make a map!" were the bird's final words as the door swung closed.

And then Griswald, the villa and the dead photographer were gone.

THIRD MOON: RAVEN MOON (OF BIRDS)
THE MEAD HALL OF TWR-Â-GÂN
SNOWDONIA, WALES, UNITED KINGDOM
WEDNESDAY 14 DECEMBER 1887 | 05:11:23

THE ROOM JOE HAD FALLEN into was full of the smell of churches and Christmas. Between a pair of giant sofas a fire was newly started in the carved fireplace. Though the room was still chilly, its woody-sweet scent of coal and pine filled the air. Heavy velvet curtains framed a candlelit casement window showing darkness outside its leaded glass. Trembling in shock, the splitting pain of gunfire still ringing in his ears, the boy saw that he was not alone. At the other end of the room a dark-haired woman all in black sat at a dining table set for breakfast. Before Joe's sudden appearance she had been reading, but now she stared up from the forgotten pages with wide eyes. To Joe, her look was one of masked panic, silent proof that she knew he was a bad child. That he was nothing but trouble.

Almost imperceptibly, the lock of the oak door clicked quietly into place behind him.

For a moment Joe managed to keep standing, to hold himself together. Then hot pain pulsed down his entire left arm, and when he looked, his shoulder was red with blood. The shock of seeing this, and the weight of everything that had happened since the raven and the roundabout, came crashing down upon him.

He was hunted. Be Invisible!

Romano was dead. Do Not Talk To Dead People!

His timer had stopped and soon he would become sick and die. A Good Boy...

Suddenly his eyes burned wet and he staggered, dropping to the nearest sofa. The pain in his arm and chest was excruciating. Curling himself into a tight ball, Joe began to cry. He had to get back. He had to find his parents. Only they could save him now.

"My goodness," said a voice close to him, and the boy felt a hand on his wounded shoulder. Squirming away, Joe forced himself deeper into the cushions.

"No!" he bawled. "Don't touch me!"

The woman ignored him and he felt her fingers on his burning skin. "How are you injured?" she asked. "Did someone cut you?"

"No," said Joe, his vision blurring. "I was shot."

The woman took a deep breath and began removing his jacket and checked shirt. Joe winced and opened his eyes. He found he was looking at the cover of her book. She had placed it on the cushion beside his head. At first he thought the name of it was *A Study in Scarlet*, as these were by far the largest words on the page, but then he saw the real title in smaller letters above: *Beeton's Christmas Annual*. He couldn't see a date.

"Am I in Wales? Is this Twr-Â-Gân?"

"Yes. Yes, you are. It is." Her hand moved to the wound and he howled. "No bullet. Just grazed," she said to herself. "That is good, Rose, but be quick."

Not wanting to look back at his bloodied shoulder, Joe looked up and tried to focus on something else. He saw a white-horned sculpture set above the mantelpiece. The face looked like some kind of horned god or devil; its mischievous grin was both smiling and freakish. Upon its head was perched a silver crown hung with holly and ivy.

"But, my, aren't you another strange one," the woman continued. "Where are you babes in the wood appearing from?"

Babes? Wood? Joe's head swam in a sea of pain. "Who are you?"

"Me?" The woman seemed struck that he would be interested enough to ask. "I am Mrs Meirion, the housekeeper. I manage the small staff here, tend to the master and his guests. I was just preparing the breakfast things."

"Where…" Joe started to ask, but she shushed the question away.

"You are hurt and must rest." Her fingers pressed and poked. Joe fought back more tears.

The housekeeper stood and started gathering branches and berries from the candelabra, the baskets and tables. As he watched her, he noticed that the room was filled with all manner of birds and beasts. There were animals everywhere: in the fabrics and figurines, chess pieces and taxidermy, in pictures and standing on shelves. There were fox heads and rabbits, carved dragons and owls, butterflies, bumblebees, and even sparkling dragonflies in the stained-glass table lamps.

As Rose moved through the room, she began what sounded like a little prayer.

"O Wild One, Goat-God Pan, both beast and man, piper at the gates of dawn here in this mighty forest, this sanctuary. I call upon the magic that is found deep beneath this ancient watchtower. Help me save this lamb from the wolves that hunt him, from the harm those beasts have done." Returning to the sofa, she picked the berries and rubbed them into his wounds. "This holly and this ivy are the symbol of eternal life during these long winter months," she explained as she worked. "Their roots drink from Blackmirror Tarn and are leavened with the water's magic. I take the life of these berries to mend this thatch of wounds. I channel the weaving god and pass hale and health back to you." Then she began to sing – a strange and foreign language that sounded more animal than human – and Joe felt himself starting to fade.

"When… is this?" Joe asked weakly, fighting the urge to just close his eyes and drift off to dreaming.

"You must be the only boy in the entire country who does not know? It is the middle of December and Christmas fast approaches."

"Christmas? What… year?"

"Ah, now I know you as a stranger."

"A stranger?"

"A *stranger*. A traveller in the labyrinth. Tell me it is not so."

"It is. I am."

Rose nodded to herself. "In answer, then: it is 1887 and the entire household prepares for the master's midwinter retreat. His guests arrive this weekend from as far as Italy and the Americas."

"Italy?"

"From all over. They are artists, writers, poets and painters. They gather here… periodically. We expect them to stay until well past Twelfth Night."

"Mrs Meirion, I need your help."

"Oh, do call me Rose, and I will help as I can. Do not be afraid to be plain with me, my boy. Your arrival was fortunate, for there are far worse people you could have chanced upon in the tower this morning. In another few hours it would be the master's tea and toast you'd have been disturbing."

Joe heard the warning in her tone and struggled to sit up. "I need to go. I can't stay here," he said as Rose tried to calm him. Looking wildly around the room, he suddenly saw something familiar. Over Rose's shoulder, perched on a branch atop a carved cabinet sat the raven.

"Griswald?" he said before he could stop himself.

Then in the next moment the boy realised the bird was stuffed, just another of the taxidermy animals in this cluttered room. Was this the same raven? And if so how could Griswald be dead in 1887 and alive at the rectory and Italian villa? One was – his foggy mind worked through the calculations – thirty-five years ago in 1852 and the other more than a century afterwards. His head hurt just thinking about it.

"Mrs Meirion!" The bellowing voice came from above. It was so loud it shook through the ceiling.

"It's the master. Now we must be thinking quick. What tale this time, Rose?" It was then that she noticed the cord around his bare neck and pulled the black gemstone out of his shirt. Her face went white with terror. "Oh my, but we will have to hide *this*."

"*Mrs Meirion!*" The tone was sharper now. Bells were ringing, distantly, but Joe was far beyond caring. A rush of gentle warmth now flowed through him, dousing the pain in his arms and legs, and finally pouring like thick honey up into his mind.

"Nowhere is safe," he breathed as he slipped into sleep. "I must not talk to dead people…"

WHEN JOE WOKE IT WAS from a world of horrors. In his nightmare he was at the barbecue and his parents were trying to force-feed him The Medicine. The hard edge of the spoon scraped against his clenched teeth. His mother's hands were locked around his face, forcing his jaws apart. His parents' shocked faces loomed large before him as his mother screamed, "You did this! You brought this on yourself! On all of us!" Then thick hairy arms were reaching for him from behind the swing bench, while the adults were swarmed with hooded figures. It was no longer summer; the apple trees were bare and dead, the air a tempest of icy winds. As he watched he saw his father grappling a giant assailant, while Aunt and Uncle B fled in terror. Over by the toppled table, his mother writhed on the hard ground, her attackers falling upon her with knives and claws. Joe thrashed against the ugly hands that held him, but he couldn't get free. There were too many. They were too strong. Romano stood by the orchard wall. He was holding the red mess of his stomach and screaming. Beyond the garden the sky flashed with blue and red sirens… And those haunting words, echoing in his mind like some terrible prophecy. "The problem with bad children is they don't listen – and they *never* learn."

Joe forced himself awake and sat up. It was dusk and he was in Rose Meirion's room. He knew they were the housekeeper's quarters instantly as her things were everywhere. He lay on a narrow brass bed and beside him was a dressing table with an oval mirror. A linen shirt and woollen trousers had been hung from a wooden frame before the smouldering fireplace. There were also some leather shoes. What little light there was came from a small arched window high upon one wall. Joe slipped out of bed and tried to stand. His head felt foggy, but when he checked, he found his shoulder was healed completely. It was still sore, but soon even the redness would be invisible.

On the wall at the bedside hung a calendar for 1887. All the months were on a single page, and at the top Queen Victoria sat in full regalia in honour of her Golden Jubilee. Almost the entire year's dates were crossed out, marking today as Saturday 17 December. Throughout the month Rose had made notes beside the days in her spidery hand. Most significant was the entry for Wednesday that read simply 'BOY'.

I've been asleep for four days, he realised. Four days? That was more than seven doses missed. Why am I not sick yet? Why am I not dead? Perhaps like the clockwork countdown, everything stopped here.

Tomorrow was annotated with 'MIDWINTER RETREAT', running all the way to the end of the year. A thought occurred to the boy, sparked by something the housekeeper had said about babes in the wood and her needing *another* tale to tell her master. And there it was. Tuesday 21 June. That single word: 'GIRL'. Had Gunner's sister found the way this far? Or was she wandering the hillsides of Italy?

That can wait, he thought. First I have to get out of this place. Yet in thinking about leaving he realised something far more chilling. His rucksack, the talisman and − by far the most distressing − *The Stranger's Guide* were gone. With increasing alarm, Joe checked every conceivable hiding place, but they were nowhere to be found.

Without the book how will I find the way out? he thought in terror. I'll be trapped in 1887 forever.

On the verge of panic, he tried to calm himself down. He had to find the housekeeper and get them back. She helped him once, hopefully she would again. But he had to keep her at a distance. He needed a way out, not friends. He would be safe if he followed The Rules. And what had Griswald said? Yes, he should make a map.

In an effort to stop shaking, Joe dressed in the clothes left out for him, then found some writing paper in a desk and began to draw. First he sketched a rough labyrinth like the one on the standing stone. Next he added what he could remember of the rectory garden and Reverend Grey's house. Finally he drew the entrance and grounds to the Italian villa and the start of a tower. He was fairly happy with the finished map. At school Joe had always enjoyed art class, and the act of drawing, of concentrating on lines and his memory, certainly helped drive away the nightmares and panic. He couldn't remember if the rectory had a name, and had no idea how to spell the one for the Welsh tower. I'll make up my own names, he thought to himself. So he marked the rectory garden 'The Labyrinth', the villa 'The Hall of Mirrors' and the castle 'The Watchtower'.

Something large crashed against the diamond glass and Joe leapt to his feet. For a moment the boy caught a glimpse of a white shape, then it was gone. Crossing cautiously to the small window, Joe saw some kind of bird which appeared to be circling the tower.

Maybe there's a way to the battlements, he thought, and slipped on the shoes, wrapped himself in a heavy woollen blanket and headed for the door. Outside was a short corridor and at the end a spiral set of steps. To the boy, leaving the room felt like trespassing along the dark alleys of an abandoned amusement park. At once both afraid and rebelliously excited, Joe headed up and emerged through a low metal door onto the roof. Bracing himself against the cold, he stared out in astonishment at the spectacular scenery.

Standing like a sentinel on a rocky hill above a mountain pass, the watchtower stood in the middle of a magnificent forest that seemed to go on forever. It was just past sunset and dusk was falling fast, but even in the gloom Joe could make out snowy peaks on every horizon. The air smelled fresh and very green. Crossing to the battlements, he looked down and saw below a second smaller tower, connected to this one by thick stone walls. Outside the gates of the castle, steep steps led down to a bridge and watermill. In the other direction the leafless trees parted to reveal a copper-blue circular lake. Beside this were pitched a group of circus tents, their pennants fluttering in the stiff wind.

In one long, powerful note, a mournful howl rose up from the forest, piercing the stillness of the evening. And in reply many others howled back.

Warily, Joe stepped back from the crenellations, catching sight of something above him. The boy forced his eyes skywards and saw a blaze of fluttering wings. It was an enormous owl, its pure white feathers flecked with black as if individually dipped in ink. For an instant it flew overhead, then disappeared out of sight over the battlements.

"Well, well, if it isn't our little *stranger*."

Joe jumped at the sound and spun around. He'd heard that voice before calling for the housekeeper. So this was the tower's master. A man emerged from the opposite corner, his dark shape slipping silently from the shadows. The figure was tall and thin. He was maybe as old as the boy's father – maybe as old as his grandfather; it was difficult to tell. His eyes were invisible, sunken as they were into the dark hollows of his pale face. A short grey beard ran around his sharp jaw, his hair silver, raked back from his temples and greased into place. He wore a long coat, his hands gloved and holding an ivory-headed cane.

"What? Cannot you speak? Wolf got your tongue? *Lupus in fabula*, perhaps."

"What does that mean?" Joe asked. Why did everyone insist on speaking in foreign languages?

"Simplicity. The ancient belief that the sight of a wolf could strike someone dumb. Speak of the wolf—" the man raised his hands to form fangs with his fingers, "—and he shall come."

"Who are you?"

"Me? Oh, nobody and everybody. I am Jonathan D'Ante, master of this castle and everyone in it." He grinned with a smile like the horned face in the hall below. "And that includes you."

Joe didn't know whether to run or cry out where he stood. In the darkness above, the owl was in flight again.

"Now," said the man. "Who are *you*?" Joe's tongue felt huge, swollen. He couldn't say a word. "Speak up. I haven't got till Christmas." Joe still stayed silent. "Well, I'll have to call you something, won't I? Names are so very important, you see."

D'Ante mused for a moment, looking the fair-haired boy up and down.

"Hmm, you look... ordinary. Very ordinary. So we need an ordinary name. Something common. Think... Think... Crank the handle, and... pop goes the weasel! Let's plump for Joe."

The boy was shocked. How could this man have known that? "That is my name!" he blurted.

"Quite so." D'Ante snatched out his hand and produced a playing card as if from behind the boy's ear. "The Knight of Swords," he said, regarding it at arm's length. There was something about the master's voice, something theatrical and enchanting. Joe found he was utterly fascinated, his previous wariness gone completely.

The man stopped laughing.

"My apologies. I am easily amused is all. Do not be amazed. I know your name and why you've come here. It's why they all come." He was deadly serious now.

"Why's that?" the boy asked, thinking, And who are *they*?

"Why to take away my crown, of course." He threw his arms open, a gesture that said the answer was obvious. "To become king of the forest."

"I don't understand."

D'Ante beamed, then changed the subject. "Tell me, Joe, do you like owls?"

The boy's mouth was moving even before he could think to stop himself.

"Yes, I love owls. They're my favourite animals."

"Birds, boy. Your favourite birds. But yes, of course they are." The man laughed again. "Here, look. Let me show you something spectacular."

Stepping forward, the bearded man lifted his cane and teased Joe's arm up until it was horizontal before him. Then he took something from his pocket and placed it in the boy's hand. It was a piece of bloody meat.

"Keep still," he ordered.

Taking a step back again, he pursed his lips and sent a piercing whistle ringing across the valley. There was a rustle of leaves. A drumming in the air. A huge ghostly shape appeared beside them both. It was the white owl.

Reaching with its talons, it alighted on Joe's extended hand. The boy was so numb with excitement that he didn't even notice the bird's claws sinking into his flesh. He hardly felt the pain, unaware of the drops of blackness that dripped to the lead roof below. Transfixed, the boy reached out his hand to touch the bird's feathers. Just as he had with the raven.

"Stone the crows!" the owl said gruffly, shrugging off his touch. "Will this child never learn?" The owl's golden eyes regarded him with contempt for a moment, then it began to eat.

"*Nyctea scandiaca*," pronounced D'Ante in his crisp accent. "Commonly known as the snowy owl." Joe watched him for a reaction to the outburst, but the man seemed completely unperturbed. "Most commonly known as Tarrow."

"She's beautiful," he breathed.

"*He's* beautiful," D'Ante corrected. "Tarrow is a boy… a male owl." The man's face warmed for the first time that evening. "I'm so glad you like him. Now, shall we make him work for his supper?" D'Ante forced Joe's arm up, setting the bird into flight. From somewhere he produced a dish scattered with more chunks of meat. "Hold up the bowl," the man said. It was like a dream. One moment the boy was staring past the rim of the bowl into blackness. The next the owl, its wings wide as a bicycle, came swooping out of the dark, snatched a chunk of meat and was gone. In its wake Joe was left with the bird's ghostly whiteness etched on his retina.

There was a long pause. His arms began to ache, but he dared not let them drop, not even slightly. Behind him D'Ante let out a contented sigh and clasped his hand upon the boy's shoulder. The bird swooped again, startling Joe with his swiftness. The owl snatched, its talons finding meat, then was gone again. Snatch, finding, gone. Snatch, finding, gone. And when the last piece was taken, the owl did not return.

"What do you think of the tower?" D'Ante asked.

"It's amazing," said Joe.

"I added the crenels and merlons myself. Almost doubled the height of the keep." The man's penetrating dark eyes sparkled mischievously. "It was built by a Welsh prince in the Middle Ages upon the site of a much older tower. The woods you see are one of the last ancient medieval hunting forests in Britain. I have reinvented this rather lonely little tower as a bohemian retreat for writers, artists, poets and those folk inspired by art, the mysteries and magic. Yet this entire watchtower is not what it appears. It is a wolf in sheep's clothing."

"It's hiding in plain sight?" asked Joe.

"We are all hiding in plain sight, my boy. What we appear is never what we are."

Another blood-chilling howl rose up from the darkness beneath the trees. Joe shivered. "I hate wolves," he muttered to himself.

"Is that so? Well, what I would say to you, my boy, is, if you're scared of the wolves, stay out of the forest."

"You said it's a hunting forest?"

"Indeed it is."

"What do you hunt?"

"Everything that is in it."

At that moment there was a gust of cold wind and looking up the man and boy noticed rain approaching from the west, piling up over the southern skirts of the mountains. The temperature was dropping as the storm approached.

"Come," said D'Ante suddenly, making for the door. "There is something I wish to show you."

The master led Joe back into the stairwell, down one floor and along past Rose's door to his study. Unlike the housekeeper's humble garret, this room was large and ornate. Completely windowless, all four walls were hidden behind towering bookcases, except one area hung with a floral tapestry. Beyond a cluttered desk, a wide fireplace blazed, and around the hearth, near enough to be warmed by the roaring flames, stood two chairs: one a worn armchair, the other a lattice-backed seat. Squatting between these was a small table set for tea. Everything smelled musty and incredibly old.

It's the sort of place a professor would own, thought Joe. Or perhaps a wizard.

Upon the desk stood a model of the tower showing the extent of the renovations. Joe crossed to it and saw how what had once been a fairly basic interior had been divided up into all manner of rooms. A kitchen had been added to the floor below the living quarters and the hall fireplace had been transformed into a huge window.

"As you can see I have made downstairs into smaller rooms, but once the whole ground floor was a feasting hall for the lords and ladies of the castle."

"The Mead Hall," Joe said, remembering the name in the guide.

"Yes, indeed. Not as great as Heorot or Din Eidyn or the mighty Valhalla, but impressive nonetheless."

"What's mead?" asked the boy.

"It is not wine and it is not beer. It is made by fermenting honey with water, and sometimes spices. Bumblebees are the sacred messengers of the gods and their drink is the brew of heroes." He produced a leather hip flask from his jacket. "The honey comes from our hives and is mixed with the water from Blackmirror Tarn, plus some rosemary, thyme and somesuch. Metheglin I call it, and it is a magical draft. Those who taste it always tell the truth…"

D'Ante sank into the armchair and invited Joe to do the same. "Sit," the master of the tower said. "Tea?"

"No, thank you," said Joe.

"No? Then perhaps something stronger?" He offered the flask.

Joe shook his head.

"Oh, I insist." D'Ante unscrewed the canteen and passed it to the boy. Feeling he had no option, Joe lifted it to his lips and sipped. The drink was thick and very sweet. It did taste of honey, but also of spices and herbs. He swallowed and felt the mouthful sink down his throat. Within seconds his whole head was on fire. Joe had once had brandy at a party, but this was far stronger. Joe put the flask back on the table and looked at it suspiciously, while the room swam around him.

Immediately D'Ante began to question him. "I spoke with the housekeeper and she informs me you were found in the forest. She told me you were wounded. Were you shot?"

"Yes," said Joe. "I think so…"

"Well, that doesn't seem the sort of thing you'd forget. Rose says you were, so let's go with that. Perhaps you know where you come from? You are obviously not Welsh." His voice was strict and cold now. "And do not lie to me. I will know you out."

"From Essex. A place called Great Dunmow. It's—"

"I know where that is. Do you realise you have slept for four days?"

"Yes, I do."

"And do you know why?"

"I was healing."

"Yes, my housekeeper has many hidden talents." He mused a while on that, then continued. "Let me tell you of the history of this place. The first record of a settlement here was in the Dark Ages. Missionaries from Ireland recorded a wooden tower called the Mead Hall of Twr-

Â-Gân. That's Welsh for 'the tower of song'. It was occupied by a tanist and bard named Huan Caius Mereddin."

"What's a tanist?"

"A Celtic prince. And before you ask what a bard is, they were poets and storytellers who trained at a special college. Do you know why he chose this site?"

"No."

D'Ante raised a disbelieving eyebrow. "This place, like only a handful left in this world, is sacred and magical. It is amaranthine, eternally beautiful and unfading; everlasting."

D'Ante indicated a large painting on the wall. It was a landscape view, probably from the battlements, showing the peaks, forest and lake. "This is the tallest mountain in Wales. We call it Snowdon, but Mereddin knew it as Yr Wyddfa. History tells us that the castle was built to defend this strategic pass through the mountains. We know differently. It is due to this." He pointed to the circle of water in the painting. "That, my boy, is Dudrychllyn, Blackmirror Tarn. It is the watering hole that draws the animals down to drink. That is why the circus is here. To sup their fill of the mystical tarn. The magic that drew them draws all of us."

Just like the magical spring beneath the temple in Italy, Joe thought.

"Don't you feel it, boy? It's in the walls and the floors. It's through these doors. It's in every handful of soil, every rock and root."

"Yes," Joe had to admit, "I do."

D'Ante nodded as if this were the answer he wanted. "It's undeniable. Why, the Celtic tanist drew a sword from that lake that fairly jangled with sorcery."

Joe ignored that. "You said you had something to show me?"

"Yes, indeed I did."

D'Ante stood and walked to the tapestried wall. Joe joined him, and as he did so, the man pulled at the heavy fabric as if revealing a commemorative statue to an expectant audience. Behind it stood an arched doorway leading into a further room. Beneath its arches stood a pair of brass lecterns, set back to back. Upon the closest of the two, open to the map pages, lay *The Stranger's Guide*.

"*You* have it!" Joe shouted.

"Yes, I do." D'Ante's eyes glittered dark and unreadable, appearing wholly untouched by the candlelight.

Eyes like lakes. Eyes like a universe.

Eyes without end.

"Aha! And here we have it. Confess to me that you are a magician come to unseat me from this sacred place."

"I am not."

D'Ante snorted and wagged a finger at him. "You are a boy wizard – an enchanter of some considerable power to so convincingly travel in such a form – arrived to steal my kingdom."

"No, I came here by accident. Just give me the book and I'll leave."

"Liar! You are no errant boy."

"I am," Joe insisted.

"Well, then how do you explain this?" With one bony finger D'Ante pointed through the archway.

Joe looked and saw for the first time that what he had assumed was a doorway was in fact the frame of an enormous mirror. There was no room beyond, it was this room. Stepping closer, he now made out the tower's master, the lectern and the bookcases, yet there was something odd about the scene. Joe stared for an age before he realised that his reflection was missing from the giant looking glass.

AFTER THIS REVELATION, D'ANTE DRAGGED Joe away and left him in the tower dungeon for safekeeping. D'Ante called the pit an oubliette, the only access through a circular barred hatch set in the ceiling. This was situated below the floor of the mead hall and smelled of damp and decay. It was also very cold. There Joe was abandoned in the darkness.

Interminable days passed. A high window showed him dusk and dawn, so he was able to keep a tally, scratching marks for Sunday, then Monday and all the way to Saturday, which by his reckoning was Christmas Eve. Heavy snow fell and guests began to arrive from all quarters. He heard them gather in the mead hall above, their conversations and after-dinner chatter, while outside the travelling players rehearsed whatever show they were to perform for the watchtower's guests. During this time Joe thought a lot of his parents, of the school bus and how simple life had been. Before he had stepped through a door to this other world and lost his way home.

His dark confinement conjured thoughts of the fateful birthday barbecue, of his parents and the promise of grilled food. That day was supposed to be a special time, a happy time. Then the dark shapes had swept from the shadows and he was fleeing for the hideaway. Why couldn't we live a normal life? he asked the blank walls. Why had they never owned a real house? Why instead did they have to move from rented flat to radical commune to weirdos' spare rooms? Joe was always on the road, always being minded or cared for by strangers. *Why didn't they come back for you?* said the darkness. *What is so wrong with you that they left you behind?* Joe missed his father's quiet companionship and even craved his mother's strictness and chores. He would have suffered anything to see them again and to prove them wrong. He could be good. He could do what he was told. And then he realised that even if they did come back to the roundabout, he was here now, held captive in a prison in the distant past. Nobody knew where he was. Nobody was coming for him.

I did this, he told the total blackness. I brought this on myself. On all of us. I wanted to be a maverick superhero and not follow The Rules. And look what happened when I didn't.

He wasn't a superhero. He was just Joe. A sick little boy who should have done what he was told. It was his fault his parents had gone. All his fault. It was why he had been forgotten at the bus and now why he was here. He had not been a good boy. He had not taken his medicine.

And before, way before, was his greatest screw-up, the one that had ruined everything.

Most of the time Joe spent sleeping or shivering in his blankets, but twice a day the grille was unlocked and a basket was lowered down to him by a servant girl. It always smelled of warm kitchens and breakfasts in bed, and held leftovers from the previous day such as meat pies, dumplings in gravy, wrapped cheeses and freshly baked bread. Whatever D'Ante's aims in imprisoning him here, obviously starvation was not one of them. All he ever saw of the young woman were flashes of her hands and long, flame-red hair. When he tried to speak to her she remained silent, moving out of sight as quickly as she could. She wouldn't even tell him her name. Then on the morning of Christmas Eve he was shaken awake and found the young woman kneeling beside him. Most of her ginger hair was tucked up inside a tight scarf, and she wore a simple dress and scuffed shoes. Her hands were filthy with soot. Yet still even under the dirt Joe could see she was exceptionally pretty. Joe had never had friends and certainly not *girl* friends. Apart from his mother and a few older daughters of people he'd stayed with, he had never been this close to a girl before. It was all he could do not to stare.

"What—" he began, but she shushed him.

"Be quiet," she said, "or they will hear you."

"Who are you?" Joe whispered.

"I'm Serene, and I want you to help me escape."

"Escape?" Joe couldn't believe what he was hearing. "How can I do that?" After all, he was the one locked in a dungeon.

"There's talk in the scullery that you're a powerful warlock," she continued. "That D'Ante might actually be scared of you. Years ago he stole this castle from its rightful owners and I think he lives in terror that someone will come and steal it back." Joe nodded. The master had said as much on the battlements. "I know where your book of spells is kept. If I return it to you, you can use your magic to get us both out of here."

Joe's heart sank. The book was about as magic as he was. Her dreams that he could whisk her away on a flying carpet were just that. "Why don't you just run away?" he suggested.

Serene looked at him like he was something she'd just stepped in. "Because D'Ante's wolves patrol the forest. I would not get from here to the first hill."

"I can't help you. I'm not—"

"You don't understand how awful it is here. Working dawn to dark in that stupid kitchen. I mean Rose is not so bad, but that horrible D'Ante… He's a nasty bully. And his henchmen… with their shaved heads and—"

Shaved heads! "Wait," Joe interrupted. "These henchmen. Do they have scars?" He reached up and tapped the back of his head. Serene nodded sombrely.

"Of course Rose has taught me little bits of household magic, things like charms and tea-leaf readings, but nothing compared to what you must be able to do. Cook says you could stop his heart with a look."

"Sorry to disappoint you, but I'm no magician. Actually, until today I didn't even know magic was actually real."

Serene let out a shocked laugh. "Oh, now you are teasing me. Why would a warlock not know magic exists? Around here, it's simply taken

77

as read. It's like in a faerie tale. There's a tower in the forest. There's an evil sorcerer and an owl. Birds talk. Swords sing. Doors open to other worlds."

"Doors—" he began, suddenly far more interested in their conversation, but Serene ignored him.

"We get all sorts. Guests from far-flung places. Arabia. Zanzibar. Darkest Peru. When I arrived here, I didn't believe in sorcery. That all changed when the owl spoke to me."

"What did it say?"

"Believe it and you'll see it." Even in the dimness of the dungeon, Serene's eyes glittered with the memory.

"Why are they keeping me prisoner?" asked Joe. "Why has nobody come for me?"

"The master is far too busy entertaining the guests. Everyone is. I'd guess you'll be down here until they're gone."

"I have to escape," Joe begged.

"So do I." The girl's face lit up with the thrill of her plan. "I want to run away with the travelling fayre. Of all the enchanted things here, they are the most extraordinary. I shall be a fortune teller and use my full name. Serene is short for Lasairfhíona." She pronounced the name 'la-sar-ee-na'. "It's Irish and comes from the old tales. Isn't it wonderful?"

"It's very beautiful." As soon as he said it, Joe knew he sounded stupid. Thankfully Serene didn't seem to notice.

"I love it, but everyone else thinks it's too high and mighty, so I just stick with Serene. That's the name I'll use in the fayre."

Stop being so wet, he chided himself. Forget the girl. You have to get out of here. "The plan?" Joe urged.

"Tonight is the start of Christmastide and everyone will be at the performance of the play. Tomorrow the travelling fayre leaves for Scandinavia. There's a large chest in the fortune teller's caravan, but I need someone's help to hide me inside. I need you, Joe."

Up above people were entering the tower.

"I have to go," Serene said, handing over the food and water from the basket. "So, if I help you, will you help me?"

"Yes," the boy promised. "I will."

The girl clapped her hands in excitement. "Be ready at dusk. That's when I'll come back for you."

THE REST OF THE DAY moved incredibly slowly for Joe. The only respite from his loneliness was when D'Ante's house guests gathered in the mead hall and he caught snatches of their conversation drifting down through the grille. Some of the most fascinating were those things that echoed other aspects of Joe's journey so far.

"Master Abraham, I heard with interest how in your manuscript the Undead have no reflection. How so?"

"Well, Doctor, folklore shows how the looking glass mirrors the soul – and the vampire has none."

"And also the sun's rays turn them to ash? So why then would they not also turn to ash in moonlight, which is, is it not, merely *reflected* sunlight?"

Then D'Ante's voice saying, "Perhaps they should travel only in the dark of the moon. For surely that is truly evil's time. The time when no light shines."

Joe's heart leapt. Were these the other travellers that Serene had mentioned? Had they too stepped from other times and places?

"In my opinion, the Ghost Club hasn't been the same since Dickens died, but in this revival we shall show how the unseen universe is a great reality, Charles. And what better place than this watchtower and its enchanted tarn for attempted communication with the world of spirits."

There was other talk: of games of logic and grand inquisitors and a society called Occultus Earth, of which many of these people appeared to be members. But mostly their chatter was incomprehensible to the boy. Then – finally – dusk fell over the tower and, as promised, the flame-haired girl came for him. One moment he was alone in the dark, the next the iron gate was lifted and the long ladder descended into the pit.

"Hurry, Joe," Serene called down. "We must be quick."

Climbing up, Joe found himself in the hall that held the stairwell. The girl was dressed for travel, wrapped in a thick hooded cloak and carrying a small bag. Everything was drab and functional, except at her neck he saw the merest glimpse of something gold shining at her throat.

"Where's Rose?" Joe asked as she led him out through the tower.

"At the fayre," Serene replied. "They all are."

With haste she led him through the empty rooms, down the stone steps and across the courtyard. Outside was bitterly cold, and ice still lay in patches, but to Joe, so long imprisoned, it felt wonderful to be in the open air. Guided by the maid's lamp, Joe kept close.

Once beyond the castle gates Serene kept to the walls, following the curve of the hill until they were above the cluster of tents and caravans near the tarn. By now it was full night, and the wolves were baying in the woods. The circus's festive lanterns could be seen clearly below, lighting a small stage that had been built under a bell-shaped awning. Here D'Ante's house guests gathered, wrapped in furs and greatcoats, smoking and talking as they waited for the spectacular to begin. While they lingered, a few jugglers and musicians provided entertaining sideshows.

"See that caravan?" Serene whispered, pointing out a painted wagon near the back of the encampment. "That's where Madame Lilith lives and where I need to be hidden when they leave tomorrow. She's the leading lady in the play, so is backstage preparing. That means the camp will be deserted. Let's go."

Joe held the eager Serene back with one hand. "Where's the book?"

"Don't worry. I have it. You'll get it back when I'm safely hidden."

The boy and girl descended the steep rocks, moving under the shadow of the trees until they stood at the edge of the fayre. As they approached, the sound of music and laughter grew stronger, then suddenly a trumpet sounded a long fanfare. The play was about to begin.

"Can you make us invisible?" Serene whispered. When Joe shook his head, she tutted and said, "OK, in that case we need to wait until the play is underway so everyone is either on stage or in the audience."

Out onto the ramshackle stage strode a tall, moustachioed man in an Elizabethan-style costume and a many-coloured cloak. He carried a heavy book and his shoes were fashioned like the feet of a rooster. He had an air of mischief about him, and between masses of lustrous black curls his eyes sparkled like those of a madman.

"That's Pandoro," said Serene. "He's the head of the troupe."

Pandoro made a great sweep of his hat, bowing low, then addressed the audience. "The fantasmagorie you are to witness this night are all cautionary tales. Fables of taboos broken and warnings ignored, and of fellows' grisly and ghoulish fates. Ladies, lords and gentlemen! Pandoro's Travelling Fayre presents 'Cautionary Tales of Dreams and Darkness'."

A small wave of excitement rippled through the onlookers. Some clapped. Someone whistled.

The ringmaster opened his large book, tossed the ringlets from his eyes, and began reading. "There are those who walk in this world, and there are those that walk in the other world, but—" he raised a finger into the air, "—this is a story of those who walk in both worlds, those who travel between the light and the dark, and of their mysterious purposes. Their land is the place you've seen only in your dreams; the land of the lost and the free. The place where Death never treads – the place between."

Joe was reminded of the conversations of D'Ante's guests in the mead hall.

"It is the place of once upon a time. You see, certain places, like certain people, seem not to be a part of the here and now, they seem to be beyond. From the realm of nowhere and everywhere all at once. They exist at all times and all places, dwelling like shadows of history. And they say that if you sit at these dwell points in the hour between the setting of the sun and the moon's rising, if you sit very still and look very hard, you can sometimes catch glimpses of these worlds through the crack in the door of reality. They say imagination is the lock and belief is the key. Do you believe enough to try it? Do you? Then join us here this evening on a magical journey into a time beyond time!"

In the audience D'Ante started to clap and, after a brief pause, almost everyone joined in.

"We need to go," said Serene.

"Wait," replied Joe. "I want to hear this…" The boy was torn between staying and going. He wanted to leave this place with Serene and never look back, but the play's talk of people who walk in both worlds might be vital for his travels. "Just a few more minutes."

From somewhere came a short drum roll, and the players emerged. Immediately they bowed and began handing out masks to the audience. Each mask represented one of the characters in the cautionary tales. There was a knight, a princess, a villain, a sorcerer and a monkey. Once all had chosen their champion and were wearing them, Pandoro began again, this time in verse.

"I am storyteller, Pandoro, I
The master of this travelling band
It is I that calls forth these enchanted tales
From the book here in my hand.

I come to tell fables, both tall and true,
From a land behind the sky
From a land on the other side of the rain
For what reason? I'll tell you why:

These are tales of dreams and darkness
Cautionary tales are they each
And within each one there's a message to hear
So listen and learn what they teach."

Five pantomime caricatures entered, each wearing copies of the masks previously distributed to the audience and each introduced by the storyteller.

"So see here the leading lady and man,
His rival, the mystic and fool
They strayed from the paths of wholesome, good lives
And foul ends shall come to them all.

Yet before I start with their stories
And before these tales come to a close
Let me say that their fates are bound tightly
In the evil of a single black rose."

From somewhere in the folds of his cloak, Pandoro produced a large midnight bloom that glistened in the torchlight.

"This flower comes not from shrewd planting
Nor a gardener, mad as a loon,
But instead is a shard of the terrible dark

That will one day extinguish the moon.

It's a darkness that waits at the end of the world
And that shakes like the leaves on a tree
And when those black leaves fall, they fall into our lives
As, my ladies, my lords, we shall see…"

"Joe!" Serene urged, and this time when she tugged his arm he went with her. There was something about the play and the words within it that disturbed the boy. At first he thought it was the ominous dark rose or the impending fates of the characters about to stray from the righteous path, but he knew it wasn't. It was the bit about the place between. That's how it felt being here – that he was standing between worlds. As if he had fallen down and got lost in the cracks in reality. Just the thought of that made him shiver.

Quickly the two children crept between the wheels, barrels and tent ropes of the encampment until they arrived at Madame Lilith's caravan. The gaily decorated wooden house was set between tall wheels with a railed porch and ladder at the rear. Inside it was easy to find the chest the girl had mentioned, for it was being used as a table in the centre of the cabin. Clearing the top, the girl drew back the long bolt and together they hauled open the lid. It took all their combined strength to lift, but inside was easily enough space for Serene to fit with comfort.

"I have food and water," the girl said, "so all you have to do now is replace the board and items on the table."

"OK."

Serene reached into her case and pulled out *The Stranger's Guide*.

"Here," she said, handing the leather volume to him, then nestled down inside the giant trunk. "A deal's a deal. But it would have been far simpler had you just turned us all invisible."

"Thanks for setting me free," said Joe in a mumble. Wanting to say more but not really sure how. Part of him yearned to go with her, to forget all about labyrinths and talking birds and Grim Grotesques. Being part of a travelling fayre would certainly be an adventure. Yet once more, The Rules echoed through his mind. Don't Make Friends, they warned. Be Invisible. "Have fun with the circus," was all he could manage.

"Awesome sauce!" Serene said with a grin and leaned forward and kissed him. She tasted of flowers and honey.

Joe was shocked. Both by the kiss, but more by the peculiar phrase. "What did you say?" There was no way *that* was a Victorian turn of phrase.

Serene's eyes sparkled; for the first time she actually looked like a child. "It's like apple sauce, only made with awesomes." She laughed. And in that moment he realised who she was. There was no doubting it.

"You're Gunner's sister!" he said, rather louder than he'd meant to.

Serene's face paled, her eyes widening in distress. "How—"

"It's true, isn't it?"

"Yes, but how do you know Scott? Is this a trick? Are you reading my mind? There's no way you could have met my brother. Unless…" She stopped and placed both hands up to her mouth in shock. "You came through the labyrinth?"

"Your brother showed me the way here. It was him who got me into this mess."

"Is he here?" The girl's eyes went wild with fear.

Joe shook his head. "No, but that didn't stop him ruining my entire day."

"It's his superpower," Serene said. "That and hurting people."

"What's your real name?" asked Joe.

"Lakelyn. Lakelyn Reeve," she replied, and Joe screwed up his nose.

"Oh, it could have been far worse. With parents like mine, I could just have easily ended up as a Princess or Kenidee or Jazzlin." The two of them exchanged smiles, then Serene remembered where she was. "You have to leave," she urged.

"I was supposed to be finding you, not letting you go."

Serene stepped back out of the chest and took both his hands. "Don't you see, Joe. I don't want to go back. My brother was a cruel and jealous bastard. He hurt me, tortured my friends, got in my bed at night…" Her voice broke, but she carried on. "The worst was my parents did nothing. I'm not like them, and I'm not going to become one of them. I want a better life."

"I'm sorry," Joe mumbled. He had no idea what to say to her.

"Don't be. I got away and the house found me. Like it does all lost things. I don't want to go back. I'm better here. It's a new start. A chance to be free."

"I don't want you to go," said Joe, and only as he said it did he realise it was true.

Serene squeezed his hands, her eyes shining as she said, "Then come with me."

Joe's heart ached. He would have given anything then to have been able to step into the chest and be close to her in the darkness. But I can't, he said to himself. I have to get back to the bus. To my parents. Joe let go of Serene's hands and stepped away from the box. It was all the answer he could give her.

"Goodbye, Joe," the girl said, releasing him. "You have to leave me now. You have to go."

"Will I see you again?"

"Maybe. Perhaps next time you go to the circus. Here." She lifted her hands and unclasped her necklace, allowing the boy to see it clearly for the first time. It was decorated with golden leaves and flowers, and at one end sat a jewelled bumblebee. It was beautiful. "Something to remember me by. Or as my scatty mother used to say, 'Keep me in your dreams'."

"Come out, come out, whatever you are." The voice was D'Ante's and it was right outside the door.

"Joe!"

"Get down," said the boy. Closing the lid, he swiftly replaced the items on the table. Once he was sure all was as before, Joe stepped out onto the balcony. It was no use hiding; they knew he was inside. Perhaps in this way Serene would remain undiscovered. Still, when the boy emerged from the painted wagon he gasped in shock. It was no surprise to see D'Ante there, holding the owl on one gloved fist, nor Pandoro, the actors or the ragged crowd of guests who stood behind them. What made Joe's blood run cold was that they were accompanied by Damfino and his band of Grim Grotesques. The rake-thin huntsmaster's face was curled with a self-satisfied grin, like a cat about to taste its cream.

"Thought you'd escaped me, wolfshead?" Damfino rasped. "Have no such fear. There is no covert from the Wild Hunt. Not there, not here, not anywhere. We will hunt for you to the end of eternity." Every one of his huntsmen grinned at this, and Joe's heart froze. He knew now that this was true. They had been hunting him since his birthday. But why? It didn't make any sense. Silently he squeezed the book to his chest until it hurt. "And my eternal thanks to Lord D'Ante," Damfino continued, "for hindering the quarry till our arrival." His men found amusement in this, but Joe just clenched his teeth and said nothing.

"Come down here, boy," D'Ante commanded. "I want to know—" Then he realised Joe was clutching *The Stranger's Guide* in his arms. "That's impossible! To translate from a locked dungeon is one thing, but my study is thrice-warded by—"

"Time enough for talk," spat Damfino. "Cock Laurel. Gilderoy Waites. Seize him."

From the pack, two wild-eyed figures stepped. Their faces shone wetly in the lantern light, giving them the look of deserters from a prison outpatients' unit. Between them they carried a rope net. Joe shrank away from their approach, pressing his back against the wooden caravan. In his head, warnings pounded. No way out! No way out!

Suddenly, the boy was blinded as the air between the crowd and the caravan exploded into fiery chaos. Everyone leapt back as vermilion, golden and acid-green flares erupted, bursting like a swarm of multicoloured molten spiders and turning the night into a kaleidoscope of noise and colours. It took Joe a heartbeat to realise they were fireworks, but then Rose was there, at the base of the wagon. The housekeeper was wearing a monkey mask, but it was clearly her. "Joe! My boy!" she shouted up at him, reaching out her hands. "To me!"

Joe didn't hesitate. As the guests, Grims and players were thrown into pandemonium, he leapt deftly over the small balcony and took her hand. Shrouded in smoke, they fled back towards the dark shadow of the watchtower, while behind them D'Ante screamed, "Damfino, follow! I want that child!" Soon enough came the sounds of pursuit, but Rose's diversion had given them a good head start. Not looking back, the pair ran as fast as they could, and both were panting as they entered the keep. Even delayed by the fireworks, the huntsmen were on their heels as they climbed the stone steps into the tower. Entering the mead hall they threw their weight against the door and tried to force it shut, but they failed miserably. They were no match for the strength of so many adults. Instead they crossed to the other door, but when Rose tried it, she found it was locked.

Another dead end! Always Have A Way Out!

Behind them, D'Ante and Damfino stepped into the hall, leaving the rest of the men outside. Joe stood very straight and clutched the guide to his chest. His eyes searched the room for something, anything that might help. To his right were just books and ornaments, but there to his left, beyond a tall candelabra, hung a finely crafted short sword.

Its silver blade was shaped like a long thin leaf with a wooden handle ringed by golden bands.

"You can stop looking for another way out, my dear boy," said the master of the house. "I assure you there are none, except the door behind me. And you haven't a prayer of escaping that-a-way." With a wide pantomime gesture, D'Ante lifted a bunch of keys from his jacket, turned and locked that door too. Joe felt tears welling in his eyes and his head throbbed. Unconsciously he took another couple of steps back.

"I must use the oracle to escape," Joe said to Rose in hushed tones.

"I don't know what it is," she replied.

"I saw a drawing in the book. It's like a black circle framed by the rays of the sun."

"There. The obsidian mirror." The housekeeper pointed to an alcove next to the table. Above a display of fir branches and festive fruits, Joe saw a circle of polished stone set within a golden frame. "It can be nothing else."

"Oh, that old thing," D'Ante said. "That was dredged from the tarn years ago. They say it's older than the keep and everything in it."

Rose ignored her master. "So, you must look into the glass and—"

"I can't," Joe almost sobbed. "I have no reflection."

Rose gave him a look of complete open-eyed wonder. "*Swyngyfareddwyr,*" she said in a whisper.

"Surrender to me," the silver-haired man said coldly. "You have no other choice. If you kill me, Damfino will kill you. If you kill him, his huntsmen will kill you. If by some divine miracle you kill us all and escape into the wildwoods, the wolves will tear you to pieces. So surrender. Give up the book and maybe you need not be dead by the dawn."

Joe stared at the man with a look of hate in his eyes. "No," he croaked.

"What?" asked D'Ante.

"No," said Joe a little louder.

"No?" D'Ante echoed, then sighed in exasperation. "So be it. Damfino! Kill them both."

Striding forward, the tall thin man marched right at the boy, sending him scuttling back behind the dining table. Seeing this, Abram Kyle stopped and laughed. It sounded like a chicken being strangled. And as he threw back his head, he changed, altered, utterly transformed. First his neck contorted, his spine snapping backwards and cracking like a rotten stick. Then his knees and elbows twisted, lengthened and grew. Within seconds the huntsman was gone, replaced by something altogether other. Where once a man had stood, now an enormous hairy wolf hunched, its claws and fangs glistening in the candlelight. In the creature's black eyes many things danced and moved. Fearful, terrible things. It was like looking into bottomless wells of blackness.

"We all have our secrets," the monstrous thing growled.

Joe clung to the housekeeper in utter terror.

Now it was D'Ante's turn to chuckle. "You see, living in this house is a dangerous game. A very dangerous game. Especially for a child. Things live here. Things that come out of the dark looking for warmer homes. Horrid, shape-shifting things…" He indicated the slavering beast beside him. "Things like Master Damfino."

The beast at his side started forward again, but Rose stepped between him and the boy. "Stay away from the child," she spat, "or so help me, God…" She dug a hand into her apron and pulled out the ebony gemstone.

Seeing this the wolf stopped, growling, "She bears the stone of shadows."

"Oh, Rose," admonished D'Ante. "You black, black Rose. This is indeed a night of cautionary tales. Tales of shattered trust and treachery."

"I served the rightwise master of this tower and serve him still. This is a sacred place. It is not to be owned. Especially by the likes of you."

"Well, well, well." D'Ante steepled his hands in delight. "Now we see your thorns." His face darkened, all trace of humour erased. "And in service of the enemy. The revelations continue. First this boy and now you."

"The boy is innocent, D'Ante. I cannot stand and watch you touch him." Feebly, she thrust the talisman out before her. Just like Reverend Grey. Recoiling, the wolf roared in her face and lashed out. Though Rose shrank back, throwing up her hands in defence, the tips of the wolf-man's claws raked across her arm. The housekeeper screamed, stumbled and almost dropped the necklace.

Seeing the woman who had helped and healed him bleeding at his feet broke Joe from his shock and horror. All the people who had aided him – the reverend, Romano and now Rose Meirion – had suffered for their kindness. He wasn't going to let that happen again. Stepping between the woman and the wolf, he reached to the wall and grabbed for the sword. As his fist found the pommel, the wolf was upon him, its great arms closing around Joe's shoulders.

"Be still," hissed the Grim Grotesque in his ear. "If you struggle, I may have to cut you more than once."

"Get away!" Joe shouted. "I'll… I'll…"

"You'll what? Stick me with your little blade?" Damfino's breath smelled of rancid meat. "You will not kill me. And you will not escape. There is no place I cannot find you. Like you, I'm a travelling man. I can come after you wherever you are. Whenever you are."

"No!" Dropping like a stone, Joe slipped from the monster's grip and slashed out at the thing's furry haunches. Damfino roared, reaching after the boy, but Joe was already scrambling away. Fumbling to keep grasp of both the book and the blade, he staggered, then managed to haul himself up. Keeping the solidness of the table beside him, he stood and found the wolf already upon him. Yelling, he struck out with the sword, flailing blindly. The swing missed the wolf completely. Instead the tip of the leaf-shaped blade clipped the green lamp and sent it crashing to the floor. Instantly the glass smashed, ignited and a sheet of flame erupted between the boy and the men. Flaming oil sprayed across the cupboards and velvet curtains, spreading like wildfire through the lavishly decorated room.

As D'Ante and Damfino were driven back, Joe snatched a glance at the housekeeper and saw that she appeared to be praying. No, not praying – casting. She was using her magic to help him. Lifting the necklace up, she touched it to the mirror. Behind him the locked door glowed and transformed, revealing an open arch into a brightly lit room.

"Run, Joe. Run! And don't look back!"

Now the fire roared unchecked, consuming the table, the carved chairs and even the copy of the Christmas annual Rose had been reading when he arrived. It was a study in scarlet indeed; scarlet tongues of flame. There was nothing for it; he had to go through that door.

He turned and fled. And in that moment the wolf leapt.

"Joe, the talisman!" shouted Rose. She sounded manic. Turning, Joe saw her throw the shadowstone to him, and as he caught it, he toppled backwards under the immense shadow of the wolf. Flames seemed to be everywhere and Joe screamed, thinking he'd be burned alive, but the blaze did not harm him. Instead, as the doorway to Wales vanished, he found himself still sprawled in the heart of a blistering inferno. There he heard voices, saw visions and somehow knew that it was the fire speaking to him. And what it said and showed was beyond incredible.

IV

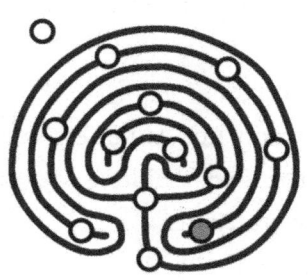

FOURTH MOON: WOLF MOON (OF BEASTS)
MANSE L'ESTRANGE
BAYOU ST JOHN, LOUISIANA, USA
MONDAY 4 JANUARY 1954 | 07:34:36

"MALEDICÉREUX! MALEDICÉREUX! LET ME GO! Let me go!"

"No, Cora. Stay here and the fire will not harm us."

Upon the other side of the door Joe found himself in a burning kitchen. It was night and the room was plain and functional with grubby tiled walls and floor, its sink, stove, cupboards and counters all painted a deep red. Above, a timbered ceiling was crusted with soot and grease, and almost hidden behind roiling black smoke. Over by the oven three figures stood huddled, cowering back from the flames. One was a black woman with a long dress and hair in a turban; the other two were little girls. The girl named Cora was fair; the other girl's hair was dark. They appeared not to notice Joe's chaotic entrance. All their attention was focused on the back door and the torches and cries from outside.

The flames engulfed the far end of the room and the heat was fierce, yet it did not burn the boy. The scene seemed indistinct, almost dreamlike, as if it were the shadow of a memory, so he stayed where he was and watched.

"Governess, you hear me?" came a man's shout from out in the night.

"I hear you, Master Louis."

"Emilia is here. She wants her daughters safe."

"Maman!" shouted the two children together, and Joe realised in that moment that they were twins.

The governess hugged the girls even tighter in her arms and shouted back, "Cora and Corvina are staying by me, Louis. Torch the house and fields and the whole wide world, but no flames will touch ol' Maledicéreux."

"Maledicéreux! My babies!" This time the voice was a woman's.

Across the roof the rafters began to burn, popping and spitting as the fire ate them up.

"I served your daughters like they were mine own. And when the evil comes calling you do nothing, 'cept hand me over to it."

"We can do nothing—"

"That," said the black woman almost to herself, "is all evil needs to make merry."

"You will have a fair trial."

"No!" shrieked the governess. "I will be strung up in that ol' Wishing Tree as sure as I'm standing here."

I've seen a mob like this before, thought Joe.

With a terrible cracking the roof timbers splintered and split, and fire erupted across the ceiling. Shrieking, the dark-haired girl – presumably Corvina – broke free of the black woman's clutches and ran for the back door. It was a brave move, for a second later great chunks of roof cascaded down in a rain of burning timber, only just missing her. Frantically the child heaved at the door but it did not budge. The heat from the fire had swollen the wood into the frame.

"Hear me now, all of the Bayou!" Maledicéreux's voice went from a whisper to booming thunder. "I call Grann Brigitte down upon this house and this family. Come now to hear my curse." Then she chanted,

"Three Things Taken! Three Things Taken!
One! Each night will Nightmares waken.
Two! Each day your Bones be broken.
Three! Each year Death's Shade shall darken
And take a loved one's Life as token.
Never shall this House be free,
Until you give your Self to me.
So mote it be!"

Between the words and the advancing fire, driven by the extremity of her fear, Joe saw Corvina heave the back door open. Outside stood a wide porch crowded with people and an ocean full of flames that poured into the kitchen like water. The black woman and the blonde-haired girl were consumed by the scorching inferno. Then the fire reached Joe. Even though he knew it was a vision, reflexively he threw up his hands to protect his face and screwed his eyes tight. There was a great blast of boiling air, a searing heat, and then… nothing.

The boy opened his eyes and blinked as bright sunlight blinded him. The fire and people were all gone. It was morning, the sky clear and fine – and he saw this because the ceiling was now made of glass. Pale morning sunshine shone through deep green slatted blinds. That was not the only change. The entire kitchen was altered, different in many ways, though obviously still the same one. The tiled floor and walls remained and even some of the furniture, but now it was painted a deep buttery cream. From a radio atop a tall refrigerator came the sound of a jazz band.

In his hands he still held the talisman, and the sight of it brought back wrenching thoughts of Rose and the tower. Not really understanding what he had just seen, Joe did know that Damfino and his huntsmen would already be on his trail. He had to get out of this room and to do that he had to find the oracle. Slipping the shadowstone around his neck, he looked around. The sight of the fridge made the boy's stomach groan. Who knew how long it was since he had last eaten. Maybe this place had halted his need for The Medicine, but it hadn't stopped him getting hungry. Surely he could spare a few minutes to get something to eat.

Inside he found the fridge was piled high with bottles, jars and plastic tubs. In one container were three cooked turkey legs. Another was filled with spicy rice. Always keeping his eyes to the doors, he began eating. As he scoffed the ice-cold food, he read more from *The Stranger's Guide*. Flipping through the pages, he found the passages about the fourth room of the labyrinth. Under the title 'Manse L'Estrange' was a photograph of a house painted all white with a jumble of steeply pitched roofs, wide porches and tall turrets. It made Joe think of the shops along Main Street, Disneyland.

"Monday 4 January," he read, "1954. Bayou St John, Louisiana." He was in the United States of America.

Next, the boy found an illustration of this place's oracle. It was a ceramic hand used for reading people's palms. The book noted that the key to leaving this place could be read in a person's moon line. Though he had skimmed the book, it made so much more sense now he was standing right here. Reading too far ahead made his brain hurt.

Finishing a slice of apple pie, Joe scanned the kitchen with his eyes. Beside the large red stove was a fabric noticeboard crowded with family photographs, magazine clippings and trinkets. There was even an advertisement for a New York private investigator. High shelves ran almost all the way around the room, and under a red-glass arched window was a ledge stuffed with candles, brightly painted bottles and all manner of dolls. Rabbits and chickens hung from pegs below this, but there was no sign of the ceramic hand.

Then he saw it.

On the other side of the kitchen directly above the sink was a bookshelf, and at one end perched a large upraised palm painted with lines and symbols. Even from where he stood Joe could see this was what he was looking for. The only problem was how he was going to reach it.

From somewhere nearby a door slammed shut and the boy heard footsteps heading his way. He knew he would have to hurry. Joe dragged one of the chairs from the table and climbed up, but he was still not tall enough to reach. The approaching steps were quite close now. They would be here any moment. Standing on tiptoe, the boy's fingertips brushed the hand's base. Desperately Joe strained upwards, reaching and grasping to gain purchase. Instead he succeeded only in knocking it forward.

Laden with brown paper shopping bags, a dark-haired maid entered the kitchen and, seeing Joe standing on the chair, she let out a high shriek and dropped everything she was carrying. The boy teetered, trying to explain, and in that moment the palmistry hand fell. Joe reached to catch it, lost his balance and watched as the hand hit the edge of the sink and smashed to pieces. The woman was shouting now, crying for help, her shopping forgotten. Joe skidded through the powdery debris, grabbed the book and rucksack, and ran for the back door. He reached it in three strides, threw it open and raced outside.

The air was humid and a fine mist hung across the gardens. Which way? he thought. Which way? Clattering across the porch, the boy leapt all but the last of the steps and ran headlong into lines of washing. Flailing through them, he didn't stop until he reached the back wall. Hauling himself over the railings, he jumped into the bushes beyond and kept on going.

As he ran, his mind throbbed out a desperate thought: with the oracle destroyed, how am I going to open the next doorway?

Finally, when he could no longer see the house or hear the screaming woman, Joe stopped. Hidden within a bank of tall grasses, he clutched his knees to his chest and shivered. He felt so alone, so abandoned and so far from anywhere he even remotely thought of as safe. A wave of self-pity welled up inside him, followed by anger and finally tears. All the pain and suffering, the trials and tensions of the past few days overcame him. He had had enough.

"Why you crying, boy?"

Joe looked up into the face of a thin, dark-skinned girl, maybe four or five years older than he was. She was eying him quizzically through the grasses, her eyes deep brown under a frizz of wild hair, forced into control under a floral headscarf. He didn't want to talk to people, so he screwed up his face and said, "I'm sick. Stay away from me and you'll be fine."

"You don't look sick," said the girl.

"It's invisible," he replied, wiping his eyes. "You can't see it from the outside. It makes me different, and different scares people." He stared at her, trying to will her away. She wore a plain black dress, white apron and carried a brightly coloured cloth bag slung over her shoulder.

"What's your tale, nightingale? You up from the Crescent City?"

"Yeah, I'm visiting from… England. Who are you?" asked Joe.

The girl's face lit up, showing a vast array of brilliant white teeth. "Why, I am Evangeline. Delighted to make your acquaintance." Stepping forward, she extended her hand to Joe. The boy paused for a second, then took it and they shook. He couldn't help noticing that her feet were bare, and she carried her shoes with the laces tied together around her neck.

"And I'm Joe. Now leave me alone," he said moodily.

"Why, ain't you in a lordly funk. You know when my mamie sees me down that great and deep well of pity, do you know what she says? She says, 'You gonna get bitter or you gonna get better?'" The beaming smile got more serious. "So, what you gonna do? Sit smaller and cry louder or stand taller and sing prouder?" Evangeline laughed at her own joke and the sound was just so infectious that Joe smiled too.

"Well, that's a whole lot better," she said and offered her hand again, helping him to his feet. "I saw you running from the house," she said, looking him up and down.

"What house?"

"*That* house. The only one you would ever be running from." Joe dropped his gaze and said nothing. "You shouldn't be messing around in there… Is that…"

"What?" he snapped.

"Is that why you're carrying a weapon?"

"I've never met a girl who asked so many questions."

"And I ain't never met a boy who carried a sword before," she shot right back. "Nor some big old book." There was something about her manner that made him trust Evangeline, even though his mind was flashing Rule #4: Don't Make Friends.

"Look, Evangeline, I need to get back to where I came from and to do that I have to find someone to read my palm. Do you know where my moon line is?"

Evangeline shook her head. "But there is a palmistry hand—" she started.

"Not any more," Joe said, morosely.

The girl slitted her eyes. "That old thing's been stuck up on that shelf ever since I've been around. How can that help you home?"

Joe heard the suspicion in Evangeline's words, but really had no way to answer it. With the oracle destroyed, Joe had no idea how – or even if – a palm reading would help him locate or open the door through the labyrinth. Yet he had to convince her to help. With no medicine and pursued by the Wild Hunt, time was priceless right now. He couldn't spend days wandering around the city of New Orleans waiting to fall ill or into Damfino's jaws. He had to be honest and convince the girl to aid him. And he had to do it quickly.

Dropping his gaze he swallowed hard, then said, "In that house is a door. It's a special door and the secret to opening it is found in the palm of my hand. In... in my moon line." Joe stopped himself. Had he said too much? "I tried to get the palmistry hand, but I dropped it. Now I need another way..." Joe winced. He sounded like an idiot, but when he looked up, he saw that Evangeline was beaming her irrepressible smile.

"Well, hasn't truth just upped sticks and come right out of her well?" Joe had expected the girl to mock him, but instead she seemed thrilled by his words. "I knew that house was hoodooed. I just knew it! Just the way the birds avoid it."

"Evangeline," Joe urged, "can you help me?"

"Maybe. For a start I know that Madame L'Estrange reads palms. She's legendary good at it."

"And you know her?" Joe asked hopefully.

"Know her? I works for the batty old pointer." To illustrate, Evangeline pointed her finger here, there and everywhere while impersonating her employer. "'Evangeline, you go fetch me my sewing basket. Evangeline, you go bring me my afternoon Old-Fashioned.'"

"You do that every day?" asked Joe.

"No. Only Mondays, Wednesdays and Saturdays."

"And today is?"

"Why, ain't you precious? Today is Monday. And I'm late. I gotta run or else boss maid Carlotta'll be tanning my hide two shades darker." Evangeline turned to go. "Anyhow, I shouldn't be seen talking with no white boy."

"No! You have to help me get to Madame L'Estrange."

"And why should I go and be doing a damn stupid thing like that? Want to get me jinxed, poxed *and* sacked, all sure as Sunday?" The girl folded her arms and raised herself on the balls of her feet. She regarded Joe for a long time as if sizing him up. "OK, here's what I'm doing. See that little path. Head right along it until you come to the shack with all the painted bird houses. That's mine. Go in and wait. I'll be back just after dark. God willing."

Joe nodded. He knew that somewhere and sometime, he had to trust someone. Just why did it have to be here and with someone as undeniably crazy as Evangeline?

Bayou St John, which was the neighbourhood of New Orleans Joe had appeared in, was a dirty, smelly place. Only a short stroll away from the white columned mansions on the waterway that connected Lake Pontchartrain and the Mississippi River, these houses were ramshackle with overgrown yards full of crazy, barking dogs and old men smoking on porches. This was a very poor area, but it took Joe a while to realise he hadn't seen another white face since back in Snowdonia. Well, unless he counted the ghosts of the twins. When he arrived at Evangeline's shack, it was pretty clear it was hers. Like she had said, within the white wooden fence were dozens of bird houses, each one painted in wild colours and stacked with corn, seeds and chunks of fruit. The tin roof of the house was crowded with birds, the air filled with their movement as they swooped and flitted from sky or tree or gables to feed. From somewhere close by a radio played, adding the music of a brass band to the dance of wings and beaks.

Opening the gate, and trying to look like this was the most natural thing for a young boy to be doing in the middle of the day, Joe walked up to the porch, opened the mesh screen and tried the door. He found it wasn't locked – indeed it didn't even have a lock, just a finger latch – and inside he found more of Evangeline's art. Every wall, ceiling and floorboard was adorned with painted flowers and animals. Some were repeated stencils, while others were larger and more detailed. Though the furniture was fairly rustic, every stick of it was daubed in bright colours, making what would have been a drab little space something altogether alive and delightful. The entire shack was just one big room, split into a living area with a small kitchen, a place for sleeping, and that was it. Outside at the back a rusted bathtub sat beside a shed that must have been the toilet.

With no idea when Evangeline would be back and nothing to do but wait, Joe sat at the kitchen table and, at last alone, found he was suddenly incredibly tired. He also found himself missing his parents. A little guiltily, he realised he missed his father more. Laverna wasn't a bad mother exactly, just strict and distant – and she grew more so every year. "Doesn't she love us, Dad?" he remembered asking his father.

"Of course she does, son," Thomas Darkin always answered. "Just in her own way." But to Joe that love was as warm and visible as the sun at midnight. What use was love like that? She had been very different before their life on the run, when Joe was younger and they had lived in the grounds of the big old empty mansion in Cornwall. The boy closed his eyes, imagining those happier times but knowing, now he was older, exactly how and when things had changed for them.

It was the night he'd failed her – and she had cut him out of her heart.

JOE STOOD STARING AT HIMSELF in the milky glass of a broken mirror. It hung beside the final flight of steps that led into the attic of the decaying mansion. He was five and this was an old dream, but the boy had no more idea that he was asleep than he had of the time in Timbuktu. Behind him the rotten stairwell swept downwards into darkness as thick as ink, but here his wind-up torch kept the worst of the blackness at bay. Caught in the murky reflection, the boy looked pale, his features angular, his eyes sparkling like sapphires in the stark torchlight.

From inside the room came a low animal sound. It was like growling. Summoning courage, Joe pushed the door and watched hypnotised as it swung open. Inside tall candles guttered and a hunched shape squatted within a scattered sea of objects. With the door half open, the growls bloomed into words.

"Sea to Forest. Forest to Sky. Eternal Flame in the Deathless Dark."

The door shuddered on its hinges and sent up a sudden, hellish creak. The hunched form squirmed and dropped whatever it had been holding. Metal clattered on the floorboards and rolled to a stop in a cloud of dust. The thing looked up and straight into the boy's eyes. It was his mother, doing some mysterious thing in this nameless old house.

"Mummy?" the boy's voice trembled. "What are you—?"

"Joe. You made me start." Laverna Darkin's stern features melted into smiles. "Come, do not be afraid. Mother is protecting us. A little ritual warding us from the evil eyes of our enemies."

"We have enemies?" he asked.

"You have no idea," was her answer. "My magic keeps you, me and Daddy safe. You want us to be safe, don't you?" The boy nodded. He wanted that always. Especially in houses as deserted and disturbing as this one. "An ancient custom for an ancient place. Come, let me show you. You'll be Mummy's little protégé."

"What's a protter-jay?" he had asked back then. Now, dreaming Joe said nothing. Did nothing. Waiting for what came next.

In the dream, the room changed. Instantly, it was night and the candles were out. His mother and father and their strange friends slept in the rooms below. Joe stepped into the foul-smelling chamber. His feet crunched on fallen parts of the ceiling as he crossed to the ritual circle. He lifted the metal object from the dust and shone his torch over its golden surface. The disc was etched with images of a serpent, its back crowded with trees. His mother had told him it was an Inca treasure, the snake a goddess. "She is the mother of forests," his memories whispered. "She channels the power in this place. Focuses it and makes it stronger. There is magic here. I will use it to protect us."

"Let me try," Joe had asked.

"No. You are too young and it is far too dangerous. Perhaps when you are older."

Or when you are sleeping.

Joe turned the cool metal over and over in his sweating hands.

Mother doesn't show me magic, so how can I believe it's real? She says it's there, all around us, but I've never seen it. He needed to prove to himself that her magic really existed and show his mother he was a big boy and could do it. He wanted to believe, but he had to see.

Five-year-old Joe lit the candles. He retraced the circle. He ignored the groaning of the attic floorboards as he squatted down beside the mother serpent and lifted the disc to his lips.

"Forest to Sea. Sky to Forest," he said, his breath frosting its golden surface. "Endless Flame in the Dreadful Dark."

"Joe?" said a low voice in the gloom behind him.

"Joe?" said another.

But it was already too late.

What happened next had never made any sense to Joe; not then and not now in this nightmare reimagining. One moment he was holding the disc, speaking the spell. The next he was turning towards the shadows of his mother and father. Watching as they ran headlong towards him, hands outstretched, eyes wide and wild. The next, the floor was falling. He was falling. His entire world was falling. Had his mother smacked him? Was the mansion collapsing? Whatever had happened, he knew he had failed. Knew he had broken something that could never be mended.

"No, no, no!" his mother's voice wailed. "My treasure! My treasure!"

Her anguish swept the boy away, erased him like footprints under a surging tide. Still falling, Joe wailed too. And in his dream, those tears became an ocean of pain and grief. Endless and unstoppable.

And every night after that night Joe wished she had been calling to him.

JOE WOKE WITH A SHUDDER, trembling and cold, and found himself slumped upon Evangeline's kitchen table. Filled with relief, he stood up, staggered and tried to shake the last of the awful dream from his head. Glad that he wasn't back in hospital and at the start of their life on the run. His meddling had drained all power from the Inca treasure, and without it, nowhere could be totally safe. Then began the time of The Medicine and The Rules. The time they discovered his sickness and all those dos and don'ts. And his parents never mentioned magic in his presence ever again.

Needing distractions, Joe turned his attention to keeping occupied – and awake. First he took the crumpled map from his pocket, drew on the castle keep and Manse L'Estrange, then stuck it inside the back cover of the book. Then he found a cloth sack that he fashioned into a makeshift bag long enough to hide the sword. Before putting it away, the boy polished the silver blade, testing its weight with a pretend battle against imaginary huntsmen. Not as awesome, perhaps, as retractable claws, but still a fine companion for the road ahead. He found an outside stand pipe and filled a jug with water, then sat back at the table and continued reading *The Stranger's Guide*.

He started with the pages on Louisiana and the USA, reading how the president was Dwight D. Eisenhower and the first television sets went on sale last December for $1,175. He learned more of the history of Bayou St John and found floor plans of the L'Estrange house. He studied them until he knew every bedroom, den and nook. He didn't want to get trapped by a rabid wolf in a dead end again anytime soon. As Joe read, each section drew him deeper into the unknown author's perilous journey of documenting the many times and places of the labyrinth. Joe was only four rooms through thirteen, and he had a long way to go. Worryingly, there were several near-blank pages of locations that hadn't been visited. What would happen when he arrived at those? The boy was curious as to who had written the guide and possibly more worrying was what had happened to him in the dark house and dangerous gardens. Of both questions there seemed not a trace of an answer in the book's pages. The most startling discovery by a mile was a photograph of Evangeline. The picture was labelled 'The Artist' and included a short description of her employ at the house and how she and Madame L'Estrange did not see eye-to-eye due to the girl's devotions to what the book called 'the old arts'. Had she recognised *The Stranger's Guide*? Or met its mysterious author? And if so, why hadn't she mentioned it?

The sun had already set by the time Evangeline came whistling through the front door. She was carrying her bag and in it was enough food to concoct a thick soup of rice, shrimps, chicken and vegetables. It was the first hot food Joe had had in days, and despite his forage in the kitchen, he ate ravenously. Afterwards, they sat by in the candlelit shack and Joe asked about the twin girls he had seen. It was all Evangeline needed to start talking of the curse of Manse L'Estrange.

"The manse is one of the oldest houses in Bayou St John, or at least the first one was before it burned to the ground. That's what started all this moonshine on the water. Back when Indians lived by the banks of the bayou, this land was sacred. That was why nobody built nothing on the site until the L'Estranges moved from France. They were slave traders and wealthy lawyers. They had the money and influence to run the natives off the land and build whatever it was they pleased.

"At this time the Voodoo Queen Marie Laveau held wild rituals and sacrifices hereabouts, up by a place called the Wishing Tree. She'd call to the tree to make people's wishes come true – which they did! – but still to this day most folks insist the woods near the bayou's mouth is a place best avoided. Who knew how the rumour spread, but it was said that the L'Estrange family fell in with Laveau and her crowd.

"About a hundred years back, two daughters were born to the family. They were twins and very beautiful. The one with blonde hair they called Cora and the other with black hair they called Corvina. To raise 'em, the family took a governess and that woman's name was Maledicéreux. As soon as she got her feet under the table, people began whispering of her rootworking powers and knowledge of things best left in boxes. Some said she drank a potion made from bat's blood that kept her eternally young and pretty."

"This is getting weird," commented Joe.

"Hush, as it's about to get a lot weirder. On the night of St John's Eve in 1875, the townsfolk reached the outside of enough and marched up to the house accusing Maledicéreux of witchcraft and devil worship. They asked that the governess be turned over to them but the family refused, so they torched the house with the governess and daughters inside."

"That's what I saw," said Joe. "The governess and the two daughters."

"You saw this? All those years ago?" Evangeline looked suspicious.

"No, today when I arrived here. When I was in the kitchen. It was like a vision."

The maid relaxed as if visions were fine with her.

"Well, then you already know what I'm going to tell you next. With the fires raging and sure as anything that no one would save her, Maledicéreux uttered a curse on the family and the house. She spoke that every year one of the family would die until her death was revenged."

"Yes, I know. It was horrible."

"Well," Evangeline admitted, "she *wanted* a life to be taken for every year, but her standing wasn't strong enough. Instead the voodoo gods granted one death every fifth year."

"How long ago was this?" Joe asked.

"Shush. When the governess spoke those words, Corvina was so terrified she fled and managed to escape the burning building. Maledicéreux and Cora were not so fortunate and were overcome by the smoke and heat. Both died when the ceiling collapsed."

"That's awful."

"Oh, that's nothing compared to what happened next. So the curse started its magic with one member of the L'Estrange family dying every five years. The family rebuilt the manse – pretty much how you see it today – but there was no happiness there for them. First off, Corvina's mother wasted away with grief, and her father followed, leaving the young woman all alone in that big, old house."

"Did she never marry?" Joe asked and Evangeline's eyes glittered with glee.

"Why, yes, she did. Twice. But she learned her lesson about that true enough."

"What do you mean?"

"Madame L'Estrange met her first husband at a Sunday dance in the summer of 1889. His name was Jean-Michel Savage and she was twenty-one. They were wed the following year, but as soon as that wedding ring joined him to the family, he withered away of yellow fever. You see, 1890 was the next five-year marker. So Corvina had now lost three people she loved: her mother in 1880, her father in 1885 and now fine Mr Savage in 1890. Yet still she was a goddamn stubborn so and so. Even after losing her uncle, Victor L'Estrange, in 1895, she was ready and marrying the very next year. She was twenty-eight, and though by then the curse was very real to her, she loved her new beau. By all telling he was a handsome one indeed. He even had a handsome name: Barthélemy Lachance. They had four fine years together and she thought she'd outwitted the curse, until he was struck by a horse and cart and killed on New Year's night just after the clocks tolled in the new year. That was how she started the twentieth century.

"After the loss of her one true love, Corvina locked herself away in the manse and nobody's seen her since. Well, 'cept Carlotta and sometimes me."

"So she's given up?" asked Joe.

"Oh no. Corvina L'Estrange is not a woman to ever give up. But she lives alone up on that sacred land with the ghosts of all those who have been taken from her. Now she is doubly obsessed with breaking that ol' Maledicéreux's curse – because she suspects she's the last and when her entire family is gone, that's when the curse will come and take her, too."

Evangeline counted on her fingers: "1905... 1910... 1915..." Each one representing another five years and another death. "1940... 1945... 1950." And when she was done, she'd used every last one. "Ten deaths in a long black river that flows right out from that accursed house. And now it's 1954 and she's indeed the last one left. She's only got a few months to break that curse otherwise she'll be meeting Maledicéreux before next St John's Eve."

"How old is she now?"

"Eighty-six. Ha!" Evangeline snorted a laugh as something dawned on her. "It's like those detective movies. Eighty-sixed at eighty-six. How righteous is that?"

"Do you think if we help her break the curse she'd help me with the palm reading? I haven't any money, and…"

Evangeline's face lit up. "Joe, I think if you help her break the curse, the grande dame would give you anything in the entire world and more besides."

"Well, then that's great," said Joe excitedly.

"Only one thing though. My guess is you sure as hell have no idea how to do that, do you?" The boy's heart sank. It was true. If Madame L'Estrange with all her money and influence hadn't been able to find a way after all these years and years, then how could he? Seeing the boy's crestfallen face, Evangeline added, "But I will help you find out, if you like."

"How?" Joe felt he would do anything.

"We can ask the Wishing Tree. Because right now it sounds like you've got a great big wish to make, my friend."

"You want me to go ask a tree for help?"

"Well, not just any ol' tree. This is an enchanted tree with roots that reach right into the magical heart of this sacred place. But actually when we go there, we'll really be speaking to Papa Legba."

"Your father can help?"

"Oh no, he's not my father," she said, laughing her infectious laugh. "This papa is the god of the crossroads where the Wishing Tree grows. He can take a message to ask for help and guidance. And we have to go tonight as Papa Legba's days are Saturday and Monday."

"And the tree or this Legba or whatever will grant my wish?" said Joe. "Like magic, right?"

"Yes. But only in that place, at that time and when the moon is darkest."

Joe sat up at this. It sounded very familiar, this story of special times and special places. "It isn't everywhere," she continued. "Take magic from its source and it slowly fades and dies. Like a branch taken from a tree. Or a chicken's head cut from its neck. You have to be careful with magic. Spells, curses... All magic is about using and losing."

"I think I lost it years ago."

"Don't be so sure. It's in these places. It's in that house. And it's in you, Joe. I am magic and so are you. I can feel it. Everyone's born magical. Just most people don't even know it. So what do you say? Shall we go get your wish?"

"I'm not sure I can do that."

"And why in heaven's name not?"

"But what if it doesn't work?"

"But what if it *does*?" Evangeline's eyes widened, and Joe knew that if it did, that would change everything. The girl moved about the room collecting items and stuffing them into a wicker basket.

"OK, well before we go, one more thing," Joe warned. "When we go out we have to be careful. Something else followed me here. It's a man who can change into a wolf, and he has my scent."

"Well now, I guess we'll have to use Evangeline's cloak of invisibility."

"You have a cloak of invisibility?"

"No, you crazy boy! But I do have this..."

She fetched from a wall cupboard a walking cane. It was painted black and red and wound with copper wire with nails and pins hammered all over it. "This will disguise our path," she said matter-of-factly as she tapped the stick three times on the table, then twice on the front door. "Let's go."

THE WAY TO THE WISHING Tree was back towards Manse L'Estrange, then off the track to a swampy area near where the river met the lake. At first, Joe tried questioning Evangeline. How long had she worked at the manse? Since Mardi Gras. Did she ever meet anyone else carrying a guide like this? No. Why did she live alone? Because no one can stand me around for long. "What, you writing a book?" she said at last, and after that Joe decided to walk in silence. It was full dark when they arrived at the great tree and the night was filled with the alien sounds of insects that the maid referred to as cicadas. The only illumination was from their lanterns and those of the boats out on the water. Looking up into the gnarled branches, Joe thought it might be an oak. It was certainly very old. Every bough was hung heavy with moss, making them look as if draped in fishermen's nets. Stumps where other trees once stood littered the area, but the ground had been cleared so that people could gather. Something about this place made Joe's skin prickle. It was too open and exposed. If Damfino and his mob appeared right now, they were as good as dead.

"Rule One," he whispered. "Nowhere Is Safe."

Evangeline cocked her head. "What did you say?"

"Nothing," Joe mumbled.

"Boy, you's more nervous than a long-tail cat on a porch full of rocking chairs."

Standing at the base of the great tree, Evangeline instructed him to climb up and sit in the junction between the biggest branches. Joe scaled the trunk and found that where the boughs split was a wide area. It was filled with coins, chalk symbols and the burned-out stubs of candles. As he got comfortable, the girl scrambled up beside him.

"Now what do we do?" asked Joe.

"We have to make nice to Papa," she said. "And I need to show you how to do some magic."

"Me?"

"Well, who else? I can't ask for nothing for you."

From her bag Evangeline produced a bottle of alcohol and a flask that steamed with hot coffee. She lit a few candles and piled what looked to be crunchy breakfast cereal into a natural bowl in the trunk. Then she started to talk-sing in a low murmur. It was a song about troubles and Christmas and happiness being a thing called Joe. It rose into the warm night air, drifting with the breeze, sending the boy into a doze. He didn't even know he was asleep until Evangeline touched his arm and woke him. "Time's now, boy," she whispered. "Grab that star at your throat and make your wish, Joe."

This is so not going to work, he thought. Pulling out the necklace, he held it tight in his fist and said, "I wish to know how to break the curse on the family of Madame Corvina L'Estrange." As his voice died in the darkness, all was silent except the sighing of the wind through the branches. Joe thought of Nature's Tongue and strained his ears harder. Incredibly, in the shivering leaves and the creaking trunk he heard a voice. It was repeating the same words over and over.

"Speak the curse. Speak the curse," the tree said.

"It says for us to speak the curse."

"I can do that," Evangeline said brightly. "There's not a swamp rat in the whole bayou who can't." She recited:

"Three Things Taken! Three Things Taken!
One! Each night will Nightmares wake you.
Two! Each day your Bones will break you.
Three! Each year as the Shadows darken
Death will come and take you.
Never shall your Self be free,
Until you give this House to me.
So mote it be!"

"That's not the curse," Joe blurted when she was done.

"What you saying?" Evangeline said, confused.

"It's almost right, but it's not the words I heard. Not exactly."

There was a lot more rustling and creaking from the tree.

"Speak the curse," the tree said again and Joe replied:

"Three Things Taken! Three Things Taken!
One! Each night will Nightmares waken.
Two! Each day your Bones be broken.
Three! Each year Death's shade shall darken
And take a loved one's Life as token.
Never shall this House be free,
Until you give your Self to me.
So mote it be!"

Hearing the true words of Maledicéreux's curse, the Wishing Tree let out a long, low splintering sound that resonated through Joe's feet and fingers. The tree was speaking again. "You think this journey will lead you to the hearth and home so lost to you. It does not. There can be no journey. You cannot be lost."

"Why not?" the boy said into the night air.

"Because you are already at the centre."

The words made no sense. It contradicted everything *The Stranger's Guide* had said.

"Joe," hissed Evangeline, "we have company." Breaking from his daze of concentration, Joe looked down and below saw the body of a massive wolf circling the base of the tree.

"He's found me," he gasped. "I told you he would."

"What? The wolf-man? That's him?" Evangeline was panicking. Joe understood why. Below the creature stood on its hind legs and raked its claws across the weathered trunk.

"I really hate wolves," Joe snarled, then to the tree asked, "Papa, can you help us?"

Softly, the tree replied,

"When the Hour is Dark, two things Remember:
The Stone of Shadows and Ilkilæmber."

"What's 'Ilkilæmber'?" asked Joe.
I am, spoke the sword.

IN THE MOMENTS AFTER THE leaf-shaped blade spoke to the boy, something changed in Joe. The words of both the sword and the tree blazed in his head, challenging him to accept another impossible thing. First doors, then birds, and now that trees spoke and metal was alive. Were these houses really standing on the last magical places on the earth? As he deliberated, Damfino prowled below, but thankfully the master huntsman looked to be alone. At the appearance of the wolf, Evangeline had flattened herself in fear into the hollow. Now she looked up at the boy and said, "Can wolves climb trees?"

"Undoubtedly," said Joe. Thinking, I can't let her be hurt. Too many people have helped me and suffered for it. Then he realised that she hadn't heard the sword. She heard the tree, but not the blade. Below, the beast that was Damfino circled, sniffing the humid air. Joe imagined he heard him sucking his teeth hungrily.

Ilkilæmber, thought Joe, did you speak to me?

By fire and ice, do you hear me speaking now?

Is Ilkilæmber your name?

It is. I am last of the Singing Swords of Albion. Blade of dark kings and dread lords. What is your need of me?

I need to kill that wolf.

And I have need to dine on our enemy's flesh.

But I don't know how to sword-fight.

Then run and die tired. The choice is yours.

Great, thought Joe, then he used every ounce of courage he had to half-jump, half-slide down the trunk to the waiting werewolf.

"Run, Evangeline!" he called as he leapt. "Get to safety. Go!"

Landing in the boggy grass, he held the silver blade in both hands and tried not to shiver. Again, Damfino in wolf form was massive. The beast's haunches stood easily as tall as the child's shoulders. As Evangeline fled, Joe's eyes darted between her and the monster, not knowing whether to fight or flee. Seeing his prey's indecision, Damfino snarled and in a rough approximation of human speech he growled, "Damned if you do, damned if you don't."

All Joe could focus on were the wolf's enormous claws, the wolf's cruel fangs. Claws like kitchen knives. Fangs like butcher's hooks.

This, thought Joe, is my initiation. My do-or-die time here in this foreign land and distant time.

And that was the moment that Ilkilæmber began to sing.

The sound was not like normal singing, or even bad karaoke singing. It wasn't the singing of drunks on the way home, or like opera or pop. Instead it was a high keening like the kind of noise a police siren would make if powered by dogs. The racket was awful, and hearing it the beast winced in pain, its ears flattening to its fur. Yet to Joe it had the opposite effect. The siren song filled his mind with fire, his arms with strength and his heart with daring and determination. As Evangeline's lantern disappeared into the misty night, Joe stepped forward and brandished the leaf blade.

"You've been hunting me since the old rectory," the boy shouted over the sword's caterwauling. "No, before." The realisation was sudden and horrible. "That was you at the bus, wasn't it?" The giant wolf grinned and began to circle the boy. "I am so sick of this."

"I, on the other hand," replied Damfino, "am sick *for* this. You have led me a merry dance, whelp. It seems we both wish for the ceremony of death."

Kill it, said the sword in Joe's mind and the boy charged. Damfino howled, rearing up to meet him. And there under the ancient tree, the two foes clashed.

Spurred on by Ilkilæmber's feral song, Joe slashed at the beast's face while the wolf deflected the leaf blade with its terrible paws. Ducking, the boy let the sword lead the attack, allowing its long experience and blatant bloodlust to guide his movements. Joe felt invincible, invulnerable, and he knew he would be as long as the sword continued its wailing.

The wolf was lightning swift, darting and leaping this way and that. Then it was at Joe's neck, its teeth scraping across his shoulder. The boy recoiled, craning to keep the wolf off his throat. The wolf's weight almost toppled him and he knew if he went down, he would never get up. He would die.

By death's dark kiss! the sword chided. *I should be wielded by a champion, not a child.*

Stabbing at the creature, Joe felt the sword find its mark and Damfino howled. The wolf leapt back and retreated, more cautious now that it had felt the blade in its belly. They fixed eyes and circled.

When the monster attacked the next time, Joe marched forward to meet it, hacking as he went. Dodging, the wolf hit the child with a mighty backhanded slap that sent Joe slamming into the trunk of the Wishing Tree. Winded and gasping, the boy almost dropped the sword, wanting to wrap his arms around his hurting sides. Instantly Damfino dropped to all fours, pressing himself to the wet ground, crouching, snarling. Joe cowered in terror, his hand reaching for the stone at his throat.

Up! demanded Ilkilæmber. *Hold me up!*

With all the effort he could muster, Joe raised the silver blade as high as his tired and aching arms could go. He was just in time, for in that heartbeat the beast sprang. The sword speared the wolf through its chest and Joe was showered in the creature's thick blood. Damfino let out a terrifying howl, then fell back and lay still on the sodden ground. Horrified, Joe pulled the blade from the monster's flesh and dragged himself to his feet. Everything hurt, but he wanted to be as far from the wolf and the tree as was possible. Using the last of the sword's adrenaline, he willed his legs into a slow, loping run. As he fled, Ilkilæmber's song fell silent, leaving only the sound of the night-time insects and the boy's running feet.

The longest of times later, Joe arrived at Manse L'Estrange but did not stop until he had the ornate ironwork of the gates between him and the terrifying darkness. Only then did he collapse, all strength and courage gone.

"Joe!" Evangeline was running down the veranda steps and across the immaculate gardens to him. "Oh, Joe! You're alive!" Then she saw the blood and her hands flew to her mouth. "Did it hurt you?"

"Why... here?" the boy said softly.

"Help! Help!" Evangeline was shouting, then to Joe she answered, "You said get somewhere safe. This is the safest place I know."

"I need to leave," the boy panted. "Now."

"What in heavens!" A dark shadow fell across them both. Joe looked up and saw the silhouette of a lady in a fur-collared dressing gown standing in the open doorway. She had her arms folded, her hair under a large, ostentatious hat. "Why, Evangeline, is that you out in my front yard? At this hour?"

The maid helped Joe to his feet and led him to the house. "This here is Joe," she said, "and he's got a need to speak to you, Madame L'Estrange. A mighty need."

Corvina L'Estrange's eyes widened at the sight of the wounded boy, but she shooed them inside without further questions. As Joe passed he saw she was much older than her photograph in the book. Her once raven-black hair was streaked with grey, her hands veined and crooked. The years had not been kind to the child Joe had seen in the burning kitchen.

Silently Madame L'Estrange led them through a foyer and into a round hall at the base of the master staircase. The manse was a grand residence, with each of the rooms stuffed with elegant furniture and antique objects. Sending her part-time maid off to fetch hot water and towels, Madame L'Estrange lifted a cloth from a side table and threw it over the smallest of the three sofas. "Sit," she said curtly, and perched herself in a giant green velvet armchair. As Evangeline returned, she tutted at the trail of dirt that followed the girl, but waved the annoyance away with a casual hand. For a while longer she held her tongue, waiting for Joe to be cleaned and calmed. Only once this was done did she speak again.

"Explain," she said firmly.

"Begging your pardon, I know it's late and you're probably very tired," babbled Evangeline. "We mean no disrespecting, and—"

Corvina waved away her jabbering with a hand. "What do you want to tell me, boy?"

Before Joe could even think to speak, Evangeline was talking again. "He knows the reason you cannot break the curse."

Madame L'Estrange sat up a little at that, but her tone was still impassive as she replied, "Why, does he now?"

"Tell her, Joe."

Taking a swallow, the boy said, "She's right. I don't know why or how it happened, but you're remembering the curse all wrong. Perhaps you were too young. Perhaps you got confused by the fire and all the commotion…"

"And how could you sit there and tell me that?" Madame L'Estrange's tone was unreadable.

"'Cause he was there!" blurted Evangeline, which broke her mistress's calm entirely.

"What? Oh, come now, how utterly, utterly preposterous."

"Tell her, Joe. Tell her what you told me."

And so Joe recounted what he had seen on his arrival in this time and place. He spoke the correct version of the governess's verse and included as much detail as he could manage. When he was done, Corvina's eyes were wide as the porcelain plates in her immaculate glass cabinets.

"Never shall this House be free..." she whispered. "Until you give your Self to me. My, my, my..."

"Does that help?" asked Joe.

"I am the last of my line. There is only me. And I'll be taken soon enough. I fear you are far too late to make much difference, you strange little boy."

But Evangeline was bursting with other ideas. "I could fashion you a poppet."

"What?"

"We could work an uncrossing. I could fashion a likeness of you and we could give the poppet to the governess. We could break the curse."

Madame L'Estrange's feigned indifference was entirely gone now. Her eyes were brimming with tears. "Oh, my darling child, to even spend these final years free of this bane... Will it work?"

"I'm sure with Papa's help it will."

"And if it does, how will I ever thank you?"

"Well," said Evangeline, "you could start by telling Carlotta and Beauregarde to stop being so mean to me." The girl thought for a moment, biting her lip, then added, "And allow me every other Saturday off."

Corvina let out a choked laugh and Joe saw that underneath all those years of pain and loss, she was still a very attractive woman. "And what do you want, boy, in return for saving me from my torment?"

Joe didn't answer right away, so Evangeline did it for him. "You have to read the fate in his moon line."

"His moon line," the woman said darkly. "So, we're a stranger, are we? Well, that explains who broke my palm-reading statuette. Give me your hand, Joe."

The boy hesitated. "Which one?" he asked.

"Why both, of course, but let's start with the right and see what God gave you. Then we'll see in your left what you're going to do with those gifts. We'll start with the Head, Heart and Fate lines, and get to the rest soon enough. The Head line is for wisdom, the Heart line for love, and the Fate line is for destiny. You are a first and only child." Her fingers trailed up and down his palm. "Good birth. Bad life. By bad, I mean hard. There is a sickness within you, but it is not what you think. I read talents in leadership and inventiveness, but no finesse in words or numbers. You have never been in love except with your father, and possibly your mother, and—" Madame L'Estrange looked up and straight at Joe, "—and a girl with flame-red hair."

Behind him, Evangeline whistled softly through her teeth, muttering, "You sly old dog." The boy felt his cheeks reddening so kept his eyes firmly on his palm.

"Your Fate line runs powerful and free like the great Mississippi and it is unmatched. I would normally think this would be an Earth hand, but it's not that. Nor is it Fire, Water or Air. You have a very rare hand, Joe. To know about you I have to read between the lines. See these two? They are the Saints and Sinners lines. And this one is for Life and Death. Up till now, you've been a practical boy, haven't you? A real average Joe." She smiled, lost in the creases in the boy's palm. "But already that's up and a-changing," she said curtly.

As if prompted by her words there came a clattering outside, followed by a crashing against the window. Everyone jumped and Joe whirled to see the monstrous form of the Damfino-wolf pressed against the glass. The thing was bloodied, its eyes wild, but it was most definitely still alive.

"Oh, by the Papa," shrieked Evangeline, "he's here!"

"Please hurry," Joe said.

Madame L'Estrange looked from the wolf back to the boy's hand. She betrayed not the slightest of panic, but her fingers trembled against Joe's palm as she continued.

"See this mount here, under your little finger? This shows the Luna is growing in you, Joe. The moon is reigning your Fate now. It is the sign of imagination – and you need it. Else you'll be lost in its Infinite Ocean."

The wolf heaved itself against the window and the whole pane shook.

"Is there anything about a door?" said Joe.

"Ah, if it's a door you need to get to, then we need to call upon the King of the Crossroads," Corvina said. "Evangeline, get the besom and conjuring oil. Let's hope Papa will reward Joe for his help with a way out of this place."

Turning their back upon the monster at the window, the three moved through the house to the kitchen. There Madame L'Estrange locked the door behind them and ordered Evangeline up to a small altar on the high shelf before the arched transom. The maid handed down a yellow broom and a crystal bottle of dark oil. "First," said Madame L'Estrange, "we must ask Papa to show us the door. We could have used the palmistry hand, but… well, never mind. There are other ways."

Back within the house there came an almighty smashing of glass and something began rampaging through the rooms towards them.

"Your hand, Joe. Hold out your hand."

Joe did as he was told and she swept the broom across his palm, then anointed it with a little of the oil. Immediately the moon line on the boy's hand shone like gold at the bottom of a wishing well. "Hold it up," Corvina said and began chanting, beseeching supernatural aid. "Papa Legba, open the gate. Your child awaits." In the far corner of the kitchen, just beside the back door, was the way to the family rooms. There was nothing extraordinary about it, but as Joe watched, molten fire ran around its frame until it was completely edged in a shimmering sunrise.

And then it opened.

As Evangeline clapped in amazement, Corvina said, "Fly swiftly and fare well. We will do all we can to delay those that hunt you." She opened her arms wide and Joe hugged her fiercely, then he turned to Evangeline and saw she had tears streaming down her cheeks.

"Why are you crying, girl?" he said and they hugged too.

Something large and terrible slammed into the kitchen door.

"Hurry, child!" the woman commanded.

Stepping up to the golden doorway, Joe saw that the next room was a small toilet and bathroom. It smelled of lemons and the ocean, and was lit by two nautical wall lamps. Above was a sloping glass roof and beyond that a clear pre-dawn sky. In the bath was a white-bearded man smoking a pipe, completely oblivious to the boy's appearance. Balanced on one soapy leg sat a model galleon with a great white sail, which the fellow was painting with curious signs and symbols.

With a terrific splintering of wood, the great wolf burst through the door and into the kitchen. Evangeline screamed and leapt to flee, crashing into Joe's back.

There was no exit, Joe observed uselessly.

"Wait!" he said, but he was already being pushed across the

threshold. Twisting, he reached out to stop himself and as he did so his hands found the young maid's. Toppling he tried to pull himself back into Louisiana, but instead fell into the sea-green bathroom. And as he did he pulled Evangeline in with him.

V

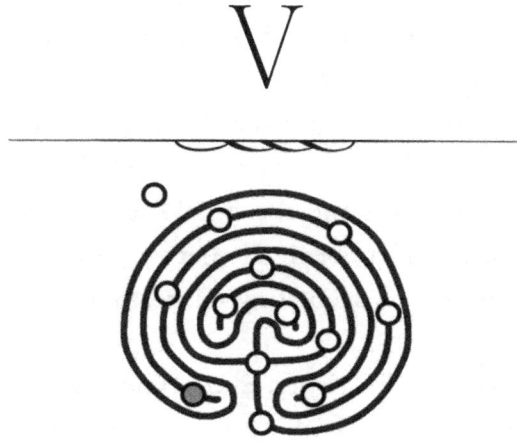

FIFTH MOON: STORM MOON (OF NATURE: SEA)
THE LIGHTKEEPER'S HOUSE
TRANØY, HAMARØY, NORWAY
SUNDAY 9 FEBRUARY 1986 | 08:29:06

QUITE HOW JOE WOULD HAVE reacted had two strangers burst in on him having a bath, he couldn't really imagine, but the bearded man's shrieking was probably a good guess. As the boy and girl picked themselves up from the wooden floor and began backing out of the room, the man replaced his initial shock with shades of embarrassment and blazing anger. Then, obviously feeling vulnerable sitting naked in the soapy water, he stood up. This final move sent Evangeline into high-pitched fits of screaming herself.

"*Hvem er du og hvor kommer du fra?*" he barked. Just by the tone of the question, Joe knew what the man was saying.

"Yeah, I get asked that a lot," he replied and fled.

They emerged on a wooden walkway that connected the bathroom to a red-painted boathouse. Outside was freezing cold, felt even more keenly compared to balmy Louisiana. The cold struck Joe like a hammer, urging him to the back door of the main building. Where was he? *When* was he? The room they entered was a stark contrast to the New Orleans opulence of Manse L'Estrange. It was a laundry with a small, shabby kitchen beyond. Everything looked rather provincial and badly made, from the cream and red painted wood panelling to the battered wooden chairs and the fitted cabinets with their sliding glass doors. It looked as if cobbled together by someone's grandmother long before the luxury of decorating entire rooms in the same style had ever been a thing.

"Where's the kitchen?" shrieked Evangeline. "Where's the mistress? Where's the *house*?" Joe said nothing and moved forward, pulling the maid by the hand. "Joe, you have to get me home!"

On from the kitchen was a pantry and sitting room. It was impossible to date any of the furniture. Everything looked so beaten and battered, but there was a strong nautical theme everywhere. In the living area every shelf, sideboard and table was stacked with all kinds of ships. The models ranged from single-masted yachts to large galleons mounted on twisted driftwood stands. The last rooms in the building were a pair of bedrooms, empty apart from iron bunk beds and small storage trunks.

"Oh, Joe," said Evangeline, her voice filled with wonder. "Just lookie here."

Out of the wide windows was a view across a rocky island. Dawn was breaking, its first light shining off a red lighthouse that towered over a cluster of fishermen's cabins and wharf houses. Between the boathouse and the cottages animal pens stood, while a thin footbridge wound its way across the rocks to the mainland. A dark ocean surrounded the island on three sides. On the fourth ran a ragged curtain of snowy mountains.

Behind them the door slammed and there was the sound of bare feet on wooden floorboards. Always Have A Way Out! Joe pressed himself against the wall, while Evangeline stood her ground scowling. She looked set to take on anything that came through the door. It was about then that Joe realised he was still spattered in Damfino's blood. Probably not the best thing for first impressions, he thought, wincing. A moment later the bearded man appeared. Now he was wearing a grey captain's cap, his waist wrapped in a crimson bath sheet. One hand held the towel, while the other grasped an old cutlass.

"*Hvem er du?*" he said firmly, brandishing the weapon menacingly. "*Hvorfor er du her?*"

"What is he saying?" asked Evangeline. "Where are we?"

"*Hvordan kom du deg hit?*" The captain or lighthouse keeper or whoever he was didn't seem angry now, just very, very puzzled.

The pair slowly backed away, while in Joe's mind Ilkilæmber was saying, *Take me up, boy. Raise me 'gainst this dread pirate before he runs you through.* Without realising he had even pulled it from his rucksack, the sword was in Joe's hand, and he was striding forward, blade raised. The man looked shocked, then brought up his cutlass, taking on a fighting stance.

"Boys, boys, boys!" shouted Evangeline and stepped between them. "This is not the way to go." To the man she said, "We are lost. Can we stay here? Just for a few days?"

"I am light keeper not child keeper," the man said in broken English. "Where are your mother and father? Where is the boat that brought you?" The boy knew what came next, so he answered the captain's questions before they were asked.

"I am Joe and from Great Britain. This is Evangeline and she's from New Orleans. In America. We arrived here... We sort of..." Joe faltered. How could he even start to explain?

The captain's face became very serious. "You are from between the walls, *ja?*" When he translated, his voice was melodic and sing-song and sounded a little like the Muppets' Swedish Chef. It was easy to imagine him bursting into a song ending in "Bork, bork, bork!" This was made especially hilarious by his cutlass, cap and towel combo. Thinking all this, Joe smiled without meaning to.

"Yes," he said, "we are from between the walls."

The boy's words seemed to decide something for the captain. "So strangers, not *Svartálfar*, yes?"

"What's 'zwartelffer'?" the girl asked, pushing the man's sword tip away from her face.

"A dark elf. Black and like dwarf. A thing of nothing but trouble."

Evangeline let out one of her wild crowing laughs. "Hah! No, sir, I ain't no dwarf!" She indicated her slim form and cotton dress. "Do I look like a thing of trouble?" The bearded man raised one eyebrow. "OK, don't answer that."

"*Nei*, no dark elf. For you are far from hideous. And—" he indicated the light that poured through the windows, "—the sun it no turns you to stones. Instead, I will call you *min huldra*. My faerie princess." Then Evangeline was smiling, and the man was smiling. Then they were laughing. And the tension was broken.

Instantly, the glamour of the sword crumbled.

"Darn right you will," said Evangeline. "So, now the big chiefs have done their war dance, how's about we all fix some breakfast? Then you tell me where I am and how in the heck I'm getting back home."

WHATEVER ELSE YOU COULD SAY about Evangeline, it had to be admitted she was an excellent cook. In no time she had organised the men into helping her serve up a delicious breakfast of soft-boiled eggs, mackerel, some kind of spiced sausages and buttered toast, followed by coffee. While they ate together, the bearded man introduced himself as Captain Lars Thorstad, lightkeeper of Tranøy *fyrstasjon*, which he said was built on the outermost island of Hamarøy in Norway. As Evangeline had never heard of Norway, the captain brought sea charts and maps to show exactly where in the world the island was. Even to Joe, who knew all about Vikings and trolls and the midnight sun, he was fascinated to discover more of the fjords and ragged coastline – and marvelled at how far north the lighthouse stood. He knew from reading *The Stranger's Guide* that somewhere on this island were rune stones that opened a doorway to Ireland and a cottage named Tigh Samhraidh. The next step through the labyrinth of this mysterious house, and another closer to his escape and reuniting with his parents.

"There always was needed a lighthouse along the Vestfjord," Lars Thorstad told them in his fractured English. "The light was a beacon for 1864. For the shipping to Tjeldsund, and Tysfjord. Boathouse and barn and... oil house. Later came an engine room and fog horn. The bridge came in 1969. Across the narrow sea strait."

"Don't you get super-lonely," asked Evangeline. "Being here all by yourself?"

"Yes, it is lonely," the captain replied. "In past times there were four workers here, but those days are gone. Now I use the hours to build boats. For boats is what I love. And now I build the biggest boat. For I make plan to sail around the world. I will do this when I finish my duties at the *fyrstasjon*."

He indicated a wooden board on the wall inscribed with all the names of the lightkeepers from Kristian Gundersen in 1864 to his own name next to the year 1971. He explained how soon the light was to be automated, the island already sold to a wealthy Japanese family. In less than three months it would be time for Lars Thorstad to leave his watch.

"Where will you go?" asked Joe.

The captain pointed at the sea charts, tracing his imagined route with his fingers. "I will go in the footsteps of my ancestors and the great Viking Erik Thorvaldsson – Erik the Red of Rogaland – here to Iceland and Greenland and then to the Americas."

"The Americas," said Evangeline. "Then you can take me home."

And that settled the friendship between the New Orleans maid and the lightkeeper. Joe and Evangeline would stay until the captain was ready to sail, but they had to earn their bed and board. Thorstad assigned them both roles, calling Joe his houseswain and Evangeline his quartermaster. The hours were filled helping around the island, the working shifts ending with more of Evangeline's delicious cooking. For lunch she served fish soup and fresh shrimp salads, while for dinner she grilled salmon and found ingredients to recreate her grandmother's meatballs. She made everything from scratch and poured Louisiana love into every dish. Each night Joe fell asleep to the sounds of the swells against the rocks. Every morning he awoke to the smells of the sea and Evangeline's hearty breakfasts. The captain was thrilled with the maid's culinary skills, especially as he had secretly feared a life eating from tins on his long voyage. Now the two planned extravagant feasts for their journey and set about making lists of provisions to pack for the long Atlantic crossing. In this way winter turned to spring. The snows thawed and the first arctic terns began to return from their Antarctic winter migrations.

Those first weeks Rule #1: Nowhere Is Safe drummed in Joe's head, but he learned to ignore it. And every day he did, the voice got less and less urgent. The Rules did not seem so important here.

With no television and only a battered radio, their evenings were spent playing board games like Mouse Trap and Go, while the captain's favourite versions of Norwegian Scrabble and Trivial Pursuit were deemed incomprehensible and gathered dust. Evangeline became captivated by a box of pop-up children's books, endlessly opening up the three-dimensional castles and forests and circus big tops in radiant disbelief. The captain, it transpired, had been a fencing champion in his youth and taught Joe the basics of parrying, cuts and thrusts. He also loved stories and songs – and the three spent long evenings telling tales from their particular cultures. The captain told of legendary warriors from Nordic history; Evangeline's were of the hoodoo gods and their tricks on the mortal world. Joe's were just rambling stories he half remembered from his childhood books, but no one appeared to feel that mattered. On those evenings Rule #4 screamed for his attention. Don't Make Friends! it clamoured. Joe told the voices to just shut up and leave him alone. With his mutant superhero powers, it was as if he regenerated. He had never felt so healthy and full of life. Even the memory of the wolf and the wild hunters seemed to be just a dream out here on this island at the edge of the world.

As winter receded, pale purple carpets of bluebells and blazing yellow clumps of bird's-foot trefoil brought sudden colour to the rocky island. The youngsters stayed in the boathouse, while Lars Thorstad lived in the lightkeeper's house. The buildings were full of items and objects that Joe found antiquated and Evangeline impossibly futuristic. Every day the captain locked himself away working on his ship. When Joe asked if they could see his secret project or where the lightkeeper kept the boat, the bearded captain just tapped his nose and answered, "Soon, all will be revealed."

Watching Lars Thorstad show Evangeline how to hoist sail or mend nets, it was clear the captain was becoming enchanted with his strange visitors. It began to be clear to the boy, and later to the girl too, that Lars Thorstad saw them as the grandchildren he had never had. Though he never told the whole story, the captain touched upon the tragedy that had brought him here to this lonely island. He said that his children were *druknet*, which Joe guessed meant drowned.

One evening the captain took the pair out to the rocky cliffs of Vesterfjell. There he showed them two stones marking the graves of his parents. "The sea orphaned me and it will get me when I am done, no doubt," he said. "But in you I have found a family again." The captain's words brought back thoughts of Joe's father and mother – and his never-ending anxiety about The Medicine.

As the days wore on, Joe still worried constantly about getting sick. It had been weeks since he had last taken his medication. Could it be true that the timelessness of this place had halted his need for The Medicine? Could it be that the screwed-up time in the labyrinth delayed the onset of his illness? Was he really that lucky? After all, 1986 was almost two decades before he was even born.

Don't Make Friends! Always Have A Way Out! Nowhere Is Safe! The Rules chimed like cathedral bells in Joe's head, but he had to admit that with Lars Thorstad and Evangeline he no longer felt like some unfixable thing, a discarded toy that no one missed.

Instead of dwelling on the past, Joe focused on the future. He returned to the bathroom regularly. Like the rest of the lighthouse, it was simple and functional, though the bath, shower, toilet and basin were noticeably more modern than the rest of the furniture and fittings. The room was decorated in greens and reds, with marbled tiles and driftwood mirrors and beams. Wooden carvings around the walls reminded Joe of Viking ships, and above, woven blinds hung like sails. On the highest part of the wall an arched transom window was framed by dried hops and there stood a bronze sculpture of an owl. Joe immediately thought of D'Ante's white pet and shivered.

It seemed odd to go there every morning to wash and brush his teeth, knowing that the pine door with its glass window and iron grille was every dark of the moon a portal to another time. He avoided the room then. There was no way back for him there. Which begged the question: where was the way forward? *The Stranger's Guide* named the god of the room to be Odin and clearly showed a bag of rune stones as being the oracle. The bag had been placed on the high shelf, but all the books Joe could find explaining about them were in that strange language of crossed Øs and haloed Ås. Though Lars Thorstad seemed the most wonderful host, Joe was not ready to share the secrets of the guide with him just yet. He would simply have to work it out for himself.

One afternoon Joe grew so frustrated he decided to seek help from Evangeline. The day was wet and they were mending fishing nets in the sitting room. "I need to tell you about all this," he began. "About the moons, rooms and doors and everything. It'll be important once you get back home. I don't know how and I don't know why, but there are thirteen places that are all linked. Each doorway is like..." he paused at the word, but there was no other, "magic, and each one leads to the next. It's a labyrinth. Here..." He opened his half-finished map showing all the rooms so far set out in their spiralling pattern. "I have to get to the end, I think." Even to himself he didn't sound sure about that.

Evangeline took the book and turned to the pages on Manse L'Estrange. "Joe," she said, pointing to her photograph. "That's me."

"Yes, I know."

"Who took that? Why am I in your book?"

"It's not my book and I have no idea. Did anyone ever take your picture?"

Evangeline gave the image a really long look. "No," she announced. "No one ever has. Never. And certainly not recently. That's how I look now."

It was true, Joe admitted to himself. She looked just like the day he'd met her. She was wearing the same dress and everything. "I can't explain it," he mumbled. "That picture was in the book all along. Whoever wrote it met you at the exact moment I did. Guess they had a camera." Evangeline wasn't in any way satisfied with his answer, and neither was Joe, but he had no other. Flipping forward a few pages, he came to the pictures and passages about the island. "There's a photograph of the captain, too," was all he could offer.

"Darn strange," the girl said. "Go on."

Joe showed her the drawing of the bag of rune stones. "There are different oracles in every room. I just need to find out how each one works. With the stones I have no idea. There is another way. If you go to the place on the dark of the moon – like if you could get to the L'Estrange kitchen right now – the doors open and you can get through."

"So why can't I just go that way? Because of the wolf?"

"Maybe, and there's not just one. We don't know what waits for us back there. It could be a trap. Anyhow, this is a labyrinth and the raven said…" Joe stopped, remembering Griswald's ominous words. "The only way out is in," he finished.

"Can that wolf-thing find us here?" Evangeline asked.

"Maybe. Maybe not. They haven't so far. Anyhow we'll be off soon. New Orleans is a port, right? The captain can take you right there."

Evangeline's eyes lit up at the thought, and seeing her hope, he suddenly realised that he didn't have to work out the rune stones at all. The next point on the labyrinth was Ireland. Somewhere called the Boyne Valley in County Meath. Joe had never heard of it, but the captain's charts showed they were sailing right past. Lars Thorstad could dock somewhere on the coast and Joe could travel the rest of the way by land. After that, it was just a case of waiting for the Dead Moon. He'd been thinking so much about magical ways of travelling, he hadn't even considered the usual ones. It was now the end of April, only a fortnight before the new owners would arrive and the captain could leave on his much-anticipated voyage. The lightkeeper promised sightings of great gatherings of pilot whales and orcas, but this was a sight Joe never got to see.

Because everything changed the day the sea eagles came to Tranøy island.

EARLY ONE MORNING IN MAY, a mere three days before the date of their departure, the captain burst into their bedrooms and woke Joe and Evangeline with his cries. "*Havørn! Havørn avkastning!*" The bearded man was almost dancing with excitement. "The King of Birds. Is coming! Is coming!" Dressing quickly, they followed him out into the breezy morning and across to the towering form of the lighthouse. Climbing to the very top, the captain led them out onto the main gallery balcony. Not for the faint-hearted, it rewarded the brave with a spectacular panorama of the surrounding coast, the mountains and even far-flung islands out to sea. The lighthouse tower had been stripped of its original mechanism and now the lens room housed a single globe of glass, at the centre of which hung a long, shining sliver of white crystal.

"See!" Captain Thorstad said, sucking on his pipe and pointing into the skies. "*Kongen av fuglene!*" The air was filled with eagles with vast fingered wings and white wedge-shaped tails. They were all squawking like crazy. As they wheeled and banked, the boy counted maybe two dozen. They were easily the largest birds Joe had ever seen. "Such majesty. Such magnificent. Haunter of the skies."

"You mean 'hunter'?" asked Evangeline.

Seeing them circling in the misty morning air, Joe didn't think Lars Thorstad did.

"There are many and they are crying. This is bad." The captain sounded worried.

"Why's that?"

"Because always are they solitary… and silent."

Swooping around the lantern room, one of the sea eagles landed on the metal railing. Its giant wings were as wide as the captain was tall, its eyes stern over its bright golden beak. For a moment it sat regarding the three of them, then looked right at Joe and said, "It is not wisdom to stop flying, little bird. When you stop flying, you fall. The wolfshead is found. The Wild Hunt are coming."

"Did that big pigeon just speak to us?" said Evangeline in disbelief, but it was Lars Thorstad who had the widest eyes. Turning to the boy, he said, "You are wolfshead? Prey to the *Odensjakt*? This is very bad."

Joe found he couldn't look the captain in the eye. He felt so ashamed. Nowhere Is Safe! Always Have A Way Out! Joe had been so stupid, thinking that he could ignore The Rules. "How do they keep finding me?" he asked. "How do I escape them?"

"I know of them from the old tales. The *Odensjakt* are led by The Vandal King. It is said that if you are the prey of the Wild Hunt, there is no escaping. Not ever. No place is a safe haven from such monsters. Not this island, not forever. Not from Time and not from *Odensjakt*. It might take them one moon or thirteen, but they will unearth you in the end."

"Does this have something to do with that big bad wolf?" asked Evangeline.

"The eagle's words are wise," said Thorstad. "We are warned, so no more waiting. We leave now." Crossing to the winding stair, the captain led them back down the curving steps of the lighthouse. Not stopping at the ground level, he continued deeper than they had gone before. Finally the steps ended in a room stacked with boxes. At the far end was a heavily bound iron door secured with a giant padlock.

"Now is time for all secrets."

Lars Thorstad produced a huge key and unlocked the door. Then, giving them a crate each, they descended even further underground. Illuminated by the captain's lantern, painted brick walls gave way to hand-carved tunnels. The air turned from cool to damp and still Thorstad led them on. Eventually the passage broadened into a wide, flat ledge at one end of a large cave. Water formed a lake at its centre, and there was moored the strangest ship Joe had ever seen. It was half-boat, half-tree, its single mast fashioned from a leafless oak. In its branches brightly coloured flags fluttered. Its hull looked to the boy like a cross between a Viking ship and a medieval galleon. Yet fantastical as it was, it was utterly eclipsed by the cave itself. The walls and ceilings of the cavern were filled with glittering crystal formations, an entire otherworldly forest of frozen light. On the floor smaller clumps carpeted like ice-covered grass, while shining wrist-thick spikes speared from above.

"Behold, *hule krystall!*" announced the captain. "The cave of crystals."

Evangeline let out a squeal of delight and the sound echoed away far across the water. Joe stood completely mesmerised. It was like stepping inside a child's dream. The cave revealed the captain's deeper purpose here. As protector of one of the last magical places on the Earth.

Starting forwards, Lars Thorstad showed them a path through the thick stalactites down to the water's edge and where to stand the boxes. The boy reached out to touch the transparent formations, finding them sharp as kitchen knives. Evangeline stepped up to an arched niche in the wall and lifted one shard of crystal that had been placed there. In its reflected light her face danced with rainbows. "What's this?" she asked.

"My guiding light," the captain answered. "It remains here for a million years. When the world was young."

"When the world was magic," Evangeline whispered.

"*Ja*. When the world was *all* magic," the captain agreed.

"Can't you feel the power here, Joe?" the girl continued. "This is like the manse. A hoodoo place. Only way stronger."

Indeed, Joe could feel it. It was intoxicating. The crystals almost physically pulsed with energy, and this close to them, the boy found he was fighting to draw breath into his lungs. The weight of the air was too thick to swallow.

Arriving at the galleon moored in the underground lagoon, Joe saw now why the captain had taken so long in finishing its construction. Every centimetre was hand cut, engraved, pegged and crafted. In its hull writhed ancient ropes and roots, while above a furled sail and rigging were strung in its twisted branches.

"Long before the Vikings in prehistoric times, my ancestors – the Sámi – were guided by their gods to this place. To the cave and the tree. Here I have sat and longed for strange lands." Lars Thorstad reached out and stroked the curved prow. "Now the eagles tell it is time to slake my wanderlust."

Joe saw that the carvings along the deck matched the ones in the bathroom, as did the shingled roof on the cabin in the stern. How long must he have worked on this? he wondered.

Stepping over the rail and into the mass of roots, Lars Thorstad slapped a hand onto the trunk of the ancient oak. "This is branch from Yggdrasil. The World Tree. Before lighthouse, there was this tree. Growing here. Now it is this ship. *Leiðarstjarna – The Lodestar*." He reached up and hung the lamp that he carried on a great chain over the bowsprit. "This is the Lanthorn. Odin's Eye. It will guide us."

"This is cooler than Kool-Aid," said Evangeline.

Above in the sunlit world came a crack of what sounded like thunder.

"What was that?" asked Joe.

"It is as the eagle say. *Odensjakt*. They come for you."

"Is there nothing we can do?" asked Evangeline.

"We do it. And the eagles will aid us. Like owls and ravens, they are corpse birds. They have some power over our enemies. Come and do only as I say. We must gather whatever we can. There is not much time."

With Joe and Evangeline hurrying in his wake, Lars Thorstad almost ran back through the tunnels and up into the lighthouse. The clear day was gone. Though they had not been in the caves for long, now the sky hung with ominous black storm clouds, grumbling with angry thunder. Quickly, the captain gave them instructions to fetch their things, pack as much food and water as they could carry and return as swiftly as they could. As they left, Lars Thorstad headed to his own lodgings. In less than ten steps his dark form disappeared inside the lightkeeper's house.

Running the short distance to the boathouse, Joe and Evangeline burst inside and began frantically packing. While the boy grabbed his sword and book, the girl went to the kitchen. He joined her there and helped stuff tins and dried goods into two crates, then filled flasks and bottles with water. When they were done, they wrapped themselves in two ill-fitting coats and raced back outside. Now the sky above the island was filled with sparrows, thousands and thousands of them, wheeling and spiralling in the late-morning air. As they turned in unison their bodies made mesmerising patterns as large as the island. Evangeline stopped and stared up into the black heart of the swarming birds, hypnotised by the whirling, ever-changing patterns.

"Come on," Joe urged, "we have to go."

"No, wait," she replied. "It's as if they're trying to tell us something."

"We don't have time." As if in agreement thunder rolled across the heavens. Distantly, Joe heard another sound: the thin, whining cry of wolves.

Screwing up his eyes, Joe scanned the horizon and saw a shape on the rocks. A lone figure stood upon the mainland, his greatcoat flapping in the wind, his face lost under the shadow of a broad-brimmed hat. He was gnawing what looked like a leg bone.

Steel thyself, child, said the sword.

"Evangeline, we have to go!" He turned back to the girl, but she still stood captivated, unable to look away from the whirling flock above. Joe noticed that now the sea eagles were swooping among them, but as he watched he saw that the great birds were attacking the sparrows, killing as many as they could grasp in their vicious talons.

Over by the keeper's house, the captain emerged laden with cases and boxes. When he saw the swarmed birds and the figure across the strait, he paled and began to shout. "Back, Sigurdsveinen! The water you cannot pass. This is sacred place and no step can you take here. The child is not for you today."

The master of the Wild Hunt finished eating and tossed the large bone into the sea. "I am the Vandal King. The boy wears a wolfish head. You know the lore." Around him on the shore hounds gathered, but of the Grim Grotesques there was no sign. Where are they? Joe thought, anxiously. Could it really be that they were safe on the island? That magic crystals would protect them? Joe remembered the policemen in Italy and the mob kept at bay outside the rectory hedge, but he couldn't be sure. Thinking of Romano, Joe felt scared. He wouldn't forgive himself if anything happened to his friends. Don't Make Friends. Do Not Talk To Dead People. The boy dragged Evangeline towards the captain. When she protested, he doubled his efforts. Finally, somehow, they reached the base of the lighthouse and the captain urged them inside.

"Are we safe?" Joe asked, but their host shook his head and pointed at Evangeline.

"Yes," she was murmuring, transfixed. "Beautiful, beautiful birds."

And Joe thought, Rule #1: Nowhere Is Safe.

To the accompaniment of thunder, Damfino raised both his arms. In one hand he held a twisted wand, in the other his yellow talisman. The master of the Wild Hunt spat out a stream of guttural sounds and every sparrow in the sky stopped flying, falling like living hailstones. And as they fell they transformed from birds to beasts. For a moment the curled shapes lay motionless in the snow, then they twitched into life and rose, a great army of Grim Grotesques, their diseased faces dreadful to behold.

"Run!" shouted Lars Thorstad and the three fled down into the underground passageways with the entire rabid horde at their backs.

Desperately they descended into the tunnels, through the crystal cave and onto *The Lodestar*. The captain began to set the vessel for escape, barking orders as he did so. Items were stowed, sails were unfurled and the lantern was placed again in the branches above the bowsprit. Behind them their pursuers roared like waves on the rocks. By the time Lars Thorstad was untying the moorings, the first of the hunters had appeared in the mouth of the tunnel. Blindly they poured into the cave, crushing the crystals beneath their boots.

Will every place I go end in this destruction? thought Joe in despair. Will everyone who helps me die?

Then as the swell of the waves caught the ship, Evangeline shouted, "Captain, we cannot go!" and leapt onto the rocks.

Lars Thorstad shouted after her, yet the girl was already racing towards the oncoming mob.

"Evangeline!" Joe shouted, but she was already out of reach. At first he couldn't understand why she had left the safety of the ship, but then he saw her purpose. She was heading for the shard of crystal in the niche. With a lurch *The Lodestar* was dragged away by the current, then caught in the swell and crashed back against the rocks.

"She will be lost!" the captain was shouting, though Joe felt he could just as well have meant the galleon as the girl.

At the hole in the wall, Evangeline lifted the shard of crystal and turned back to the boat. The warriors were mere hand-widths behind her, clawing at her neck and shoulders as she ran to the water's edge.

Now the boat was easily five metres from the shore, but she did not hesitate. With the whole host of Damfino's frenzied horde behind her, she threw herself off the high rocks and landed in the captain's arms on *The Lodestar's* flooded deck.

"Ah, *min huldra*." Thorstad was crying and stroking her hair. "You are safe now. Safe now."

Retrieving the crystal from Evangeline's trembling hands, Joe placed it into the heart of the Lanthorn and at once a deep power flowed like sap into the ship. Every piece of wood and metal shivered, then the boat surged forward and they were away. Within moments they were emerging from the shadow of the cliffs and slamming through the waves of the ocean currents.

Upon the stony shore behind them, the Grim Grotesques watched them go in seething silence.

SCUDDING BEFORE A STIFF NORTHERLY wind, *The Lodestar* drew away from Tranøy and into the haze of the open ocean. At their backs the silent lighthouse watched them go, as did the figure upon the rocks. Joe stood against the rails and looked grimly back as the island shrank and faded behind, then went and joined the girl and the captain on the quarterdeck.

"It feels like we're flying!" Evangeline said, her face one big smile.

"This is dreaming come true, my princess," Thorstad replied to her happiness.

The galley was a marvel to Joe, and as soon as the land was lost on the eastern horizon, it became the focus for everything in their lives. The *Lodestar* measured forty-five paces from stem to stern, a complex mix of endless coils of hemp rope and vast, hand-woven sail. The captain said the keel and stems were Danish oak, and the rest Norwegian pine, but the boy could not believe such a fine vessel could be constructed from ordinary wood. That night, as they ate cold meatballs from a tin, Thorstad explained the route they would take to deliver Joe to Ireland and Evangeline to Louisiana.

"We relive a mythic sea voyage. The Viking discovery of the New World. We will first sail the icy North Sea." He indicated the way on a map marked with tiny red arrows that arced across vast stretches of ocean. "Here to Faroe Islands and Tórshavn, then to west of Scotland and down to Ireland. From here we go back, cross to Reykjavik. From Iceland, we go for Greenland and the Cape Farewell. Most dangerous waters there. Then we dodge icebergs set for Newfoundland and Canada. Land ho, America! Finally, we find the Mississippi and from there your home."

"How long will all that take?" asked Evangeline.

"It is an epic expedition. At a maximum fifteen knots, maybe two hundred nautical miles per day in good conditions…" The captain mused and calculated. "Three weeks to Ireland and then another six to cross to the Americas. Probably far longer. Oceans are voyage of discovery, not facts."

"That's a long time. We haven't food or water for more than a couple of days," said the boy.

"Then we must be inspired, little Joe, to go beyond our imaginable horizons. To take from the sea and find landfall. To do what is impossible. We are in modern Viking saga. I will be Erik The Red. And you will be my crew."

"Aye aye, Cap'n!" said Evangeline, saluting.

"Joe will be boatswain. You, Evangeline, will stay quartermaster and everybody else. We must hold fast and bless that we are escaped." The girl crossed herself, as the captain continued. "But our fast fleeing has left us without things. We have compasses, but no communications. We must fare as my ancestors fared. We use the sun, the moon and the stars. I know of the chants and rhymes that show the way, but I need to know more…" He hesitated, then finished, "I will learn."

"We will help you all we can," said Joe.

"*Ja*, and I will teach you. Like all our life, we must open to our senses. We must keep our ears keen for waves and birds. That is how we know shore is nearing. We must sense the touch of the wind when it changes. Taste to tell if fresh water is mixed with salt. And a good sailor can smell plants and animals on the smallest of breezes. We will watch for the fins of whales. For shapes in the clouds. We will follow the flight of birds. This tells us the way to go."

"If only I could speak Nature's Tongue," said Joe.

"What is this, First Mate Joe?" Thorstad asked.

"It is the language of the natural world. The magical speech of rare, untamed beauty."

"Ah, I have knowing of this in a different name. The ancestors spoke in the secret language of birds and beasts; they called it *dark tale*. It is found in the flight of birds and the movement of nature."

Like a swarm of sparrows, the boy thought. And look what their message was. "Yes, that's it. Can you teach it to me?"

"I will," promised Thorstad. "The ocean is full of songs. Can't you hear them, little Joe? We must know the sea's dark secrets. And we must know them quickly."

So began their arduous sea voyage. The work onboard was heavy, wet and cold, and demanded tons of physical strength to get through the days. Though there was a captain's cabin of sorts under the tiller, all three were exposed to rain and cold weather with only short breaks to sleep. Every day and every night Lars Thorstad kept his eye on the charts and the skies, and when the fog was heaviest or the seas unreadable, he always somehow found a clue to the way ahead.

In the brief times when the weather was calmer, Joe read *The Stranger's Guide* and reflected on the Wishing Tree's warning. When the hour is dark, it had said, two things remember: the sword and the shadowstone. Was there anything in the book about those? As Serene had mentioned there was indeed a chapter on household magick in the book. There he found sketches of the thirteen clocks from the Hall of Mirrors, and also drawings of five alchemical talismans. The shadowstone was one, but there were four others, one for each of the elements of Earth, Air, Fire and Water. He remembered clearly the Reverend Grey drawing the black talisman to ward off the Grim Grotesques in the rectory garden. Grey had spoken a verse of protection. What was it? Scanning the book, he found it calligraphed in the back pages.

FORGED IN FIRE. CARVED IN ICE.
ROOTED IN ROCK. WILD AS WIND.
SHIELDED IN SHADOW.
THE WALLS OF THESE ROOMS WARD US.
THE POWER OF THESE DOORS PROTECT US.
THE MAGIC OF THESE MOONS ENCLOAK US.
WHEREVER WE ARE; WHENEVER WE ARE;
TALLISTON IS.

And he realised he knew far more what these words meant now than he had done when first he heard them. Abram Kyle's yellow-white gem was citrine and represented the element of air. Not surprisingly it was linked to the realms of blood and success. Joe knew Norway wouldn't be the last time he'd encounter the Vandal King or his Wild Hunt. Next time I will have to be ready, he said to himself, and that led to thoughts of his mother and father. Here, at this point of the labyrinth, he was the closest he had travelled back to his original time. It was almost as if that nearness in years equalled a nearness in feeling. By the captain's almanac it was May 1986, sixteen years before

Joe was born, but his parents would be alive. Perhaps they had met. He couldn't remember. They rarely talked about the time before he was born and Joe suddenly realised that he had never asked. If only I knew their phone number, he thought, I could call them. And had a phone. It would be wonderful just to hear their voices. His father would no doubt crack some awkward joke. His mother would scold him for being out way past bedtime. Joe longed for some kind of connection, then one evening it came to him.

It was dusk, about two weeks out from Hamarøy, and the great orange ball of the sun was disappearing into the honey-gold ocean over the prow. The wind-up radio was on, the sound of American swing drifting up into the perfect evening skies. The captain and Evangeline were dancing on the deck, the maid showing the merry Norwegian how to Lindy hop. As the sea swelled, a green bottle of whatever the captain drank on the nights he danced rolled up beside Joe.

"Ah, to be young again," Lars Thorstad said. "To join you in the dance hall and rock around the clock."

Evangeline blew him a kiss, not missing a step. "Why, eggs in moonshine, I do declare Joe's smiling." It was true. The boy was indeed grinning at their crazy antics. The girl stopped flailing and caught her breath. "So what's up? Why the change?"

Joe thought for a moment, then said, "Because, for the first time, life's suddenly..." He stopped, unsure.

"What?" Evangeline urged. "Magic?"

Joe looked away, sheepish. "Yeah," he mumbled.

"There's no more magic than there was before," Evangeline said. "You've just opened your eyes to it. Look here." She handed him one of the children's books she had saved from the lightkeeper's house. Though written in Norwegian, the pop-up tale of a travelling circus was easily understandable. She turned to a vertically slatted page showing an empty cage on wheels. "This is how you saw the world."

She pulled the tab marked '*Trekk Meg!*' and the slats slid under and over each other, transforming the scene. Instantly the cage was filled with performing monkeys. "This is how you see it now. Nothing has changed. Except you."

Joe looked from the book to the ship, then off across the ocean towards the dazzling sunset. His heart felt swollen and bruised. He had never imagined living could feel this good. Yet all the while his head throbbed warnings. This is not your family, it said. You need to find them. He knew this was true, and now he had seen what a happy family was like, he could make it happen. He could make things right.

At his feet the empty bottle rolled away, then back. And that's when the idea clicked in his mind.

Taking up pen and paper, he wrote out his message.

Friday 23 May 1986

To Mum and Dad,

I am writing this from somewhere in the middle of the ocean.

I miss you.

Don't be angry when you come back and find me gone. I had no choice. I wanted to stay like I promised, but I couldn't. The people after you came after me too. They knew about the hideout. About the bus. About me.

Where I'm going I don't know if I'll see you again. Mummy, if you are gone for good, I want to say that I am very, very sorry. I tried very hard to be the son you would have wanted to have around. For you to be proud of me. I'm sorry I was never good enough. I'm sorry if I was a burden.

I didn't follow The Rules. I didn't take The Medicine. The reason I acted bad was that I hated you always leaving me behind. Of people moving me around like a box of stuff they have no space for. Every day I feel these things. Like I don't belong in your life. Like you don't want me.

I hid everything, and wish I'd told you what it was doing to me. I'm sorry I did not tell you this until this letter. I did not want you to worry about me. This was the only way I could think of to tell you this now.

I hope that you will forgive me for whatever I've done. If I get the chance and I get back, I will become the son you always wanted. I promise.

I love you more than you will ever know. Thank you for giving me life and for letting me see this world. I thought life was dark and ugly. But out here, Mum, right now, the world's very beautiful.

That's all I wanted to write, so I will say goodbye now. Don't be sad that I'm gone. Please never be sad. I am happy. I am really happy now. I will be no more burden for you. Everything will be fine. I am with good people and they are good to me. They've taught me lots of things. But there is one thing I taught myself – and that is, it's never too late to have a happy life.

Goodbye.

I love you, Mum. I love you, Dad.

I am happy now.

I miss you.

Joe.

When he was done, he folded the letter up, pushed it inside the glass bottle, corked it and threw it without ceremony into the ocean. There it bobbed in and out of sight for a while, then was swallowed by the waves and was gone.

Two days later – and seventeen since they had fled the Tranøy *fyrstasjon* – they arrived at another lighthouse. This one marked the shallows surrounding Rathlin Island, a place of impossibly green hillsides and cliffs stuffed with seabirds. At the small port they dined on hot food and Lars Thorstad secured Joe passage by ferry to the Irish mainland. That night sleeping in a real bed, Joe's mood turned heavy. He knew tomorrow it would be the time for farewells. Don't Make Friends. Do Not Talk To Dead People. The Rules were back in his head, louder than ever. Tolling out their dark commandments. And his heart ached every time they did.

The next morning was overcast and bleak, with ashen clouds hanging over the fishermen's houses. Standing on the stony shore among the weathered shacks, trying to ignore the way everyone gawked and pointed at the strange wooden ship, Lars Thorstad, Evangeline and Joe gathered to say their farewells.

"Here." The captain handed over a battered duffel bag. "I do not have much that we will not need on our voyage, but perhaps I spare these." Inside were provisions and a few gold coins that looked like they had been plundered from a pirate's treasure chest. Joe took the bag and saluted. "It's been an honour serving with you, Captain."

"*Ja*, my boy," the captain mused. "I am only head of the ship. You are its heart." He gave the boy and girl a curt salute. "And any time you want to crew again…" Lars Thorstad reached into his pocket and pulled from it a tiny fragment of Odin's Eye. Solemnly he handed it to the boy. "When all paths are gone and there is nowhere else to go, this will show the way." Joe took the crystal and held it in both palms. It was the greatest gift he had ever been given. Then the captain was shaking his hand and saying, "I am so happy that you fell into my bathtime."

Joe turned to Evangeline, but didn't know the first thing to say to her. Everything seemed impossibly stupid or totally irrelevant. Thankfully, Evangeline saved the day by just throwing her arms around him and hugging him fiercely. "Well, you sure voodooed up my Monday morning," she said, then pulling back, added, "Now, go catch that rainbow by its tail."

"Goodbye, Evangeline," said Joe. His voice croaked with sadness. He wanted to stay with them both, to travel the seas and forget all about rules and medication, but he couldn't. This is not my family, he told himself over and over. I need to find them.

"No, no, no," she scolded. "No tears. I need to get home. And you need to get to what's at the end of your adventure too."

"Yes, I do," he said. "Promise I'll see you again."

"Maybe we'll find each other one day. Somewhere else in the labyrinth." They embraced a second time. "D'you know what?" she whispered in his ear.

"What?" the boy asked.

"Happiness is just a thing called Joe." The girl's eyes were wet as she pushed him away. "Go," she said, "before I do something bat-crazy like come with you."

WITH THE CAPTAIN'S COINS, JOE bartered rides in everything from cars to carts as he made his way from Northern Ireland to the south. Staying at inns he found himself telling the tale of the captain and how the sea orphaned him, of how he was travelling to stay with a distant aunt in the Boyne Valley. It took five days to make the journey, but finally it was over. He was eventually dropped off by a farmer in a rusty tractor in torrential rain at the hilltop cottage of Tigh Samhraidh. The place looked as if it had been deserted for years. Beside it stood an even more derelict chapel that overlooked a tiny village below. Hanging from the ivy-tangled gates was a metal sign that read DANGER. UNSAFE BUILDING. KEEP OUT. Joe couldn't help being reminded of a similar sign back in Great Dunmow.

"This is the house of Mrs MacGeraghty," said the rain-soaked fellow from beneath his dripping hat. "Or it was. The old witch died thirty years ago." The man didn't sound upset by this, and mention of the word 'witch' made Joe think of a female Jonathan D'Ante. "This house is a ruin. No one's here. Let's get you out of this rain. Come back to ours. My wife—"

"Don't wait," said the boy, still gazing at the derelict cottage. "I can walk back down myself." The farmer shrugged, obviously thinking the boy utterly mad to want to stay here a moment longer. Starting up the tractor, he reversed down the hill, turning back to the village.

Joe found the courtyard mentioned in *The Stranger's Guide* at the back of the house. Climbing over a wall choked with brambles and creepers, he dropped into the wilderness of a long-forgotten garden. Centred by a cracked font, purple rambling roses bloomed everywhere, while ivy scrambled across pieces of white church stonework. The book told little of the woman who had once lived here beyond her fiery temper and reclusiveness, though it did mention a fortune-telling tea cup that was undeniably her oracle. It also said that the next door was found through the leaves. Perhaps another tree? Still, the main thing was he had made it. It was still several days until the dark of the moon when the cottage and gardens would transform and he could step from 1986 into 1933. Pulling up the collar of his fisherman's coat, he tried not to shiver in the cold night.

So now all he had to do was wait. Perhaps he'd take up the grumpy farmer's offer after all.

VI

SIXTH MOON: EAGLE MOON (OF BIRDS)
TIGH SAMHRAIDH
BOYNE VALLEY, COUNTY MEATH, IRELAND
SUNDAY 26 MARCH 1933 | 11:45:21

UPON THE NIGHT OF THE next Dead Moon, Joe translated back a further fifty-three years into the past. Yet as soon as the darkness parted, revealing a grey misty morning, he knew it was a trap. The 1930s courtyard was pretty much as before, just far less wild. The months had wound back from spring to winter and now the leaves on the trees were gone. Every branch was bare, except one tall, thin tree that was hung with ribbons and pennants of all sizes and colours. The barn was restored, as was its wooden summerhouse, its diamond-latticed roof wound with bare vines. The nearby church was still derelict, but the cottage was restored, its latticed windows and tiled roof in good repair. Smoke rose from the chimney. The garden was littered with carved toy horses, torn theatrical posters and even a cartwheel pinned with faded playing cards. Cold rain fell from heavy clouds, each drop as large as a penny. In moments the boy was drenched.

Yet different as this courtyard was, the thing that alerted him to danger was not the stonework or buildings or the barn roof crowned with its hare and moon weathervane. It was the strings of nautical signal flags that criss-crossed the tall trees above him. He had last seen a set of these in the rigging of *The Lodestar*, could clearly hear the captain telling him of 'ship speakings' and, more importantly, how they were flown in times of danger and distress.

How were they here? How had they arrived in this place? When and why?

The only question he could answer for sure was what they represented. By now Joe was learning the ways of this tricksy labyrinth and suspected this was a message for him, or at least for any similar travellers through Talliston's labyrinth. He could not read them, had no idea what message they might spell, but he knew their presence was a warning. Beware, Joe, he thought; remember this is the house of a witch. Already in his head had been burned that image of a female Jonathan D'Ante, seeking out and buying this property to feed on whatever magic was buried here.

Joe was determined not to get caught again. He was done making friends and playing happy families. That was all over. He'd learned his lesson. Just get in, get the oracle and get out, he thought.

The back door of the cottage opened and an old woman emerged. She was wrapped in an enormous checkered cloak, her wrinkled face shadowed by its hood. In her wake came several cats, peering from around the folds of her voluminous gown. Joe stiffened and took an involuntary step back. Wiping the water from his eyes, he grasped his pack and made ready. The witch's silvery hair streamed from beneath her hood, her round spectacles shining like the eyes of an owl. She leaned on a carved stick with an eagle's head and was carrying something held close to her chest to protect it from the downpour.

The boy watched as the woman left the shelter of the porch and crossed the courtyard towards him. The cats stayed in the dry. He couldn't be sure, but looking up at the house, were those more feline faces peering from the dark windows?

"In a winter so long, we lost all thought of spring..." The witch's voice was dry and cracked, as if this were the first time she'd spoken in a very long while. "I have waited for you to come."

"Who are you?" Joe asked.

"I am..." the woman started, then trailed off. "Mrs MacGeraghty, that's right. It has been such a time since I've been asked I barely know myself. Most know me as Granny Em."

"How old are you?"

"Oh, now, now there's a question." Her face screwed up in concentration. "Old," she concluded finally. "Very, very old."

Which prompted the thought: I know when you die.

Granny Em pointed up at the tree covered in multicoloured decorations. "This is the Kissing Tree," she said with conviction, reminding Joe immediately of Papa Legba's ancient oak. "There's a ribbon for every boon or bane the village folk have asked me to be given or taken."

"Don't people leave you alone?"

"They do, but it's amazing how quickly that's forgotten when they want something. A sick infant cured. A curse lifted. A girl to fall in love with them..." She gave the boy a sly wink. "See all this stonework? Churchwardens used to live here."

"When was that?"

"Long, long ago when the world was young."

"Where is here?" Joe asked, knowing the answer, but trying to see if she did.

"Six days east of the sun, and three nights west of the moon," said the old woman dreamily. In the throat of the porch, more of her pets appeared. "Have you seen the cats?"

"What? Yes. They're right behind you."

Mrs MacGeraghty stopped and supported herself on the intricately carved font in the centre of the garden. For a moment she regarded the sprawling lavender planted within it, then stiffly looked behind her. "No, Timalons, no," she said. "You stay out of the wet, my loves." But it was clear the cats had no intention of venturing into the torrential downpour.

There was something odd about the old woman and more than just seeming mad as a March hare. Her skin was grey and clammy, making her look sick or diseased. Joe didn't want to be near her at all.

Turning back to the boy, she said, "Come inside. The kettle's on – or is it the oven?" As if for the first time she seemed to notice the rain. "Why, we need to get you out of this fierce wet." Her breath caught in her chest and she let out a series of racking coughs. During the fit Joe saw what she was holding. It was a silver-framed photograph of a man in military uniform. Her husband?

Joe didn't want to enter the house, but he had to find the oracle. And if he was looking for a tea cup, what better place to start than the kitchen?

Inside the house stank. At first Joe thought the rank smell was coming from a blocked drain or rotting rubbish, but then he saw that the entire house was full of cats. They were everywhere. As were bowls and bowls of food. On tables, under chairs, even placed strategically in little lines along the hallway. The cottage was simply furnished, the only decoration being ornately framed images of the man. Above the wood-burning stove was an oil painting of him with a beard in his later years, while the walls and mantelpieces were crowded with photographs of him at all stages of his life. In one of him as a younger man Joe noticed he was standing at the entrance to a circus sideshow tent. He was wearing a simple set of trousers and waistcoat, his face serious. Had Pandoro's fantastical fayre travelled here?

"Is this your husband?" asked Joe.

The woman regarded the photographs intently, then sighed. "That is my angel, my sweet," she said confidently. "We met under a paper moon at a penny arcade. He was a navy man, very handsome. His ship was lost at sea. I have no idea which one."

Joe was reminded of the captain and the graves on the cliffs. He went to ask about the signal flags and who put them there, but right then there was a scrambling sound next to the boy's head. It was coming from behind the peeling wallpaper.

"What was that?" he asked.

Mrs MacGeraghty stopped fussing with the kettle and looked up. "What, my angel, my sweet?" she asked. "Are you back with the messages, my love?"

Joe looked down at his thick seaman's coat. Does she think I'm her husband? The sound came again. A noise like scuttling or shuffling. He had heard such sounds before, back at the Italian villa in the Hall of Mirrors.

"There's something in the walls," he said, backing away.

"Oh no. That's just the old house speaking."

"It sounds like... Are there cats in the walls?"

The old woman crossed the room and pressed her ear against the floral wallpaper. The sound came again, a little fainter this time as if moving off. She made a series of low grumbling noises, like rattling in her thickly veined throat. There was a pause and... an answering sound.

"You speak to the house?"

"Why not? It's as alive as me or you."

"Houses aren't alive."

The old woman tutted. "Why isn't a house alive? Why do you think a tree or stone can't be just as conscious as you or I?" She had another coughing fit, recovered, then added, "Anyways, that's not in the walls. Because *we* are in the walls. That's outside."

"Outside?"

"Like you were once," she explained. Her face changed, like a cloud had passed from it. With perfect clarity she said, "Many get lost in the walls of the labyrinth, but there are many, many others still out there in the world. Searching for the right door to get in. They all know it's there. They can feel it in their water. Everyone tells them it's a myth, but that doesn't make it a fantasy. And it doesn't stop them searching."

The walls of the labyrinth. Joe reached into his pack and drew out *The Stranger's Guide*. Turning to the page with the drawing of the earth-fast stone, he showed it to the old woman. "Yes. See," she said, pointing. "We are in the walls." It was with a certain fascination that he realised Mrs MacGeraghty was correct. The design on the Tallis Stone clearly showed the rooms as circles drawn upon the lines of the walls, not on the spiralling path. Hadn't Saturn said something about being within the walls of all worlds?

"Obviously, I can't speak house," said Joe, still a little stunned. "What's it saying?"

The witch listened, then shrugged. "The door is found through the hill of heroes. Under the stone where once it was," she said. "Whatever that means."

"Can you help me?"

"I think I can." Granny Em frowned. "Or I could once. I suppose it all depends on what you want."

"I want to get out of this house and back to my own time and place." Is that true? he asked himself. Is that really true? He thought of Serene and how she didn't want to go back. Then he thought of his words from the message in the bottle.

It's a trap, said the sword from his pack. *You know it is. Get out now.* She's just a dotty old lady.

But the cats, Ilkilæmber insisted. *The cats!*

"All this chatter is making me fair parched. Perhaps some tea first, my loves." MacGeraghty opened the cupboards, but each one was bare. She started to cry a little. "What is to become of us? How can we feed our children when we have nothing for ourselves?" A few of the cats moved towards the woman, leaping onto chairs and tables to be closer to her. Perhaps they were hungry, but that couldn't be true as there was plenty of food everywhere.

With a pounce a massive brown and black feline appeared, jumping onto the cluttered dresser. Joe jumped too. The animal was massive, easily as large as a Border collie.

"Ah, now that's Timalon," she announced, stroking the giant creature. "He's a forest cat and his ancestors travelled to Ireland with the Norsemen. And that's…" She pointed to a hairless grey cat with impressively long ears, obviously searching for its name. Then she had it. "Timalon." The kettle began to whistle and she looked around in sudden alarm. "Have you seen the cats?"

They're everywhere, thought Joe. And apparently, they're all called Timalon. Why can't she see them? Or perhaps – an unsettling thought struck him – that wasn't the question. Joe looked at the nearest of MacGeraghty's pets and it stared right back at him with yellow slitty eyes. In this new world he travelled he had to consider that maybe they weren't cats at all.

"Do it," the cat said to the old woman as the kettle shrieked on.

"Timalon," Granny Em scolded. "It's tea first. Always tea first."

"How… human," sneered the creature.

Joe stepped to the stove and turned off the gas. The screeching died away, but when he turned back every one of the creatures was facing him. Mrs MacGeraghty was facing him too, her eyes wide with terror.

"Go, my loves," she whispered. "My angel. My sweet."

As one, the cats bent low and began to retch. Joe expected hairballs, but this was no trapped fur. Gagging and hacking, the animals started expelling dark fluid from their fanged mouths, and as they did so began shape-shifting back into their human forms.

Grim Grotesques!

From the table, a ginger tom that was transmuting into something far uglier pounced right at them both. Joe pushed the old woman out of its way with one hand, while the other swept up the kettle. It struck the cat mid-leap, knocking it to the floor while boiling water flew everywhere. The writhing things recoiled and Joe grabbed the book and Granny Em's trembling hands and headed for the door. Kicking anything that came close, Joe and Mrs MacGeraghty fled across the courtyard to the barn. At his back the huntsmen yowled. Hauling the old woman into the outbuilding, the boy slammed the door and snapped the bolt into its iron keep.

Click.

The sound of the door closing was one of the sweetest the boy had ever heard. Panting, he leaned his drenched back against the cold wood and breathed steam. Granny Em's confused face peeked from under the tangled disarray of her hair. Even over the smell of oil and mildew in the barn, Joe could still smell the stink of that foul black sick.

The Wild Hunt had been waiting for him. Of course, the clues were everywhere – the flags, the sword, the woman's inability to perceive them as cats – it's just Joe had not seen them.

With a resounding slam something large hit the door at his back. Making it jump. Making him jump.

Outside, the shrieks of the cats or shape-shifters or whatever the hell the Grim Grotesques truly were wailed in frustration. Joe ached with relief that he had escaped, had managed to get from the chaos of the kitchen and find somewhere secure. He knew it was only a brief respite, but it did buy him a little time. Looking around, Joe saw the barn was filled with piles of timber, steamer trunks and wicker chests, even a cobwebbed lawnmower. It didn't look as if anyone had been out here in a long time. The good news was that the outbuilding had only two doors: the one they had entered and a double set at the back. As one was locked and the other barred with a great wooden brace, they were safe.

Trapped, but safe.

"Are you OK, Granny Em?" Joe asked.

"I'm fine," the old woman replied in a voice of all shades of everything but fine. Then, after a pause, "Do we have any cats?" She still appeared in shock, her face solid and unsmiling. After this, Joe doubted she'd ever smile again.

How were they going to get out? He could run, but the woman wouldn't get ten metres without them catching her, and then... It was all too terrifying for him to consider what would happen if they were caught out in the open. Frantically, Joe checked the woman over with his eyes. Her messed hair, her stiff shoulders, the way her hands shivered as she forced them against her chest. She didn't seem injured, but she still looked very sick. What should he do? And when did he decide to trust her?

Draw me and attack, said the blade. *I am no sword to sleep in your hand.*

"Did you hang the flags?" he asked. "Did you try to warn me?" Mrs MacGeraghty looked back at Joe as if he were speaking Arabic.

"I knew you would return, my angel, my sweet. The tea leaves told me. The dagger for warning, the cats for deceit..." Her voice trailed off. "It's only the two cats, isn't it?" she added absently.

Crossing to the double doors, Joe pressed his ear to them and heard clawing at the wood. Already there too, he thought. On every side of the barn, the walls were alive with Damfino's henchmen. Over the

·

rain, the boy could even hear them crawling over the roof. He could easily imagine the things covering the oak barn completely, making it appear as if built of bodies. He could also imagine them getting inside and what would happen to them if they did.

"Don't worry," he said more to himself than to her. "They're not getting in here." For now, he added in his mind.

Granny Em shuddered, suddenly in the grips of a violent spasm. Joe rushed back to where the old woman was standing by the door. Her whole body shook and when he tried to take her hand, she drew it away. In the dim light, her eyes looked as dead as stones at the bottom of the ocean. Then she reached out, but not to him.

"Granny Em, what's happening. Are you—"

Click.

In one movement, Mrs MacGeraghty drew back the bolt and threw the door wide open. Now it was Joe's turn to look shocked. Outside dozens of Grim Grotesques stood waiting in the downpour. Of course, the clues were everywhere – her pallid features, the cat's command, her conflict – it was just he had not seen them. Both the old woman's hands locked onto Joe's wrists with impossible strength. As her lips met his, Joe saw the trap for what it was, but it was far too late. Her throat was already convulsing. Suddenly his mouth was full of stinking black bile. It was at the back of his throat and its stench was in his nose. He was drowning in it. His mind flashed images of Damfino and Nathaniel Grey, their faces locked together in the rectory gardens. The boy had thought Abram Kyle was biting the reverend, but now he knew different.

Instantly hysterical, Joe struggled to break free of the terrible kiss, trying not to swallow. He failed in both tasks. Involuntarily, Joe's throat opened and he drank the broth-thick liquid in one noisy gulp. Her job done, MacGeraghty – or whatever the woman was now – collapsed, slumping to the floor like a lifeless doll. At that moment the Grims began towards him.

Gagging and spitting, Joe lurched backwards, hefted the brace off its iron supports and threw the barn doors wide. Outside the hill dropped away into the green valley. It was crowded with cats and huntsmen. Finally heeding Ilkilæmber's cries, Joe drew the sword. Leaping out into the torrential rain, he swung blindly as the bile churned like snakes in his belly. The enemy drew away from his wild thrusts, and Joe ran from the witch's cottage, the ruined church and all the terrors he had found there. He didn't get far. His legs felt as weak as milky tea. The dark shapes watched him stagger. They did not follow. They know I won't get far, thought Joe, not now the infection is within me. I'm almost as good as theirs. Already the boy felt his limbs turning cold as ice. Looking towards the tiny lights of the village, Joe saw a car's headlights on the lane. If only he could get to the road. Joe shouted for help, but merely croaked. He stumbled on numb legs, his head woozy, and fell towards the rain-slick grass.

"Help me," he managed. His voice was cracked and barely a whisper. "You have to help me."

He was unconscious before his head hit the ground.

OPENING HIS EYES, THE FIRST thing Joe saw was a giant eagle watching him. Shocked awake, he struggled against the tightness around his arms and legs. Imagining ropes or chains, he writhed and kicked, only to find his bindings to be crisp linen sheets and blankets. He was in an attic bedroom. Above, the ceiling was thatch, the walls rough plaster. Grey light seeped in through a small open window. Outside it was grey and ghostly. The enormous bird sat on the end of the bed with talons sunk deep into the wooden footboard. Its yellow eyes regarded the boy severely, the curve of its eyebrows making it look stern and judging. "You," Joe said. "The eagles. You warned us."

The bird opened its formidable beak and let out a low cry.

"Kuk-kuk-kuk."

Joe stopped struggling and sat up. Below, voices filtered through the floorboards and then came the sound of approaching footsteps. A woman entered the bedroom up a set of stairs that emerged through the floor. Her head was wrapped in a scarf. Her face and hands showed signs of cuts and bruises.

"So, the little master is awake," she said in a broad Irish accent. "A hundred thousand welcomes. How do you feel? You took quite a tumble."

Joe stared at her coldly, not knowing who he could possibly trust after the attack at the cottage. He felt very ill. There was a heaviness in his head and stomach and he could not properly focus his eyes.

"Where is this?" he said accusingly. "How did I get here?"

"Iolairn has a keen eye. When you fell, we were already on the road. And lucky for you that we were."

"*Yu-lar-en*," Joe said slowly. "The eagle?"

"Exactly so."

"Why can't I understand what he's saying?"

"Because you are no longer in a place that allows such wonders. This is The Sun, Moon and Stars and my name is Boann."

"This is a hotel?" Joe asked.

The eagle let out a little cackle in its throat.

"Oh, hush, Iolairn," she scolded. "You may be surpassed only by the salmon in wisdom, but you have such ugly manners." Turning back to Joe, she went on. "This is a tavern and I its innkeeper. I live here with my partner, Jana, who tends to me while I tend to the customers. The old woman who lives on the hill is the third of us, and we watch over her."

"Are you all sisters?" he asked.

"Oh no, nothing like that," said Boann with a wry smile. "We are as individual as fingerprints, but together we are the sun, moon and stars. You have no reason to fear while within these walls." The boy was still unconvinced and she saw this clearly. "I am a friend of Talliston," she added, and the way she said this was filled with unspoken meaning. While Joe was familiar with the name of the labyrinth from the title of the guide, who its friends were he had no idea. "Those that pass this way say there are others, in different times and places. Others that call themselves friends."

"I'm having a hard time trusting anyone right now," Joe said. "But thank you for saving me." He cast a glance at Iolairn. "You too. Thank you."

"I would say it was nothing—" she indicated her wounds, "—but as you can see, it was not." Joe flinched. The burden of all the people who'd risked their lives for him was almost unbearable.

"Is Granny Em really a witch?" asked Joe.

"Well, she knows every plant to quell fevers and reduce swelling. And she can tell your fortune from the tea leaves in your cup. Does that make her a witch? She keeps to herself and lets the valley folks have their gossip. She lived up in that house with her fella for many years, but he was conscripted into the navy as an officer in the Great War and never came home from sea."

"That was the First World War, wasn't it?"

"First? What are you saying to me, child? It was the war to end all wars." Joe winced as he realised his mistake. "His death broke her mind as well as her heart. She was never the same after. Now we do our best to help her; take her food and gladly suffer her forgetfulness and eccentricities. War does that to people." The way Boann said this made Joe think she had also seen its horrors. "Right, enough questions. Let's fix you some supper."

Boann wanted to feed Joe in bed, but, though weak, the boy insisted he felt well enough to get up for his meal. Helping Joe out of the bed, the innkeeper shooed Iolairn out of the window and headed off to the kitchens. These were two floors down through bars and common rooms busy with customers and the smell of food and wood fires. Everyone was smoking and the air was choked with the smell of tobacco, an easy reminder that he was back in the 1930s. All the cooks and waiting staff were women, dressed like Boann in simple skirts, their hair tied back in scarves. In the tiled cookhouse, the innkeeper found a spot for the boy on a stool beside an enormous stove, and began spooning broth and vegetables into a large earthenware bowl.

"You've been poisoned by our foes, the tainted *sídhe*. *Sídhe* are faerie folk, but like us some are light and some are dark. Their venom is dark also – and you need to keep up your strength."

"You mean the Grim Grotesques?"

"I do not know this name, but the dark *sídhe* have many, here and in other places – Fomhóraigh, Dearg-Dur, Púca. Many names, but one wicked heart. To us they are the Sluagh, the haunted dead who rise up to ride with their hellish master."

"Abram Kyle," said Joe bitterly.

"Abram Kyle is gone," Boann snapped. "He lost the right to his mortal name when he joined the ranks of the Wild Hunt. His story is a dire telling – and there is no time for it here. What must be said is this: he entered the throat of the labyrinth and walked between its walls, but not all who do find its centre. Many stray. Many die. And some find darker doorways on the path. Abram Kyle is only Damfino now. Only Ghûl. He and his kin have existed for centuries beyond counting. They are the ancient dark folk that my ancestors drove into the underworld but never vanquished. And know this: terrifying as he is, he is not their monarch, but one of the restless dead like all the rest." Which begged the question: who was Damfino's master?

"Why are they hunting me?"

"I have no notion. Do you?" The boy shook his head. "They are servants of those who attack, steal and control the last sacred places of the world. They draw the land's power and use it for ill."

"And I suppose you use it only for good?" Joe said suspiciously, thinking of the fayre.

"Oh no. We do not use it at all. We defend it. Well, as best we can. Now eat." She handed him the bowl and a wooden spoon. The sight of the broth filled Joe with nausea. He pushed the food away.

"I'm not hungry," he said.

"Eat or your death will be all the quicker," Boann warned. "And after you die your corpse will rise and swell the ranks of your enemies. There's something important you need to know about the folk you call the Grim Grotesques. They have existed as long as the fear of them. The disease within them, the poison that is inside you now, is inescapably fatal in one hundred percent of cases. No one survives. Once down your throat it gets into the blood, then works its way to the brain and there wreaks its havoc."

"Sounds great," said Joe.

"Do not affect that sarcastic tone," Boann warned. "For it is a terrible thing you carry within you. You may feel weak now, but soon it will take hold of your mind and your body will rebel. It manifests as a fear of the elements: of water, earth, fire and air. Even fear of shadows." She placed the back of her hand against his forehead. "Their venom is in you, son, and if your life force fades, you have witnessed what will fill its place. Eat."

Joe took the bowl and lifted the spoon to his dry lips. The thick soup tasted like someone had tipped an ashtray into it. It brought back terrible memories of the attack in the barn and the face of Mrs MacGeraghty.

"Will Granny Em die too?"

"Yes," said Boann. "She will."

"How? How long?"

"Her or you?"

"Her."

"By morning. You'll follow sometime after noon."

Joe dropped the spoon in shock.

"You mean we're going to die *tomorrow*?" Joe yelled. The effort made his head spin, reminding him he was still as weak as a kitten.

Everyone in the kitchen stopped working and stared at Joe. Boann grabbed the boy's food and led him back up to his room. There the innkeeper put Joe back to bed, seating herself on a cushioned window seat with diamond leaded panes that looked out over the valley side. Joe could clearly see the cottage on the crown of the hill and beside it the derelict church.

"See that ruined chapel?" said Boann once he was settled. "It's just rubble now, but it was a fine house of worship once. When I was a child, we went there every Sunday and I marvelled at its craftsmanship. All that beauty is gone now. The only fragments of its former glories are found in Granny Em's courtyard – the font and parts of the nave balustrade – the rest is lost to time. Beneath the garden lies the secret: the Well of Destiny, an entrance to the Otherworld. The church was dedicated to St Patrick, but everyone around here knows it by a much older name: Ráith Sídhe." The story made Joe think of the hidden spring in Italy. How each culture made sense of the forces at work in these places. Forces far older than humans and their histories. "When the high kings of Ireland came to this island, this was the hallowed heart of their kingdom. This hill has been a place of heroes and power for over five and a half thousand years." Heroes, thought Joe. The hill of heroes. "Yet here you will find no grand temples or fallen palaces. To find true wonders, you must go deeper."

Boann produced a half-smoked cigar from her breast pocket and lit it. Immediately the room was filled with its bitter leathery smell.

"Did you know you carry a magical sword?" she asked.

"Yes, and I guess you've seen *The Stranger's Guide* too?"

"I have indeed. Now don't tell me *you* wrote that, little man?"

"No. Do you know who did?"

"I have no idea, but they seem only to have visited the cottage and met Granny Em. This place is not mentioned at all."

Joe flipped through the book and found the section on Ireland 1933. There at the bottom of the page was a drawing of a tea cup and saucer.

"That's the oracle I need to find. It's my only way out of here."

"That's the cup Granny Em uses to read fortunes," said Boann.

"Then I need to get back to the cottage and find it. We have to rescue Granny Em. You have to help me."

"Not so fast. The cottage is teeming with dark *sidhe*."

"You mean the cats?"

"Cats, hounds, devils on horseback… They can appear in many guises, even as you and me." Joe sat bolt upright, making Boann laugh clouds of smoke. "Iolairn has eyes that see through all glamour and illusion. We are as you see us."

"Can you help me? Can anything cure us?"

Boann smoked for a while, looking over the boy as if judging if she could trust him. Finally, she said, "See that lone monolith up there?" The innkeeper pointed to the crest at the far end of the hill that held the cottage and the chapel. "That is Lia Fáil, the Stone of Destiny. The legends say that when a true born king put his feet upon it, the stone would roar in joy, but that was a story dreamed up to protect the true secret of the well. The stone once stood upon the Mound of Hostages, entrance to a great underground temple, but was moved to hide the doorway and the place was sealed. To drink from the well's waters cures all sickness, heals all wounds. In the hands of magicians, it could be made to wash away old age, even death. But there is always a price for such potency."

169

The boy didn't like the sound of that, but he had more pressing questions. "Will it cure me and Granny Em?"

"Yes," Boann said simply.

"Then you have to get me there, and—"

The woman's face darkened. "Were you not listening to me? We are guardians here. We do not use the magic of this sacred place."

Joe couldn't believe what he was hearing. "What? You have to. Otherwise we'll both die." No, worse, he thought. We'll both turn into one of those *things*.

"We do not use the magic," Boann repeated.

Joe's eyes stung, feeling suddenly close to tears. He didn't want to die. Why wouldn't they help him?

"There may be a way." The voice came from the doorway. It was a young blonde-haired girl. She was watching Joe with quizzical interest, her arms folded.

"This is my daughter, Jana," said Boann.

"Adopted daughter," the girl corrected. "And part-owner of this inn. So, this is the stranger?"

Boann stubbed out her cigar and stood up, scraping the chair across the wooden floor. "Yes, and he says he wants to drink from the Well of Destiny."

"Good luck with that," Jana mocked. "The hill is crawling with the restless dead. He might just as well want to eat cheese from the moon."

"You said there might be a way," said Joe.

"Yes, I did. I'm willing to take you to the sacred well."

The boy's chest heaved with relief. "How do we get there?"

"With great difficulty," said Jana.

"Not helpful."

"There is another entrance. It lies through a sealed portal in the crypt of the ruined chapel. Only us three hold the enchantments to pass that door. We will go there tonight. It's just past the dark of the moon, so—"

"I know," Joe blurted. "We'll use the near-darkness, creep in unseen, get the water, then go up to the house and save Granny Em."

Boann and Jana passed a glance. "You still underestimate our foemen," said the daughter. "And the well. This is not like buying lime squash from the local shop."

"I can use the sword," Joe insisted. "Not well, but I've been learning."

"Have you now?"

Boann interrupted the pair. "This will need all our number to achieve, and maybe not even then."

"How many are you?" asked Joe.

"We are nineteen. I will send Iolairn to gather the company. We will meet at oh-dark-hundred." Joe looked puzzled. "That's midnight to you, civvie."

MIDNIGHT ARRIVED QUICKLY FOR THERE was much to do before the attack to take back Tigh Samhraidh cottage from the enemy. To Joe the hours passed in an eye-blink. Whatever medicines or balms were contained in his food and drink had eased the writhing pain in his stomach, but Joe knew this was a temporary respite from the venom's possession of him. The boy spent the time adding sketches to his map of The Boathouse and The Fountain Courtyard, reading the guide and practising his swordsmanship with Jana. As well as being a formidable opponent, Boann's daughter was super-knowledgeable about the savage history of Irish warfare and also knew a little of the legend of Ilkilæmber. She told him how the name meant 'Death's Kiss' and showed Joe the silver coating on the leaf-shaped edge. "These short swords were too proud for scabbards," she said, testing the blade's weight in her hand. "Instead they hung from baldrics – here – under the left arm. They are close-combat weapons, efficient and deadly at both cutting and thrusting. The Singing Swords were the blades of dark kings and dread lords, infused with wild spirits that cared only for adventure, battle and bloodshed. And you," she said raising an eyebrow, "keep it in a duffel bag."

When the last hour of the day came, Joe stowed his scant belongings in his room, then went down to join the others. Emerging from the inn, the boy found all nineteen of Boann's company gathered in the cobbled courtyard. Each wore black, their clothes thick and tightly fitted. Joe saw weapons ranging from bats to hayforks, and three of the group carried wide nets on poles, the kind used to land large fish. It was difficult to tell for certain the sex of each individual, but there were all manner of heights and ages. In a low voice and chewing an unlit cigar, Boann addressed the group.

"This night we go to fight our darkest foes. There are two reasons. One is that our eldest sister is captured and poisoned. She is the lure, the struggling hare that is meant to make us reckless and devil-may-care. We must not let this blind us. We must be decisive and cautious. Two is this boy. He is infected also and is prey to the Wild Hunt. Wherever he is, they will come, so he cannot stay here. I feel the only reason they are not already at our gates is that they set a trap at the cottage. So we shall go to meet them. And while we engage our ancient enemy, Jana and he will enter the chamber of the sacred well."

The group said nothing while she talked, just looked on in silence. Joe could almost feel the mounting foreboding at what the next few hours held for them all. The boy couldn't help but imagine the anxious and distrusting stares all around him.

"Iolandra, Brielle, you are to guard the chapel. Jana, take Joe. The rest of you will join me in regaining the cottage. When this is done, we will all rendezvous beneath the Kissing Tree. Live long and hard and when you die, die well." At his side, Joe's sword joined in the rousing chorus of cheers. "Let us go!"

The group of masked figures began to run, and Joe was swept along with them. Immediately outside the courtyard, they plunged into the pitch blackness. Though the rain had stopped, the hillside was wet and muddy. Without lights, the boy struggled to keep up without slipping or falling. Where the ridge and sky met Joe could make out the faintest outlines of the ruined chapel and cottage, but even though his vision adjusted to the dark, he could see nothing of the countryside around him. All he could do was keep Jana ahead, and Iolandra and Brielle on either side, rely on blind faith and just keep moving. Halfway up the slope the women veered off from the rest of the group and headed directly for the ruins of Ráith Sídhe. As they went, Joe heard them whispering under their breath. At first he thought the words sounded like poems, but knew they were more likely to be invocations or spells of protection. He was grateful they were not relying on the fabled luck of the Irish to pass undetected by the Grim Grotesques.

Arriving at the chapel, Brielle led them through a collapsed portion of the wall. Inside trees and ferns grew, but thankfully all seemed silent and empty. Dimly the great chancel window loomed above as they picked their way across the nave. Suddenly both women froze and Joe was about to ask why when he heard movement everywhere.

"Hurry!" hissed Iolandra. "It's the cats. Watching from the trees."

"Quickly. Here!" Immediately, Jana grabbed Joe's hand and dragged him behind a great mass of stone. The boy didn't get to see the entrance to the crypts. One moment he was standing waist-high in undergrowth, the next he was being dragged down a set of spiral steps. Behind came the sound of wailing creatures and Iolandra's battle cry. The attack had begun.

Back encased in impenetrable blackness, Joe stumbled after Jana, his hand on her shoulder like a blind man. He kept all his concentration focused on not falling down the uneven stairs. At the bottom of the steps Joe found his footing on level ground, then the woman was speaking some strange language and there was a scraping of stone on stone. Feeling his way through a narrow doorway he felt himself step into a larger space. Only then did Jana turn on her torch. Shielding his eyes, through his fingers Joe saw they had entered a domed chamber. It was roughly circular with sill-stones in the walls marking five ledges. Like at the palazzo, roots had ruptured the ceiling, snaking their way down to the centre of the room. There stood the sacred well. It was simple and unadorned, constructed from wedges of stone, pressed together like pizza slices to form a circular shelf. It was towards this well-head that the criss-crossing web of roots extended. The place seemed prehistoric; the air hung thick with the same potency as the captain's cave of crystals.

The only problem was that the well looked completely dry.

"Where's the water?" asked Joe. His head was already ringing with warnings. Always Have A Way Out!

Jana placed her torch on one of the shelves so that its beam illuminated the room. When she turned back to the boy, her face was an emotionless mask. "This is the part we didn't explain," she said. "The secret of calling the well water." Joe said nothing. He dreaded what she would say next. In his bag the sword thrummed with anticipation. "Did you think such gifts would be given up for free?" Jana continued. "Like for like is the lore of this place. You know what that means, don't you?"

Joe nodded. "A life for a life."

"A life for a life," Jana repeated. "Yes."

It made a kind of grim sense. That to imbue the water with life-giving properties there should be some similar sacrifice. It wasn't difficult to understand now whose life that would be. A stranger's for a friend's. His for hers. The boy thought to run, to escape and save himself, but already he heard sounds in the tunnels; a soft, low whisper like the rustling of dead leaves. Was it Iolandra and Brielle? Boann and her cronies? Whoever it was made no difference. Rule Two! Rule Two! pounded in his head. He was so stupid. He was trapped.

Jana smiled and drew her sword and at that moment the shadows in the mouth of the doorway shifted and moved, then a terrifying shape detached itself from the darkness and entered the chamber. It was neither Iolandra or Brielle. It was the Vandal King himself. The thing that would not rest until it found him and killed him. From it, waves of horror poured like overflowing sewage from a forgotten drain. At the ends of its bony hands talons glittered like butcher's knives.

"Back, Joe!" Jana shouted. "It is the Sluagh's black lord."

The leader of the Wild Hunt stepped fully into the shining torchlight, illuminating his new and most terrifying form. In England he was an outlaw. At the tower and bayou, a werewolf. In Norway a bearded wizard in a wide-brimmed hat. Now, in Ireland, he resembled a half-man, half-beast. His chest was naked and white, while his lower body was covered in matted fur and ended in muddy, goat-like hoofs. Upon his head, rising from a mane of thick, lank hair, rose a pair of ram's horns. His eyes were as red as the dark sprays of blood upon his claws and fangs. A nightmare version of the Pan sculpture at the watchtower.

"Well, well, well." The man that was once Abram Kyle smirked. "Look here, the bunnies all trapped in their pretty burrow. For sure, here is the end of the hunt. It has been long beyond enduring, but that makes the kill so much sweeter, don't you find?"

I long for a taste of the blood of such an ancient foe, said the sword.

Joe felt his body turn to ice. Terrified, he drew Ilkilæmber as if under a sorcerer's spell, and adopted a fighting stance. If Damfino was here, both Iolandra and Brielle must have fallen. What chance did they have against this shape-changing huntsman? This was not a fight in the open under the Wishing Tree. Here they were cornered in a stone tomb.

"I entered this labyrinth a lovesick fool, hunting my heart's love, but I soon saw the folly of that petal-strewn path. Now I hunt in many forms. Kill in many names. And now – here in this moment – I am become the horned king of death, my final form for thee." Raising talons as long and terrible as Wolverine's adamantium claws, Damfino roared. The sound was deafening in the circular chamber. Only the sword's strength upheld the boy, allowing him to face the fearsome monster. All of Joe's instincts told him to curl into a tight ball or tear through the stone walls with his bare fingers. If not for the sphere of invincibility flowing from the blade, he would doubtless have crawled into a corner and waited to be slaughtered.

"For the water to quicken, this thing needs to die," said Jana through clenched teeth.

The antlered beast took another step into the room.

"What?" said Joe, realising what she was saying. "So you weren't going to kill me?"

"Kill you?" Jana replied, for a moment puzzled. "Lord, no! We knew bringing you here, this fool would follow. That his life would save others. Did you really think…?" She stopped. It was clear that the boy had thought exactly that.

Jana and Joe moved forwards to meet the master of the Wild Hunt. As they approached, Damfino's lipless mouth opened and he began to sing: "Joe and Serene sitting in the tree. K-I-S-S-I-N-G." The boy was shocked to hear Serene's name and the mocking rhyme, but he kept walking. "First comes love, then comes marriage…" Crossing the room to where the grotesque figure gloated was the hardest thing he had ever done. "Then comes death in a pitch-black carriage."

Joe and Damfino faced each other, one with a blade, the other with raised talons.

When the hour is dark, said the sword, and Joe remembered. With his free hand the boy pulled the talisman from beneath his coat. It shone like a star. Upon Damfino's chest his own yellow crystal throbbed in response. Presented with the shadowstone, the antlered figure shrank back a little, then sprang. The taunting was over. The fight to the death had begun.

Throwing up his leaf blade, Joe blocked the creature's talons, while Jana swung at its hairy flank. Without turning, Damfino grabbed her blade, tore it from her hands and flung it to the floor. Sparks flew as it skittered across the stones. Jana retreated while Joe hacked and slashed, trying to keep from despair. Damfino knocked his blows away, using his long claws to turn every thrust, foil every swipe. The boy found he was retreating, the red-eyed monster advancing.

Leaping from the shadows, Jana launched herself at Damfino's neck and ripped at the thing's throat. The horned man-goat batted her away like a doll, but not before her fingers found purchase on the waxed cord of the necklace. She fell hard upon the floor, winded and twisted. Joe thought she might even be dead. Damfino bellowed at the loss of his talisman, but could do nothing to retrieve it while Joe stood before him.

Drawing on Ilkilæmber's fortitude and the half-remembered lessons from the captain, Joe tried to hold his ground, but he was no match for the fiend who had led the Wild Hunt over untold years of conflict and killing. As the boy and beast clashed steel and claw again, Joe was beaten back and back, until he felt the cold stone of the tomb wall against his shoulders. The air was heavy with the goat-thing's imminent victory, and only the sword's strength kept the boy standing.

Then there beside the well stood Jana. Her face was bloodied and bruised, but in her hands she held the yellow talisman as if her life depended on it. *It does*, spoke the sword, and Joe didn't doubt it. She was chanting. It was a verse far older and more potent than Damfino's doggerel.

"Forged in Fire. Carved in Ice.
Rooted in Rock. Wild as Wind.
Shielded in Shadow."

At these words something changed. Something in the air, felt through the earth. Pale golden lightning glittered across the stonework and the darkness, and dread shrank back in its presence. The roots shivered, then flexed, as if somewhere up on the crown of the hill something awoke in the ribboned tree.

"The Walls of these Rooms ward us.
The Power of these Doors protect us.
The Magic of these Moons encloak us.
Wherever we are; whenever we are; Talliston is."

Damfino snarled at the words, drew away from the amber fire in her hand. Joe lowered his blade, grabbed at his own necklace, and they began the invocation together. Damfino howled, lashing out and shrinking back to the mouth of the tunnel. His eyes were wild and sightless, his body twisted in agony.

I'm using magic, thought the boy as the gem's power flooded through his fingers. Mother, I'm using magic.

"Now, Joe, now!" shouted Jana, and in that moment Ilkilæmber took hold of Joe with its iron will and forced his arms forward. The boy watched numbly as the blade speared Damfino in the centre of his bare chest, not stopping until the cross of the hilt rested against his flesh. The boy held the blade there for a moment then pulled it free of the dying beast. The creature let out a vile hiss, and as the life ran out of the thing's grotesque body, its blood spilled down the slope toward the middle of the room. As soon as the thick fluid reached the channels, there came a gurgling chuckle from the well. Suddenly water burst from the centre, flowing across the stone and splashing onto the floor and roots.

As Joe shuddered in disgust, the lifeless carcass of the Vandal King withered and shrank, passing from goat to wolf to young man, and finally collapsing into dirt and dust.

"Here is the magic of Tigh Samhraidh," Jana continued quietly. "The sacred well has stood here for over three thousand years. Now these waters feed the Kissing Tree above. You must drink. We do not have much time."

Joe approached the fountain and stooped down to the fast-moving spring. Jana swept the torch to illuminate his path and in its silver light he saw that the water was a rich red. He reached out and found that it was warm to the touch.

Like blood, he thought. The blood of the earth.

Jana pressed an ornate chalice into his hand, and taking it he dipped it into the stream and then raised the cup to his lips. He paused. It was no surprise that it smelled like blood, too. The water had a sweet metallic scent.

"Drink," Jana commanded.

Joe drank. It was like swallowing warm cream, if cream also tasted of salt and copper. It ran like slime down his throat – so much like the venom that had poisoned him – and when it hit his stomach it churned like the worst belly ache imaginable. Suddenly his gut convulsed and the boy was hit by a savage series of cramps. Yelling, he dropped the chalice and folded to his knees in the flowing water. The pain was excruciating.

"Help me!" he shouted. "It burns!" This wasn't curing him, it was killing him. Jana watched him impassively.

"You are not dying. You are fighting back," she said. Joe writhed, his head spinning. His hands grasped for something solid and, finding the roots of the tree, gripped onto them until his knuckles throbbed. In the midst of his agony, he saw another vision. Around him figures entered the chamber and stood before the well. There were kings and queens, their wizards and warriors, all brought in secret to drink from the blood-dark waters. They watched him bent double on the ground and smiled. The pain lessened, then vanished completely. In its place was a warmth like summer in his stomach.

Seeing Joe's anguish had ended, Jana said, "Hurry. The water will not flow forever." She offered back the cup, but Joe pulled the empty medicine bottle from his bag and filled it with the thick liquid. Then they were hurrying off again, heading back through the tunnels toward the church. This time the light from their talismans lit the way.

Back in the upper world, Iolandra and Brielle were dead. Their bodies lay in the grass, while the creatures that were not cats waited in silence around the entrance to the crypt. Their septic eyes reflected in the torchlight, and Joe recoiled back into the shadows when he saw them. At his waist the well water in the bottle sloshed audibly.

"What should we do?" asked Joe.

"Die well?" Jana replied with a smirk. She raised her sword. "Follow me, and when I engage them, you run for the…"

Outside, every one of the felines' heads turned. Something was approaching through the wet grasses of the graveyard. There in the ruined doorway to the chapel stood Boann and Mrs MacGeraghty. The innkeeper supported the old woman, who was the pure personification of sickness and disease. In her hands she held her walking stick in clenched fists.

Through pale lips Boann cried, "Back to Hell with thee, devils. We have no more need of ye here." As she spoke, Granny Em raised her wand and the end burst into eerie fire.

She *is* a witch, thought Joe thankfully.

All around the skulking forms hissed and spat. There were so many of them it sounded as loud as the sea. Behind the pair Joe could see others from the group. They carried lanterns, illuminating the church and the crouching shape-shifters. Above these flared the power of the wand, pulsing in the woman's gnarled hands. Aided by Boann, Mrs MacGeraghty raised the stick into the air and the night crackled in response. At this and as one, the Grim Grotesques transformed from cats to monstrous hounds to fiery-eyed horses and finally into the air itself. As they vanished into the darkness, Joe sagged in relief. It was done.

With a convulsion that shook her entire body, Mrs MacGeraghty collapsed. Shouting in alarm, Joe ran across to the old woman and lifted her head in his arms. Jana and the rest joined him, watching as the boy brought the medicine bottle to her lips. The gasping woman drank weakly and the boy held her as the pains came, the sacred waters destroying the taint within her. Joe's breath caught in his throat as she spasmed and kicked. Was she too frail to survive? You cannot die today, he thought. I know when you die. Or did he? Was time a solid or a liquid? In this place, after all that he had seen, he had no idea. Granny Em shook one final time and then, with a great gasping shriek, the terrible cure was done.

In the sky the first shreds of palest purple announced the coming of the new day.

OF THE NINETEEN WHO HAD gone to fight Damfino and his fiends, all but three returned to The Sun, Moon and Stars. Joe knew that number would have been far greater had Damfino not been vanquished. Jana was the last to leave for the inn, lingering to speak to Joe. While Mrs MacGeraghty sat in her kitchen, making that long-

181

overdue cup of tea, they stood under the leafless branches of the fabric-hung tree in the courtyard. "Well, well, well," Jana said sarcastically, her thumbs tucked into her sword belt. "That was a bit of a holy show. Do you always make such unforgettable visits?"

Joe nodded. "This is the Kissing Tree, right?"

"That's right. It doesn't look much now, but its leaves are redder than berries come autumn. It's pretty rare. Granny Em says it was brought here from Japan." Joe placed his hands upon the slim trunk. It was pleasing to think of its roots drinking from the well deep in the earth below where he stood. Then, just like the one in New Orleans, the tree shivered and spoke to him:

"When the Hour is Darker, three things Remember:
The Stone of Shadows,
The Staff, Arthiæ
And Ilkilæmber."

It's going to get darker? thought Joe in despair. How is that even possible?

"Goodbye, Joe. And thank you for your help back there."

"Goodbye, Jana," Joe replied. They shook hands.

"Did you really think I was going to kill you?" she asked playfully.

"No. Yes… Whatever I thought, you still used me as bait." The blonde-haired young woman gave him a 'fair enough' shrug and turned to go.

"Oh, I almost forgot." She pulled out Damfino's talisman and held it out to him. "Victor's spoils."

"No, you keep it. You earned it."

Jana tied the talisman around her neck. "That I did." She dug around in her bag and pulled out the chalice. "Gift for a gift. Think of this as a parting glass."

Joe took the engraved cup and smiled. It was a fine trophy.

"Thank you, Jana," he said. His cheeks were stinging. Was he blushing?

"Right, time to be off." Jana passed under the arch and around the side of the barn, whistling as she went. As she moved out of sight, she called, "Be strong or stay clever, and may your troubles be as few and as far apart as Granny Em's teeth."

The old woman tutted loudly from the back door as Jana left. "That there is a wilful child," she muttered, "but come. Let us see another use for the well waters beyond mending the thatch of wounds." Taking the medicine bottle, she poured almost all the remaining liquid into her kettle and lit the gas beneath it. While the water boiled, she handed the glass container back to Joe.

"One more mouthful left. Just in case," she said. "Of course, Boann would fair scream my house down if she knew about this. So say nothing, eh?" Again, that sly wink. Then she placed a few scoops of dark leaves into her teapot, and when the kettle whistled she made her brew with the magical waters.

"This—" she indicated the pot, "—is the magic of my readings." She seemed possessed of perfect clarity now, as if fortune telling was a thing her dementia would never touch. Perhaps *could* never touch. Or perhaps it was the power of the curing waters. Deftly she placed the cup of fortune, the teapot and her deck of cards upon a floral tray and carried them to the overgrown summerhouse. There she and Joe sat at the small circular table and Granny Em asked the boy to pour a cup. The liquid from the kettle was far thicker and darker than any normal brew.

"Wouldst thou learn thy future with thy tea? This magic cup will show it thee," she read from the writing around the rim. Joe liked the simplicity of the cup with its red, black and white designs. "Do you have something for payment? Cross my palm with coin or gold?"

Joe had bartered away the captain's coins, and had little else of value that he would be willing to give away... No, wait. He reached into his pack and brought out Serene's golden necklace. Thinking about it, Joe also thought about Damfino's horrible rhyme. For a moment he was back in the dark caravan with the girl, saying their goodbyes. He had no wish to part with it, but he had to progress in the labyrinth. "Here," he said, handing it to her. "This is all I have." The old woman's face glittered in the reflected sunlight off the necklace. She stared at it for the longest time, her eyes swimming with tears. Finally, she reached out and pushed his hand away.

"No," she said quietly, "that is far too precious. Let us say this first one is on the house."

She requested Joe to drink a little of the tea, then pour the rest into the cup of fortune and swirl the remaining mess of wet leaves. She stared at the dark patterns, then she sat up and spoke softly, saying, "I see three things here. I see a girl, a woman and a crone."

As she said this, an image of Serene appeared in Joe's mind. Damfino's cruel song had brought back thoughts of her, and the boy realised he wanted to know she was safe and well.

"What girl?" Joe said sheepishly, his eyes not meeting hers.

"There is a cluster around the symbol of the heart. Ah, first love is a very powerful thing."

"Ugh, no. It wasn't anything like that," said Joe.

"As you will."

"What else does it say? Will I find the girl again?"

"Yes. In my past and your future."

The boy didn't understand that. "So, I'll meet her again? And..." He paused, unsure. "Will anything... happen?"

"No, it's too late, child." The woman's voice was calm, but her eyes were wet with tears. "Far too late."

"Oh." He couldn't keep the disappointment from his voice. "What about the Wild Hunt. With Damfino dead, am I safe?"

"No," the old woman said immediately. "The hunt goes on. The Cat's Head indicates their evil... and the Spider shows much courage is required to prevail against them."

Joe groaned, then asked, "Who sent them?"

"See the dark shape between the Eye and the Envelope? This shows all that was hidden will be revealed — and soon, for the leaves are near the rim. And the one who draws the cloak of night across your eyes is here... See? This is the figure of a woman."

"Who?" asked Joe. "Who is this woman?"

"Oh, my loves, my angel. I am so sorry." Granny Em's hands shook as she held the tea cup.

"Who is this woman?" the boy insisted.

"It is your mother," Mrs MacGeraghty said quietly.

"What?" Joe stood up in surprise. "No, that's not possible. These are all lies."

"So be it." With a flick of her wrist Mrs MacGeraghty tossed the dregs of water and leaves from the cup towards the barn door. Obviously the fortune telling was over. Yet where they landed, the air shimmered like a mirage and as he watched, the arched entrance became a rustic log door.

"The door is found through the leaves!" Joe cried and stepped towards it. Then, remembering his manners, he turned back to the old woman. "I have to go now. Perhaps someday we might meet again?"

"We already have, my love." The old woman leaned forward and kissed him sweetly on the forehead, then nodded towards the barn. "May your road rise to meet you, my love," she whispered as the boy reached the threshold, the veil of dementia once more in her rheumy eyes. "My angel, my sweet..."

Joe took another step, crossed the threshold, and then she and Ireland and the entire courtyard were gone.

VII

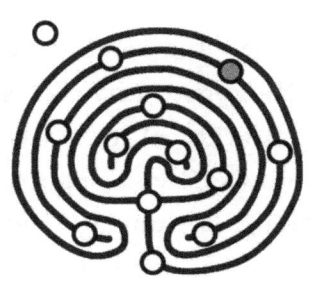

SEVENTH MOON: SNOW (OF NATURE: LAND)
WISAKEDJAK LODGE
KINGSMERE LAKE, SASKATCHEWAN, CANADA
FRIDAY 9 APRIL 1948 | 13:07:05

THE DOORWAY OPENED INTO A rustic log cabin. Newly fallen snow glittered outside the windows, illuminating an entirely wooden room. Everything smelled of smoke and forests. The small space held all the rough comforts, though skins, cushions and painted beams added some homely touches. An unlit oil lantern hung overhead, while heat radiated from a roaring stove. A few pieces of furniture – the dresser, sideboard and chairs – looked well made, while the rest looked crude and primitive. At the back of the narrow room, set above a small store, a stepladder led into a galleried sleeping area. Even with the white light reflected off the snow, it was still dim inside.

Joe crossed to the window and looked out. The cabin was built on the shore of a lake surrounded by a forest wilderness. No other buildings were visible, though a few conical tents clustered between the trees. Down at the water's edge was a pair of canoes.

Sitting at the table, the boy pulled *The Stranger's Guide* from his pack. He wasn't looking forward to revisiting the pages for the seventh room. For these were almost entirely blank. The book's mysterious author had never visited this part of the labyrinth. All that had been added was a copy of the calendar page from the Hall of Mirrors and the information it contained: the name of the cabin as Wisakedjak Lodge, the location as Kingsmere Lake, Saskatchewan, Canada, and the dark of the moon on Friday 9 April 1948. But apart from that and a brief note about Whiskey Jack being a folk hero, the rest of the page was empty. This was the first time Joe had entered a location not described in the book. How was he to find the oracle and escape? He had no idea.

From outside there came a low bellowing, and looking up Joe saw that a baby bear had entered the clearing. The little cub rambled between the house and the tents, finally investigating a pile of newly chopped wood. Fascinated, Joe left the cabin to get a better look. Outside sunlight filtered through low clouds and birds filled the woods with life. Though early afternoon, it was still very chilly. At the sound of the cabin door opening the bear looked up, then turned its attention back to the logs. Perhaps the cub was just out of hibernation and hungry, but this was just a wild guess. The boy had never seen wild animals before. He didn't even think he had been to a zoo and if he had he was too young to recall it. Stepping from the shadow of the building, he walked cautiously forward. The cub ignored his slow approach, completely focused on his foraging. Joe was focused too, so much so that when a firm hand wrapped around his mouth, he almost leapt out of his skin.

"Shush there," a voice said close to his ear. "Don't move a whisker."

Behind him the muscular figure pressed itself close to his back. Joe struggled yet strong arms held him motionless. He tried to yell out or break free, but it was useless. The man – it had to be a man – smelled of wood smoke and alcohol.

"Shush," the man said again, and finally the boy saw why. At the edge of the clearing was the cub's enormous mother. "Back up, sonny. Slow and steady. You don't want to be stepping between a she-bear and her baby." With deliberate movements they retreated to the log cabin, and once inside, Joe was released and turned to face the man. He was tall, lean and dressed head to toe in buckskins and furs, though Joe knew his own clothes must look just as eccentric. "You with the authorities?"

"No," said the boy, all too familiar with these questions. "Just passing through."

The man's eyes narrowed at this, but he did not challenge Joe. "Well, if you want to live to send postcards, you should leave cubs and their mothers well alone. Playing with bears is mighty dangerous. As is wandering about alone in the woods. You ain't in no *Jungle Book* now, fella." Though the man had a twang to his voice and looked like a pioneer from the Wild West, underneath his accent was definitely British.

"Are you Whiskey Jack?" asked Joe to change the subject.

"Me? No. What makes you say that?"

"This is Wisakedjak Lodge, isn't it?"

The man was taken aback. "Why yes, it is. How in hell did you know that?"

Joe shrugged.

"Whiskey Jack is a storybook hero, a kind of benevolent trickster. The Woodland Cree tell tales about him."

"I'm Joe."

"Pleased to make your acquaintance. I'm William Henry Megquier," said the man. "But I haven't gone by that name for ten years o' more. Now I'm Tipiskisiw."

"That's your Indian name?" Joe asked.

"Yessir. To the Cree I am He Who Walks By Night, but you can call me Megquier if that's your preference. I'm in my forties now, was much younger when I came over. Was late 1932 and that first mighty winter damn near finished me."

"You're from England?"

"Cornwall." Megquier seemed to drift in memory. "Always fantasised of a life in the wilderness. Trekked all the way out here to be a fur trapper, guide and woodsman. Then there was wartime and that near finished me off, too." The trapper slapped his left leg. "Sniper bullet. Lucky I still can walk."

"War sounds horrible," said Joe.

"True enough. But it did one lick of good. Made my mind up good and proper."

"About what?"

"When I was conscripted I walked in two worlds. Man's world and this one." He indicated the trees, the forest and the entire wilderness. "But that's not possible. We must choose. The white man only takes from the forest. Their trap, rifle and poison are anathema to me. I am of Nature, not of Man. But look at me flapping my tongue like a washerwoman. I have to go to council, and don't think for a minute I'm leaving you here."

"I won't be any trouble," Joe said.

The man raised a quizzical eyebrow. "The village is thataways." He pointed vaguely off through the trees.

"Will we walk?"

"No, the only sensible way to get anywhere around here is by water."

"The canoes?"

"Yessir. And if you're coming with me, you need something warmer than that rinky-dink jacket." Megquier produced a fur-lined poncho and handed it to the boy. "And remember, lad, out here you belong to nature, and not it to you."

"Yessir," mimicked Joe, and they headed for the door.

OUT ON THE STILL HALF-FROZEN lake, the true immensity of the Canadian wilderness struck Joe. Yes, he had sailed a ship across the Norwegian Sea with Captain Thorstad, but somehow this felt far larger. Perhaps it was that the canoe was lower to the water or more exposed to the elements. The boy sat up front with the trapper behind, the only sounds the splash of Megquier's paddle and the odd bump of ice against the sides. Even the buzz of the birds and animals was silenced here. Back over the boy's shoulder, the cabin with its shingle roof and weathered log walls was already the size of a postage stamp.

"This is so beautiful," said Joe, feeling excited and calm both at once.

In the waves, in the wind, in the wilds, we are our true selves, the forest said.

"There's where the Woodland Cree are living," said Megquier, pointing towards the shore. Joe looked and saw a small village set upon a defensible bluff with the lake on one side and a river on the other. The place was centred around a wooden longhouse, and as they grew nearer he saw how huge poles speared the roof of the building, matching others set at the boundary of the dwellings. Atop each one was a monstrous owl with spreading wings.

"This is—" Megquier paused, translating in his head, "—Bear-Blade-Bone. The Cree winter residence. About sixty families or thereabouts. That's all the hunting the land can support."

"The village seems a long way from the cabin," said Joe.

"Only the holy men can go *there*. Wisakedjak is sacred land."

191

Of course it is, thought Joe. And that makes you more than just a trapper and hunter.

As they approached, the settlement on the hill grew larger. After only crossing half the distance, already Joe's fingers and toes felt numb with cold. He imagined falling into the icy water and knew he'd be dead in seconds. The trapper kept them moving with strong, swift strokes. He didn't get out of breath or look tired. Joe guessed living out here made this journey easier than a pedalo ride. Only once they were closer to the village did Megquier speak again.

"Saskatchewan was first explored by Europeans in the 1700s," he explained, "but these folks have been around for more than seven thousand years." Yes, the Viking ancestors of Lars Thorstad, Joe thought with a smile. "Now with the railroads, more and more Western settlers come. It is not a good time. Trouble is the Cree don't own this land."

"Why not? They've been here forever."

"They don't own it because they don't understand why they need to. To them the land is not something we possess."

The village was right above them now and Joe could see it was comprised mostly of tall tents; the central smokehouse the trapper said was home to the elders. Each tent was constructed of light sapling poles with a covering of birch bark, skins or reed mats. Some were conical, others domed. Most were plain with a few ornamented with images.

"Are those wigwams?" asked the boy.

"Only the plain ones. The rest are tipis. Those designs transform them into sacred lodges. See how their doors open to the east? They are used for ceremonies and holy occasions."

"One for each family?"

"Clever boy. The dark portion at the top represents the sky, the dark band at the bottom represents the earth, and—"

Remembering the Tallis Stone rhyme and the three realms of

Saturn's sons, Joe couldn't help but blurt out, "Immortal Sky, Eternal Forest and Infinite Ocean."

"*Very* clever boy," the woodsman said, clearly impressed. "These folk are hunter-gatherers. They winter here, but soon the snows will be gone and so will they. Most of what you see will be packed up and they'll be off."

"On horses?"

"No, horses are too expensive for these Indians. They use travois pulled by dogs. Right-o. Here we are. Now, let's see what they make of you."

A crowd was gathering by a reed gate, watching the canoe approach. There were three men at the centre of the group, and they were obviously important figures. Their hair was woven with feathers and two of them carried bows. Leaving the canoe in the icy shallows, Joe and Megquier climbed the rocky bluff and arrived at the gate into the village. At once they were introduced, and Megquier translated.

"This is Atahkakohp Starblanket, chief of the Bear-Blade Cree. These are his two sons, One Arrow and Grey Wolf. They welcome you to their winter village on Little Trout Lake."

"Isn't this Kingsmere Lake?" Joe asked in a whisper.

"To the mapmakers, maybe. To the Woodland Cree, it is not. Chief Atahkakohp, this is Joe, a visitor to these parts. While he remains here, he is in my charge."

The chieftain answered, questioning, then nodding. Finally, they were done and he turned to face the boy.

Joe didn't know the proper greeting for Native Canadian tribesmen so he just placed his hands together and gave what he hoped was a reverential bow. The men exchanged looks, then stiffly returned the gesture. Behind him, he heard the trapper chuckle. "And this..." Megquier indicated a woman in ochre robes who stood off to the right, "is Kaliska Daystar." He paused, as if unsure how to say the next thing. "My wife."

The woman had judging eyes, her hair curled at her shoulders. She wore a pinafore dress under her cloak, but her most striking feature was a pattern of dark red tattooed lines that ran from her mouth around her chin. She also looked as if she walked in two worlds, yet it was still a surprise when she spoke English.

"You are most welcome here, stranger." The way she said 'stranger' was brimful with meaning. Joe was reminded of Rose Meirion and guessed he wasn't the first child to appear in these woods either. "Yet you come at a terrible time for us."

"Kaliska," her husband warned, then they spoke in Cree. It sounded like they were arguing. Joe wanted to ask if they had seen other people come through here, but there was no time. Already the small group was making its way to the longhouse.

Inside was a single space divided into several functional areas. The hearth occupied the centre, and cooking equipment hung from a rack below the smoke hole. The floor was scattered with fir boughs, and animal skins were placed on top of these for sleeping. Painted family crests hung above the doors and what scant possessions they owned were stored against the walls. Starblanket sat in a large wooden throne crowned with white curved bones.

"What's that?"

"Bear's ribcage. It conveys the spirit of Torngarsuk, a white bear spirit of the Inuit that haunted these hunting grounds. It is spoken that the spirit is invisible to everyone but Anguekkoks, the shamans of the far north.

"What's a shaman?" Joe asked.

"A shaman's a medicine man – a healer, really – and a guide who walks the other worlds and speaks to the spirits."

"Can you?" Joe asked, wondering if Megquier had knowledge of the oracle and doorway at the cabin.

"Sometimes," was the man's only answer, but Joe knew that if the man lived in that lodge on that land, he was one of these Anguekkok spirit men too. Maybe also he knew of the labyrinth, but the boy thought it best to wait before asking that particular question. Joe, Megquier and Kaliska sat in the lower portion of the room on a row of woven mats. Fragrant smoke rose from a fire pit, wreathing the other tribesmen in sunlit haloes. When all were ready, the woodsman stood and was handed a carved wooden baton.

"It's a talking stick," Kaliska whispered to Joe. "They mark the one who can speak." Megquier addressed the Cree chief, his sons and gathered villagers, and while he spoke, his wife translated what was said to Joe. The story she conveyed was dire indeed. People had come with papers of ownership for Bear-Blade-Bone and the land around Wisakedjak Lodge.

"These claims are signed by the lawmakers," Megquier explained. "Even though you are of the Great Spirit, you are bound within the fabric of Canadian political society and law."

The chieftain held out his hand and was passed the stick. "This is a fear we have lived with for more than five hundred seasons. We are people who know what is truly sacred. We believe a mountain or a river or a rock can be a place of the spirit. Now we are told we shall be arrested for trespassing on our own land." He offered the baton and One Arrow took it.

"All we have is this land and this forest," said his son. "If there is a problem, where should we go?"

"And why should we go?" echoed Grey Wolf, and many voices rumbled in agreement.

"Who is there to hear our call?" said another tribesman. Every time the stick was handed from person to person.

"Tipiskisiw comes. He learns our traditions, our ways and some of our language," continued Starblanket. "He knows our hearts. He should go and speak with these white strangers."

The Cree were to be moved on before winter's end, and had been told they could never return. It seemed obvious to Joe that these strangers wanted to own the sacred land and all the magic it contained. After more incomprehensible discussion, it was agreed that Megquier and Starblanket would meet the man and woman who led the authorities and discuss terms for their eviction. Once the trapper had spoken, Joe thought the room would dissolve into noisy discussion, but there was only silence. Megquier passed the carved stick to the chief, who stood and addressed the room.

"No man owns Whiskey Jack," Kaliska translated. "No man owns this land or us. We will speak to these strangers and tell them this. And tell them also why we cannot go." Everyone nodded.

"Why?" asked Joe, confused. "Why can't they go?"

"Because," said William Henry Megquier to the boy, "we are the keepers of the Thirteenth Door."

A ripple of excitement shot through Joe. They did know of the labyrinth and the house and everything. Before the boy could question further, a sudden commotion cut through the council. From outside came the gunning of an engine, breaking the quiet with its mechanical roar. Everyone stood and headed outside. A vehicle was pulling out of the forest, emerging from the fir trees like a giant animal. Everyone watched stunned at the sight, but of them all Joe was the most shocked.

For the vehicle was an emerald-green GMC school bus.

SUDDENLY EVERYONE WAS IN MOTION. As Joe watched, the engine died with a ragged splutter and uniformed men began to emerge from within. They were dressed in navy with gold lettering on their jackets and they carried pistols and rifles. It was too far to read the words, but they looked very official. Upon this side of the bluff, steep banks dropped down to the river that made this thin peninsula almost an island. The men ran along the top of the far slope, headed for the place where they could cross. Chief Atahkakohp was shouting at his sons, who were themselves grabbing their bows and racing off towards the forest. Villagers were streaming outside, their voices raised as the men called out to their wives and families. Everywhere was movement and panic, but amid the chaos Joe stood staring at the school bus. His father's voice filled his mind as he wondered how a 1940s American vehicle came to be abandoned in the middle of a wooded roundabout in England. But this bus was not old and rusted, it was shining new, and somehow Joe understood its appearance was fantastically important. His mind filled with a whirl of questions and confusion, Joe could do nothing but stare at the bus in disbelief. Was this *the* bus or another one just like it? Could it really be the vehicle he had lived in for all those months?

The sound of a gunshot split the air like thunder. It broke the spell the boy was under, snapped him out of his trance and back into the present moment. He saw that the Cree had taken off in all directions. Megquier and Kaliska were gone too. How long had he been standing there? A minute? An hour? It felt like his entire life.

Looking around wildly, Joe searched the tents and trees for some sign of where everyone had vanished and saw a flash of Kaliska's cloak disappearing into the wilderness on the other side of the water. Joe dodged past the wigwams and down the bank in pursuit. There he found several camouflaged canoes had been roped together to ford the river. Crossing carefully, he climbed the opposite bank and followed into the forest as swiftly as he could. Ahead he heard angry voices and moved towards them. In only a short while the undergrowth ended and beyond was a large open glade. In its centre a conical lodge had been constructed, the totems and paintings marking it as a sacred sanctuary. In the clearing four adults stood. Two of these people were Megquier and Kaliska.

The other two were his mother and father.

Joe gaped, unable to grasp what he was seeing. First the bus, now this! Instantly his mind threw up images of the roundabout, the barbecue and the final time they had been together. Of the raid and his father's last words. "Go, son, run! Go to the hideout and never look back. We'll get there when we can." And now they were here. In this time and place. And they looked just as he remembered them, as if he saw them only yesterday. How was any of this possible? His parents were clothed for the wilderness in heavy coats and boots. His mother's long black hair was tucked into a fur-lined hood. His father's sombre face shadowed beneath a feathered hat. Beside them the trapper and his wife looked as if they had stepped from a different century.

The boy wanted to dash forward and throw his arms around his parents and only a few weeks ago that would have been exactly what he would have done. Now things were different. He was different. While their appearance filled him with bursting happiness, it also struck him as indescribably bizarre. Joe felt as if his heart was set to burst right out of his chest, but he fought to control the pounding and just watched.

The grown-ups were engaged in heated debate. His mother was talking and pointing out across the lake. Megquier had his arms folded and was shaking his head defiantly. Joe heard snatches, but the wind in the trees made it impossible to tell what they were saying. Then everyone looked off to the underbrush and three Cree stepped into the clearing. It was Starblanket and his two sons. The chief shouted something in Cree and Megquier replied with an obvious warning. There were more angry words. Starblanket raised a fist and his sons raised their bows. Then Joe's parents pulled guns from their coats and everyone was pointing weapons at everyone else. Joe seemed to remember from his comics and Westerns that this was called a

Mexican stand-off, where no one could make a move without getting shot. In every film he ever watched, those situations never ended well for anyone.

"Mum!" he shouted, unable to stop himself. "Dad!"

Breaking cover, he ran full pelt towards his parents. Everyone stopped and turned, their eyes wide. Joe stopped too. Between him and the adults, one of the uniformed figures lay on the ground, the words SHARK EYE SECURITY embroidered across the back of his jacket. The body had been invisible from his hiding place in the trees. Now Joe saw it lay face down unmoving on the snowy ground. Beside the figure lay a large revolver.

"Joe," his mother said. Now she was facing him, her voice crystal clear in the crisp air. "Get the gun." The boy did nothing. Just looked from the group to the body and the black weapon. "Pick up the gun, Joe," she insisted through clenched teeth. "Or we will all die."

"*Kahgee pohn noten took*," said the trapper, his rifle pointed at Joe's mother's face. "We want no war."

"Joe?" his father said in a low voice. "Do as your mother says."

Joe crouched down and reached for the weapon. With trembling fingers he touched the handle and wrapped his hand around it. The revolver was heavy in his grip, but slowly he stood up and pointed it vaguely towards the Cree. Joe found he couldn't look at the adults, all his focus was on the gun.

"Put your weapons down," shouted his mother. "We come for your land, not your lives."

Somewhere distant, above the wind in the trees and wilderness insects, there was a thrum-swooshing sound, then a dull thud.

"Laverna!"

Joe jerked his head at his father's shout. Everyone stood as before. Everyone except Joe's mother. Now she no longer held out a gun. Now the bloodied tip of an arrow extended through her chest. She gazed at the shaft with incomprehension, lifted one hand to touch it, then collapsed. Grey Wolf let out a barked grunt of satisfaction.

"Mum!" Dropping the gun, Joe ran across the clearing and threw himself down at his mother's side. Already her face was sickly white, her coat smeared in red. "Oh, Mum, Mum, Mum!" he babbled. These people were not his friends. They had shot his mother. Guns exploded all around him. Bodies rushed and fled. The air was filled with birds taking wing. But all the boy's attention was on his mother. It was clear the wound was fatal. She was dying.

"No, no, no, no!" was all he could say.

Suddenly his father was at his side. "Joe, we have to go. It's not safe."

"No!" Moving was unthinkable. Everything was unthinkable. Everything but kneeling here. Joe was crying and struggling. Dimly he was aware that someone was trying to lift him to his feet.

Then he remembered the medicine bottle and the water.

One more mouthful left, the witch had said. Just in case.

"Wait!" he said. With panicked hands the boy scrabbled through his things and found the bottle. With fumbling fingers he unscrewed the top and poured the last of the liquid into his mother's mouth. Then he tore at his mother's coat and clothes, and made himself look at her bloodied wound. The arrow stuck like an accusing finger towards him, so he grabbed it with both hands and pulled. It took more strength and courage than he ever thought he possessed, but he did it.

"Joseph Darkin!" his father insisted. "We have to go…"

Though his blood pounded in his head, Joe did not move. He would not be dragged away. For him in that moment, time itself stopped. And then, as if by a miracle, Joe watched his mother's terrible chest wound heal and vanish. Slowly she opened her eyes and saw him leaning over her.

"You…" she said softly. "What happened?"

"I saved you, Mum," he said. "I thought magic didn't exist, but it does. And it saved you." He showed her the empty bottle as if that explained everything.

"We have to get to the boat," Joe's father said, his voice tinged with wonder. "They could come back at any moment."

"Mum, are you OK?" Joe asked.

"This," his mother said weakly, "is what happens when boys don't take their medicine." Stunned, Joe allowed his father to lift her, then trailed behind as they moved out of the clearing.

Arriving at the lake's edge, they struggled aboard a waiting motorboat. Joe's father started the engine and turned the craft away from the shore, the Cree village and that terrible encounter with the savages in the woods.

WITHIN MINUTES, JOE AND HIS parents were far out on the vast lake. Through his feet the outboard motor filled Joe with its velvety surge of power. Seeing him looking at the engine, his father said, "Evinrude Zephyr. It's a real powerhouse."

His mother was less than impressed. She slumped on the bench seating, her pale face a mask of disdain. "It's deafening, Thomas, and I cannot think. Turn it off." Her husband complied without a word. As the engine died, she said, "That's so much better, isn't it, Joe?" There was a pause as she took in the vast sky above the trees. "It's so silent here. So calm."

It was true that without the engine the wild beauty of the landscape dominated, but to Joe's awakened senses there was no stillness or quiet. Instead he became aware again of the countless sounds that made up the silence of the wilderness.

Whatever you do, the forest said, *do not show them the book.*

"Now," said his mother. "Let's talk."

"Mum?" Joe asked dumbly. The boy was numb, his whole body hollow after his mother's words. *This is what happens...*

"Your father and I just want to ask you some questions."

"Like what?"

"Well, let's start with, why are you here? Or more importantly, *how* are you here?"

"No." Joe knew he sounded like a child, but he couldn't help it. "You don't get to ask the questions."

"Joe," his father said warningly.

The boy could not deny his heart-churning excitement at having them back, but out of his gloom another emotion was overriding everything. It was anger. "You left me all alone in that bus. Where did you go after that night when those people came?"

"On the run, Joe. Like we always do."

"So where did you go? And why didn't you come back for me?" His parents exchanged unreadable glances. "I know you got here through the house. How else could you possibly be here."

"We used the abandoned house as a hideout," his father blurted.

"So did I. And now I'm trying to escape. Are you?"

"Let's get out together," his father said, but his wife ignored this.

"I specifically told you not to leave the bus. You were safe there," she said.

"I was attacked."

"By whom?" said his father.

"By Grim Grotesques!" Joe almost gagged on Gunner's nickname. Almost broke into tears with the memories that name conjured.

"Who?" His mother actually seemed dismayed.

"The bad people. The ones who are trying to destroy the house. Damfino. The Wild Hunt. Everybody!"

His parents said nothing.

"Do you have any of my medicine?" Joe asked quietly into the silence.

Thomas Darkin looked alarmed at this, but Laverna waved the question away like an insignificant bug.

"There's no need for that now," she said.

"What?" The boy was shocked, then his mind grasped an answer. "Is it because time has stopped for me? Did the sacred well water cure me completely?" Now it was his mother's turn to look shocked, but again Joe's questions remained unanswered.

The motorboat had lost speed, was drifting on invisible currents. The boy gazed down into the deep water and it terrified him. Nowhere Is Safe, he thought. Don't Make Friends. Where was his rising sense of anxiety coming from? It felt like the forest was shivering like a frightened animal. Wasn't it his father who had taught him The Rules? Wasn't his mother the one who insisted he take The Medicine?

"Were the Grim Grotesques after you?" He had a flash of his own journey here. "I know it sounds crazy, but… did a bird lead you here?"

"Did it lead *you*?" asked his mother.

"Yes, a big black raven."

"I see."

"Why are you here?" the boy asked again.

"It's time to tell your son," Laverna said. Thomas Darkin gave his wife a pleading look, but she did not relent. "Tell him."

"Joe," his father said finally, "come and sit with me." The boy crossed to the stern and sat down at the tiller. When they were facing each other, his father began to explain. As he spoke, his tone was level and deadly serious. "There is a battle for the last sacred places upon the earth. Do you understand what sacred means?" Joe felt insulted that he thought he didn't, but just nodded, not wanting to interrupt. "There are two sides: the Maje and the Ghûl." The names seemed familiar, as if perhaps he'd heard them before. It was clear who they referred to.

"The ones who protect and the ones who destroy," said Joe.

"Not destroy," his mother corrected. "Utilise."

His father continued. "These natives are occupying this sacred land. That is why we are here."

"So, they are using the magic?" the boy asked. "They are the bad people?"

"Yes, Joe. That's it," his mother said. "Isn't it, Thomas?"

"Why don't we team up, kiddo," his father said. "No leaving you behind this time. You can come with us."

Joe remembered the words he'd written in the bottled message. How, if he got the chance, he'd be the son they always wanted. Here and now he saw how to make good on that promise. To start that happy life together. To be told his mother and father were involved in the very fight he was… it was like discovering his parents were superheroes. It was so much to take in, but it all made sense now. The bus, his parents' appearance, the oncoming battle between the Cree and the security men. Yet there was still something wrong with this discovery. Something *very* wrong. "I met their chief and went to their council. I thought they were right to stay here, but they're not. They shot you, Mum. I can never forgive them for that." He paused, mulling everything over in his mind. "I want to help you," he said at last.

"Excellent," his father said. "And when we're done here, we'll all go back together as one big family."

"How?"

"Maybe we could take the bus," his father quipped.

"The bus?"

"It's the only way to travel."

"Thomas!" Laverna snapped, and, like always, that was the end of the conversation.

SHARK EYE SECURITY'S MAKESHIFT ENCAMPMENT had been hastily constructed at the north end of the great lake. It consisted of perhaps twenty camouflaged pavilions centred around a larger sea-green marquee. Between the tents were black jeeps and trucks. It was so like the Cree homestead, and so unlike it all at the same time. Joe's father moored the motorboat on a shingle beach and helped his wife and son from the swaying deck to the shore. Ahead the pine trees flickered in the sunshine like emerald tinsel. The sun was warm on the boy's face as he climbed the steep bank, but the wind was fresh, making the day cold.

Ware, ware the grizzly bear, sighed the needles.

"Do you hear that, Dad?" he asked as they started for the tree line.

"Hear what, son?" his father replied.

"Nothing," the boy said.

Joe sensed the dogs just before he saw them. There were about two dozen waiting for them on the ridge, chained together collar to collar. As soon as they sensed them, the hounds leapt into a wild barking chaos, straining at their leashes. The boy shrank back, but his mother ignored the animals. Raising her hand, she let out a single sharp command. Immediately the frenzied ruckus of yelps was silenced. Beyond the dogs, the entire taskforce was preparing for the eviction. Uniformed figures were everywhere, readying vehicles to come by land and by water. No one mentioned the dead man. There was no talk of calling the police or forest rangers or whatever authority you would report a murder to. These people looked as if taking the law into their own hands was second nature to them.

Following his parents, Joe passed a series of cages. Cree prisoners sat in them, their sullen faces gazing in open hatred at the woman and her guards. Seeing people imprisoned did not sit well with Joe. He knew exactly what that felt like. In the last cage sat Kaliska Daystar. Thankfully, the trapper's wife was gazing at the ground and didn't look up as they walked by. Joe wondered what had happened to Megquier. Was he alive or dead? And if alive, was he off plotting an attack of his own?

Inside the main tent the centre of operations was a hive of activity. Maps and desks crowded one end, while the other was divided into individual rooms. Joe's mother made straight for a speaking platform and called everyone to attention. Joe watched in surprise as the security men fell silent; this was a side of his mother he had never witnessed. What is this? thought Joe. It's like they're going to war…

"Commander Váth, gentlemen, the time has come. All preparations are made and further negotiations have failed. Now we must move to the next phase. The plan is simple. I will go with the task team to the cabin and secure the site. Thomas and the commander will lead the main force to the settlement. I want that group dispersed into the woods with immediate effect." As she spoke, Joe was reminded of Chief Starblanket speaking with his tribesmen. So like the Cree council, yet so unlike. "Once each has accomplished their designated assignment, report via radio. If you need to abort, signal via flare. The rest is as planned. Any questions?" No one said anything.

"What about me?" asked Joe.

His mother looked at him blankly. "You? You stay here. Private Blackthorn, your duty is to mind the boy in my absence." One of the uniformed men stood to attention and saluted.

"What?" Joe was astounded to hear he wasn't going with the security men. "You said I could go with you!"

"No. Your father said that, not me. I want you to stay. We lost you once and I have no intention of letting that happen again." As always, Laverna's tone ended all argument. "OK, people," she concluded, "let's get this done."

The members of Shark Eye Security began to file out of the tent. Blackthorn crossed to Joe and indicated that the boy must go with him. The private was young, his face serious and tense. Outside car engines roared into life. Again the dogs began barking. His parents turned to join their teams.

"Mum? Dad?" Joe called out. "Let me come. I can help."

"Don't worry, son," his father said as they went. "We'll be back before you even know it."

And then they were gone, leaving Joe alone with Private Blackthorn.

"Unbelievable," the boy said under his breath.

"This way," the security guard said. Joe followed. What else could he do? Cars roared past them, already leaving for the winter encampment, while down on the water he saw his mother climbing back aboard the motorboat. Now it held a trio of armed men. Once she was onboard, the craft pulled away from the shore and headed out onto the great lake. The boy watched her go with that old, familiar gnawing feeling of abandonment in his stomach.

Blackthorn led Joe to one of the many bell-shaped tents and opened the flap to allow him inside. Within there was a camp bed and small trunk, but little else. The boy spent a few minutes looking around. He sat on the bed. He lay on the bed. The quiet of the forest resumed. Joe got bored.

So I'm a prisoner again, he thought. I can't just sit here. I need to do something.

Looking out of the tent he saw that the guard sat on a folding stool just to the right of the door. The young man had taken off his cap and was staring off into space. Now Joe saw that upon the back of his shaved head a short scar ran vertically just behind one ear.

The sight struck Joe cold as ice.

The security man was a Grim Grotesque! What if all of them were? Did his parents know? How could they? For if they did... No, that was too hideous to contemplate. Whatever the truth, there was danger here. A danger far greater than grizzly bears in the woods. His thoughts left him with a head full of questions and doubts. Who was on his side? Was anybody? He couldn't trust his parents. He couldn't trust the people who protected this labyrinth world. Nowhere Is Safe. Do Not Talk To Dead People.

Retreating back inside, Joe gathered his things and wriggled out under the canvas at the back of the tent. Reaching into his bag, his fingers found the hilt of the sword.

So, I will drink today at the last, Ilkilæmber said.

Moving quickly, Joe made his way around the edge of the encampment, finally arriving at the shore. All the boats were gone, but Joe saw a single canoe remained. Slipping into it, he lifted the paddle and set out onto the lake. Knowing that he might already be too late, Joe paddled as quickly as his arms would allow. By the time he reached the other shore, he had blisters on his hands and he was completely exhausted. Yet he could not stop to rest. Slipping between the motorboats, the boy crept up the stony beach and, seeing that nobody was about, stalked through the undergrowth right up to the back of Wisakedjak Lodge. Moving around to the front, he found the door open and inside heard voices. One of them was clearly his mother's.

"We have purchased this land. We are here to claim it. Already my men are dismantling the Cree settlement. You are just stalling the inevitable."

Joe stepped up to the door and peered inside.

Within the room stood Laverna and her three guards. All four were armed. William Henry Megquier stood at the back of the small room. In his hands he held a round water flask and a short staff. The rod was about as long as his arm, decorated with feathers and carved with the head of a bear. Before him the rug had been thrown back to reveal a trapdoor and he was guarding it fiercely.

"Don't do anything stupid, Megquier," Laverna warned. "Remember, we have your precious Daystar."

"I am He Who Walks By Night," the trapper replied. "I am Anguekkok, medicine man and shaman. Take one more step and I will unleash the spirit of Torngarsuk from this flask."

"Oh, please." Joe's mother rolled her eyes. "You think I believe you've contained the power of your Sky God in that little bottle?" Is she bluffing? Joe wondered. Surely she knows such things are possible?

"During my initiation I brought the bear spirit of Torngasuk from the Inuit of the north. We are one, and I will invoke him should you not agree to leave this sacred place." He sneered, then added, "Forever."

"That is not going to happen," said the woman.

"You will not possess the Thirteenth Door while I live," the man insisted.

"Well, that's easily remedied." Then to her men, "Kill him." Instantly the guards raised their guns and aimed them at Megquier.

"Wisakedjak, protect me!" he shouted as in unison three shots rang out. The bullets slammed into the shaman and he fell, his call to the spirit of the cabin still on his lips. The staff and spirit bottle, however, did not fall with him. Instead the shaman threw them towards Joe. Both items clattered across the floor, coming to rest at the boy's feet. Everyone turned, noticing Joe for the first time.

"Joe," Laverna said. "Don't touch anything."

"Pick up the flask, Joe," Megquier gasped between breaths, "or we will all die."

Caught by a terrible indecision, the boy did nothing. He looked between the bleeding trapper and his mother, feeling the emptiness of his own bottle intensely.

Joe stooped down and picked up the two objects. The flat, circular flask was intricately carved with symbols, while the bear-topped cane thrummed with radiated energy. One held a rage as fierce as a storm, the other the feeling of slipping into a warm lagoon. Suddenly his head was filled with voices.

I and the shaman's spirit are one, said whatever was inside the flask. *He will not die while I yet live.*

Forget the flask. Use me! said the sword.

Violence is not the only path, said the staff.

"Arthiæ?" Joe questioned, the name appearing in his head even as his fingers wrapped around the wood.

Yes, the soft female voice replied. *I am the Staff of Lore.*

And I the Sword of War! said the sword. *Draw me now and let me feed. I am hungry still!*

"Joseph," his mother warned, her face hard with disgust.

Joe's head burned with anger and resentment, while his mind threw up images of tea cups and tea leaves, and of Granny Em foretelling the one who drew the cloak of night across his eyes. "Who are you, mother?" her son asked. "Who are you really?"

"Mother?" The trapper's voice was a gurgle in his throat. "No... She is Laverna-Vel Beltaræ... Black Queen of the Ghûl."

Joe felt every square centimetre of his body turn cold. His mother head of the Grim Grotesques. And worse, Damfino's master. "You're lying!" he shouted. "That can't be true."

He looked at his mother, then at the black-clad security men, then back to the wounded Megquier.

Lies without. Truth within, the staff said.

The boy's heart stopped beating. "You!" he screamed at his mother. "I saved you! I should've let you die!" And with that he threw the spirit bottle with as much force as his arms could manage. The ceramic flask hit the floor and shattered, splintering into pieces. At once a great and terrible tempest blasted through the log cabin. It blew the glass from the windows and howled like the wind at the world's end. Everyone still standing was flattened by its supernatural force. Joe was thrown back into a corner where he sheltered from flying objects behind a carved chair. In the eye of the storm, he could make out the ghostly form of a giant animal. The magic of this place was bear-shaped and primal. Its roar thundered through the forest and was echoed by many others. It was a summoning to the grizzlies of the wilderness, and they were compelled to answer the spirit's call.

Even the shaman.

"Get back! Get back!" Laverna was screaming. "He assumes Nature's Form."

Tipiskisiw was a man no longer – now he took the guise of a giant bear himself. Seeing this the security men fled in fear, firing as they struggled to escape. Joe cowered from the beast, his mother the only one who rose to face it. Then the boy fled too, heading outside to find that the woods were already brimming with huge brown bears. They emerged from the trees on all sides, each one taller than the eaves of the roof. Some were on all fours and some reared on hind legs. All were starving after their winter-long sleep. The mere sight of so many wild creatures was terrifying. They were approaching fast, running as swift as racehorses, the cabin their obvious target. And they bellowed as they came. Joe watched as the security guards tried to escape and were attacked at once. Though the men kicked, punched and even shot at the bears, it was no use. They were toys in the animals' ferocious paws. In no time at all, the three men were dragged off into the undergrowth.

Paralysed as he was by the chaos and carnage, Joe didn't see the bear rearing behind him until it was too late. The first he was aware of the impending danger was when the creature's shadow eclipsed the sun. The boy turned and saw the ferocious creature's great clawed arms thrown wide, its mouth a roaring tunnel of teeth. Joe screamed and felt wetness soak his trousers. He wanted to run, but he was frozen in horror. All he could manage was to wrap his arms against his chest and howl.

With a sudden roar of power, the green bus drove straight out of the wildwoods and crashed into the mammoth animal, knocking it away from the tiny boy. As the cantilever doors hissed open, Joe saw his father sitting in the driver's seat, his face white.

"Joe! Joe! Joe!" he was shouting, but his son needed no encouragement. Even as the great grizzly picked itself up and howled, Joe swung his pack inside and leapt up the metal steps. Immediately the doors slammed behind him. Outside the bear heaved its weight against the glass, clawing wildly, but could not get in.

"No," Joe was stammering. "No, no, no, no…"

"Joe?" His father's tone was iron. "Where's your mother?"

The boy was crying with relief, and could only point towards the lodge. There emerged Laverna. In her hand she held a large knife and it looked as if she had been using it. Claws had shredded her clothing and she was badly hurt. Seeing this, Thomas rose from the driver's seat and headed for the door.

"No, Dad!" Joe said. "You don't know who she really is. She's—"

"Yes I do, son. She's my wife."

Outside Laverna was backing away as the bear-form of Tipiskisiw lumbered into view. It was hard to tell which of the two was more injured. To Joe, both looked in need of emergency services.

"Dad, what's the Thirteenth Door?"

"It's too complicated. You wouldn't understand."

"Dad! I know about the house. I know about the labyrinth. You *have* to tell me."

Thomas was not listening. "I tried to keep you out of all this," he said over and over.

Throwing the lever to open the doors, Joe's father moved down the steps, but before he went he pulled a long splinter of crystal from his satchel.

"I have to save her," he said to his son, "but maybe this way I can save you both." He stabbed the glittering shard down upon the dashboard, embedding it into the metalwork. "Twenty-two. Eighty-two," he growled. "*Michi No Eki Tzu.*" Immediately, the vehicle thrummed with the crystal's energy. Had his father been to the caves beneath the lighthouse? There was no time to wonder. Already the vehicle shuddered and bucked, the air in the driver's cab crisp as ice.

"Goodbye, son," Thomas Darkin said, and leapt from the bus into the bear-infested woods.

"Dad!" Joe shouted after him, but it was too late.

As the folding doors clanked shut, there was a sudden sensation of plummeting, the crest and plunge feeling of riding a rattling rollercoaster. Metal ground against metal, the engine over-revving.

Joe wailed, hammering against the door.

Outside his father grimaced. "Go, son. I'm sending you to someone who can save you."

Staggering back, Joe grabbed the steering wheel and clung on. He was not a moment too soon, for then the bus and everything in it was transported out of the Canadian wilderness and into a world of blinding golden sunlight.

VIII

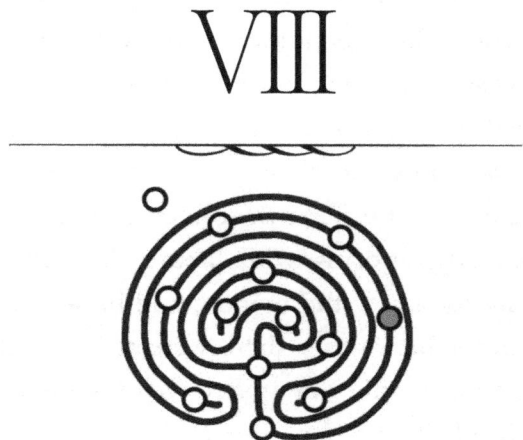

EIGHTH MOON: HARE MOON (OF BEASTS)
THE WAYSTATION AT TZU
D'ARKADIA, 12TH MOON, MALORIAN STARSTATION
MONDAY 8 MAY 2282 | 14:59:12

WITH A SICKENING LURCH, THE school bus was jerked into its new reality. Glorious sunlight immediately fogged the windscreen as the temperature leapt from freezing to sweltering summer. In a spray of sparks, the dashboard erupted as the whole bus shook violently. Suddenly the crystal blazed brilliantly, then dimmed. When all the light had gone, the shard was burned-out and black. After that, Joe expected the shaking to stop, but it did not. Instead the vehicle skidded and twisted as it slid down some invisible slope. Wiping his hand over the window, the boy was shocked to see the bus was slipping towards an enormous cliff face. Ahead the rocky ground ended at a jagged precipice and beyond all Joe could see was grey-green ocean and cloudless sky. Hitting the lever for the doors, Joe threw his rucksack through the opening and leapt after it. Rolling on the ground, he grabbed for handfuls of grass and slid to a stop. Behind him the green vehicle skidded a few more metres then halted about two bus lengths from the cliff's edge. This time it seemed to be stopped for good. The boy stood up, swaying giddily, and looked around. He was standing above the rugged coastline of a wholly new place and time. A place and time that was easily the most strange of them all. Out to sea, from the great expanse of water, rose immense black towers. Each was crested with domed platforms, while above the heavens were filled with hazy moons. Joe knew the moon could be seen during the day, but here – wherever here was – there were at least a dozen. He had just started to count exactly how many when, with a sound clear as crystal on the air, a bell rang out a single note.

Joe shielded his eyes from the blazing sun and looked towards the sound. At the top of the slope, almost obscured behind the bus, was a red tower set within a circle of blossoming trees. It clung to the edge of the bluffs, its sweeping tiled roofs, dog-like statues and elaborate gates apparently all part of a large temple. The entrance was via a tunnel of orange-painted gateways.

Picking up his pack, Joe went to start for the mysterious tower, but at that moment all the weight of the Canadian wilderness and what had happened there fell upon the boy, crushing him. It hit like a wave, sweeping him out into a sea of loneliness and distress. The pain of loss and betrayal staggered him and he wanted to get as far away from it as he could. It was that or just fall apart where he stood. Joe started to run, fleeing the bus and all it represented. Heading for the strange temple, the boy cried as he went, great aching sobs that felt as if his heart was coming out of his chest. Clutching his rucksack in his arms, he gritted his teeth against the agony and forced himself up the slope.

At such a pace it did not take long to reach the tower's boundary.

Stone steps started just beyond the tree line, rising in tiers beneath the endless parallel rows of gates. The path inclined slightly too, leading up to the main shrine at the top of the hill.

"*Ohayou!*"

Joe whirled, startled by the voice.

A robed woman stood beneath the first open gate. She was dressed all in white, except for a colourful fabric panel that hung from her waist and a spray of red spiky hair. She looked to be in her late twenties, though it was difficult to tell for her face was painted with pale powder.

"Sorry, I'm not trespassing." Joe forced the words through the tightness of his throat. "I got lost... I..."

The woman waved away his explanations as unnecessary. Then she said, "In the labyrinth, you are not lost. You are found."

Hearing this, Joe's father's last words echoed in his head.

I'm sending you to someone who can save you.

"Help me," the boy said in a tiny voice.

The woman frowned slightly at his words, then reached out her hand and placed it against his forehead. Joe flinched, but her touch was gentle and unthreatening. She nodded, concentrating. "Yes," she said. "I am the shrine maiden, Jin-Lin. Welcome to the Waystation at Tzu, mythical sanctuary of the *kami* Amen and most important grand temple in Japan." She completed her greeting by touching her heart, mouth and forehead, then extended her arms, indicating that he should go with her. Joe started to climb the path, following the red-haired lady. As he went he wiped his eyes on Megquier's fur-lined poncho and forced himself to stop crying and concentrate on his new surroundings. Each of the arches was constructed from two wooden poles topped with a horizontal rail. Every single surface was painted with black script, written with names in unintelligible symbols and also in English.

There must be hundreds, thought Joe. As they walked, he began reading the names and saw that each arch was dedicated to distinct buildings and places:

YUMBU LAKHANG, LHOKA PREFECTURE, TIBET

ROOM 21 CHATEAU MARMONT, CALIFORNIA, UNITED STATES OF AMERICA

BASILIQUE SAINT-NAZAIRE, CARCASSONNE, FRANCE

At first he didn't know what these could be, but then he saw a name he actually recognised: THE MEAD HALL OF TWR-Â-GÂN, SNOWDONIA, WALES, UNITED KINGDOM. Joe stopped in his tracks. This arch was dedicated to the Welsh watchtower! He wanted to halt the maiden and question her more, but she was already far ahead of him.

Arriving at the end of the tunnel, the woman paused to allow him to catch up. Beyond lay a view of the gardens and tower, and what struck Joe was not the immaculate beds of plants and flowers, but a pair of dog-like statues. Upon the head of one of them sat the snowy owl. The sight made Joe instantly suspicious. Griswald, Iolairn and now Tarrow again. These birds kept popping up everywhere. First the raven and his warnings at the bus. Next the owl, pet to the magician in the tower. Then the sea eagles in Norway and Ireland. Joe had no idea if he could trust any of these creatures or the people they accompanied. Only one thing was for sure: whatever game they were playing, these birds were shadowing his every move.

"You are most welcome here. Follow and you will see," Jin-Lin said.

Ignoring her subtle urging, Joe asked, "Don't you want to ask me who I am and where I come from?"

"Why need I ask this, Joseph Elijah Darkin? There is only here and there is only now."

The boy started at the use of his name, then gave Tarrow a stern look. "You know who I am?" he said.

"Yes." The woman seemed amused.

"I suppose *he* told you." He nodded towards the white bird.

"Oh, my stars," muttered Tarrow and turned his back on the boy.

The woman raised her painted eyebrows in mock exasperation, then answered, "No night's herald was needed to announce you, little master."

Joe wasn't so sure, but he had other, more pressing questions. "The names on the gateways? The watchtower... Where exactly is this?"

"This—" Jin-Lin indicated the gates, the trees and the entire complex, "—is the last magical place on earth."

The last? "What date is it?" Joe said, itching to consult the guide in his bag and remind himself of it.

"Today is Monday 8 May. Twenty-two eighty-two."

"What?" The boy experienced a pang of astonishment, but then he recalled the calendar page in the hallway. The year marked as 2282, the exact numbers his father had used in the bus. He must have sent Joe to the next place in the labyrinth. To someone who could save him. However anxious he felt, the boy held on to that fact as his only comfort. Like the cabin in the woods, he knew that this was another location the guide's author had not discovered. "What is this place? And why are there so many moons?"

The woman looked up at the sky as if seeing the pale white discs for the very first time. "Those are not moons," she said. "Near space is made up of thirteen distinct starstations. They are the places of the macrocorporations, wealthy individuals or private companies. Grown from crystals, they are home to many billions of former Earth inhabitants. But come, we should continue our journey." Jin-Lin turned and began to walk towards the inner temple with delicate, shuffling steps.

"No, wait," said Joe, his head so full of questions he didn't know which one to ask next. "These names on the poles... What are they?"

"The outer and inner worlds of the *jinja* shrine are linked by the *torii* gates. This shrine doesn't actually exist in this world. Well, it does, but it doesn't. These are the boundary between the ordinary and infinite worlds."

"How can they be gates?" the boy asked. "They haven't got any doors."

"Not all doors are visible, Joseph Elijah Darkin. They make obvious that the temple is always open."

"But the names, what do they signify?"

"The names make memory. It is the purpose of the gateway and the *miya* – the palace. The waystation is a god-shrine to all the lost places of the Earth."

"But there are hundreds," Joe said.

"Thousands," corrected Jin-Lin. "Upon thousands."

Joe was dumbfounded. If each one of the gates was a sacred place that had been drained of its power...

So this is the ultimate end point of using up the magic, he thought. And what had happened to all the guardians like Boann and the trapper? Had the Ghûl won?

Following the shrine maiden, Joe stepped out from under the last of the gates and into the immaculate garden. Red and white blossom hung heavy on the trees, while shrubs had been arranged in a weave of patterns. The stone path continued and there straight ahead rose the central tower. He recalled these were pagodas, but to Joe the building looked more like a giant beehive. This resemblance seemed appropriate as the air was filled with bumblebees moving to and from the enormous structure.

"In my time they told us bees were dying out," Joe said. "Guess that never happened."

Jin-Lin lifted her palm and immediately her fingers were full of the insects. "No, it did. These are not bees that you would know. They are all gone. These have a special purpose. We will see soon. Come inside."

Then he had another thought. If this was future Japan, how could Joe understand her? Yet in thinking this he realised the woman was speaking Nature's Tongue. Silently Joe thanked the captain and Evangeline for all those interminable lessons on the *Lodestar*, but underneath he knew this was not a language you learned; you just had to awaken to its existence.

Passing through the gardens, Jin-Lin led Joe up a wide flight of wooden steps into the first level of the temple. Inside the entire space was a single hall, supported with what Joe first thought were pillars, but then saw were living trees. Each one was hung with fabrics and offerings, reminding him of Granny Em's Kissing Tree. The room was entirely constructed of squares, each exactly the same. The wall panels were grey frosted glass, the ceilings red lattice, the floors a complex trellis of black honeycomb tiles. Somewhere a plucked instrument was being played, heard above a deep humming like that of a giant engine. Every centimetre of the room was decorated with rivets and designs from old ships. It looked like the offspring of mating a Japanese tea house with an ocean liner.

All the while, Jin-Lin explained their journey.

"Welcome to the Hall of Pillars. The Waystation at Tzu is like a stepping-stone place, linking the Within, the Between and the Without. This is the place of the last tree, the last flowers, the last rock and river. There is no out there, only in here. No future, only history. Of everything else there remains no trace, neither memory nor regret."

Joe didn't really understand fully what she meant. Perhaps the real meaning was lost in translation. Instead he asked, "What are all these trees?"

"This section of the waystation is a sacred place where the *kami*

– the spirits – live. These trees are many thousands of years old and were planted when this temple was built by my master. The straw rope and paper flags show that a tree has been sanctified and a spirit dwells within. To reach the temple you walk through the primeval forest." She directed him to the centre of the hall and there loomed a massive tree that grew up through the entire temple. It was so old deep cracks like fissures ran up its twisted trunk, revealing the heartwood within. Around the tree a spiral set of steps wound upwards and at its base a granite bowl babbled with flowing water. "This tree is the oldest of all. It is holy camphor. If you wish you may enter inside and hear the beating of its ancient heart." Jin-Lin laughed again. It sounded like the tinkling of little bells. The owl flew in through the doorway on snow-white wings and up into the branches of the tree. "But, to begin the process of your departure. Step the first: *Temizuya.*" The maiden indicated the granite water bowl and a bamboo cup on a long handle. "This is *tsukubai.* Your road has been long and…" She searched for the appropriate word. "Dirty," she said at last.

Joe looked down at himself and had to agree. He looked as if he'd been pulled through the wilderness backwards. Since leaving present-day England, he'd changed several times. He'd been wearing his current clothes since the ship. His navy coat was bloodied and torn, his boots scuffed and muddy. He shuddered to think what his hair looked like. He couldn't even recall the last time it had been combed. Norway in 1986 was his best guess. Now Jin-Lin was offering him a chance to wash and perhaps even rest, which when compared with many of the other places he'd visited felt like an absolute miracle.

"Like this," said the woman and knelt by the bowl. Taking the cup she poured water on her hands then lifted it to her mouth. Joe did the same. "Now, step the second: *Haiden.* Here you set aside your heavy burden. This hall is one for the safekeeping of sacred objects." She reached out and lifted Joe's pack from his shoulders. Looking inside she tutted when she saw the sword and staff. "No weapons into temple," she said. Carefully and with great reverence she placed his equipment in the base of the camphor tree.

"Step the third: *Kōkūken*. Here is your very special *katamichi kippu*." From her white robes she produced a golden square of paper upon which were figures and more of the magical script from the *torii* gates. "Your ticket," she said simply. Joe took the pass, shaking his head in confusion. What was this place? A Japanese temple or futuristic version of King's Cross station or Stansted Airport? Was he walking a sacred path to enlightenment or checking in his luggage? Perhaps I'm doing both, he thought.

Silently Jin-Lin accompanied the boy up the spiralling steps around the venerable tree. It led to the first floor of the pagoda. This level was split into four rooms around the central chamber for the trunk. Each was viewed through giant oval hatches and inside descended into what looked like oddly shaped baths.

"This is the Hall of the Five Always." She indicated each area, the four rooms and the central space. "The Everlasting Flame, the Infinite Ocean, the Immortal Sky, the Eternal Forest and the Deathless Dark." The boy recognised a couple of these names, but not the entire list. "These are steps four, five, six and seven. Here you will prepare your physical body."

Joe stepped tentatively into the first chamber. This was marked with the symbol of a burning ball of fire. Oh boy, he thought, here goes nothing. Walking slowly down into the first empty pool, he stood at the centre and looked for some indication as to what he should do next. There was nothing; the place was completely featureless. There wasn't even a plug.

"Jin-Lin," he said, "what am I supposed—"

With a sudden explosion of amber, flames materialised in the air, engulfing him. Scared, Joe let out a shriek, but though intensely hot, like the fire in the Manse L'Estrange kitchen, the flames did not burn his skin. Unfortunately the same could not be said for his hair and clothes; everything was instantly immolated. Everything, that is, but the talisman around his neck. The next moment the fire was gone and Joe was standing bald and naked in the empty chamber. Stupidly he covered himself with his hands, embarrassed.

"Work moonwise," the shrine maiden said from the central hall.

"Moon-what?"

"The wrong way of the clock," Jin-Lin explained.

Emerging through the open door, Joe moved into the room to the right. This was marked with the sign of Water. Once he was in the pool he experienced a similar transformation, but this time the air around him transmuted into liquid. The touch of it was cool and refreshing, but afterwards his skin tingled with cleanliness as if he'd been scrubbed raw then left to soak in a hot bath for hours.

"And so, the next," said the maiden.

The third chamber was the room of Air, and here Joe was dried upon the warmest of winds. After the breeze had vanished the boy felt as if he was the cleanest he'd ever been. He felt vital and alive.

"And, to the last."

The final chamber was marked with the sign of a tree, signifying the Earth. What could happen in here? Joe wondered. As soon as he reached the base of the pool he was cloaked in roots and leaves upon which caterpillars swarmed. For a moment the creatures crawled across his body, making him shiver in disgust. Then they were gone and he was dressed in long silver robes tied at the waist with blue and gold belts. He looked down at his comfortable attire. Welcome to the cult, Joey D, he thought with a smile. On a more serious note, he wondered if anyone else he'd met on his travels had been here. Or more importantly, how they had got back.

Outside, he found Jin-Lin at the base of the stairs, ready to lead him up to the next level.

This room was again constructed of square windows, but arranged in a series of chambers that formed one enormous circular arena. The entire area was scattered with straw mats, the air above filled with tiny golden spheres of light that hung in the air like fireflies. Each was reflected in the glass and highly polished floor and woodwork, making the room feel infinite.

"This is the Hall of Stars. Here you will prepare your mind. Step the eighth: *Kagura-den*." Joe saw cushions and a low table set with a delicate tea service. The teapot steamed in the cool air, its handle and spout fashioned like a coiled dragon. "Please be seated, Joseph Elijah Darkin," said Jin-Lin. The boy knelt upon one of the cushions and arranged himself cross-legged like in school assembly. The woman poured the tea and they drank for a while in silence. On the edges of Joe's vision he began to see movement in the corners of the room, then between the stars shapes began to form. Swimming in the shadows, they danced a rhythmic ballet, but every time Joe turned to see them better they vanished like morning mist.

"This is the place to look within yourself. To see and understand the inner world you are living in. This landscape is always an island, a private place in a private sea where we run and sail and fly. Out here—" she indicated the room and the entire temple, "—is just… *mu*."

"*Mu?*"

"Nothingness," the shrine maiden whispered. "So now, imagine." Jin-Lin passed her hand softly across the boy's eyes. Joe's mind went blank. The room and temple, his body and everything in the entire universe vanished. He experienced the briefest seconds of weightlessness, then his eyelids felt as heavy as dustbin lids and he closed them for a moment and sighed.

Images like lightning speared Joe's inner darkness. Scenes sprang into life. Visions of a storm-lashed isle hanging at the edge of the world. A place of foam and spray before a final plunge into nothingness. The island before him was not made of earth and rock; it was made of skulls. It was a place of abandonment and loneliness and there was no way to reach it. There was no way to escape. At its centre stood a volcano, its boiling heart spewing lava and smoke. And there upon that bone-white mountain Joe saw himself. Almost torn in half by the ferocious tempest, the boy stood, his arms wide, his mouth the perfect O of a silent, endless scream…

"Awaken, Joseph Elijah Darkin," said Jin-Lin.

Joe sat bolt upright and opened his eyes. Instantly, the awful scene was shattered, swept away by sudden golden light. The stars were gone from the room. Now only the late-afternoon sunshine filtered through the walls.

"Sorry," he said. "Must have dozed off a moment there."

"You have slept for an entire moon's turn," said the woman in white. "The Moon of the Hare is now the Moon of Thunder. That was step the ninth: *Komainu*."

"What?" Joe said, struggling to his feet. "I just closed my eyes for a second."

"You know that is not truth," said Jin-Lin. "Search within." She was right. Joe felt completely and utterly rested, as if he had returned from a long holiday to far-off lands. He reached for his head and found even his hair was growing back. It was then that Joe noticed the shrine maiden was staring at him intently, as if looking at him for the first time. "I thought you were dead," she said in a whisper.

"So did I," the boy replied. "Several times. And I should be, I really should. It's been weeks since I took my medicine. I think the sacred well water cured me."

Jin-Lin shook her head, confused at what she was hearing. "Cured? What medicine?"

"*The* Medicine," Joe explained. "The one I had to take every thirteen hours. A good boy always takes his medicine."

"A good boy…" the woman said dreamily. "And you say you have not taken it?"

"Yes. I ran out. Weeks and weeks ago." He really had no idea how long; it felt like centuries.

"This reveals much… No, everything."

"Yes, it was what kept me alive."

"No," Jin-Lin interrupted. "It was what kept you hidden. And now this is how you can be found. How they keep finding you. It masked your Nature's Scent. Now those dogs have it, they can track you to the ends of the earth." Joe had sudden flashes of memory. Of Damfino sniffing the air in the Old Rectory gardens. Of his alarm shrieking him awake in the middle of the night. More invention and lies. Was everything he believed in a fable? Just something made up to deceive him?

The woman and boy climbed the next set of spiral stairs and Joe saw that the fourth level was split again into separate rooms. They were arranged much like the second, but these four had submarine-like hatches instead of openings. On each were celestial symbols. Here the topmost branches of the camphor tree spread and the hexagonal floor was scattered with tiny leaves.

"These are the Halls of the Moon and Sun. The places of sleep and dreams. My master's chamber is there and mine is here. You will rest in this other place." She crossed to a hatch marked with a symbol like a crown and turned a wheel. Inside was a large, airy apartment with a bed, table, cushions and large cupboard. Everywhere was filled with ferns, orchids and other plants Joe had no names for. Decorative stone lanterns held amber flames for light, and just inside the door stood another granite bowl brimming with bubbling water.

"Step the tenth: *Sessha*. You will await your calling here."

"Is this the topmost level?" he asked.

"No, there is one more. The arkspace." She pointed up. "You have cleansed body and mind. This Jin-Lin can do. Now, spirit. But only my master can shape the shadows of the Deathless Dark. The last three steps are ones for you and he alone."

"Who is your master?"

"He is the Black King of the Maje." But more than this she would not say.

Joe stepped into the room and crossed to the sleeping area.

"One last thing," said the woman. "Something important."

"What's that?"

"We cannot fix you, Joseph Elijah Darkin."

Something caught in Joe's throat. "Why?" he croaked.

"Because you are not broken."

JIN-LIN RETURNED THE NEXT MORNING and informed Joe that her master was ready to receive him. Joe had spent the time initially pacing, unable to sleep much past a restless doze. After that he had filled the hours updating his map and consulting *The Stranger's Guide*. He confirmed that futuristic Japan was another location the unknown author had not travelled, so no help was found as to the oracle or the way forward. The name, time and location were recorded from the calendar page, but the only other information was that Tzu was located at the very tip of the Shiretoko Peninsula on Hokkaido Island. None of this was very helpful.

Leaving his room, Joe climbed the final flight of steps and entered the topmost floor of the temple shrine. The last level was directly situated above the main living hub, and like the one below, four doors stood around the central vaulted chamber. These looked less like submarine hatches, and more like spaceship gateways. Each was inset with a porthole window, bordered with illuminated orange panels and carved wooden fretwork, both antique and futuristic at the same time. As the boy wondered how he was supposed to choose which one to enter, the wheel on the left-hand door began to turn and the portal split open, spilling golden light. Joe stepped through and found himself in a room very much like his own quarters, but larger and more resembling a garden than a living and sleeping area. Opposite the hatchway was a wooden bookcase topped with an altarpiece fashioned like a galleon. It bore an uncanny resemblance to *The Lodestar*, right down to the miniature tree as a central mast. Surely that's one of Lars Thorstad's models? Joe thought with a pang of sadness.

Inside the latticed top of the cabinet fine sand had been raked into a Japanese garden and at its centre stood a white shard of crystal. It was unmistakably the one Evangeline had taken from the cave below the lighthouse on Tranøy island. It was even missing the sliver that the captain had broken off and given him. The fragment that he now carried in his rucksack. It was pulsing slowly like a beating heart, illuminated with a soft red inner glow.

"Behold," said a deep voice from further within the room, "the last shard of magic left in the world."

No, Joe thought, not quite. Distinctly he heard the captain saying, "When all paths are gone and there is nowhere else to go, this will show the way." He couldn't help thinking that maybe he could use it to get back to Lars Thorstad and Evangeline. After the discovery of his parents' secrets, the boy ached to be back on *The Lodestar*, and Joe realised the girl and the captain felt more like his family now. Perhaps they could all sail off and find Serene again? In his heart Joe wanted that more than anything.

Beyond the cabinet was an area centred on a low polished table inset with a bronze sphere. Around the table cushions were scattered while above hung rows of silk lanterns. Seated cross-legged at the table was a man dressed in midnight robes. He looked African or Caribbean, his skin the darkest shade of chocolate the boy had ever seen, but in contrast he had the purest piercing blue eyes.

Joe looked back at the crystal and watched as a bumblebee buzzed past his ear, through the latticed wooden panels and alighted on the white surface. As it did so, there was a tiny flare of golden light, then the bee took flight and swept through the curtains, over the parapet and was gone.

"What are they doing?" Joe asked.

"That is simple," said the robed figure. "They are gathering grains of magic for the crystal sentience. Nourishing and expanding it."

"Sentience?"

"Here in this time bio-anima constructs govern our world. Like computers govern yours. It's just our computers are alive and powered by light. This is the central core of the waystation. We call it Home."

As the man said that word, Joe's stomach knotted like coiled rope. Home was something he so needed, just the mention of it made him yearn inwardly. To the boy that word was the promise of everything he wanted. It seemed to ask him, could this waystation ever be home? This island at the end of the world?

"Do you know who I am?" asked the man.

"Yes. You are the Black King of the Maje."

"I am. Just as Laverna-Vel Beltaræ is the Black Queen of the Ghûl."

"So is my father her White King and Jin-Lin your White Queen?"

"Exactly so."

"So that makes me special, does it? Or somehow cursed?"

"Not at all. We are each our own selves. Welcome to the arkspace vivarium, Joseph Elijah Darkin."

"Just call me Joe."

"In our time, with so many trillions of people, the norm is to use all three names. In this way we differentiate…"

"Joe's fine."

"Joe it is, then. In that case you may address me as Nirromelhe. And know that you have taken step the eleventh: *Shamusho*."

"That's great, but you've got to remember all this is two centuries in the future for me. Everything is so… *weird*."

"Then just ask Home." Nirromelhe indicated the crystal.

"Home, what is an arkspace?"

Joe felt stupid talking to a rock, but as soon as he had spoken a male voice emanated all around him. It was as if the very air were speaking. "Arkspace. An organically grown, stable-orbiting satellite. These structures are built from particles of space dust accumulated within interstellar clouds. They range in size from single homes to entire cities."

"Like I said, weird."

Nirromelhe beckoned for Joe to sit. "This arkspace – what you assume is the topmost level of the pagoda shrine – is currently docked at the Tzu waystation, but this vivarium is part of D'Arkadia, the near-space laboratory starstation of Malorian Industries."

"You mean you come from outer space?"

"Near-space. Outer *atmosphere*. The moons you saw when you arrived, these are the starstations."

"Wow," was all Joe could manage.

"You thought magic was dead, then you found Talliston. Or perhaps it is better to say then Talliston found you. Because, in truth, we find things not because the path is there, but because the path is revealed to us."

"Are you saying I was meant to come here?"

"Not really. There is no luck or fate or destiny. These are man-made ideas. The universe is always in motion. Think of it like an infinite ocean whose tides and currents move and shape our lives and worlds. The labyrinth of the house is the place into which all lost things go."

"So you're saying all my pens and gloves turned up here, too?"

"Let me explain another way. Just because we cannot see or feel a thing does not make it imaginary. Talliston is a world trapped within four walls of an invisible labyrinth. Like a prehistoric fly encased in amber. Can you feel its presence and power? Indeed. But can you see it? No. Think of it as an island; things wash up here all the time. Places, people... even objects." He raised both hands and clapped them. The door opened and Jin-Lin entered. She was carrying something. When she held it up, Joe could do nothing but gape. It was his message in a bottle, the one he had tossed into the Norwegian Sea. Even under two centuries of brine and barnacles, the rolled-up note was visible inside.

"Do you want to read it, Joe?" the shrine maiden said softly.

Anger flared in the boy. "What? No." He remembered clearly what he had written in that letter. His words to his parents. Now he knew that those words were wasted. "Everything I wrote is meaningless now."

Jin-Lin shook her head. "You are wrong. Any mother in the world would want to read those words."

"Not my one."

Bitterly, he snatched for the bottle, but Jin-Lin moved it out of reach.

"Do not destroy. Learn," said the shrine maiden. "The secret lies within all of us."

"What secret?"

"That is for you to discover," Nirromelhe answered. "All have the power to be a creator, to be a destroyer. To be Maje or Ghûl."

"Is it my—" Joe stopped himself from saying 'destiny' "—job to do something? To help save the house?"

"You must choose your own path."

"But you can train me."

"You do not need training. What can any man teach another? We are the acorn and when planted hold within us everything required to grow into a mighty oak. Everything you need for your journey already exists – has always existed. Here, here and here." Nirromelhe pointed at Joe's head, heart and stomach. "All I can possibly do is help you to see your world not as it is, but as it should be."

"Jin-Lin mentioned how only you could take me on these last steps."

"No, only *you* can take them. And to do this you must go into the Deathless Dark."

Nirromelhe raised his arms and indicated the entire ceiling.

"You mean we're going into space?"

The Black King of the Maje said nothing. He just smiled.

"This place is amazing!" Joe said, laughing.

"No, this place is nothing. It is nowhere," the man replied. "It is only amazing when we step into it."

"Master." Jin-Lin backed away, heading for the door. Her voice was tinged with apprehension.

"What is it?" he asked calmly.

"Outside. Dread forces gather."

"Ah, speaking of the dark…" said Nirromelhe without a hint of anxiety. "As I mentioned, all lost things wash up here."

Joe sat up straight. Had the Grim Grotesques managed to follow him again? Even here? But he knew that they had. They were hunters. Did he think they would give up just because he had killed their leader? Another would take Damfino's place. When Joe stopped and concentrated, he could sense them coming. It was not a pleasant sensation. It was a lot like how he imagined it would feel diving into a swimming pool filled with spiders.

"But I am not finished with our talk," Nirromelhe continued. "I need to tell you about the thirteen doors of the labyrinth." Joe's ears pricked up at mention of the doors, and he listened intently, yet his attention wandered under the feeling of approaching doom. "Before the labyrinth was created to protect these last places, there were many ways to travel – the Hwythrevane, the Room Atlas – many ways and many doors. Yet those ways are gone now. Now there are only thirteen."

"How do they work?" Joe asked.

"There are three ways. One: upon the dark of the moon, all the doors open. Then any can step between worlds. As you know, this is the way evil travels."

"How *evil* travels?" the boy repeated.

"Yes, the path of the Ghûl and the Wild Hunt. It takes longer – far longer – but it can be accomplished. Some of these moments the enemy know of. Some they don't. For the Maje, there are the oracles. These allow us to open the spiralling path of the labyrinth, to walk between walls. And then there is the last way." The robed man pointed to the talisman that hung around the boy's neck.

"The Stone of Shadows?" Joe asked. "It's used for travelling?"

"There are five talismans. They once adorned an Inca helm of great potency. These were hidden long ago in a sacred temple carved inside a volcano. Once all five were held by the monarchy of the Maje. Sadly, this is not now the case." Joe's mind flashed a memory of Damfino holding the yellow necklace. "The Maje created the labyrinth from the power of the helm and its elemental doorways. If we had time, I could teach you more of this stone's powers…"

"My king!" urged Jin-Lin.

"Perhaps later," said Nirromelhe to the boy. "Home, initiate externals."

The paper-like opaque glass faded to transparency, revealing a vista that encompassed the temple gardens, the sacred forest and the ominous towers. The cliffs were already a mass of dark shapes. The sky too. The gathering army of the Ghûl swarming down upon the shrine. Upon the last magical place on earth.

"It's the Grim Grotesques," Joe cried. "Millions of them."

"Yes. The age of Man is over. Now is a world only of Ghûl. To find people we must look to the stars and the new moons."

The swarm came on, unstoppable as the imagined zombie plague he'd invented back at the roundabout.

Do Not Talk to Dead People…

"This place will be overrun. You can't hope to stand against so many. There's only two of you."

"No, Joseph Elijah Darkin," said the Black King of the Maje. "There are three."

"We're going to fight them?"

"No, that would be foolish. Our task is to protect the last shard."

Already the first of the enemy were crashing through the *torii* gate tunnel, emerging into the garden. With a sick churning in his stomach Joe saw that they were clad in Japanese armour, a sea of samurai or ninjas or whatever Far Eastern warriors were called. At the head of the group strode his mother, her black hair streaming from beneath an ebony horned helm. Upon her shoulder sat the raven. At that moment she looked straight up and at them, her face contorted into a mask of hatred.

Jin-Lin stepped to the boy's side. "Joe," she said calmly. "This is step the twelfth: *Honden*. You may want to prepare."

"Prepare?" asked Joe, confused and sickened by Laverna's appearance. "What for?"

"For *this*," said her robed master. "Home, take us out."

And with that the arkspace vivarium departed the Waystation at Tzu and in one clear, perfect arc launched into space. Instantly the blood rushed from Joe's head to the furthest reaches of his toes. Outside the sky turned pale, then purple, then black, while Joe, who had no idea what else he could possibly do in such a situation, howled and then passed out.

JOE STOOD BESIDE THE TRUNK of a giant tree. It was impossibly old, impossibly tall. Beside it, skyscrapers and mountains would have been dwarfed. In its branches all four seasons were displayed, from bare twigs to blossoms, fruits to golden leaves of autumn. Its thick, gnarled roots twisted deep into the bare earth and between them stood a small arched door. Butterflies crowded everywhere, their wings a thousand hues. Beside the trunk stood a golden four-poster bed and seated on its multicoloured silks was a robed man. His skin was dark and lined with age and wisdom.

"Set down your burdens, weary traveller. Rest," he said. His voice was the voice of the crystal.

"Am I asleep?" Joe asked the man.

"After a fashion, but you will awaken."

"Why am I here?"

"That is a question only you can answer. As are all questions. I am Hrishikeshr, Wych and Guardian of the Tree of Life. Nothing more."

"Wych? Are there three sides now?"

"Only the misguided take sides," said Hrishikeshr. "The Grey House of the Wych are far more ancient than Maje or Ghûl. The Maje are formed to use the magic within, the Ghûl the magic without. But it's all magic. It is all from one source. Like the Wych. Like all things."

"Is this the Tree of Life?" Joe looked up into the branches of the immense tree. It looked as if it had been growing since the dawn of time.

"In the beginning," spoke the ancient man, "the entire Earth was a magical place. Every part of it was infused with power. All the lands were one, and at the centre of that vast continent was this tree. When man unearthed the ways to harness its magic, great were the forces they unleashed. Witch doctors, shamans, holy men and warlocks, each drew from that innate power. There were battles, and the tree – their home – was destroyed. From that destruction, its seeds and splinters were scattered across the lands."

Joe shifted in the darkness. So magical places could be anywhere? he thought.

"Yes, at first. Now they are nowhere. Once there were thousands of rooms. Now there are only thirteen. Gone are the doors to the temples in India, to Peru and Egypt. The Maje built the labyrinth to guard the last magical places and connected each house with doorways, hoping to save what little power remained. That proved impossible."

"But surely the Ghûl can see where this all leads?"

"Yes, they know the consequences of their actions, but still they lust for control of such powers. That is the nature of their folly. Like a watering hole that is drying up, Talliston draws animals both good and ill forever to its dwindling waters."

"Like the travelling fayre," said Joe in his dream, thinking of the tents set up around Blackmirror Tarn.

"Exactly. For it is far, far easier to use the magic of the earth than unlock one's own power. So the Waystation at Tzu is no more. This ark is the last place. Gone are Reverend Grey, He Who Walks By Night and signore Balthazard. Now there are only the shadows of magic within us."

"So the tree is… lost?"

"Not yet. It is the thing that connects the three worlds. The water of the Infinite Ocean nourishes its roots. It stands sentinel at the centre of the Eternal Forest. Its branches reach like dreams into the Immortal Sky. It grows through everything, even the labyrinth. The tree is the concept you call Time. Do you understand?"

"No," said Joe.

"Though the roots are unseen by us, they are still there. Just like the topmost branches which are invisible overhead as we stand on the ground. It, like you, is a whole universe of moments, each one a droplet making up an infinite ocean of all things past. Each one an acorn making up an eternal forest of the here and now. Each one a star making up an immortal sky of the future. All these moments exist, all at once, and their magic makes them free from the unbroken path of hours, days and years."

"But what does all this mean?"

"It means history does not change, *you* change. It means do not seek to change the world, change *your* world. There is no good. Nor evil. There is only right and wrong. You are your only guide, so seek within. And do what you believe."

"AWAKEN, JOSEPH ELIJAH DARKIN."

Joe sat bolt upright, his mind still full with the story of his dreams. Tarrow perched beside him on the black railings. Nirromelhe and Jin-Lin sat close by at the low table, apparently navigating the craft via the bronze globe set into it. Upon the surface of the sphere were several tiny points of golden light.

"Oh, you," Joe said.

"Charming," said the owl.

The boy rose and went to join the others. "What are those?" he asked, pointing at the lights within the golden sphere.

"This is the view of the planet below us," said Jin-Lin. "We are above the North Pole looking down on the northern hemisphere. Those points of light are the geographical locations of the houses of the labyrinth."

"They all seem clustered around Europe. Are there none in the south?"

"The first Maje were from England and their influence spread from there. When the work to protect the temples began, the southern hemisphere, Russia and China were already lost completely." As if from nowhere Jin-Lin produced the boy's pack and objects.

"You said weapons weren't allowed in the temple?"

The shrine maiden shrugged. "This is not the temple. Now you are ready to take step the thirteenth: *Himitsu*," said Jin-Lin. "Let the universal tide take you, Joseph Elijah Darkin. It is always there, but to feel its flow we must stop, sit and listen."

"Is that the mission of the Waystation at Tzu?"

"Yes. To do what the house does."

"And what is that?"

"Embrace all. Follow none," said Jin-Lin with a bow.

"Open yourself to every knowledge, every faith, every creed," said the robed man. "Draw from every time and every place. Seek the road of every writer and artist and prophet. Then follow your own."

"Ticket, please," said the woman. Dumbly Joe produced the golden square of parchment and handed it to her. "And the crystal."

"The… How did you know?" Jin-Lin smiled as if to say knowing was what she did best. The boy reached into his bag and pulled out the small shard. The shrine maiden took it and bowed, while Nirromelhe explained.

"As each of the places have lost their magic, the paths and doors are lost also. This is the last place. There are no doors back."

"What?" Joe said, shocked.

"Don't be afraid. As I said, these crystals create their own paths. And you carry the shadowstone. You have a way."

When all paths are gone… When there is nowhere else to go…

Jin-Lin set the crystal inside a wall-mounted lamp above the hatch and the entire wall shone in red. Joe faced the oval doorway then stepped forward. Grasping the wheel he turned it and the bolt clicked out of its lock. Slowly the boy pulled the hatch open. "Is the future set?" he asked. "Can it be changed?" Then he added, "Can *I* change it?"

"There is no past or future. There are only these moments," said Nirromelhe.

Faces flashed in his mind. Evangeline. Captain Lars Thorstad. Serene and Granny Em.

"That's enough," Joe said. "That's worth fighting for."

I'm ready, he thought. Ready and determined to reach the centre of the labyrinth and find the way to save the house and everything in it. And if that means fighting my mother, my father, Jonathan D'Ante and every last one of the Grim Grotesques, then so be it.

"I know what I have to do," said Joe suddenly. "I need to go. Keep the crystal safe."

"Until the end of time, Joe," said Nirromelhe, then indicating the door added, "Passing this threshold marks the end of the outer circle of the labyrinth. Those eight locations are done. Now you must spiral back through three more, and make one final turn to reach Talliston's heart."

Joe's mouth was dry as he asked quietly, "What lies at the centre of the labyrinth? What is its secret?"

"You are, Joseph Elijah Darkin," Jin-Lin said, her eyes both smiling and wet with tears. Softly she reached up and brushed her fingers against his cheek, then placed both hands together in prayer and bowed.

"*Ki wo tsukete!*" she said. "Bon voyage, Joseph Elijah Darkin."

"Goodbye, Jin-Lin." Joe touched his heart, mouth and head, repeating the gesture she had used when they met. The boy drew his sword, gripped the bear-headed staff and stepped through the open doorway. One moment he was standing upon the polished wooden floors of a crystal starstation, the next he was stepping onto a chequerboard of marble tiles.

This was the Palazzo di Ombre. He was back in the Italian Hall of Mirrors!

II

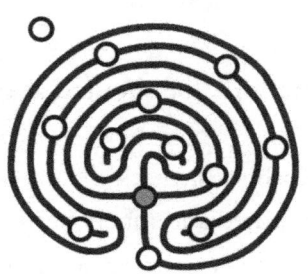

SECOND MOON: BLOOD MOON (OF MAN)
PALAZZO DI OMBRE
SACRO MONTE DI VARESE, LOMBARDY, ITALY
TUESDAY 24 NOVEMBER 1992 | 02:42:16

THE BOY STOOD AT THE bottom of the stone steps beneath the magnificent chandelier and stained-glass skylight. In the faint illumination, each of the ornate mirrors was filled with ghostly shadows. At his back the hatchway dissolved, replaced by the door that led to the vaulted room he had hidden in all that time ago. Joe appraised the room sternly. Had he really returned to signore Balthazard's palatial home? Right back to the beginning of his journeying? Here was the steep stone staircase with its gold-green curtains. The twisted tree roots breaking through the plasterwork ceiling. The marble-tiled floor. The thirteen clocks. There was no mistaking any of it. This was the Palazzo di Ombre. Exactly as he had left it.

No, not *exactly*.

Joe looked again. Where were the bullet holes? The chaos of masonry?

No, not as he had left it. The room was just as he had *found* it.

Yet even that was wrong. Where were the raven and the scattered calendar pages?

"Cru-uuk," came a familiar sound. Griswald hopped onto the topmost step and cocked his head down at the boy. "Having troubles, are we?" the bird said.

"Just shut it, you… traitor!" Joe shouted at the dark-winged bird.

"How so?"

"I saw you on my mother's shoulder."

"That's not for two hundred and ninety years," the raven pointed out.

"Once I couldn't decide if you were helping me or leading me into danger. Well, now I know."

"Ye gods! It's true you have travelled far, but have you learned nothing?"

"But I saw—"

Griswald cut him off with an indignant cluck. "You have seen many birds, many beasts, too. You have seen moons and rooms and doors. Do you actually understand any of it? There is no need of terms such as good or evil. We birds do not consume the magic of the Earth. We do not plunder its riches or destroy its sanctity. Don't deign to judge us until you can say the same."

Joe's mind tried to take this all in. "I… I'm—"

"And don't say you're sorry. Still, at least this is an improvement on our first conversation." It was only then that Joe realised he was speaking to the bird in Nature's Tongue. "Instead solve the puzzle of the here and now."

"This room is neither how I found it, nor how I left it. I'm back here, when I should be in the next room."

"Why?"

"Because the labyrinth is not a maze. It has one path."

"A straight path?"

"No, it spirals... Of course!" Then he had it. It was as Nirromelhe had said. He had completed the first circuit and was back at the cross point. "But that still doesn't explain—"

"It explains everything. How did you enter the room just now?" Joe pointed to the side door. "And how did you enter this room before?"

"By the front door."

"So?"

"So... *that's* why the calendar pages blew off the shelf."

Griswald waggled his body as if actually excited. Joe felt that if the raven could clap his wings to applaud, he would.

"Your mistake, young man, if I may be plain, is this: you are trying to think of these moments as somehow linked to time. But time is a human invention. It does not exist. That is why this place makes no sense to you. This is a time behind the clock, a world beyond the glass. Here you are far, far across the darkness of the mirrored sea." Griswald made the short flight down the stairs to stand beside the shelves of timepieces. "These clocks mark sacred moments. They transcend the everyday stupidity of linear minutes, hours and days. They are as different as dreaming and waking."

"So, the labyrinth chooses the moments? How? Why were Serene's moments different from mine? And why are the moments in the book the same?"

"Do not be vexed. These things of which I speak are Byzantine in their complexity. And you just a seventeen-year-old boy."

"I'm thirteen," Joe insisted.

"Not any more," the raven replied.

As Joe scrabbled for a response, the raven's head darted up, at once alert and stiff with fear. An instant later, Joe heard the rumbling sounds within the walls.

"He is coming," said the bird.

"He?"

"Just hurry."

Joe strode up the stairs, acutely aware of his lack of reflection. Retrieving the snake-headed bowl from the shelf, he called the Roman god's name. As before, images poured into the mirrors, and again when the voice spoke it was clear and calm.

"I am the Oracle of the Sacred Mountain. Offer up your sacrifice and speak your question."

"What sacrifice, O Saturn?"

"One of three things must be offered. One of the three things that Time cannot kill."

"I offer air," said Joe and held out the bronze cup.

"No! That offering has been made. One of the *other* things that Time cannot kill."

The front door to the palazzo burst open and a figure entered. As the calendar pages scattered like the first leaves of autumn, Joe's breath caught in his throat. For there in the entrance hall stood Gunner. Upon the boy's face was a look of death and in his eyes was the maniacal sickness of the Grim Grotesques. In his hands he held a pair of axes. "Maje," spoke Gunner. He made the word 'Maje' sound like 'Judas'. "You left me. Out there. To them! Who cares that they want you alive. I'm going to kill you, you little runt."

Joe faltered, panicking. Immediately his mind was a mess of facts and fears.

Axes are no match for a thrice-forged blade, said the sword, further confusing his thoughts.

"Jupiter, Pluto and Neptune. Come on, Joe. Think!" the raven chided. "What did I say before?"

That the answer was right in front of him, yet all the boy saw when he looked down was his ragged shape cast across the steps. It was too late. Gunner was already running up the stairs.

"Remember the Five Always," fussed the bird. "Remember what you have learned."

"Shadow!" he blurted, but as soon as he spoke he knew it was the wrong answer.

"Done!" boomed Saturn. Instantly the boy's shadow disappeared from the stonework. "Yet..." the voice continued, "that is not the correct sacrifice."

The raven almost screamed in frustration. "Joseph Elijah Darkin! Earth or Water. Now!"

Joe backed up a few steps, clumsy in his Japanese robes. He tried to pull out the sword, but Gunner was already upon him. Joe cowered against the railings. The blade of the Ghûl's axe hovered before Joe's throat. Gunner was enjoying this, which only fuelled Joe's anger.

"I met your sister. I know what you did to her. I know why she ran away. And—" he drew Ilkilæmber and held it between them "—I know who you serve."

"Now you die," Gunner spat, and there was a hideous gurgling in the thug's throat. Then, he looked up and the sneer faded from his sweaty face. Joe looked up too.

There on the landing above them the bearded photographer stood. He wore his oversized dressing gown and carried a Polaroid camera.

Romano!

It was no surprise, not really. The photographer's bedroom was only down the hall and the commotion would surely have woken him. Yet there was no recognition in his eyes. That's because for him we've never met, thought Joe. He probably thinks we're burglars. Or did until he saw this.

"*Ho chiamato la polizia! La polizia, hai capito?*" Romano said, then lifting his camera he took the boys' picture. Immediately the flash went off and a print popped out. The sudden brilliance blinded both boys, but Gunner cried out as if the light actually hurt him. He toppled back, misplaced his step and fell. He landed heavily, face down, and something cracked. When his body reached the bottom of the steep steps, he didn't move. Romano let out a startled cry and dropped the camera, then turned and fled. Joe stooped and picked up the Polaroid. As it finished developing it showed the stone hallway clearly with Gunner poised to strike, but of Joe there was no trace.

"Joseph Elijah Darkin," the raven said, "you know what must be done."

The boy took the snake-headed bowl and spat into it. He replaced the cup on the shelf and cried, "O mighty Saturn. I offer water."

"What is it you wish to ask the Oracle?" boomed the mask.

Joe flipped through the guide. "How do I open the door to the next room? To Room Nine. Ravnsbrae Manor in Scotland."

"It is as you wish. Step forward and enter into the land of sleep, dreams and nightmares." In the hallway above Joe heard an unseen door creak open. He started climbing the stairs, then stopped and turned back.

"Wait, I almost forgot." Joe descended past the unmoving Gunner to the telephone and yanked the wire out of its socket. The cable tore from its plaster channel and the boy sliced it cleanly in two with Ilkilæmber's keen blade. Preventing the photographer from phoning the police was the only thing Joe could think of to save Romano's life. He hoped this telephone was the only one. Returning upstairs, he found a small arched door had opened in the stonework and it led into a room of almost complete darkness.

The boy didn't pause one heartbeat.

IX

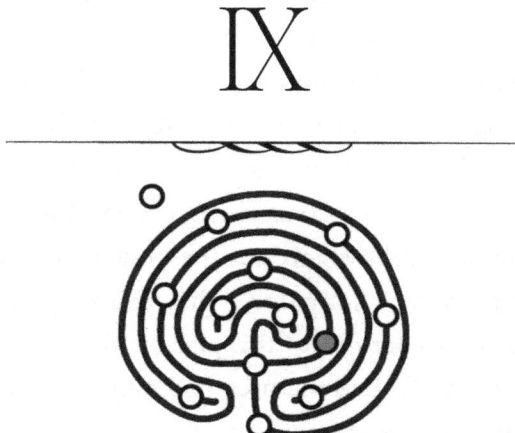

NINTH MOON: THUNDER MOON (OF NATURE: SKY)
RAVNSBRAE MANOR
STONEHAVEN, SCOTLAND, UNITED KINGDOM
MONDAY 26 JUNE 1911 | 17:23:49

STEPPING FROM THE STONE HALLWAY in Italy, Joe once more entered the unknown – and this time the unknown was very dark. Allowing his eyes to adjust, he saw he was standing in a bedroom, intricately carved and painted almost entirely black. The only hint of colour was a red tartan carpet and green fabric walls, but these did little to raise the overall air of gloom. Though it was obviously still daytime, outside the sky was grey and murky and a distant storm rumbled. Joe had long ago lost his torch, but on the window sill stood a candle lamp and matches. Once lit, he was able to start his search for the next oracle, a heart-shaped object named as a planchette.

A carved bed took up most of the room. It was hung with black curtains and at each corner rose wicked wooden spires. Upon the counterpane was a book of fairy tales held open by a stag's antler. The rumpled sheets showed where someone had recently lain there reading. There was also a wardrobe that looked big enough to house a small country and a scary black fireplace with a carved mantelpiece. Joe kicked something in the dimness. Looking down he saw a small wooden locomotive. Its coal truck was filled with shells and beach stones. The boy righted the train and then noticed a pair of tiny black shoes poking from beneath a chair in the corner. Taking another look around the room, Joe realised this was the bedchamber of a child.

Increasingly, there was something that felt very wrong here. He had a growing need to get out of this place and retreated to the door. Beside it were various framed pictures, including one concealed under black lace. Lifting it, Joe found beneath a photograph of a family standing outside an old house. They were dressed in formal clothes, as if off to church, and at the centre of the group stood a thin, sickly-looking boy. He was younger than Joe, maybe seven or eight. He was wearing a suit, his unblinking eyes staring from the photograph as if blaming the world for some awful tragedy. And it was then that Joe's mind put the pieces together: the depression on the bed, the abandoned toys and eerie photograph. Stepping back, he trod on a loose floorboard that creaked as if in agony. Instantly Joe had a feeling of suffocation and mounting dread. Grabbing the latch, he threw open the door and saw to his horror that beyond the arched frame was solid brickwork. Someone had walled up the room!

Almost dropping the lamp, the boy pushed at the bricks, finding them immovable. He couldn't budge them at all. Joe started to panic. He was trapped in a dead child's bedroom and he couldn't get out. Dropping to his knees, he found his pack and pulled out *The Stranger's Guide*. He turned to the pages for Room Nine and found they were almost blank. Like the Canadian cabin and Japanese temple, the mysterious author had never travelled here. All the book contained was the usual information from the calendar page: the name of the house – Ravnsbrae Manor – the location and the time and date of the dark of the moon.

Monday 26 June 1911.

Crossing to the window, Joe opened it to reveal a ceaseless grey sea and sky. Salt-wet winds tore at the heavy lace and curtains, buffeting the boy's face. The house sat on the very edge of immense cliffs, and far below waves the colour of slate slammed against savage rocks. Joe looked out across the immensity of the ocean and thought of Evangeline and the captain and how in seventy-five years they would be sailing north of here and he could watch them pass. It was a crushing thought and did nothing to disguise that he had come to a dead end. He was trapped.

Joe sat in the light of the single candle and tried not to cry out in panic. Hadn't Nirromelhe said there were no dead ends in the labyrinth? Was this the work of the Grims? What was he going to do?

In the hall outside he heard loud footsteps on floorboards.

Standing up Joe ran over and hammered on the brickwork. He started yelling. There was a loud crash and running feet – and it was then that Joe realised just how his commotion would have sounded.

As if the ghost of the dead boy were trying to break free.

MUCH LATER, WHEN THE BOY'S alarm had subsided, he searched the room more thoroughly. It didn't take long. Set into the wall above a carved throne was a bookcase, while either side of the metal fireplace were shelves and a pair of cupboards set into the wall. Inside the wardrobe hung the child's clothes while under the bed was a discarded doll and a school book with the name Seathan Macpherson written in elaborate handwriting on the cover. If I wanted to hide something in this room, Joe thought, where would I put it? Immediately his eyes were drawn to one of the cupboards. Inside the space was empty except for some metal water pipes, until he found that the back was hollow. The entire rear panel was loose, and when removed, revealed a narrow passageway within the walls of the mansion.

We are in the walls, said Granny Em's voice in his head.

Sighing with relief, Joe squeezed himself into the tiny space and pulled his pack in behind him. He knew he should be searching for the oracle, but something in his gut wanted to be out of the room. Just for a minute, he told himself.

The dusty passage was very narrow and was a squeeze for Joe, though the younger, thinner Seathan would have been able to fit through easily. As he inched forwards, the boy found he could look out through cracks in the woodwork or plaster into other rooms and chambers. Most held beds or baths, while others were pitch black or piled with boxes. Eventually Joe found another loose panel and emerged into the back of a closet filled with sheets and towels. Outside was a small servant's room that looked like it was used for ironing and led onto a gallery overlooking a central hall right at the heart of the house. Above, stained-glass windows were set in an octagonal tower, each one showing suns, moons and stars with constellations made of crystals. Even on such a dismal day the hall was filled with rainbows. Below sofas and palms were set around low tables crowded with vases of flowers. Even if Joe invited everyone he had ever met for a birthday party there would still be plenty of room for more. Yet on this gloomy afternoon, the vast space was empty and eerily quiet.

Moving around the railed balcony past towering oil paintings of dour gentlemen on horseback and ladies in ballgowns, Joe found the walled-up door. The brickwork had been concealed behind a velvet curtain. In front of this was a dropped tray of crockery. As he stood

looking at the spilled milk and shattered blue and white china Joe
heard voices below, talking in hushed whispers.

"It's the boy, I tell you. He's back. Back in that room."

"Now, you listen to yourself, Mary MacConall. All this talk of
ghosts and goblins. What'll it be next, I wonder?"

"But I tell you, Ailsa. True as I stand here. That room is haunted."

"Well, what I say is you'd be better served cleaning up that God-
awful mess. And best stop blaming your butterfingers on that poor *did
bairn.*"

Did bairn? Dead child! He knew it.

Moving quickly along to the staircase, Joe crept down some
enormous wooden steps to the hall below, then passed quietly across
to the grand entrance doors. As stealthily as he could, he pulled back
the giant bolt and slipped outside, only to find himself stepping into
gardens transformed into a carnival world of circus entertainments.
A fayre! Joe had a pang of anxiety. Was it *the* fayre? Between flagstone
paths, hedges and stone ornaments, brightly painted tents and
sideshows had been pitched. Everything was strung with bunting and
pennants. All manner of people milled about, some in suits and dresses,
others in gaudily ostentatious finery. The air was filled with fairground
music, thunder and raucous laughter in equal parts. The gardens and
amusements ran all the way to the dramatic cliff tops while the rest of
the estate was surrounded by tall hedges and beyond that fir woodland.
Looking up Joe saw that the house was just as creepy on the outside
as the inside. It would come as no surprise to discover its witch's-
hat-shaped towers and Gothic spires had been inspiration for Bram
Stoker's *Dracula*.

Feeling awkward and exposed on the steps of the old house, Joe
searched for somewhere to hide and that was when he saw the first of
the posters. They were displayed on every post, tree and tent, and each
one announced:

FOR ONE WEEK ONLY!

DANGER, DARING & MYSTERY!

SWINGING TO THE TUNE OF 'MEET ME TONIGHT IN DREAMLAND'

ENGLAND • APRIL

WALES • MAY

SCOTLAND • JUNE

And there at the top, between images of acrobats, horses and elephants, was the name of the great circus: PANDORO'S TRAVELLING FAYRE.

Joe groaned inwardly, then began counting on his fingers. Obviously in the twenty-four years since he first encountered the troupe at Twr-Â-Gân, the fayre had gone from strength to strength. On either side of the poster were panels listing all the extraordinary acts and attractions that were now part of the fayre. Joe read with growing incredulity of Jules's Troop of Trampolining Elephants, Ianivo the Cannibal Human Cannonball, and Sahara Waragg, who was apparently Last of the Sword-Swallowing Midget Triplets. Yet as he read the fantastical list of sideshows, he was left with one overriding thought: what had happened to Lasairfhíona? Did she still travel with the circus? It was with some astonishment that the thought of seeing her again filled his belly with churning butterflies.

Reaching into his bag he pulled out Serene's necklace and the bear-headed staff. The wood felt strong and sturdy in his hands, but unlike the leaf blade its vitality held no hint of aggression. Instead it emanated a sense of safety and sanctuary. Gripping the staff tightly, Joe asked, can you help me find Serene?

I am Arthiæ, the female voice replied, *aegis of chieftains and priestesses of kingdoms long lost to history. I am a symbol of wisdom and learning and those who bear me beside them are warded from the eyes of evil, thrice-protected from dark magic and able to farsee the path ahead.*

Then tell me, he asked, will I meet Serene here in the fayre?

The staff rippled in his hands, and for a moment it seemed as if the eyes of the bear shone deep amber. In Joe's hand the golden necklace glowed warm against his skin, and he knew that its original owner was near. Slipping it over his head, he moved into the crowds, eager to find the girl. As he went, Joe did his best attempt to blend in. It was not difficult. Hadn't he spent most of his life observing Rule #3: Be Invisible? Additionally, his futuristic Japanese robes made him look wonderfully theatrical. In any normal situation he would have stuck out like a sore thumb, but here he was camouflaged perfectly.

"Trying to be invisible, are we?" said a voice close to his ear.

Shocked, Joe turned and found that walking beside him was a bearded man dressed in a diamond-chequered cloak trimmed with black feathers, carrying a goat-headed cane. His face was hidden behind a black mask topped with horns, and his mad eyes sparkled like gemstones under the shadow of his hood. The last time the boy had seen those eyes was back at the watchtower. They belonged to the flamboyant master of the travelling fayre.

"Hello, Pandoro," said Joe, trying to keep the tremble from his voice.

"Hello, boy," said the harlequin, taking his arm. "Shall we walk?" The masked man's over-familiarity was faintly disturbing.

"How did you…" Joe hesitated.

"Find you?" asked Pandoro. "Oh, I seem to make a habit of finding lost children. Wouldn't you agree?" Joe didn't answer that. "And of course losing them. But you're back now, and no doubt want to see Lasairfhíona."

"She's still here?"

"Of course she's still here. We shall see her presently, but there's something we just *have* to do first."

Ducking through the legs of a passing column of elephants laden with passengers inside glittering carriages, they strolled through the crowded walled gardens. They made quite a pair: the man with his cane and the boy with his staff.

"This is Scotland, right?" asked Joe, thinking back to his parents. "We were going to move here once." That fact suddenly seemed laden with meaning.

"Yes, I think that's what they're calling it now. First time I was here it was Caledonia. How times change. Aberdeen is that way." Pandoro pointed along the cliffs to the left. "Dundee, the other. And out there—" he indicated the grey ocean, "—is Francia, then Iberia, and our next engagement."

"Where's that?"

"Spain. A place known as the Moon's Nest." The ringmaster's voice was soft and dreamy, almost inaudible over the music, crowds and thunder.

"You transport this entire circus all over Europe?"

"The world, boy, the world! And yes, but don't fuss. It all packs quite neatly."

Joe had visions of Pandoro waving a magic wand and miniaturising all the helter-skelters, Chair-O-Planes, big tops and sideshows into a bottomless carpet bag, but knew that wasn't what he meant. Or was it? This new and improved version of the travelling fayre was an endlessly wonder-filled place, like walking inside a grown-up fairy tale. The alternating black and red diamonds on Pandoro's cloak seemed to dance, flowing like water in the torchlight. Even the torches appeared to illuminate without flame. Everywhere was laced with the whiff of enchantment. They passed two flamboyant tents announcing DOUG MCMAMBA SNAKE-THROWING KNIFE CHARMER and G'ARTH THE GARRULOUS MIME in ornately flowered lettering.

"We are the most spectacular show on Earth," Pandoro was saying.

"The most magnificent and the most excellent. The competition is fervent, each showman vying with the other as to who should be the wildest and most eccentric. Barnum and Bailey practically seethe with envy whenever we pass on the highways. Yet while their fayres use steam as if Air and Water are the only elements, we use all five. We have Jubilee Fire Yachts, Lightning-powered Gallopers – and then there are the Dark Rides—"

"The Dark Rides?" asked Joe.

"The ones of Shadow. Those haunted trails in car or on foot."

"Haunted?" Immediately Joe thought of the bedroom.

"Practically jam-packed with ghosts and ghoulies."

"Is the labyrinth one of them?" asked Joe. "One of your sideshows?"

Pandoro stopped in his tracks and turned his madman's eyes on the boy. "Bravo," he replied. "That's the first sensible thing you've said since Queen Victoria's Golden Jubilee. God rest her soul. But no, the labyrinth of the house is far older than any magic I know or conjure. Much older. Practically prehistoric." They skirted a Western sharpshooter's booth, entering an avenue of bearded ladies and flea circuses. "This is our grand tour – and we the grand tourists; our itinerary is not fixed, though the focus is principally on Europe. There magic wells from deep roots and is long to fade. One day we will travel east to Asia or west to the Americas. But why expend efforts making for distant oases when there is water right at your feet?"

"What about Africa, Australia and South America?" asked Joe, remembering the golden sphere at the waystation.

"Magic is now only in the north with Italy as its centre. We have the Medici to thank for that."

Perhaps that is why it's the staircase, thought Joe as they passed between the Palais de Danse Mystère and the Déjà Rêvé Tea Rooms.

"For me, the turning point was when Rome was gone," said

255

Pandoro wistfully. "Ah, the place where Romulus stood and Caesar fell. Each of its seven hills mined of its beauty and mystery. Such, such a shame. Once the papal city was brimful with potency, but no more. Now it is just as much a circus as my own."

Yes, but aren't you and this entire fayre part of that very problem? Joe thought. Out loud he asked, "What is the magic of Ravnsbrae?"

"It is a sacred eternal flame that burns in buried caves. There are tunnels beneath the manor that descend to it, and those are the easiest ways, but there are others. It is one of only three such fires left in all the world. And before you ask, the others are in Wales and New York."

"What makes them special?"

"They come from the Everlasting Flame. They are the fire that does not die by day or by night. The amaranthine flame that burns in the heart and hearth of every thing in the universe. Aha, here we are."

Circling a steam-powered carousel, the pair arrived at the Bête Noire pavilion. Merry music filled the air, drawing crowds to this place for whatever unknown entertainments waited within. Everyone wore masks, their faces veiled behind several designs.

"Ta-dah!" said Pandoro with a flourish.

There on a candlelit stall Joe saw piles of disguises in five different styles: a handsome knight, a beautiful princess, a moustachioed rogue, a sorcerer in a tall hat and a monkey in a turban. Dimly Joe remembered them and realised he had last seen them worn by D'Ante's guests for the cautionary tales. They were all displayed under a large sign that proclaimed that all guests must: CHOOSE YOUR MASKS.

"As must you," said Pandoro.

Joe looked them over while the ringmaster pointed out the options. "Leading Man, Leading Lady, The Rival, The Mystic and The Fool."

"What's it for?" Joe asked suspiciously.

Pandoro laughed. "When we take up a mask we transform our

yahoo selves into our true selves." Joe reached for the swashbuckling hero, then paused, his eyes strangely drawn to the conical hat of the sorcerer. "Take your time, but *do* hurry," Pandoro urged. Joe reached for the Leading Man, but the harlequin slapped it away. "Here," he said and handed Joe the monkey mask. The boy gave the ringmaster a cold look and tied it around his head.

Suitably attired, Joe and Pandoro entered the darkness of the pavilion.

Within, the audience sat upon tiered benches set out around a space like a gladiatorial arena, and there in the centre grew an ancient oak tree that filled the giant tent to the roof. Beneath its festooned branches stood Madame Lilith's painted caravan and beside that were set various tables and chairs. A celebration of some kind was being held, and in attendance were a colourful cast of characters, including Lasairfhíona in a white lace dress and matching mask.

"Serene!" Joe called and ran into the sawdust-strewn ring. Immediately, a blinding spotlight caught him in its beam and the crowd began applauding. It was as if he were a famous actor taking the stage of the London Palladium. He stopped, suddenly self-conscious, but the young woman had already seen him and her delight swept away his embarrassment. They met under the branches and threw their arms around each other, laughing.

"But you mistake me, foolish Jaxy," Serene said. "I am Madame Lilith, Voice of Prophecy. But remember the mask is just a mask. You must make it alive. The pointy hat does not make the magician."

"I'm beginning to realise that," he said. Out in the crowd people laughed, but Joe ignored them – as he ignored the way his voice appeared to be projected to every ear in the room. He was too overjoyed about seeing the girl again. "You were no more than sixteen when I met you in 1887, and now you're no older. Well, a little, but you should be… forty."

"Today is my eighteenth birthday," Serene said to him, and also to the audience. "Yet a few weeks ago I celebrated my twenty-fourth anniversary with the fayre."

"But you're not aging?"

"Yes, isn't it magical?" she said.

"But how?"

"To understand that you must first understand the fayre's rhyme and reason. We, the travelling players, voyage from site to site, visiting the last magical places on Earth."

"Yes, that's quite and correctly right," announced Pandoro, stepping onto the stage. "The world of yore was filled with miracles, yet to use magic is to use it up. Weave a feather from a winged stallion into your hem and you have a flying coat. Yet there is only one Pegasus and only so many of its wondrous feathers."

Throwing his multicoloured cloak wide, with a great leap the harlequin launched his slight frame into the air. Soaring like an eagle, he flew once around the branches of the tree and landed back at the table to the rapt amazement of the audience.

"The same is true of the world," continued the fortune teller. "Slowly magic fades and in time it will all be gone."

"Eradicated," said Pandoro.

"Forever," said Serene.

"Just look at my story," said Pandoro. "I started as a trick cyclist giving exhibitions at the forum in Londinium. Riding iron-rimmed boneshakers for the amusement of free-born citizens. It was quite a spectacle, not least because the bicycle was not to be invented for another two millennia. As I say, I began in London, but alas, no more. Why, you ask?" He cupped his ear.

"Why?" asked Joe dutifully along with the audience.

"Because, my furry friend, London is all dead now. No magic in it. Not a single scrap. Just pockets out here in the wilds of the world. We drink from magical wells, cook by eternal flames, light our way with enchanted crystals…"

They have crystals? thought Joe.

"Yes," said Serene. "And that magic sustains the fayre and nourishes its players. Like faeries from the enchanted woods, we age more slowly. And the longer we stay, the slower we age. Until finally…"

"We're practically immortal," finished Pandoro.

Like the speed of light, Joe thought. The further you travel the older the world is when you return. The boy looked from the players to the audience, knowing that every word they spoke was true. Knowing also that the onlookers thought it was mere theatre. Once I would have thought so too, he realised.

"Pandoro has been a devoted father to me." Serene continued her act. "He has provided me with a good education, which includes music, singing and classical dancing. He also allows me to develop my own ambitions."

"It is true; but from the first moment I beheld her lucky eyes I knew there was nothing but the stage for her."

Serene bowed low to the audience. "Come, let us start the party."

"But wait!" shouted Pandoro, throwing his arms wide. "There is something I have to do first. And it concerns you, little Jaxy." He pointed an accusing finger at Joe and produced the book of tales from beneath his robes.

"Oh, come now," said Serene. "Surely it can wait until after I've opened my presents?"

"No," said the cloaked figure. "Justice must prevail, for do you not recall the cautionary tale of why you should not wander in the woods?"

Instantly the lighting darkened and the other players stepped forward to enact the play within a play. Pandoro became the narrator, while the leading man transformed into the King of the Faeries, with the Mystic his herald and the Rival an executioner with a comically large double-bladed axe. Joe realised *he* was playing the Fool.

"Now Jaxy was a proper clown
A foolish ape, a kid
Who, despite being told a thousand times
Not to enter the forest, he did.

He went a-chasing bluebirds
And picking bluebells just for a joke
But he did not expect to trespass the court
Of the King of the Faerie Folk."

The leading man stepped forward, followed by his two cohorts, and produced a pair of brass scales. To the boy he seemed to have gained two feet in height, his mask now green and ghastly, his forehead topped with giant antlers. The resemblance to Damfino made Joe shudder.

"You should not have entered my faerie dell," the Faerie King bellowed. "Now my executioner will grind your bones to dust!" The lord's assassin smiled and raised his fearsome blade, while the herald pushed Joe over a tree stump so that his neck was exposed.

There were gasps and shrieks from the audience.

"Should the monkey be slain?" Pandoro beseeched them. "Should he?" Joe cowered, unable to fathom the change in his fortunes. Surely this was just a play. Wasn't it? Luckily on this night, the crowds seemed to be rooting for the dumb ape. Pandoro continued: "Seeing the pitiful creature, the king was moved by a whim – and audience sympathies! – that he would let the creature live… If he'd bring the meaning of life to him.

"To achieve this impossible task
The dim chimp was given one thing

A pair of scales in which to weigh
Both rhyme and reason in..."

Joe was pulled roughly to his feet and the Faerie King thrust the brass scales into his hands.

"And answer the question to life itself! What is the rhyme of reason?" finished the narrator.

"You have thirteen hours!" roared the king.

Suddenly, Serene was at Joe's side, hurrying him into the painted wagon. "Oh, Jaxy, come! Let us start your quest by reading your fortune."

And in a dozen steps they left the mad theatre and applause behind and found themselves alone in the interior of the Voice of Prophecy gypsy caravan. Taking off their masks, they stood for a moment in the candlelit room catching their breath.

"So, what's the answer?" asked Joe.

"What answer?"

"In the play. The answer Jaxy gives to be saved?"

"It's different every time. I think they make it up. He sings a song about what is the rhyme of reason, then gives some hokum, and it all ends with 'For the woods are dangerous, the woods are bad. Don't go wandering off, or you'll wish you never had.'"

"Great. Sounds like a threat. I have to tell you something." The way he said it made the young woman frown.

"What?"

"It's your brother. Gunner. He's... He fell. It was an accident, but he's dead."

Serene was silent. Her eyes were the only part of her that betrayed any emotion at all. "He was a dumb and selfish bully, but I still feel terrible," she said at last. "Guilty too. Because the news makes me feel free. I always had nightmares that he would eventually find me. Joe, we don't have much time. What I said out there was only the half of it. The better half." At once Serene's face was a wreck of sorrow. "Yes, today is my birthday, and I would be forty, but there's more. I have met someone – his name is Ruairí." Joe's heart sank. "He works with the fire-breathing mermaid."

"The what?"

"Never mind that. The point is he's not part of the fayre. He's aging and I am not. We're in love and want to leave, to start a life together away from the circus."

"Why? This place is wonderful."

"I know it seems 'all prizes and no blanks' as they shout on the sideshows, but if I stay not only do I not age, I also cannot conceive. We are both old beyond our years and want to start a family. The only way is to leave – now. Before it is too late."

"Where will you go?" asked Joe, but then he was hit with a sudden blinding thought. Why had he not seen it before?

"Ireland," Serene said simply.

"You're her!" Joe exclaimed. "It was you!"

"What are you talking about?"

"The old witch on the hill."

"What?" The young woman had no idea what he was talking about.

Of course she didn't. How could she? But she would have known *then*. Why didn't she tell him? And then he remembered how he had spoken of falling for the young girl and the wetness in the woman's eyes. That was what she was trying to tell him.

"Forget it," he said, suddenly reddening in embarrassment. He felt like a stupid child. Fumbling for the chain around his neck, he pulled out the bumblebee necklace and offered it back to Serene.

"Here," he growled.

The woman looked puzzled. "Joe? No, you keep it. I gave it to you. Anyhow, it's not gold or precious or anything. I got it ages ago from Woolworths."

The boy's fist closed around the necklace and he stuffed it in his pack. "We have to get out of here. Pandoro, the fayre, this whole thing is using up the magic in the last sacred places. Soon it will all be gone. I've seen where this all leads."

Serene looked doubtful.

"I don't think Pandoro has plans that Ruairí and I will leave the travelling fayre. And now after that monkey scene, I think that includes you too."

"So we're prisoners?"

"No, not prisoners. It's just the reasons for staying are incredibly persuasive."

"You mean because if you leave you'd instantly be an old woman."

"Forty's not old," she said.

"Still," Joe agreed, "very persuasive."

"Ruairí and I have to work out our own fortune, but I think it is time for me to return a favour. One time you helped me join this strange and magical circus. Now I'm gonna help you escape it."

"You have a plan?"

"Yes, we'll make our getaway in the elaborate magical transformation scene during the Harlequinade."

"When's that?"

"It's the part of the pantomime when the eloping lovers are pursued by the girl's father and his comic servant."

"How appropriate," Joe said a little too bitterly.

"My life as commedia dell'arte," she said and smiled.

"Perhaps I have a better idea," Joe said. "I need to get back into the manor and locate the oracle. If you can help me, I can get us all to the Hall of Mirrors. And from there you can get practically everywhere."

"Awesome sauce," she said quietly and hugged Joe tightly. And so it was agreed.

THE FAYRE CLOSED FOR THE night just as the storm broke over the North Sea. There was no rain, just a roiling thunder filled with ripples of silver sparks that turned the dark back to day. Serene and Joe slipped away from the supper tent and made their way back to the creepy cliff-top mansion. They found an unlocked door in the base of the tower topped by its great black spire. Retracing his steps, the boy led Serene into the passage between the walls and out through the cupboard to the room where seven-year-old Seathan Macpherson had died.

The girl lit the gas lamps and candles and looked around the oppressive bedchamber, with its black woodwork, carved panelling and emerald fabric walls. She crossed to the bed and inspected the open book.

"*Beauty and the Beast*," she said. "Left just at this page."

"Obviously he never finished it."

"Do you know how he died?" she asked.

"Not a clue, but just being locked in this room would be enough to finish me off. Let's get searching."

"What are we looking for?"

"The oracle is something called a planchette." He showed Serene the image from the guide. The sketch pictured a wooden heart with a circular window in its centre.

"Right," she said and they began combing the bedroom. It did not take long. Apart from the child's books, stuffed toys, skittles and picture blocks, the room was empty. Even the wardrobe and cupboards held nothing except a few clothes and pairs of shoes. To Joe, everything looked as if it belonged in a Chamber of Horrors, especially the corner with the low chair, its back carved into a black cross. Upon its embroidered seat stood a school bell, a candlestick and a copy of the Bible. The boy imagined a priest leaving them here after fleeing for his life.

Serene let out a grunt of triumph and pulled something from

behind the wardrobe. "It's a Ouija board," she said, holding it out to Joe. "You use it to contact the dead."

"Great," Joe mumbled, turning it in his hands. On the front were all the letters of the alphabet, the single-digit numbers and the words 'Yes' and 'No' at the top, and 'Good Bye' at the bottom. Fortuitously, on the reverse were instructions as to how everything worked. "Place the board upon the knees of two persons, lady and gentleman preferred," he read. "Place the planchette in the centre of the board, resting fingers lightly upon it. A question may be asked, and the spirit's message is indicated in the planchette's window."

But where was the planchette?

Continuing their search, it took another ten minutes to locate Seathan's secret stash.

In the cupboard with the door into the walls, the fayre's fortune teller found a false panel and hidden beneath were the dead boy's most treasured possessions. There was a much-loved copy of Beatrix Potter's *The Tale of Tom Kitten*, a rather sinister statuette of an eagle-faced idol and a wooden box. Lifting these out, Joe tried the lid, but it was locked. Beneath it was the heart-shaped planchette.

"Give that here," said Serene, and sitting on the bed, the boy and girl followed the instructions.

Joe asked the first question. "Is anybody there?" Nothing happened.

He tried again, then Serene asked, "Is Seathan there?" but still nothing happened. Just the silence and shadows.

Shadows? thought Joe. What was it Pandoro had said about shadows? It was about the Dark Rides, the haunted acts…

"I can use the shadowstone," he said and pulled the talisman from within his shirt. "I command the spirit of Seathan Macpherson. We are in dire need. Can you hear me?"

With a sudden sharp tug the planchette skidded to 'Yes' on the board.

"It's working," said Serene. "Is this Seathan?"

I prefer Jack, the board spelled out.

"Jack it is, then."

Joe began to hear something over the sound of the storm and sea. It was very quiet and it took a while before he realised it was the sound of a woman sobbing. The shadowstone was showing him another vision. There on the tartan throne sat a woman in a black robe, her head in her hands. Joe guessed this was the child's grieving mother. Someone else who had died in this room? Weeping over her lost son? Then Joe could see other spirits. Many, many spirits. The boy saw Jack lying upon the bed beneath a thick black shroud. There was also a priest blessing the room – the owner of the bell, book and candle that now sat on the chair. Had he too died? Beside him was a Viking warrior, and in his hand he held the Everlasting Flame, the magic source from which the house drew its chaotic power.

Then there were two other figures in the vision, but these were not spirits. One was a white-haired man in a grey suit and thick tie, the other was younger in a bowler hat. They were setting up a cumbersome camera on a tripod while the last light of some distant or future day bled through the shredded lace in the windows. The room was empty now, abandoned and derelict, the carpet and furniture gone. On the floorboards a red circle filled with arcane symbols had been painted, and around its edge stood the stubs of burned-out candles.

"Well, ain't this a terrible tableau?" said the younger man in a thick American accent. "Two men, a circle protecting from a Babylonian wind demon, all here in this black Scottish vault." He glanced at the rapidly fading sunlight. "Ah, apple sauce! The sun's setting. We gotta hurry."

"Time has no meaning in a place of death," said the older man. His voice was husky and deliberate.

"That may be so for you, Mr Kane," his nervous companion

replied, "but try telling that to a Kodak Junior. We need light."

"True, son – I forget myself. Swiftly then. We need to document this awful…" The man named Kane turned and looked right at Joe and stiffened in terror. "Who?" he managed.

"What?" said the younger man.

"There," said Kane and pointed right at the boy.

Focus, Joe, focus! Using all his concentration, his vision slurred back to the present, filled as it was with the spirits of the dead that the eternal fire drew moth-like to its flame.

"How must I open the door to the labyrinth?" he asked Jack. "What must be done?"

The ghostly boy sat up from his eternal slumber on the embroidered counterpane and pointed to a painting on the wall. It was a hand-drawn pastel of three figures flying above a pirate ship in an island bay. Joe recognised them as Peter Pan, Wendy and Tinkerbell. In the drawing Peter held out his hand, beckoning the viewer into the painting. Joe stood and went towards the picture, but Serene pulled him back. "Wait," she said. "Perhaps the spirit can answer the Jaxy question."

Of course. Why hadn't he thought of that?

"What," he asked the empty shadows, "is the travelling fayre's rhyme and reason?" For the first time the question initiated no response. The planchette did not move a whisker. Joe asked the question again, but still nothing.

"Why isn't it moving?" said the girl.

"Perhaps Jack doesn't know. Or isn't telling," said Joe. "We don't have time for this, Serene. We have to go."

He lifted the board onto the bed and stood up. He was halfway to the painting when he noticed the dark shape seated on the carved throne.

"Going somewhere, my loves?" said Pandoro from the shadows.

"Well," the ringmaster indicated the room with his goat-headed cane, "how ravishingly crepuscular." Joe and Serene flinched back. "Don't make me use the gigglestick, boy."

At his back, Joe felt Ilkilæmber's battle anger rise. "I don't want to fight you," he said, raising the bear-headed staff.

Yes, we do, said the sword.

"Joe," warned Serene. "Be careful."

The master of the fayre stood up and his feathered cloak fell about his frame. "Well, this is what you get when you trespass into this night-shadowed land. When you start opening doors to danger."

"Why are you here, ringmaster?" Serene asked.

"It's been thirteen hours and I need an answer. Joe?"

Joe stared up into the man's beatific eyes. "What?" he said softly.

"What is the answer to the question of life itself? What—" he opened his arms wide "—is the rhyme of reason?"

"I... I..." said Joe.

"Speak up, boy. We all wish to know. Answer me and you walk free. The gypsy girl too if she wants to go. Her *and* her lover. I am not an evil man. Indeed, I am quite fair. It all rests with you."

The tension between the two was palpable and combat seemed almost inevitable.

I am your defender, said Arthiæ.

"I will not fight you!" said Joe, fiercely.

Snarling, the boy stuck out his free left hand and grabbed at the painting. It was almost no surprise when the hand in the drawing met and clasped his. As Joe and Peter Pan's fingers touched, the gap between the bedroom door and its frame shone argent.

Every door has a silver lining, Joe thought, then drew back and grabbed Serene's hand. "Come on!" he shouted. "Let's go!"

Stepping to the door, he threw it open and where once had been the hastily built wall, now the palazzo hallway lay beyond. The two ran for the doorway but at the threshold they found they could not pass. Some force or spell held them back.

"Joe? What's happening?" said Serene.

"I… I don't know," he confessed.

Pandoro laughed, genuinely amused. "You, boy, are duty-bound to the travelling fayre. Your service binds you. You cannot leave. And my little fortune teller won't, else she will age quick as an autumn leaf."

At these words, Serene screamed in frustration and Joe turned to see Pandoro clutching her by the throat.

"Leave her alone," Joe spat and lashed out with the staff. It cracked the harlequin's knuckles, allowing the girl to slip from his grasp, but in such a small chamber there was nowhere for her to go. Pandoro raised one gloved hand and pointed a menacing finger at the boy, but Serene leapt onto his back and started pounding him in wild rage. She succeeded only in dragging the cloak from his shoulders, which the ringmaster sloughed off like a second skin. With a lunge of his own cane, Pandoro knocked the staff from the boy's hands. Unable to retrieve it, Joe drew Ilkilæmber and held the leaf blade before him.

By tooth and claw, said the sword. *I am hungry still.*

A sudden gust of wind extinguished every candle in the room. Even the gaslights guttered almost into nothingness. Joe and Pandoro turned to see Serene at the window. She had thrown both panes wide and squatted on the narrow ledge, wrapped in the parti-coloured cloak. Outside the storm raged while from below came the savage sound of the ocean crashing against the rocks.

"Serene!" Joe gasped.

"My angel, my sweet!" Pandoro exclaimed.

"I'm not going back," Serene said coldly. "You don't own me. Nobody owns me."

With not even a final glance, Serene leapt from the window. For a moment her dark form was silhouetted against the lightning, then she was gone, falling out of sight like a stone. Both man and boy sprang to the window, peering out and down the precipitous cliff face. Far below, Serene's tiny shape soared in the flying cloak, arcing over the ocean and out to sea.

And that was the last Joe ever saw of her, sailing off into the blackness above the rippling glitter of the dark ocean.

X

TENTH MOON: HONEY MOON (OF MAN)
EISH AL KAMAR
ALHAMBRA, GRANADA, SPAIN
SATURDAY 16 JULY 1977 | 18:56:01

PANDORO'S TRAVELLING FAYRE DEPARTED FROM beneath the macabre shadow of Ravnsbrae Manor with all the flamboyance, pageantry and chaos Joe would have expected of a circus leaving town. He watched wide-eyed as the marquees and sideshows were dismantled and efficiently packed, stashed and bundled upon a variety of conveyances. He had to admit to being a little disappointed that the ringmaster did not wave a magic wand and zip the entire spectacular freak show into a commonplace carpet bag. Yet it could not be doubted that the sight of the fayre wending its way from Aberdeen to Liverpool, before being stowed aboard the Booth Steamship Company's SS *Hildebrand*, was a sight to behold. Joe felt detached from the entire affair, a stranger both to the people and this century. While the Edwardian passengers were dazzled by such ocean-going luxury, all Joe could think of was Leonardo DiCaprio in *Titanic*.

During the voyage – and ultimately for the entire journey that followed – Joe kept his head down, slavishly observing Rule #3: Be Invisible, and Rule #4: Don't Make Friends. He kept calling to mind Serene's hate-filled face and then her leap to freedom from the bedchamber window. The feelings that accompanied these thoughts were a strange mixture of rejection and envy. Joe's memories of his former self seemed impossibly distant, almost as if they had happened to a completely different person.

Of course, Joe knew from the book the fayre's final destination. They were heading for the ancient kingdom of Granada and ultimately to its Moorish citadel and palace. The Alhambra was described in the guide with wonder as a ninth-century Arabian fortress, where an American author called Washington Irving had stayed as far back as 1829. The room Joe had to locate was the Moon's Nest, in Arabic a squiggle that when transcribed became 'Eish Al Kamar'. It was another bedchamber, this time situated in the Court of the Myrtles at the heart of the Casa Real Vieja. The guide's author had travelled to the Alhambra through the Palazzo di Ombre, arriving on a balmy evening in July 1977. That was more than sixty years into the future, and left Joe wondering if the room would even exist in this time and place.

A few days later the ship arrived at the port city of Vigo in northern Spain. From here the fayre travelled by train along the West Galicia Railway on a sweltering journey to the city of Santiago de Compostela. Here Pandoro's phantasmagoria began its tour, reconstructing its multicoloured attraction for the edification and delight of the locals and tourists. On a route that took them to Salamanca, Toledo and Seville, the fayre enchanted everyone from kings to commoners, but such squandering of precious magic sickened Joe, especially now he was acutely aware of the cost and conclusion of such extravagance.

Joe was forced to work with a strange band of itinerants who ran the beer and entertainment pavilions. Led by the iron but fair Madame Shazza (Miracle Cures & Hexes) and her husband, Christo (the Original German Clown), the rag-tag group called themselves the Family Zingari, though the boy could not imagine for a moment that they were all actually related.

Over the coming months, the travelling fayre became their lives as the troupe moved through the provinces of Galicia, León, La Mancha and Andalusia. Through indescribably silent mountains and boundless sandy wastelands, the fayre wound its way from north to south. Most days there were just the gilded carriages and wagons, and the deep blue, endless sky. The boy rued every day of this journey as time utterly wasted. Any free moments were spent trying to solve the puzzle that bound him to Pandoro and his stupid circus. If he had his way, he would have crushed the fayre and Pandoro and everything in it into the Spanish dust. That said, Joe did not view the ringmaster and his fellows as wicked or evil, more misguided. By its very nature, the circus had to run on magic, just as a car ran on petrol. Both needed fuel and, in the case of the travelling fayre, there was only one way to get it. Still, Joe was consumed with the desire to break free of the binding spell that kept him within the fayre's bounds. He just had to get away and start the task of saving the house. He had faced and defeated Damfino, and soon, he knew, he would have to face the Vandal King's masters.

He had to face his parents.

The travelling fayre arrived at the gates of the Alhambra under the pink skies on the night of the September full moon. The ancient citadel stood atop the highest hills of the city of Granada. While the main troupe piled into lodgings on the Vivarrambla Square, Pandoro, Garivinda, Lady Lindini, Joe and a few of the other noteworthy performers were met and escorted by a pair of uniformed guards to the palace. The elder of the two was dour, moustachioed and named

Gonzalo, the other the young and dark-haired Alejandro. The guards guided them through the Great Bazaar, along a deep ravine and up the winding street towards the looming fortress. Joe let the others pace ahead, lingering at the back along with Alejandro, who brought up the rear of the small group. The climb was steep, but finally they emerged onto the crest of the hill. In the last of the day's sunlight the citadel shone a deep gold against the lush woodland surrounding it.

"The Alhambra is a beauty rare," the younger guard said to Joe in a rough-accented English. "The poets called it 'a pearl set in emeralds'."

From the edge of the plateau, Joe marvelled at the expanse of ragged roofs that made up the Moorish city, while above rose the hazy forms of impressive mountains.

"Those are the Sierra Nevada," Alejandro explained. "And this is the Alcazába, the archaic citadel of Al-Hamar Muhammad One. To enter we go here, through the Puerta Judiciaria – the Gate of Justice."

"Impressive," said Garivinda, the Great Swami Hypnotist.

"Gargantuan," said Lady Lindini, the World's Smallest Giant.

The entrance to the alcazar was a massive horseshoe arch, easily half the height of the tall square tower that held it. At the gate Pandoro was being introduced to a bespectacled old woman in a multicoloured wrap who the guard said was Luna Izquierdo, custodian of the Alhambra. The pair were exchanging pleasantries, then Pandoro bowed extravagantly and said, "Yes, yes, and thrice yes! We will humbly accept your generous offer to stay within this palace. We are here for a month – by far our longest engagement – and straight after we are to travel to Austria, Switzerland, then over to the fabled Sacro Monte in Italy."

I don't want to go back to Italy, thought Joe bitterly. I just left there.

The woman mumbled something back, then made a small bow and indicated that the company of performers should enter.

The unremarkable exterior masked within a magnificent courtyard stuffed to overflowing with roses, orange trees and fountains. Crossing the gardens, the company entered the main palace and were led through a series of ever more impressive chambers, marble galleries, tiled summer rooms and columned courtyards. Every floor, wall and ceiling was coloured in rich blues and reds, and accented with golden yellow. Everyone cooed in admiration, and while Joe was grudgingly impressed, all his attention was focused on locating the Moon's Nest. His patience was rewarded when they emerged from another fabulously carved hall into a simpler open courtyard. In the centre of the walled space was a large pool set in the marble pavement and surrounded by rose hedges. In its waters Joe saw great numbers of golden fish, their scales gleaming even in the dusky light.

"This is Patio de la Alberca," announced Alejandro. "Court of the Pond. It is part of the Comares Palace and this name means: 'Open your eyes and see.' Here you will all stay as guests of the marquis." Joe said nothing, already too busy looking for a clue to the whereabouts of the bedchamber. A photograph of this courtyard was in *The Stranger's Guide*, so it must be close. "You not like?" the guard questioned the sullen boy.

"What? No... Yes. It's..."

And then he saw it. The door to the Moon's Nest. It could be no other. As Pandoro and the others fussed over the staterooms at the head of the courtyard, Joe crossed to an open door in the far corner. This led to a short corridor, at the end of which was a deep-blue door inset with stained glass in the shape of a crescent moon. He felt Alejandro at his back, urging him to rejoin the company.

"Master, this empty room is small and merits no attention. We have—"

"I'll take it," Joe said, far more loudly than he intended. In the enclosed space his voice rang in echoes. Everyone stopped what they were doing and stared at him. "If it's so small, I mean." He tried to cover his enthusiasm with what he hoped sounded like a willingness to please.

"Jaxy, I really think…" started Pandoro, smelling a rat.

"Ah, but perhaps the little prince has good taste," said their benevolent host. "This is Eish Al Kamar, a room long used by dreamers and their dreamings."

"But, he—" started the ringmaster.

"Will find it most comfortable," finished the marquis' assistant. And that was that.

Within the room the air was tinged with the scent of oranges and a deeper, heavier perfume Joe did not recognise. Exhausted by the day's journeying, including the long trek up and through the Moorish palace, he wanted nothing more than to rest. Throwing himself on a wide brass bed that took up almost a third of the room, the dusty boy sprawled on his back, kicked off his shoes and let out a slow breath. Only then did he survey the room more thoroughly.

It was, on the face of it, a simple bedroom – small, white and with diamonds of amber tiles on the floor. The only embellishment to its bare plaster walls and wooden ceiling were two intricate starred panels of blue tiles. Outside the window sat a roof garden centred by a giant stone bowl from which a fountain bubbled. The chuckling of the water drifted in through the windows, along with the sounds of creatures and the scent of lavender and rosemary.

Joe pulled out his map and by the light of the oil lamps began to add this room to the others. Unable to spell the Arabic original, as before he chose his own nickname. 'The Room of Dreams' he added in capital letters below the sketch. The next location was an office in New York, but how he was going to get there was an even bigger mystery.

There was a knock at the door, breaking Joe from his concentration. It was Alejandro, checking all was to his satisfaction.

"Everything's more than fine," Joe said. "It's great to have a room that's not on wheels."

The young guard smiled and was about to go when he looked past the boy, out into the night.

"Ah," he said and crawled up onto the bed. "You have arrived at auspicious times." Joe looked out and saw the moon rising above the mountains. It appeared as a great disc of dark silvery gold, far larger than he ever remembered. "This is the full moon of honey. And there is the place where this room gets its name. The image on the door. Eish Al Kamar. The moon's nest." As they watched the moon ascended until it crested the mountain's inky silhouette. There it rested, an ivory egg cradled in a dark nest.

Joe looked from the window to Alejandro, his face full of wonder.

"I know," the young man said. "Sleep well. If Allah wills."

Then he bowed and left.

Looking back to the pale moon, Joe was filled with a sudden sense of overwhelming loneliness. It felt like being lost in a fearsome forest or adrift on an endless ocean. Unbidden, Serene's face drifted into his mind, and that brought a different sense of loneliness and loss. Fumbling in his pack he pulled out her golden bumblebee necklace and held it in his hands.

"I miss you, Serene," he whispered, then blew out the lanterns and sprawled back on the moon-washed bed. Joe relaxed. His face sank into the feather pillows, his tired limbs curled upon the crisp cotton sheets. In minutes he was asleep.

LESS THAN A SINGLE MOMENT seemed to pass between the closing and opening of his eyelids, but in that time the entire bedchamber was transformed. Gone were the oil lanterns and bare walls. Now forged sconces shone harsh electric light, illuminating an eclectic collection of artefacts that crowded every available surface. They looked as if they came from every region around the globe, ranging from African masks, Mexican statues, Egyptian swords and Indian idols to Asian stonework, Native Indian arrowheads, pouches and even an entire feathered headdress. The bed was newly made and sat beneath a canopy of mosquito netting. A wardrobe and chest of drawers had also somehow miraculously appeared, as had a small bench upon which a thin, dark-haired woman sat watching him.

Seeing her, Joe sat bolt upright at once, totally awake. "Where am I? What are you doing here? How—?" Joe stopped, realising that the woman did not seem shocked or surprised to find a teenager in her bedroom.

"So, from where are you coming into my room?" the woman said slowly. Despite her slight form and advancing years, the woman's gaze was fierce and calmly self-assured. She reminded Joe of the way his school teacher addressed her class. It was clear some transition had been made, but it was the full not the dark of the moon. How had that happened? He tried to look out of the window, but now the shutters were closed and no moon was visible.

"I don't know how I got here. Is this the Room of Dreams?" When the woman did not respond to that, Joe added, "Is this the Alhambra? The Patio de la…" he couldn't recall the Spanish name. "The Court of the Pond?"

"Yes, but it is called the Court of Myrtles now."

"And when is 'now'?"

"It is Saturday. Just coming up to seven o'clock."

Joe asked again. "No, I mean the date. And…" he hesitated, "…the year."

The woman looked surprised by the question, but answered, "It is 16 July 1977. Who are you?"

"I'm Joe."

"And I am Lìa Josefina." Her voice sounded vaguely foreign, but the boy had no idea of its origins. With her long dark hair and olive skin, Lìa looked Spanish, but could just as easily have been from anywhere in Europe, or even Asia. "I am a travel writer, and for these past weeks a guest of the Alhambra palace."

Then Joe noticed that in her hand she held Serene's precious gift. At once he leapt off the bed shouting, "Hey, that's mine! Give it back!"

Surprised, the journalist sat back on her seat, looking at the golden necklace in her hand. "I am sorry. I found it here in this room when I arrived. It was hanging on the wall…" She held it out for Joe. "I was not going to take it. I meant no harm."

The boy reached forward for the pendant, but his fingers passed straight through Lìa's hand. Wide-eyed he tried again. It was no use. He was as solid as a ghost.

"What is happening?" he wailed.

Lìa regarded him sympathetically. "Can you not touch anything?" she asked. Joe walked to the chest of drawers atop which stood several statues, a crystal ball on a stand and a blue book. Its title was etched in gold above an ornate illustration. The book was *Crusader Castles* by T. E. Lawrence.

The writer stood at his back watching him.

"This is my guide," she said. "I am on an expedition that retraces Lawrence's journey visiting important castle strongholds, from England all the way to the Holy Land. He is the man who became Lawrence of Arabia. Can you not touch this also?" Joe tried, but again his fingers could not grasp the volume. Lìa reached out to Joe's arm and found it as insubstantial as a raincloud.

The woman and boy stood staring at each other for a while, not sure what to say or do. "I think I'm dreaming," Lìa said at last.

"Of course. It is the Room of Dreams, after all."

"So you say."

"I think this has something to do with the necklace. It was given to me by a… friend. I was holding it when I fell asleep." But, he asked himself, if that were the case, how did Serene's necklace come to be in 1977?

"I think I am dreaming you," said the woman.

"What?"

"I had an aunt when I was young who taught me the scrying art. She called it her 'orbuculum', which I felt was wonderfully mysterious. Many know of the crystal ball's ability to reveal distant places, but she was a clairsentient, not a clairvoyant."

"What are they?"

"One is clear seeing, the other clear sensing," Lìa explained. "I never believed I had inherited that gift, but I found this crystal ball here in this room, and these past days when I gazed into it, the glass misted. I meditate and slip into sleep – and then I see people and places far off and long ago." It's not you that's magical, thought Joe, it's the room. But he said nothing. "Through trial and error, I found that different objects show different times and places. Today I chose this necklace, and here you are."

"Well, I can tell you, I'm real. Not a dream. And right now I am standing in this very room. Just in 1911."

"So the necklace links to the same place but a different time," said the woman, frowning. "That is new."

"Where else have you been?"

The travel writer stood up and turned to face the objects upon the tiled wall. She pointed at each one in turn as she spoke. "The wooden carving of the archer and the monkey took me to somewhere in Asia. There was a temple in the treetops and a bearded hulk of a man who spoke only Russian. I think it was Russian. I do not know that language. I suppose it could've been anywhere in the Eastern Bloc. And this." She indicated a cow's horn hanging from the wall light. "This conjured the image of a Viking warrior. He was very scary."

"So what do you think is happening?" Joe asked.

"I believe that the crystal ball is a vehicle for channelling dreams, and through each object in this room I can travel spiritually anywhere."

"Dreams that we are aware of dreaming."

"Yes, very much so, but dreams nonetheless."

Joe wasn't so sure. The crystal ball was this room's oracle, but it wasn't in the bedroom of 1911. Even so, perhaps there was a way he could still use it, either to reach the next location in the labyrinth or – and his heart leapt at the thought – to escape the travelling fayre.

"It's time to wake up now, Joseph Elijah Darkin," a voice behind him said. Joe turned and found the snowy owl was perched within the arch of the open window.

"You?" Joe spluttered. "Again? How did you get here?"

"Boy?" the woman was saying. "What is it? What do you see?" It was clear the bird was not in Lìa's dream.

The owl swivelled its head almost completely around. "Your vision will become clear only when you look into your heart. Who looks outside, dreams. Who looks inside, awakens."

"Who do you belong to? The White King or the White Queen?"

"I am a creature of the dream world. My doors are windows. You know that."

"What is the rhyme of reason?" said Joe coldly. Then turning to the journalist, he repeated the question. "Do you know?"

"What? No, I have no idea."

"Then I am trapped until you do."

"Wake up, Joe! Wake up!"

Unseen hands were shaking the boy, and as the owl took wing and disappeared into the night – and Lìa and the future bedroom splintered into fragments – he burst up from his dreaming, out of the infinite waters of the night and into the golden brightness of a new day. Alejandro, a concerned look on his face, stood over Joe as he thrashed into wakefulness. The covers and pillows were everywhere, and the boy's arms were wrapped in the twisted sheets. Seeing this, Joe stopped struggling. With a growing sense of embarrassment, he watched as Alejandro helped free him.

"Bad dreams?" asked the young guard.

"Yeah. I guess."

"I am asked that you come to eat. Breakfast."

"I'll be right there."

After Alejandro had left the room, Joe got up and went to get dressed, only to find he had fallen asleep fully clothed. He found the bumblebee necklace buried in the bedding and set it upon the bedside table. The oddest thing the boy realised about his night-time travelling was how it felt to wake up. When rousing from a normal dream it was instantly obvious that all that had gone before was just imagination. Awakening from his meeting with Lìa Josefina, it didn't feel like this at all. It felt very, very real.

Tonight, he vowed, he would attempt to travel himself.

THE FOLLOWING DAY WAS A long and curious mix of touring the terrestrial paradise of the Casa Real, residence of the Moorish kings, and working at the circus, dressed as Jaxy the monkey and surrounded by clowns. The fortress was almost a little world in itself, having streets and houses, a convent and a church. Small doors often led to ever larger and more exquisite rooms, until Joe was sure he could never find his way back to his bedroom. As ever, Alejandro was his guide, though it became increasingly obvious that the young guard had been given the task of watching over his every move. Still, Joe liked the young man's company, and even if he was under constant surveillance, at least he wasn't leaping out of thin air for the hundredth time at the command of Marco the Psychic Monkey-Juggler.

The two wandered, eventually finding themselves within the clipped hedges and water gardens of the Palacio de Generalife. From its walls the main citadel could be viewed in its entirety. While the city below scorched in the noontide heat, here was cooled by the mountain breeze, and the tall arches and arbours softened the sun's powerful blaze. Way down below the flags and turrets of Pandoro's big top, tents and sideshows crowded the square at the base of the fortress. Guests strolled here: ladies with parasols and gentlemen in suits, each taking in the glory of the gardens.

"It is strange to imagine," Alejandro was saying, "but not long years distant the Alhambra was deserted by the Spaniard kings and all this was in ruins."

"Seems impossible. Why was it saved?"

"Because below, in the deepest places of the fortress, are Roman tombs, and beneath that caves and hollows from times beyond human imagining. It is said there are the Alhambra's treasures."

And, no doubt, the source of its magic, thought Joe.

"This garden was built during the reign of Muhammad Three and the summer palace also contains—"

"Wait! Don't tell me. Even *more* elegance and grandeur?"

"What is it, Monkey Joe? Does the Alhambra leave you unhappy?"

"You could say that," the boy replied absently, not even hearing the sly nickname. More and more it felt as if the waking world were now the dream, and vice versa. "I feel like a ghost in this place."

"Is that," said a loud American voice just behind them, "why you cast no shadow?" Both Joe and the guard turned and found themselves being addressed by a slim, middle-aged man with slicked-down hair. Upon his arm was a beautiful young woman that the boy hoped was his daughter.

"You are in the circus, aren't you?" she asked, smiling.

"He's none other than Jaxy the ape!" said the man. "From the cautionary tales."

"Such a fun show," she replied. "But it still does not explain the shadow."

"Or lack of it," added the man.

"It's a magic trick," mumbled Joe, wanting to be away from this pair's questions. "The travelling fayre is full of the unexplainable." He just wanted the day to be over so he could return to the bedchamber.

"I'm an impresario myself. Name's Thanhouser. Let's shake!" Joe and the man shook hands. "This is Miss Snow. That Pandoro is some showman."

"Yeah," Joe replied. "He'd be odds-on favourite at the Oscars." The man and woman gave Joe blank looks. "Best Over-Actor Award? The movies? It isn't as funny when you have to explain it."

Thanhouser and Miss Snow beamed. "Now, *movies* are something we know all about."

"You make motion pictures?" asked Alejandro.

"Indeed we do," said Thanhouser, taking the woman's arm and continuing their stroll through the water gardens. "I've a fine studio in New York City."

Joe's interest pricked at that, but they were already almost through the next rose-covered archway. "Well, if you need a magical circus, you know where to find one," he called after them as they went.

It was almost evening when Joe and Alejandro completed their tour of the summer palace and returned to the boy's room. Pandoro and other members of the fayre were dispersed enjoying the luxuries of the Alhambra, allowing Joe to slip unseen into his bedchamber. He found Tarrow waiting for him upon the lip of the fountain bowl.

"I thought this day would never end," Joe admitted, crossing to the bed and laying his head upon the pillow.

"Time to dream," the bird said. Again, Joe felt his eyelids grow heavy, close, then open in the other version of the bedroom. All was as before except now he was alone.

"Which item do you choose?" said Tarrow.

"I need to answer the riddle of rhyme and reason."

"That is nothing," said the owl dismissively. "Now concentrate on the question at hand."

"You're no better than that stupid raven," mumbled Joe, which seemed to ruffle the owl's feathers a good deal.

"The answer to every question you will ever ask is known to you," Tarrow instructed, now sounding more like Griswald than ever. "It is tempting to think that the real world and the world of dreams are totally separate. That it is replaced by some kind of imaginary replica. That is not the case. The object you touch in Eish Al Kamar, the one that sparkles the brightest and draws you the most, that is the place you will go in your dreams."

"That's stupid," said Joe indignantly.

"Imagination is the lock," spelled out the bird. "Belief is the key. All you have to do is believe enough to try it." The words surprised Joe. They were from the prologue of Pandoro's *Cautionary Tales*.

"I need to go to New York," said Joe, looking around the room. "What object is from there?"

"Forget all that. What object are you drawn to?"

Joe looked around the walls at all the multifarious things. There was a fencing mask, a copper jug and a leather quiver full with feathered arrows. Yet his eyes kept returning to two small stone statues that flanked the blue door into the room. One was black and represented an eagle, the other was the colour of desert sand with the head of a dog.

"I see you've made your choice," said the owl. "Or at least you will have when you choose between the bird and the beast."

"They're Egyptian, right?" asked Joe.

"Correctly spoken. Horus is the falcon god of the Overworld. Anubis the jackal lord of the Underworld."

"Oh, then I choose Horus," the boy blurted, even though his eyes were ever drawn to the other statue.

"The worst lies are the ones to ourselves," said Tarrow. "He might be of funerals, death and the dead, but there is no evil in such things."

"Anubis," Joe said.

"Reach down, boy. It's time."

So Joe did as he was commanded and, kneeling, he brushed the stone figurine of the dark god with his transparent fingers. Returning to the brass bed, he climbed onto its mattress and settled down to sleep. The sheets were silken, the night cool, and from somewhere distant came the sound of mournful music, which poured tiredness over him. Sinking into the mattress's softness, he almost floated towards sleep, as sand flowed through his outstretched fingers.

Sand?

Joe sat up with a start.

He was no longer in the tiled bedroom. Now guttering torchlight illuminated a stone chamber, its walls covered with hieroglyphics and paintings of pharaohs sitting on golden boats while jaguars and snakes attended them. In the walls were many openings. In these stood painted jars. At the far end of the massive hall the roof curved around a colossal version of the jackal god. Easily three metres tall, the Anubis statue dominated the room, its massive arms held forth and grasping a long staff and a set of scales. At the foot of the imposing stone beast stood two figures, both of whom Joe was surprised to see he recognised.

One was a white-haired man in a khaki suit and spats, the other was younger in a bowler hat. They were fussing over a series of maps and charts from various volumes. The pair were the men he had seen with the camera in Seathan Macpherson's bedroom.

"This is a terrible tableau," said Joe. "Two men, a god of death and an Egyptian tomb."

Both men cried out, dropping their papers in panic.

"Hot nuts, kid!" the younger man said. "You scared me shirtless." Stooping, he began collecting the fallen books and documents.

The older man muttered an oath, took off his hat and wiped his forehead. Regarding Joe with tired eyes, he addressed the boy. "How did you...? No, wait, you're the ghost of the dead child at Ravnsbrae Manor we saw all those years ago. Did you follow to haunt us here, spirit?"

"I'm no ghost." Joe held up the granite statue of Anubis in his hand. "This statue came from this place, I think. It's like I'm dreaming myself here."

"That's some trick."

"My name is Joe. And I think I need your help."

The older man walked over to where the boy stood and stuck out his hand. "I am Antony R. Kane. Criminal, esoteric and occult investigations at your service." He watched as Joe's fingers passed through his own. "So, no apparition, eh?"

"I'm in Spain in 1911."

The younger man shuffled over, obviously more suspicious than his boss. Seeing him approach, Kane introduced him as William B. Bastiani.

"Folks call me Billy," the younger man growled.

"Don't mind him," the investigator said. "He's Italian."

Joe smirked. Billy frowned.

"Now, boys," Kane said, "don't go all hard-boiled on me. We have much work, the hour is late and we are trapped in a cursèd tomb."

"Trapped?" asked Joe.

"Oh yeah," said Billy. "Like birds in a cage. And the whole kit and caboodle reeks a ghoulish stench." Joe could smell nothing. Apparently aroma was not part of his dreaming experience.

"Where are you?" Joe asked. "And when?"

"Why, in Egypt, son. Beneath the desert sands of Saqqara. This hidden tomb is part of a funeral catacomb for ancient Memphis. And as to the date, it is early February, 1928."

"Yeah, swell. That's all fine and dandy," said Billy. "But isn't anyone curious as to who this kid is and why he just popped up here?"

"Perhaps it's a rare and potent aspect of my psychometry," said Kane.

"What's... psychometry?" asked Joe.

The investigator raised his hand in a flourish. "Aha, and well you would do to ask. It is a form of extrasensory perception, a gift like a mental telescope that may pierce the veil of an object's spirit to reveal the grand or tragic events of its distant past."

"It's reading stuff like you'd read books," Billy simplified.

"And now *seeing* stuff too, evidently," Kane added.

"Still," argued Bastiani. "This big shot was at the creepy manor. Now he's here. That's some fluke."

"Absolutely," said Kane. "Well, Joe?"

"It's no coincidence. All this is connected somehow. Are you searching for thirteen doors?" It was a wild shot in the dark, but as soon as he said it, both men's eyes widened like saucers.

"Holy moly!" said his shocked apprentice.

"Well, publish and be damned," said the investigator. Suddenly Antony Kane became super-animated, his excitement plain and palpable in the painted room. "Yes, yes, and thrice yes! Indeed we are. I found the first door in New York and took it for my office. Then, while I was employed to solve the mysterious haunting at Ravnsbrae, I found the second. My object reading and the ghost – *you!* – spurred me further on this quest. It is a crusade that has obsessed me for nigh on a decade. At the Scottish house I confirmed that the manor was just one of many ancient locations. This trail contains tomes of ancient law, seals of power and a malevolent evil stretching back untold centuries." He produced a pendant on a long, thick chain and held it out for Joe to see. It was some kind of jewel-encrusted beetle carved with inscriptions. "The following year I unearthed this scarabaeus – a prodigious talisman of occult virtues – which along with these charts and parchments have led us to discovering this tomb." He read from an engraving on the back of the amulet. "'For Lord Anubis holds the keys to life and death. He is the Claviger of the Thirty-Fifth Door.' And before you ask, a claviger is a keyholder."

"There were thousands of doors once," said Joe. "Now there are only thirteen. I bet this crypt led to another room in Talliston long ago. But that magic is gone. It's been drained. This is one of the dead places now."

"You know of..." Kane paused, unsure, "*Tal Istia'on?*" He pronounced the labyrinth's name as if he spoke it in some long-forgotten language.

"Yes, I think that's the same place."

"We can only hope against hope. Did you say there were only thirteen doors?"

"Yes."

"Alas, so very few?" Kane paused, lost in thought. "Right, Billy, that's that. Our work is done here." Kane began packing the pendant and papers into a battered satchel.

"Yeah, boss, I get that, and it's swell and all, but don't be a bunny. Remember we're trapped in here."

"Ah, yes. The collapsed obelisks..." Kane's face lit up. "Joe," he said, the thought almost visible in his mind. "Do you know the location of the Thirteenth Room?"

"I think my mother has it," said Joe quietly.

"Your mother?" Kane appeared a little incredulous. "Son, I have seen that the Thirteenth Door is possessed by a monstrous deity, an impossibly ancient being worshipped by deranged inhuman cults and hell-bent on the total annihilation of all that is good and sacred."

"Yep, that sounds like her."

"But, even so. Are you saying the room is conveyable? That it can be transported from place to place?"

"I don't know exactly what it is, but I think so. It was in a root cellar in Saskatchewan. At least in 1948 it *will* be. She was there to steal it. I have this book—" Joe pulled out *The Stranger's Guide* for the men to see.

"Great Scott!" Kane exclaimed loudly, the echoes of his words shattering the eternal silence of the subterranean tomb. "I need to see that book!"

"It's with me in Spain."

"Then we will come to you… No, I forget *you* are in the past. You must come to me."

"But how?"

"Forget how. Find a way. Get to New York City. Find Trevelyan Vean. It's a chateau on Fifth Avenue and East 86th Street."

"I'll do my best. It's just I'm kind of trapped too."

Occult investigator Antony R. Kane looked Joe straight in the face. "You *must*. Otherwise, they will unleash a shard of the terrible dark—"

"—that will one day extinguish the moon," Joe finished. In his mind flashed an image of the ringmaster holding up a single black rose. Of the open trapdoor from the cabin in the woods. Of hordes of Grim Grotesques swarming towards the red tower of the Tzu waystation. "I know," he said quietly.

"Splendid! Splendid! Splendid!" said Kane. But no, it wasn't Kane. His lips were closed. The detective had not spoken. With a sickening jolt, the boy snapped awake. Immediately the torch-lit tomb, the investigator, Billy B. Bastiani and the vast statue of the underworld god were gone. In their place were the white bedchamber and the ringmaster's theatrical figure in full harlequin mask and cape standing over him.

"Pandoro?" Joe mumbled. "What…"

"You are a clever, clever monkey. A verifiable genius, my boy."

"I don't understand."

"What's to understand? Forget dusty old, stuffy old Europe. We have a great new destination. A new magical adventure!"

"A new—"

"That odd character you met in the water garden. He's none other than American theatrical impresario Edwin Thanhouser. He absolutely loved your wild and crazy proposition."

"I have no clue what you're talking about," said Joe drowsily.

"Why, of course you do. We're booked to star in his next moving-picture circus extravaganza. Pandoro's Travelling Fayre is setting sail for the Americas!"

XI

ELEVENTH MOON: OWL MOON (OF BIRDS)
TREVELYAN VEAN
NEW YORK, NEW YORK, USA
MONDAY 5 AUGUST 1929 | 21:18:09

NINE WEEKS AND MANY THOUSANDS of kilometres later, Joe stepped into the shadowy office of Antony R. Kane, and placed his copy of *The Stranger's Guide* on the investigator's crowded roll-top desk. Shifting aside the bulky black typewriter, the white-haired detective reached out his hands and, almost reverently, touched the engraved cover. Letting out a sigh, he glanced at the boy, indicated the leather armchair, then slowly opened the book and began to read. "Well," the investigator said in a growl, "you took your time."

The room was filled with cigar smoke and beneath that the smell of antiquity, of old books and ancient objects — a musky smell, slightly dry, slightly damp, slightly in between. Though very late it was still feverishly hot in the small study. Cooler air was being pumped through a grille in the ceiling, but it did nothing to ease the heat. From someplace on the floor below jazz played. Probably Billy, the young assistant who had acted as doorman when Joe arrived.

The wooden desk calendar showed Monday 5 August. Joe already knew the year. One moment he'd been standing in 1911, then the dark of the moon had translated him here. The boy wondered how long the investigator was going to take. "I don't have much time," Joe said. "The fayre's in 1911 New York and any minute I might get pulled back."

Kane ignored this and continued reading, leaving the boy to look idly around the office. It hardly seemed grand enough for such an important and wealthy person. In the light of a single green lamp, the bookcase, desk and wallpapered walls were mere shadows. The room's mix of wooden panelling and cabinetry was drab and unassuming, though that could not be said of the objects the walls and furniture showcased. Everywhere were items of the peculiar, the exotic and strange: shrunken heads, strangely dressed puppets, and ancient books set alongside sepia photographs and framed paintings hung from shining chains. Some were fine art; some were photos of buildings with a New York feel to them. But in the middle of these was a large, heavily framed photograph of an owl seated behind a wire fence. The brass plaque at its base announced this to be TARROW, NYCTEA SCANDIACA, SNOWY OWL.

You get everywhere, don't you, Joe thought to himself, but decided against disturbing the man from his reading a second time.

The detective tsked and turned another page.

As he waited, Joe's mind drifted back to the long and arduous journey between the Alhambra and where he now sat. It was a route that included another overland to the south coast of Spain, then a ship to Southampton. From there the fayre boarded the SS *George Washington* for the crossing of the Atlantic. Memories of Evangeline and the captain were never far from Joe's mind during the voyage, and he knew that forever forward any journey by sea would remind him of the time he spent aboard the *Lodestar*.

The whole trip, Pandoro was beside himself with glee at securing paid passage to the United States of America. Edwin Thanhouser's movie studio was the biggest film maker in the whole of the East Coast, cranking out reels at a rate of more than a hundred a year. His silent moving pictures were mostly Westerns and romances, and plans were afoot to move everything to the Sunshine State of California. The proposed picture was going to make stars of Pandoro – *obviously* – and Eriqué, the fayre's silent but deadly sharpshooter, plus heavily feature the talents of Pennie Drops Flying Trapeze Troupe and Ianivo the Cannibal Human Cannonball. Though, Joe thought, they'd probably downplay the cannibalism.

But not everyone in the troupe had been happy with arrangements.

"New York City is a dark pool from which to drink," muttered Queenie Jeannie the fire-breathing mermaid during a game of gin rummy on the first evening of the voyage.

"That magic is old and dangerous," said Ronaldo, Memory Man Extraordinaire. "We leave too much behind."

The boy knew all too well that feeling. It was only as Joe had scrambled up the gangplank and the horn was sounding that he realised he'd left the bumblebee necklace on the bedside cabinet in the Alhambra bedroom.

The arrival at Staten Island was crazy, but without issue. Joe marvelled at the chaos of the immigration offices and the way the fayre navigated borders and flipped continents without one single document or passport. Ably arranged, no doubt, by conjuror and prestidigitator Lucky Lucas. Expense seemed to be immaterial to the travellers as they took over three floors of the grand dame of Madison Avenue, The Roosevelt Hotel. In the comings and goings, Joe found it impossibly easy to slip away and half-run the two dozen or so blocks to 1046 Fifth Avenue. There he waited for the Dead Moon and the gateway to this time and place.

Somewhere on the floor below, the jazz music cut off. A short while later a voice called up the stairwell, "That's it for me tonight, boss." But still Kane said nothing. Just turned another page.

On his desk the cigar smoked into ash. The cars outside and the odd raised voice of late-night revellers were the only sounds, then even these faded away.

Suddenly Kane finished reading and slapped closed the book, breaking Joe from his half-sleep. The investigator rocked back into his swivel chair, faced the boy, and said, "Now it's your turn. Tell it from the beginning."

So Joe started his story. He began and finished with his mother, from the barbecue to the encounter in Japan. He left out the details of the moons, rooms and doors, knowing that was all in the book. Instead he described his path through the labyrinth and his current predicament. "I need your help to escape the travelling fayre and get to the next room. I need to stop her."

"What a two-bit hullabaloo!" said Kane. "Well, my fee's forty-five dollars a day plus expenses. Here's my card…" Seeing the boy's face, he slapped Joe on his knees. "Only ribbing you, son."

Joe looked down at the yellowing rectangle.

ANTONY R. KANE DETECTIVE BUREAU

NIGHT TELEPHONE
VANDERBILT 3-3937

EXECUTIVE OFFICES
1046 FIFTH AVE., E. 86TH ST.

CRIMINAL — CIVIL — CONFIDENTIAL
ESOTERIC — OCCULT — INVESTIGATIONS

"I've seen this before. It was on the wall at Manse L'Estrange."

"When was that?"

"Nineteen fifty-four."

"Well, guess I'm not retiring anytime soon," said Kane wryly. "Look, son. Just because you're broke, doesn't mean I can't help you. And it just might end up helping me, too."

Joe saw the investigator's eyes unfocus. He was quiet for a long time then continued: "For me, all this started with the cards." Kane sat back and opened one of the doors to the bookcase. From inside he retrieved a black velvet bag adorned with a purple brooch, and from that he pulled a pack of oversized playing cards, laying them out on the desk. Joe saw they showed intricate paintings rather than numbers and suits. Each had a title such as *The Magus*, *The Æon* and *Knight of Discs*.

"They're for divining. They call them Tarot."

Joe glanced up at the portrait of the white bird. "Like the owl?" he asked.

"No. Same sound, spelled different. In that book of yours, the deck is listed as being this location's oracle. There's a drawing of the cards and a layout, but it's not complete. Whoever wrote this guide didn't work out how to leave this room. The twelfth and thirteenth sections are both unwritten."

"But do you know how to use the cards? To open the next doorway?"

"No."

"What did you mean when you said everything started with the cards?"

"Let me show you." Kane presented Joe with the box that the cards came in. "Look there. At the side panel."

The boy read. "Published in New York. Cards printed in Belgium. So?"

"When I found them I tried to track down the distributor. The

Thoth Tarot Deck was created between 1938 and 1943, and this particular pack won't be on sale until 1969."

"Oh," said Joe.

"The same is true of these books." Kane indicated the bookcase behind him. "Some are ancient volumes of forgotten lore. Others won't be around until next century."

Like me, thought Joe, but in reply he just repeated what Nirromelhe had told him. "Think of this place as an island; things get wrecked here all the time. Places, people… and books too, I guess."

"Is that right? Well, when I try to read them with my psychometry, it's like touching a void. Very disconcerting. So, unable to divine their origins, I gets to searching. Fortuitously, I got hired by the family who used to own this place." He pointed behind the boy, up at the reeded-glass door. Joe turned and saw lettered in reverse the pristine gold words:

II

J E TREVILLIAN

& ASSOCIATES

EST. 1925

"I'd wondered at that," Joe said. "Why it didn't say 'A. R. Kane'."

"Because I only rent this place. I head up a society called Occultus Earth and specialise in investigating the exotic and esoteric." The name sounded familiar to Joe, but he had no idea where he had first heard it. "I was over in Midtown, then one day this woman named Trevillian hires me to look into a crooked inheritance. She was a notorious gangster's moll, so I knew right off it was trouble. Took it anyway, just to get a peek in this house. Story goes that her millionaire father

Jedediah – a real nasty curmudgeon, apparently – died in his home in Cornwall. Hel Trevelyan it was called. And do you know what he did on his deathbed? He disinherited his entire squabbling family and left his estate, company and entire fortune to a boy caught trespassing in the grounds on the day he died."

"A boy?"

"Was it you?"

"No, of course not."

"Well, the fortune included this pile. Astors and Vanderbilts as neighbours. Fancy that. So Betsy and her killer husband got me shaking down Daddy's Fifth Avenue mansion trying to find a loophole, a reason for contesting that final amendment to the will."

"What did you find?"

"Nothing on the case. But while I was digging I found this study. How it was a real cabinet of curiosities, packed full to the gunwales of the weird and wonderful from the world today... and tomorrow."

"This Trevillian must have known how to travel in the labyrinth."

"That's what we know now. It explains the cards and the books. At the time I had other ideas. In that digging I found many keys to many doors, but not one inkling of how to find the locks they fitted. But—" Kane pulled out a great sheaf of notes and pages, "—I did find this."

From the great pile he removed a single sheet. It was written on skin-like parchment and looked very old. "This speaks of the Demonym. The things your book calls the Ghûl."

"The Grim Grotesques," said Joe.

"Seems they have many names. This parchment speaks of a place known as *Tal Istia'on*. I think it refers to a tree of all life, a world tree that was so colossal its roots stretched from the underworld and its branches supported the heavens."

"There's a picture of an oak in the guide," Joe said. "It shows the three things that Time cannot kill."

"Yes, indeed it does. The scroll also speaks of a darkness that waits at the end of the world, and of a bunch of folks hell-bent on summoning it up. Whatever destroyed the tree wants to destroy everything else too." The investigator gave Joe a long look.

"And you think my mother serves that evil. And the Ghûl – the Demonym – serve her."

Kane nodded dourly. "All we know for sure is that these gateways are everywhere – America, England, even Egypt. Some are dead, some are not. And every time one dies, our world shifts one step closer to theirs."

Joe thought of the *torii* gates and how they represented all the doorways that were now dead. And how in that far future only one remained.

"So we're searching for the same thing." Joe indicated the office door. "And that's the next one. These Tarot cards must be the way to get out of this room and closer to my destination. Can you help me?"

Kane swung back on his creaky chair and let out a long sigh.

"No," he said finally. "But I know a guy who can."

"Where will we find him?"

"In this town there are just two evils, boy, and we can always find them together."

"So, where we going?" said Joe, his voice already mimicking the man's gruff drawl.

"To the Landmark."

"Wow, the Empire State Building!"

"What's that?"

"You know, tallest building in the world, King Kong and all that," said Joe.

"Stop being ridiculous. That's the Woolworth Building. By next year, undoubtedly the Chrysler. And who's King Kong?"

Joe looked up at the New York skyline. Yes, there were skyscrapers but the iconic building was not one of them.

"So, another landmark?"

"No, *the* Landmark, son. The Landmark Tavern. Or more specifically its third-floor speakeasy."

"And where's that?"

"Hell's Kitchen, the lowest and filthiest corner in all of this low, filthy city. If crime was a cyclone, the Kitchen would be the eye of the hurricane."

"Great."

Kane stood and grabbed his hat and coat. "Oh, one more thing," he said, as if some insignificant afterthought. "There's a crawling bat-beast abomination loose in New York City. And I released it."

"You?"

"That scarabaeus disc I showed you when you appeared to us in Egypt? In using that at the tomb I kinda broke something. Didn't open no door or nothing, but I did set something free. Some terrible supernatural guardian or entity."

"Oh boy," said Joe, thinking, But why wouldn't there be a monster? This was a labyrinth, after all.

"Now it's hunting me down. It shows up…" Kane paused, searching for the right word, "…periodically." He pulled up one shirtsleeve and Joe saw the raking, scalding scars running all the way up his left arm. "Just want you to know what a balled-up wad of baloney you're walking into."

Joe nodded. "OK, boss," he said solemnly.

The detective or whatever he was smiled grimly. "I like you, kid. Enough to let you tag along." Kane rose from his seat and pulled on his greatcoat. "Just don't bring Lulu."

"What?"

"Drop it. I keep forgetting you're not from around here." Kane eyed Joe's circus attire disapprovingly. "Now look, son, I don't know you from nothing, but if we're heading out to Hell's Kitchen, you're gonna seriously need some new rags."

WRAPPED IN ONE OF BILLY B. BASTIANI'S raincoats, Joe went with the investigator in search of The Landmark Tavern. They hailed a yellow cab on Fifth Avenue and set out for the Irish saloon. Leaving behind the glowing street lamps of Central Park, they sped through dark streets, down to the waterfront and along the wharfs and docks of the Hudson River. When he was a boy, Joe had watched films set in New York with a sense of wonder. It was a mythical place, a movie set. And now he was here it seemed the most unreal of all the times and places he had visited. Kane smoked the whole way, filling the cab with grey smog. Joe was forced to crack open the window and try not to breathe as much. Their first task, Kane told the boy, was to secure a password for the speakeasy. "You see, in this time and place alcohol is illegal," he explained. "They call it prohibition and it's the perfect excuse for everyone to run wild. Top of the heap is New York, the booze capital of a country that apparently doesn't drink. All this craziness started in 1920. Lord knows when it will end."

Deep in a corner of the night-time city, they pulled up next to a large sign that announced: GENUINE IMPORTED RUSSIAN CAVIAR. It was a service dairy, and the shop front read:

TODE & CO.
1028 THIRD AVE., SW COR. 61 ST.
WHOLESALE AND RETAIL

"This is Gustav's gaff," said Kane. "He knows Lucky Luciano. Luciano knows the Carleys. And *they* own the tavern. He's sure to get us in."

The investigator was gone no more than five minutes, in which time the taxi meter clicked through the fare. It was now a whole ten cents. When he returned, Kane carried a newspaper folded inside a large ledger. He told the cabbie to head for a corner two blocks away and they walked from there. Hell's Kitchen crouched beside the Hudson River wharfs, a place of factories, lumber mills and slaughterhouses. The air smelled of the docks and coal smoke, and even at this late hour dark figures shuffled through the midnight streets. The Landmark Tavern rose above the waterfront on the corner of Eleventh Avenue and West 46th Street, but Kane didn't lead them there. Instead he picked a non-descript door in a cobbled alley that ran between the buildings. The door had a large letterbox at its centre and the investigator posted the book and paper through it.

"This is a desperately dangerous adventure, Joe," Kane said while they waited. "Don't talk to anyone. Just stick close."

"OK."

The boy had the strongest feeling of being watched, then the door was opened. In the dim light Joe saw an overly made-up woman in a shawl who directed them to a tiny staircase. Silently they climbed to the third floor and from there emerged into a smoky, noisy saloon. Circular tables crowded the room, as did its customers, all of whom twitched nervously when Kane and Joe entered. The makeshift bar was a serving hatch into a kitchen of sorts, and every one of its windows was sealed in black.

"Are there many speakeasies like this?" asked Joe.

"More than Catholic children," Kane replied.

The investigator ignored the stares and crossed to a wooden booth on the other side of the room. There sat a moustachioed man in a cowboy hat across from a ginger-haired woman who wouldn't have looked out of place in a Hollywood blockbuster. Both were smoking and drinking some unidentifiable cocktail from what looked like jam jars.

"What's new," said Kane to them both, slipping onto the bench beside the suited man.

"Well, if it isn't Antony R. Kane hisself. What's with you, fellah? Being hired by little boys now?"

Kane showed all his teeth. It wasn't a smile. "No, just the usual clowns and bozos." He indicated for Joe to edge in beside the redhead.

"Hey there," the woman said between sips. She sounded drunk. "What's your name?"

"Just Joe," said Joe.

"And does Just Joe want a drop of the old white lightning? Get him started?"

"He don't want to get started," answered Kane.

"Well," said the man, "at the least introduce us."

"Joe, this is Claudius. He's an ex-client and, by the by, the finest stage magician in the US. Drusilla is his flunky."

"I prefer the title 'glamorous apprentice'," said the woman, producing a red lizard from midair and stroking it across her cheek.

"I'm sure you do," said Kane, then to Joe, "May I introduce Blood and Bones. She's Drew Blood and he's Claude Bones."

"Mistress of the Macabre and Master of Mystery!" finished Drew, blowing smoke rings. With a wave of her hand the woman's scaly pet vanished back into thin air. I know a circus you'd be so at home in, thought Joe.

A barman appeared at Kane's shoulder, and he ordered panther sweat and a soda. "In two glasses."

Claude stubbed out his cigarette, immediately lit another. "So, how'd you know to find me here?" he said between puffs.

"Where else would a dark beast lair, except in the most murderous area in the country?" Drew laughed at that, but Claude ignored them both.

"Turn off the New York charm, dick, and tell me what you want."

Kane told Joe to show them the cards, so the boy pulled out the Tarot and fanned them on the table. Seeing the deck, Claude's face turned to a look of intrigue. The magician picked up a few and scrutinised them, then he said, "Never seen anything quite like these before."

"Nor will you for another forty years," said Joe.

"The case I'm working on," the investigator added, "has a puzzle. A puzzle including this deck. It's a special layout. Five cards. Set like this... Show him, kid."

Checking they weren't overlooked, Joe placed four cards in a square, with a fifth card at their centre. Kane took a napkin from the table and drew a similar design. "The only clue is this drawing. It's incomplete, but I know you read fortunes with cards just like this. Wondered if you could fill in the blanks."

"What's it worth?" said Drew.

Kane tipped back in his seat and gave her one of his stares. "Worth? It's worth not jawing to the DA about that little stunt you both pulled in East River."

"Now, now," said Claude, "I'm sure that's all water under the Brooklyn Bridge."

"Just look at the picture. Any of this mumbo jumbo mean anything to you?"

"One man's gobbledygook is another man's Grail," Claude mumbled, but at least he was concentrating on the cards again. Slowly he examined the investigator's copy of the drawing from *The Stranger's Guide* and scanned the cards for clues.

"Well," he said after a long pause, "these are referring to actual cards. The four outer ones are the elements. Fire top left, then Air; Water and Earth down the bottom. The symbols on the top two – the ones that have been marked – are a wand and a sword, I think. The other two are missing. Could be anything."

"And what about the middle one?" asked Joe. "What's that?" He pointed to the single shape on the diagram.

"Looks like a letter O. Or an egg. Or a ring. Again, could be anything."

"That is not helpful," said Kane.

Dark shadows fell across the table of the booth. Joe glanced up into the screwed-up faces of five pinstripe-suited men. All were hiding machine pistols tucked into their coats.

"Howdy, Miss Blood, Mr Bones… And who's this? Ah, the guy who gave my Betsy the bum's rush." Everyone looked at the detective, especially Joe, who had no idea what they were saying, but it sounded pretty dreadful.

"Well, if it isn't Barney 'The Killer' Bambini," said Kane.

The head mobster sneered. "Why, you worthless hawkshaw piece of… It's Bambino and you know it."

"Ah, that's what I love about the Big Apple," said Kane. "Everyone's just so happy to see me." All the other gangsters tensed at this. Fingers twitching around their weapons.

Involuntarily, Claude Bones stood up. "Now, now, now, gentlemen. Easy on those triggers."

"Sit down, Sim Sala Bim," said Bambino. "And listen to the story. This shamus took my Betsy to the cleaners."

"Betsy?" said Drew, startled. "Not *the* Betsy? Betsy *Trevillian*."

"She's Betsy Bambino now. And this guy was supposed to be the key to unlocking her old man's fortune."

"That's right," Drew said under her breath. "That sugar daddy was loaded." Joe watched on, incredulous, and started carefully scooping up the Tarot deck.

Claude sat back down. "I heard some say you only married her for that inheritance."

"Is that so?"

"So someone said."

"Those someones is dead," said Bambino, and behind him all the gangsters snickered. "Anyhow, this shyster didn't satisfactorily finish what I paid him for. And there's the rub."

"I ran into complications," said Kane.

"What... *complications?*" said the mobster, as if there was nothing on earth that should have stood in the way of getting his hands on his wife's money.

"I found something in Egypt. It was a scarabaeus set across a dark doorway sealed with wax. When I removed it, I broke that seal and released a monstrosity. I cannot stay anywhere for too long. The beast is drawn to that cursed object."

"And where is the disc?" said Bambino, obviously playing along with such ridiculous hogwash.

"It's in my pocket."

Kane reached into his jacket and everyone freaked out. Drew shrieked and knocked over her cocktail. Weapons were raised. In the commotion Joe swept the last of the deck into his lap. Instead of a firearm, Kane drew out a large, round disc. It looked like it was made of clay or pottery with a hole right through its middle, through which was threaded a rusted metal chain.

The mobster looked more shocked that the investigator hadn't pulled out a gun, than that such a thing actually existed. He bent closer and inspected the monstrous images that covered the amulet.

"Surely you don't expect me to believe—"

Barney 'The Killer' Bambino didn't get to finish his sentence, for Kane cut him off. Shouting a single word in some ancient language, he tossed the amulet at the gangster. Bambino caught it by reflex and in that moment all the taped-up casements ruptured inwards. Glass fragments glittered like snowfall. Across the holes where once there had been windows was a writhing and pulsating mass of legs and feelers of some hideous giant creature. Immediately two of the drinkers were seized in its claws and dragged screaming out into the night. As one, Bambino's men turned and machine guns blazed, while the rest of the room was left to erupt into pandemonium.

"Joe!" shouted Kane above the chaos. "This way!"

"Wait!" said Claude, dragging Drew with him. "We're coming too!"

In seconds they were at the door and careening down the steep wooden stairs. Taking them two and three at a time. Above came the staccato sounds of gunfire and screaming.

"Well, I'll give you one thing," laughed the magician as they fled. "You ain't no liar."

"Actually, I am," said Kane matter-of-factly. "The beast hunts me, not the disc."

Bursting out of the secret door of the speakeasy, the four of them stumbled into the cobbled alley and there in the shadows stood the most bizarre car Joe could have ever imagined. Blood & Bones's vehicle was a midnight-black hearse that was more Gothic temple than motor car. Built upon standard wheels and body, the cab was smothered in ornate columns, vases and sculptures, and crowned with a huge crucifix. At its oval windows life-sized winged angels clung to the bodywork, their weeping faces pressed against the shadowy glass.

All Kane and Joe could do was gape.

"Admiring good old La Llorona, eh?" said Claude as he followed them onto the street. "Ain't she just the bees?"

"Pulling rabbits out of hats must be more lucrative than I thought," replied Kane.

"It's a Studebaker Phaeton," crowed the magician. "Top of the line. Custom classic. With a few personal touches."

"Enough of the jalopy already," urged Drew. "You can paw and dribble once we're home free."

Her words broke everyone into action. Claude and Kane leapt into the front seats, leaving Joe and the Mistress of the Macabre to open the rear hatch and climb in the back. The boy tried not to notice the brass rails where the coffin would normally sit; yet instead of a casket the area held all manner of black crates stencilled with red mystical symbols. Obviously, this was the magician's stage equipment.

With a roar of the engine, Claude gunned the Studebaker into life and sped off across the muddy cobbles. Unbalanced by the sudden movement, Joe fell sideways into the boxes, while Drew clung on for grim death. Out the back window the boy saw a host of shapes spill out into the alley and start firing. Bullets ricocheted off the carved wreaths, brickwork and even the road itself. Luckily none hit the glass. Almost immediately the magician threw a hard left and was racing down towards the wharfs and the dark line of water, then he threw the car right and was speeding along the avenue on the edge of the Hudson.

"This beauty cruises at fifty-five," Claude was bragging, "but she'll go eighty, no sweat."

Joe watched frantically as the ships and warehouses flashed past, searching the street and rooftops for signs of pursuit. At first there was nothing, but then four black sedans burst around the corner and into view. From their side windows shapes leaned out and started to take aim.

"Kane," he warned, but Claude had already seen them in his wing mirrors.

"Hey, bearcat," he called to his assistant, "got anything back there that'll help?"

Bouncing about like she was on a trampoline, Drew started opening boxes, spilling their multicoloured contents, looking for something – *anything!* – that might thwart their pursuers. Joe joined her to help, expecting doves, interlocking rings and endless lines of bunting, but it soon became obvious that Blood & Bones was a very different kind of magic act. In the first crate they searched were blood-covered throwing knives. In the next ruptured boxes of live tarantulas.

"Bloody hell!" he shouted, suddenly aware of crawling shapes all around him. "There are giant spiders back here!"

The detective ignored this. "Joe, by the time we get back home, you'd better have worked out the symbols on those cards."

"Stage smokes," said Drew. In her hands she held three oddly shaped canisters. Each was marked by a quivering grey ghost rising from a heavy-coloured mist. "Pop the top!" she ordered.

Joe looked blankly back at the red-haired woman. "The top!" she said again as if he were a dog that wasn't obeying a simple command. She pointed to a crank handle on the roof panel. Joe grabbed it and began pumping it round. This operated some hidden mechanism opening the entire top of the cabin.

"The Fire and Air cards," he called to the magician. "What were those symbols?"

"Don't know the deck, but might be aces. One for each element. Search for those first."

"Monster incoming!" screamed Kane and there ahead, crawling spider-like around the corner of a meat-packing warehouse, was the abominable creature. A Frankenstein mess of insect, bat and octopus, it clenched every one of its oozing muscles and leapt, landing in the street ahead of them. Claude set the hearse into a spin, lost control then righted and crashed through a newspaper stand, missing the monster by a whisker.

At first sight of the thing, Joe pushed himself into a corner as far away from the windows, bullets, spiders and monster as he could manage, then started rifling through the cards. He found there were four suits, but instead of hearts, diamonds, clubs and spades, these were drawn as coins, cups, swords and staffs.

"Swords and staffs," he shouted. "I have those things! Back at the house."

Kane turned in his seat and said, "Great, kid. Then this is not about cards. It's about objects. Maybe to open the door you must have things from the other times and places. Five things."

"What things?"

"Things of sacred power," said Claude. "So get to finding those missing symbols. Something of Water. Something of Earth. And something maybe marked with a letter O."

Shuffling through cards while trying to stop himself from sliding towards the tarantulas was not easy, yet he managed at last to find the other two suits. Cups and Coins. Was the cup the chalice from the sacred well in Ireland? It had to be. That just left—

"West Ninety-Sixth! Right! Right!" yelled the investigator, and Claude skidded the car in compliance. Now the river was at their backs, ahead the skyscraper skyline rising from illuminated trees. "Cross Central Park. That's the quickest. We'll be on Museum Mile in a jiffy."

"We don't have a jiffy!" shouted the Mistress of the Macabre, her arms full of pickled things in jars. "Between the mobsters and the monsters, we're zotzed!"

"Zotzed?" said Joe.

"Blown to hell. Sent to the farm. Killed, kid. Whacked. Dead and done."

Joe knelt up and took a peek out of the oval windows. At this time in the early hours he was relieved the streets were relatively clear of pedestrians and vehicles. But not, it seemed, police. For there behind them and the mob, screaming into view, came three black and white law-enforcement vehicles, sirens blaring.

"Cops!" said Drew.

"Ford Model Ts," said Claude. "Phooey!"

Then Drew was lobbing the canisters and the avenue was filled with billowing smoke. The first was a septic greenish-yellow, the second a glorious orange, the third a noxious ebony. The mobsters and the police swerved to avoid the Hallowe'en smokescreen, but hit the cloud full tilt. Brakes screeched, and there came the thunderclap of vehicles crashing into each other and breaking into pieces. From within the billowing heart of the cloud fire erupted, turning the dark to day. Eight cars went in. Three came out. And all of those were cops.

"What you got for me, Joe?" shouted Kane.

"It's Cups and Coins," the boy called back. "I've got the cup. Have no idea about the coins."

"Let me see." Joe held up the Ace card for the investigator to look at. "Read the card, boy. They're not coins, it says 'Disks'. It's the clay disc I found in the cellar."

La Llorona skidded sideways and Drew screamed, falling back into the cabin. From somewhere above the monster landed atop the vehicle, all wet feelers and razor-tooth jaws, the car tipping under the weight of the humungous thing clinging to it. The hearse was sliding, screeching. There was a hellish crunch from the undercarriage and then a whine from the engine as it laboured under the extra weight. The creature's tentacles curled around one of the weeping angels, and with a horrendous ripping sound tore it from the bodywork. As it crammed the winged figure into its odious maw, its limbs sought new targets. One of the tentacles found Joe and attached itself to his borrowed coat with powerful suckers. In seconds he was pinned to the floor, scrabbling to get away from the hideous thing. Dragging himself up, the boy was just in time to see the vehicle leave the roadway and careen over grass and through flowerbeds. Everyone was screaming and shouting and then they were skidding along a footpath beside a row of tall railings.

A heartbeat later the car lurched sideways, broke through the metal fence and slammed nose first into the dark lake. Immediately the hearse flooded, and Joe was swept out into the open water. Thrashing, he broke above the surface, and managed to haul himself to the weed-slick bank. Out on the lake the magician and his assistant bobbed to the surface like apples.

"Run!" Kane was screaming from somewhere close by. "Run for your lives!"

Checking he still had the Tarot cards, Joe dragged himself onto the grassy bank, got to his feet and started run-limping through the park. The boy's borrowed clothes were waterlogged, awkward and heavy. Shrugging off the sodden jacket, he forced himself on, the stink of the weeds and water filling his nostrils. In a few strides the investigator caught up with him and they fled towards the sparkling lights of Fifth Avenue. With a feral scream that pressed like heat upon their backs, the horror hauled its bloated body from the water and began pursuit.

Between the tree line Joe could see the châteauesque mansion of Trevelyan Vean. Its carved stone exterior was lit by the lights of a dozen Victorian lamp posts that ran this length of Fifth Avenue. Each and every window in the place was dark, giving the house a haunted, abandoned feel, yet it was so close that the boy felt he could reach out and touch it. He was so sure they were home free that when he slammed into the iron railings that bordered the edge of the park, he almost wailed in despair. Bushes and branches crashed and snapped at their backs. The creature was storming on. At once Kane was at his side.

"Gates are locked. We'll have to go over."

"We're not going to make it. They're too high. It's too close."

"We have to try," said the man. "To die trying."

"No," said Joe. "I've got this." He turned and planted both feet firmly on the ground. And in Nature's Tongue he let out a long, keening call.

Illuminated by the hazy street lights, the rippling, wet body of the monster broke from the undergrowth and towered above them. Its tentacles flailing, its giant mouth quivering with expectation.

"Joe!" Kane was intent on forcing himself through the ironwork at his back. "Joe!"

The behemoth's shadow fell upon the little figures of the man and the boy, like a tsunami wave upon tiny crabs. Though his bones were shaking with fear, the boy faced the huge thing and kept calling. He had left his staff. He had left his sword. Now there was just him and the things he had learned on a magical ship many worlds away.

From the darkness birds and animals appeared. Crows and pigeons, rats, stray dogs and mangy cats. There was even a green parakeet with a crown of red plumage. They swarmed down upon the abomination, attacking it from all sides. Beaks poked, teeth bit and clawed feet scratched. It was a distraction only – these tiny creatures could not hope to do more than merely frustrate such a monstrous form – but that was enough. Grabbing Kane's trembling hand, Joe dragged the white-haired man away, down to the gates while the thing tried to follow. Birds harassed it at every step and then it was falling, tripping on its own flailing bulk. It crashed into the wrought-iron gates, scything them from their ornate hinges. Joe leapt through the resulting gap and, dragging the investigator behind him, raced across the road and into the Gothic building. Once inside, with the heavy wooden door closed at their backs, they caught their breath, then started for the stairs. Joe was sad he'd had to call the animals, but even with their help, he knew the beast was only stalled, not stopped. It was no doubt right behind them, and followed by the remaining police cars and all the mess that would entail.

Joe's legs felt heavy as concrete as he slapped his wet shoes up the stairs, Kane groaning beside him. "I gotta stop," he kept saying over and over. "I just gotta."

"We still don't have the final object," said Joe dejectedly.

"Show me that drawing again," Kane asked, and the boy pulled out the soggy paper. "It could be anything. An O, an egg, a zero—"

"Zero!" Joe gasped. "Yes! Of course. Of course. It's this one!" The first card in the deck was marked with a zero. It was the Fool. Joe didn't think he'd ever been as pleased to find something in his life.

"So now you have everything, son." Kane's voice sounded sad under the exhaustion. "Whatcha say we go bust that door wide open?"

Somehow, Joe knew not how, they arrived at the investigator's office, just as the monster's first hammered blows sounded on the front door below. Turning the handle, the two fell exhausted into the small room and lay panting on the rug.

"Ill met by moonlight, proud, foolish Jaxy," came a familiar voice. "Hast thou stolen away from Dreamland?"

Joe raised his pounding head and saw it was the ringmaster. Swathed in full harlequin attire, Pandoro was seated in the swivel chair, his feet up on the desk, a glass of Scotch in one hand. In the other he held a massive six-shooter.

"How did *you* get here?" Joe growled.

"I came the long way round, little monkey."

"You know this clown?" hissed Kane from his knees.

"My fairground is the greatest in the world. It was built upon the burnt-out ruins of Coney Island's Dreamland, which, sadly and unexpectedly—" Pandoro threw up his hands in mock horror, "—burst into flames in 1911." It was clear to all present just how and why the amusement park got destroyed.

With a colossal splintering of timbers the monster reduced the oak front doors to kindling. With an awful squealing it forced its massive, wet bulk across the polished wooden floors of the hallway. Joe wanted to run but there was nowhere left to go.

"New York is an unplundered cave of wonders. The fire in its depths is so, so strong. Like a fine vintage bourbon." Pandoro tossed the liquid in the crystal glass. "Not like this bilge." Beneath them, the creature howled, the roar rattling the windows in their frames. Pandoro seemed unperturbed.

315

Kane lurched to his feet, but the harlequin was too quick. The investigator found himself staring down the barrel of Pandoro's gun. "Sit," he ordered, indicating the leather chair. "And be silent. This is between me and the monkey."

More crashes and the sound of tentacles heaving against the banisters. As Pandoro talked Joe inched his fingers into his pack, which was propped against the desk where he had left it.

"I cannot let you and this buffoon go bimbling around," the ringmaster said. "For if you do there's a danger all this magnificent, immeasurable magic will drain away like a plug being pulled from the bottom of a bath." His face screwed into an evil grimace. "I will not let that happen."

In the dark doorway a tentacle flailed, seeking purchase on something, somebody, then the massive black carapace of the thing's underbelly was filling the door frame as it forced its way into the upper hall.

"I'd shut the door if I were you," said Pandoro dryly.

Joe heaved his body against the door, pushing the writhing monster back. The talons at the end of its limbs scratched at the woodwork, but it was outside. For now.

"Anyhow, Joe," Pandoro continued without pause, "you cannot leave. We have our little agreement—"

"Just watch me!" shouted Joe and, grabbing his bag, he pulled the Fool from his pocket. Now he had all five items: the sword, the staff, the cup, the disc and the Tarot. Then Joe had a odd thought and he put the card away. He was the acorn, the egg, the zero and the fool. The fifth object wasn't the Tarot. It was him. Holding everything in his arms, he stepped towards the doorway. There was a brief pause, then the heaving blackness beyond the glass was gone. In its place early-morning light shone through. Joe threw open the door and gazed out. Once more he was looking down the stone staircase in the Palazzo di Ombre.

"Go," Kane spat. "And let's hope you're right about 1954…"

With a quickening of his heart Joe clutched his pack to his chest and started forward, but the curse still held him. He could not approach the empty doorway; something restrained him as if with giant hands. Pandoro began laughing, a cruel, maniacal sound that filled the room with its lunacy. "Oh, my!" he said between chuckles. "Something holding you back?"

The boy pushed with all his strength, but it was useless. Rule #2. Rule #2. Always Have A Way Out. Swept to the very edge of despair, Joe screamed, "No! No! No! This is all madness. There is no rhyme or reason to any of it!"

"What did you say?" shouted Pandoro, and Joe knew he had it. It was like the owl had said: the answer was nothing!

"There is no rhyme or reason!" Joe cried. A wild gust of icy wind blew out from the boy, and it was as if great invisible shackles fell from his wrists and ankles. He was free! The leader of the fayre was silenced in a wink. Standing, he pointed the revolver and fired. The bullet hit the side window, shattering glass. At the same moment Kane crashed into Pandoro and the two started wrestling for the weapon.

"Kane!" said Joe, but the investigator shouted back, saying, "Go! I can't hold him for long. And the beast is almost upon us."

The boy lingered for a second longer then touched his heart, mouth and head, and stepped out into the Hall of Mirrors. Behind him and more than sixty years in the past, he heard the breaking of wood and glass as the monster crashed into the investigator's office. Then the sounds receded as the doorway faded back into blank stone wall.

II

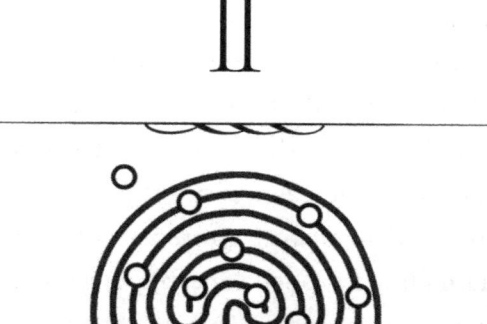

SECOND MOON: BLOOD MOON (OF MAN)
PALAZZO DI OMBRE
SACRO MONTE DI VARESE, LOMBARDY, ITALY
TUESDAY 24 NOVEMBER 1992 | 02:42:16

BREATHLESS AND ALONE, JOE STOOD at the top of the stone staircase in the Italian villa. Unlike before, he was not surprised to be back here for a third time. This meant he'd completed the second circuit of the labyrinth. Now he was just one room away from the centre. What would he discover there? he wondered. He could not guess, knew only that he was so close to finishing his journey. Slowly, the roars of the great beast faded from his ears. As his heart rate calmed, Joe gazed into the verdigris face of the great god Saturn and knew he must make the last sacrifice. As he rested, there was the sudden slam of a car door, the clank of the gates and steps walking up to the house.

"Cru-uuk," said the raven from the shadows. "He's here."

"I'm ready for him this time," Joe said. Instinctively talking in Nature's Tongue now. The large black bird flapped into the air and hopped onto the boy's shoulder. "Joseph Elijah Darkin, you know what must be done."

Joe reached into his pack and pulled out the bear-headed staff.

As both of them watched, the front door to the palazzo opened, and a figure entered. Joe gasped. As the calendar pages scattered across the marble tiles, he saw that this was not the Essex thug. Instead, there stood a white-bearded man in a greatcoat with golden buttons. He was carrying a ram's horn-topped cane, his hair slicked back beneath a fanciful hat. Where was Gunner? What was happening?

The man looked up with milky eyes. He was very old, yet still tall and broad-shouldered. He saw Joe and Griswald standing in shocked silence at the top of the stairs and gave both a small nod. Out of the dark at the man's back swooped the snow-white Tarrow. It made no sound as it settled on his shoulder. The owl was followed by Iolairn, who landed on the bottom-most stair.

"Joseph Elijah Darkin," cawed the raven, "meet Zacarias Adriano Balthazard. He is Argent Wizard of the Maje and master of this house."

"Maje," spoke the aged man. He made the word sound like 'Your Grace'. "You have travelled so far."

"I'm no Maje," said Joe, still a little in shock. "But I think I know who you are. You're the guardian of the labyrinth."

"God's hooks," said the owl from Balthazard's shoulder. "The boy *is* learning."

"Indeed," the raven replied. "Just very, very slowly."

"Agreed," said the eagle.

"Tarrow! Griswald! Iolairn! Have respect," chided the man. "After all, he is just a twenty-one-year-old boy."

Oh no! thought Joe. No! "How old will I be at the end of this journey?" he said anxiously.

"That depends how fast you can run," Griswald said enigmatically.

"Signore Balthazard, I—"

"No time, no time," Balthazard said. "Do you have the key to the Thirteenth Room yet?"

"No, I—"

"What do you know of it?"

"Practically nothing."

Balthazard looked down at his feet. Upon the marble tiles lay the calendar pages. He stooped and sifted through them, then lifted one and held it out. "Maybe this will help. This is the last page of the calendar, the thirteenth month."

"But there's only—" started Joe.

"Don't," warned the raven. "You'll just sound stupid."

"Do you see what date is circled here? What time?" said the master of the house.

Joe walked down the stairs, trying to resist the urge to look into the ornate bronze glass of the mirrors. Knowing he would not find himself looking back. Or cast any shadow on the stonework. When he got closer he sat on the stairs and examined the calendar page. It showed the exact day and time this craziness all started. Had his entire journey happened in a single moment?

"It's now," said Joe. "Or at least the now it was… then."

"*Tempus edax rerum*," said Griswald. "Time devours all things. Even itself."

"Except?" Balthazard raised a judging finger.

"Except… the three things Time cannot kill," said Joe. Then he had it. "The Maje have mastered Time. It cannot kill them."

"*Molto bello!*" The man applauded. "*Rocambolesco!*" Balthazard waved a hand to indicate the many timepieces behind him. "Talliston is a place where Time has no power. The labyrinth simply does not exist in history or any chronology. Within there is *only* now. Sadly, that doesn't mean we are immortal, for we cannot step beyond these walls. What it does mean is we can exist within the labyrinth forever. Except…" the old man repeated, "when a new guardian must be found."

A figure appeared at the top of the stairs. It was Romano, dressed in the oversized gown and carrying his camera.

"*Chi c'è? È lei, signore?*" he asked.

"*Sì, sono io, Romano. Sono a casa,*" the palazzo's master answered.

Joe looked up and smiled at the photographer, and for a moment, there appeared to be a flicker of recognition in his eyes. But then Romano saw the owl, the raven and eagle and it was gone.

"Go back to bed," said Balthazard in Nature's Tongue. "I will be the teacher today." Obediently, Romano placed the Polaroid camera on the floor and turned away, his eyes already heavy and closing. Like a sleepwalker he shuffled back along the hallway towards his room.

"There's just one thing that doesn't make sense," Joe said after the man had gone. Balthazard and his birds all cocked their heads to face him. "I didn't write *The Stranger's Guide.*"

"That is correct."

"So why are they the same moments as mine?"

The Maje gave the boy a brilliant smile.

"Now that," Balthazard announced, "is an excellent question."

Joe looked up into the man's rheumy eyes. "So, what's the answer?"

"That is for you to learn. Have you not been told you have all the answers within you?"

His mother's voice rang in his head. *The problem with bad children is they don't listen – and they never learn.*

"I don't feel I'm closer to what I want. More like being further away from what I don't. My parents want me captured. I've lost my reflection and my shadow…"

The wizard looked at the birds and they looked just as blankly back at him. "Yes, about that," said the Maje. "Here I can help. There are five gateways through which the Ghûl can pass," said Balthazard slowly and precisely. "These are our greatest strength, but also theirs. The Infinite Ocean of Water is the gate of our reflection. The Eternal Forest of Earth is the gate of clocks and time. The Immortal Sky of Air is the gate of sleep and dreams. The Everlasting Flame of Fire is the gate of fear and nightmares. That gate is the one created by our screams. And the Deathless Dark of Shadow is darkness itself. You have no reflection. You have no shadow. So two of the gateways are closed to them. Now you must protect from the remaining three."

"Stop all clocks," said the eagle.

"Do not sleep," said the owl.

"Show no fear," said the raven.

"In this way will you be immune to their magics."

Joe looked down and saw that the Maje also had no shadow. He knew he would have no reflection either. Three things taken, he thought. Two gone already, and now there was just one to go. Something that would render him invulnerable to the attacks of the Ghûl. "So this is what you were teaching me."

"Yes."

"Joseph Elijah Darkin," said the raven, "do you know what must be done?"

Joe frowned. What sacrifice would rid him of time and sleep and fear? Then he had it, and the knowledge chilled him to the bone. "Yes," he said with a shiver. "I know what must be done."

"Saturnus!" commanded Balthazard.

Every mirror shivered into life.

"I am the Oracle of the Sacred Mountain. Offer up your sacrifice and speak your question."

"What sacrifice, O Saturn?"

"One of three things must be offered. One of the three things that Time cannot kill."

Joe took the snake-handled cup, then looked around for soil. At the top of the stairs, two iron urns stood on the columns that supported the stair rails. From these grew a variety of trailing plants. The boy scooped a little dirt into the receptacle and faced the oracle mask once more. So there was one last thing he had to offer, and he didn't need to be tricked to do so this time. Night terrors he could maybe master, but little boys were the one thing that Time would always kill.

Never shall this House be free, the rhyme resounded in his head. *Until you give your Self to me.* Maledicéreux wasn't an evil sorceress, he realised, she was trying to protect Cora and Corvina from the ravages of the Ghûl.

Taking a deep breath, he said, "O Saturn, I offer up my self." Not that it was much of a life, anyway, he thought sarcastically. When this all started, I wanted to die just to get back at my parents. I would have died at the well to save Granny Em. But now I am dying for something far more important.

"Done!" boomed the Roman godhead. Outwardly nothing changed or happened, yet inside the boy felt a faint rippling tingle like his insides had been left out in the snow.

"Yet..." continued the bronze mask.

"I know," said Joe in a whisper. "That is not the correct sacrifice."

"Indeed. You have sacrificed what you are for what you need to become. You are truly one of our company. Invisible to the attacks of the Ghûl. One of the Maje."

For once the raven said nothing. Instead it bowed and spread its wings. When Joe looked around, he saw that Iolairn and Tarrow were doing the same. The master of the palazzo did not bow, but in his eyes was a glorious smiling glow.

"That was bravely done, little master," he said. "Bravely done."

"I offer earth," said Joe, and held out the bronze cup.

"What is it you wish to ask the Oracle?" boomed the mask.

"How do I open the door to the next room? To Room Twelve. San Phra Phum in Cambodia."

"It is as you wish." In the ceiling above the landing, the plasterwork transformed to wooden planks supported on bamboo poles. Against the blank wall a rope ladder descended from an intricately carved trapdoor braced with iron and shaped like a curved archway. The boy began up the stone staircase.

"Joseph Elijah Darkin," Balthazard said in an iron tone, "in this final test, remember: a Maje's magic is not wishing, it is doing. It is not without, it is within."

Grabbing the rope ladder in both hands, Joe pulled himself onto the first rung and started to ascend. And as he climbed, though the book contained nothing of this location and nothing of the country that contained it, the boy knew who and what would be waiting for him in Cambodia.

The Black Queen of the Ghûl and the Thirteenth Door.

TWELFTH MOON: STAG MOON (OF BEASTS)
SAN PHRA PHUM
KAMPONG PHLUK, TONLÉ SAP, CAMBODIA
SATURDAY 25 SEPTEMBER 1965 | 23:17:51

BEYOND THE HATCH, JOE CRAWLED into the humid night-time world of a bamboo treehouse. The air was alive with the sounds of insects and bird calls that rose above the wind and creaking trunks. The boy dragged himself up and into the small room. Beyond a wooden railing, the spirit house was filled with lights and colours. Everything smelled of the white flowers that grew through the woven walls. Flags of every hue hung from the rush roof, itself supported by a framework of bamboo poles as thick as drainpipes. At the far end of the room stood a simple altar, draped in netting and curtains. This was crowded with offering bowls and crowned by a carved stone figure, obviously the god of this treetop shrine. Beside this was a pile of books in a strange alphabet that Joe thought was Russian. Rugs covered the floor and a low hexagonal table stood in the centre surrounded by cushions and bedding. Rather than a place of worship it was being used as a makeshift lodging, but the room held no occupant. Joe was thankful for that. He could do without another forced introduction. At his back the silvery Italian light from the hallway faded, replaced by an ebony well of darkness.

Beyond all the hanging flags, flowered garlands, telescopes and offerings, one thing was obviously missing. There was no door from this room. Always Have A Way Out... Consulting *The Stranger's Guide*, Joe double-checked its position and verified that this was the final stop on the labyrinth trail. An additional thirteenth room was marked, but its circle was off to the top left of the drawing, not linked in any way to the other locations. So how could anyone ever reach it? The treehouse's oracle was listed as a pot of fortune-telling sticks called the Oracle of Kuan Yin. Joe hunted, but after an extensive search, they didn't appear to be anywhere.

Looking at the bedding, all the boy wanted to do was curl up beneath the brightly coloured sheets and sleep forever. He was impossibly weary but knew he could not rest now until he was done – and that meant keeping moving.

Joe opened the guide and turned to the almost blank pages marked as Room XIII. There was scant information. Just the usual calendar page and one passage of notes.

The lost room?
    Of all the locations within the house, this room does not
sit inside the whole, but is set apart and separate from it.
As shown on the earth-fast stone, the thirteenth room is an
enigma – the centre, representing shadow, all times and all
places. The place of the within and the without, it represents
the place of spirit, the universe, deity, god.

As on all the other calendar pages, the date was ringed in red pencil: Monday 12 October 2015. Except on this page the author had added another word: 'Today!' Joe shut the book. It was time. He couldn't delay any longer. Crossing back to the trapdoor, the boy looked down into the darkness. Now through the hatch the rope ladder descended the trunk of an ancient tree. Distantly a generator motor chugged, providing illumination for both the treehouse and a criss-crossing web of wires and bulbs below. The scene was like something out of his wildest Indiana Jones fantasy. The mighty tree grew from the ruins of an ancient temple, though most of the sprawling buildings had now been swallowed by the jungle. Everywhere green invaded, as the power of nature flexed its awesome muscles. There was a dreamlike otherworldliness to the roots of the massive tree, how they flowed like molten living webs across, under and between the carved stonework. The bulbs illuminated a makeshift series of walkways that wove between the maze-like stone corridors and roots. Somewhere off in the distance, those paths converged on a central plaza, and Joe saw that there the radiance collected. Voices sounded, shouts and commotion, pointing exactly to the place he needed to go.

Unconsciously, Joe ran over The Rules in his head, knowing what he would find in the pool of light, and in part knowing what he would have to do when he got there.

RULE #1: NOWHERE IS SAFE

RULE #2: ALWAYS HAVE A WAY OUT

RULE #3: BE INVISIBLE

RULE #4: DON'T MAKE FRIENDS

RULE #5: DO NOT TALK TO DEAD PEOPLE

And in reciting them, he realised something. It was so clear to him suddenly that he laughed in shocked surprise. The Rules were wrong.

His journey had shown him that. It had proved to him that there were places of safety. That those places did not need an escape route. It had taught him the dangers of being invisible and not making friends. How talking to dead people is sometimes the one thing that will save your life. The Rules did not keep him safe. They kept him imprisoned. The Medicine did not keep him alive. It kept him hidden.

I will keep you safe, said the staff.

I will keep you alive, said the sword.

Checking his pack, he descended the rope ladder into the ruined temple.

He was only halfway down when he noticed the first body. In the dim light from the strings of bulbs, Joe saw its shape hanging off to his right. It was tied to a thick rope which creaked in the night breeze, silently swinging like a living pendulum, except that the figure was dead. It was also not alone. There were others. Many others. As his eyes adjusted to the gloom Joe saw that the tree was filled with hanging bodies. The boy recoiled in horror and quickened his descent. Then he stopped. Could this tree…

Joe extended his hand and pressed it flat against the rough bark. Into the silence the tree spoke. Its message was not at all unfamiliar.

"I am the Killing Tree, though some call me the banyan. This spirit house sits within my sacred boughs. My flowers are scattered on the tombs through which my roots feed. I drink of death."

"O great tree, I seek the Thirteenth Room. Can you offer me aid?"

"Of all the places left upon the earth, the magic of this place is by far the strongest. That is what draws them here. Yet it is not power that gains entrance. Only knowledge."

"I carry a book." Joe held up the guide. "It says nothing of what the last location is."

"Why would it? Its author did not find the cabin in the woods, so never had the means to discover what lay in its cellars."

"Who wrote the book?" Joe asked. He hardly felt it relevant right now, but he had to ask.

"His name was Thomas Quinn Darkin. He was a dear friend of Reverend Nathaniel Grey, until his obsession with the doors of the labyrinth undid him. Not all who enter these passages find the path to its centre." Joe was shocked. His father wrote *The Stranger's Guide*? That hardly seemed possible. But the tree was not finished. Slowly, the ancient banyan continued:

"When the Hour is Darkest, five things Remember:
The Stone of Shadows
The Staff, the Birds
The Secret Within
And Ilkilæmber."

Joe shut his eyes and took a deep breath. First it was two, then three and now five. The rhyme was changing, growing, as the dangers changed and grew. He knew he would need every last one in the hours ahead. "What about Laverna-Vel Beltaræ? Is she here?" he asked through gritted teeth.

"They are all here gathered. All the monarchy of the Ghûl."

"All of them?" Joe wasn't prepared for that. "How many are there?"

"They are the Black Queen and the White King." His mother and father. "The Amaranth Prince, the Argent Warrior and the Golden Wizard. Before this night is finished, I will feed deeply," the Killing Tree concluded. Joe felt it could only be right.

Reaching the base of the gigantic trunk, the boy crossed a stone roof smothered with votive offerings and jumped down to ground level. Fearful of meeting guards or sentries, he moved off the walkways. Creeping over piles of finely chiselled sandstone blocks, keeping to dark chambers and slipping between hanging vines, he made his way to the central plaza. Everywhere was cloaked in green moss. Be Invisible, his mind cautioned, but, here in the shadows, Joe was in his element. As he neared the blaze of light, the sounds of voices, chanting and cheers increased. At times Joe even thought he heard his mother's voice above the others, but could never be sure.

The power was so potent here, the elemental magic so strong that Joe almost choked on its presence. From his time with Pandoro, he knew that this watering hole was unknown to the ringmaster. He feared what such an untapped well, so freshly cut from the jungle, would do to increase the Ghûl's magics.

Passing between giant blocks and carved colonnades, Joe clambered over strangling tree roots, finally arriving at the illuminated centre of the ruins. Here the boy found an area crowded with cars and three-wheeled scooters. The chaotic mass of electric wires converged here, dipping from trees and buildings at just above electrocution height and connecting to three noisy generators. There were even two elephants with carriages on their backs standing at the edge of the clearing. Beyond the vehicles gathered a throng of figures, rendered mere silhouettes by the overhead lighting. All the strings of bulbs intertwined around a tall stone statue draped in golden cloth. The statue looked human, though it had four arms and was carrying various objects and weapons.

Beside the statue and above the crowd rose the conical shape of a tall and stately tipi. Its canvas was pure white, though it had been painted, marking it – Joe remembered – as a shaman's house. At the base was an earth-red, saw-tooth pattern, the top deep blue. From its black poles ribbons and feathers hung. It was bizarre to see a Native American tent in this Asian jungle temple. It looked so alien and strange. It too emanated its own power, an almost touchable force that overshadowed even the ancient ruins. The plaza crackled with its energy. As soon as Joe's eyes fell upon the tipi he knew this was what

He Who Walks By Night had hidden in the cabin cellar. This was the Thirteenth Room and that meant, however improbable it seemed, that the half-circle animal-skin flap was the Thirteenth Door. That was the way out. The way back. He had to get through that last entrance and he was home.

Sneaking closer, Joe climbed a cascade of fallen masonry and found himself on a stone balcony that overlooked the heart of the temple. From this vantage point he saw that the plaza was formed of four pools, each choked with green slime and guarded by a stone figure. Behind them all, the four-armed statue loomed up before a mountain of rubble that looked as if it was once a sentinel tower.

From a carved doorway his mother and father emerged into the light. The Black Queen and her White King wore long robes, their necks hung with green and white talismans, their hands gripping long staffs. Behind them came three more Ghûl dignitaries: a prince dressed in scarlet with a red gemstone necklace, a swordsman marked by a silver moon, and Jonathan D'Ante, his garb adorned with a golden sun. Around his neck hung the talisman of Earth. Once they were all gathered upon each side of the tipi, Laverna called for quiet, then threw open the animal-skin flap. Raising the red jewel at her neck, she passed it across the doorway. Instantly the interior rippled with a fiery light and a way was opened.

"Make the next attempt," Laverna commanded.

From over behind the elephants, a dark-skinned man was dragged towards the tipi. Joe had no idea what the local people looked like, but it was a fair guess that this was one of them. The wild-eyed man was being manhandled by two Grim Grotesques with spears and forced to wade through each of the pools in turn. Next he was presented to the large statue, handed two objects – a woven pouch and a carved animal – and ordered to enter the tent.

They're trying to find the correct object to open the door, Joe thought, knowing that neither of these were the correct oracle. Joe silently berated himself for not making a more thorough search of the treehouse. Were the fortune-telling sticks still in the bamboo room? Or had they already been taken by the room's occupant and guardian?

Back before the tipi, the man cowered for a while as the crowd shouted and pointed, then with tentative steps he walked forward and peered cautiously inside. Seeing nothing untoward, and after further goading, the villager ducked down and stepped across the threshold.

The result was instant and irrevocable.

Immediately the man's body was wrapped in a burst of deep grey light, then he began to age. The effect was something like a flickbook or silent movie. As Joe watched in horror, the man's face wrinkled and his hair turned white. Joe expected the villager to turn into a skeleton and fall to dust, but the magic stopped at the moment of the man's death. Clutching his chest, the thin figure dropped the objects he had been given and fell to the ground, dead. As he was unceremoniously dragged away, Joe got an inkling as to where all the bodies in the tree had come from.

The Black Queen growled in frustration.

"Perhaps we can try someone younger?" said D'Ante, the Golden Wizard.

"Perhaps we could try you," said Laverna bitterly. "This is not a matter of age. The Thirteenth Door is the centre of the labyrinth. It holds the key to all its power. If we can breach its doorway, its magic will be ours. We need the key and we need it now. Fetch the Russian. Bring forth the Claviger of the Twelfth Door."

At the sound of that strange title, the boy remembered Kane in the Egyptian tomb reading from the amulet. "Lord Anubis is the Claviger of the Thirty-Fifth Door." These keyholders, the other guardians of the doors through the labyrinth, were suddenly clear to Joe. Rose Meirion. Granny Em. The captain and the trapper in the woods.

Out from the same dark doorway was dragged a scarecrow of a man who looked as if he was in sore need of a long bath. His wild hair and beard matched his tramp-like clothes. His hands were chained behind him and his feet were shackled. He was brought before the Black Queen and made to kneel.

"Who are you?" Laverna asked. "What were you doing in the spirit house?"

The man began babbling and if any of the onlookers understood what he said, none gave any hint whatsoever. After a while of his incomprehensible gibberish, Joe's mother waved her hand and commanded the prisoner to be silent. "I don't speak Russian, so you will speak English," she said in a voice Joe recognised from his childhood. "What is your name?"

There was a pause, and the boy was certain the reply would be more jabbering, so it came as quite a surprise when the scruffy fellow answered, "My name is very hard to speak for you, so call me Mr Sharky."

"Ah, progress. Good. Now, tell me your mission here. Are you Maje?"

"What is this Maje? No, I came from Minsk after hearing stories of the magnificent Cambodian temples in the jungles of East Asia. I travel here in search of the fabled Angkor Wat. I visit and now I explore more. I tour the Tonlé Sap Lake, and the villagers of Kampong Phluk show me this lodging in converted spirit house."

"Utter lies. Confess that you are a Maje occupant and a keyholder. Tell me of the way through the Thirteenth Door. What is the oracle?"

"I am just a stranger," said the bearded man. "Nothing more."

Without warning, Joe's mother turned to the noble in red. "Lazard," she said simply and the man bowed and lifted his hands towards the talisman at his throat. Instantly fire erupted from the ground, hissing and spitting like meat on an open barbecue. Mr Sharky cried out, and tried to rise, but Laverna cracked her staff upon his shoulder, forcing him back to his knees. With another nod, the crackling flames were gone, leaving only the whimperings of the Russian.

"Tell us of this lost room!" she commanded. "What do you know of it?" There was a brief pause where the bearded man stared daggers at her. "And if you say you know nothing again, I will kill you." She sounded utterly convincing.

Mr Sharky gritted his teeth.

The Black Queen nodded. The fires returned. She indicated with her free hand that the flames should go higher. The Amaranth Prince complied. Mr Sharky screamed.

"Stop! Stop! I tell. I tell. This is Bah-Has-Tkih, the Thirteenth Room. It draws its power from the sacred lands of the Navajo and is most powerful source. The tipi is a no-place in a no-time. It sits outside the walls of the labyrinth. It is the thing that is not connected to anything and yet is connected to everything. It is the symbol of the mystery of life and time and space. Of existence itself."

"I know all that. Is it the gate to the Within?" asked the Black Queen.

"It is the gate to all other worlds," Mr Sharky replied.

"Tell me how to enter it."

"I…" The Russian was struck speechless by what she was asking. "I do not know. I—"

The Black Queen signalled for the flames to continue. "This time there is no need to stop, Lazard," she said to the red-garbed prince. As quick as lightning, the fire roared as bright as a furnace. Mr Sharky cried out and writhed in agony, struggling to escape. Joe could not bear to hear the man's screams of torment. He couldn't sit by and let them torture people. Before he knew what he was doing, the boy leapt up.

"Stop!" Joe shouted. "Stop hurting him!"

Every one of the gathered Ghûl looked up, their diseased faces a sea of grotesque hatred, a hatred fuelled by leading them on a wild and merry dance across the best part of three centuries.

"Joe!" his father called up to his son, frantic. "No! Go, son, run! Get out of here!"

Joe drew both sword and staff and stepped further out of hiding. "No, Dad," he said. "I don't need The Medicine or The Rules." He pointed at himself. "My only power is *this*." Below in the fierce light, his father paled visibly and his mother smiled a wicked smile.

The boy knew that the only way forward was to enter the tipi and it was not lost on him that this was the exact same mission as the Ghûl. Up on the balcony he would never achieve this. For that he would have to be down there, with them. It was true he was scared, but the lonely, abandoned boy that had begun this labyrinthine path was gone. Now there was someone else standing before his enemies. And one thing he knew was that he could not do this alone.

When the hour is darkest, he thought, then with a hoarse cry, half-howl, half-laugh, Joe sent out a call into the night. And within heartbeats that call was answered.

From out of the oppressive darkness the three birds flew. Iolairn came first, and in the shadow of its great wings followed Griswald and Tarrow. While the eagle and owl chose the stone balcony for a perch, the raven landed on Joe's shoulder, a gesture that was in no way missed by the Black Queen. Seeing this, Laverna's face contorted with anger and before she could curb that fury she brought down the heel of her staff upon the floor of the temple. Great cracks snaked across the plaza, splitting the age-old rock, and from somewhere far above in the ink-black heavens thunder rolled. A moment later the air was full of rain, a sudden and frigid downpour. Within seconds everyone in the clearing was wet through, though it did nothing to lessen Mr Sharky's flame prison.

"This will end, boy," she sneered. "You are not yet too old for a good thrashing."

Joe almost fled then. He wanted to. He was not strong enough for this, but the inner strength of his five companions upheld him.

Joe vaulted from the balcony and into the midst of his enemies, then walked across the dark rock of the plaza. Between the green pools and beneath the unforgiving gaze of the four-armed god, he walked slowly and deliberately towards his mother. In his hand Ilkilæmber sang its keening song and the staff flowed its strength into him. The eagle and owl and raven were with him too. The five things remembered. At this, his darkest hour.

Show no fear, he kept thinking. And do not scream.

"Call again, little prince," said Griswald at his ear.

And so Joe did.

In answer, a thousand birds took wing above the dark shadow of the ruined temple. Into the wet night air they rose, massing together as one great living cloud that blotted out the sky. Under their weight of numbers, even the rain was halted. Some Joe recognised – pelicans and doves, swallows and crows – but there were many he didn't. There were birds of paradise, birds of prey, birds of the land and the sea. Through the air they skimmed and soared and swooped, descending, spiralling and ultimately surrounding the boy on all sides.

Joe felt them close in around him and as he strode forward, they enveloped his chest, arms and legs, creating a living suit of armour with their feathered bodies. He was finally Wolverine, a maverick superhero. As he walked, the berserk huntsman of the Ghûl swarmed forward, slashing at him with claws and knives and spears. Each fatal blow was blocked by the body of a bird, each slice obstructed and thrust intercepted. When one creature fell, another took its place, and it was through that tunnel of blood and death that Joe continued, knowing that this was his moment, here at the centre of this labyrinth.

With a look of hatred, his mother watched him come, while his father shrank back at the sight of his son and all those dying birds. The prince, wizard and warrior next stepped forward to block the boy's path, yet they were driven back by the owl, eagle and raven, allowing Joe to pass without danger. Finally, the boy stood facing the Black Queen of the Ghûl.

"Mother," Joe said, "I—"

"No," Laverna cut him off. "The problem with bad children is they don't listen — and they never learn."

His mother raised her long staff and Joe raised Arthiæ and Ilkilæmber.

As a child Joe had used sticks found in the forest to fight imaginary foes, but he was no King Arthur or Robin Hood. Instead, as the boy thrust and lunged, he let the weapons guide him. As Laverna swung at his head, Joe dodged while the staff leapt to block the blow and the sword darted forward towards the queen's chest.

Use your whole body, not just your arms, said the sword.

Block, counter-attack, return to guard, said the staff.

I don't want to kill her, the boy thought, and Ilkilæmber snorted in derision.

His mother rained blows on the boy, and each one he deflected. Or rather Arthiæ did. Being a weapon of defence rather than attack, the bear-headed staff turned the Black Queen's strikes, anticipated her feints and deceptions. Growling in frustration, Laverna tried a different course of action. She drew on the power of the temple and blasted the boy with ice-blue might. Joe tried to stand against it, but it hit the multicoloured breastplate shimmering like feathered waves across his chest and broke like a tidal wave. Scowling, the Black Queen barked a guttural spell and swept her arms wide. It was so like Nature's Tongue and yet so unlike it, all at once. It was a language made only of curses. With a cacophony of caws, squawks and shrieks like some hellish dawn chorus, the living armour split apart, the birds whirling and circling into the jungle night.

Laverna loomed over Joe and something flashed in her eyes. Something vicious and poisonous. It promised no mercy and contained all the horror and madness of her minions, the source of all their sickness and disease. Joe lifted Ilkilæmber and Arthiæ to shield him from the pitch blackness of that gaze. Under her ebony glare the sacred weapons felt as effectual as forks and spoons. A second eruption of force knocked Joe back, sending him sprawling. Distantly he heard the sword and staff clatter across the stone.

"Laverna, no!" said the White King from somewhere outside the battle. "He is my son!"

The Black Queen ignored her husband and continued towards Joe. The boy felt his courage fail. Under her shadow, he was no longer the indestructible Wolverine. Now he was tiny, insignificant, utterly human and utterly terrified. Through tear-filled eyes, he watched as his father stepped out of the driving storm to stand between Joe and the Black Queen.

"No, Laverna. You cannot."

"Move aside, Thomas."

"He—"

"Move aside!"

In the ruined plaza her words were like thunder. Thomas visibly quailed, but he stood his ground. Joe's mother did not ask a third time. Instead, in a quick, fluid movement, she brought back her staff and swung it at her husband's head. Unprepared for such an attack, Thomas raised his arm, but was nowhere near quick enough. The heel of the weapon hit him against his temple. The sound was like a breaking branch. Joe winced, and watched as his father let out a cry, then stumbled backwards, clutching his head. When he drew his hand away it was dark with blood.

"Laverna?" he said, utterly dumbfounded.

The woman turned upon her husband and hit him again, this time with the back of her hand, hard across his face. This knocked the man to the ground. His own staff clattered across the stone and dropped into the nearest pool. Thomas Darkin did not rise again to challenge her. Something had broken in him. Something in him had been close to breaking for some time. And now it had.

"I am Laverna-Vel Beltaræ, Black Queen and Ensorcellor of the Sunken City of Bziath-Karhn. I am the Unholy Mistress of the Ghûl and I will not be defied by a tenderfoot whelp. Water is my element and it shall be your death." She let out another stream of profanities, but within it Joe heard two words that he knew.

She was calling forth the Infinite Ocean.

Above the savage onslaught of the Grims and the birds, the clashing of talons and blades, the wild shrieking of both human and animal, came a sound like great stone doors opening; massive fingernails on a monstrous blackboard. Joe covered his ears against the deafening, high-pitched noise. And then the water began to rise. The pools quickly overflowed their stone sills, but that was just the beginning. Crashing through the ruins, spouting between fallen masonry, water bubbled until the entire temple floor was flooded. And it did not stop there. Dark waves of water crested over the tipi and temple buildings, came gushing around pillars and out of hollow doorways. Within seconds salty brine was washing around Joe's shins, surging quickly up to his knees. Panic was rising like the ocean all around him. Everyone was running, shouting, fleeing. Joe staggered back to higher ground. As he went he searched for the sword and staff, but could not find them in the midnight. Retreating towards the balconied temple, he climbed out of the swelling water. As Laverna barked orders at her servants, Joe searched for his father. He found him in the shadows beside Mr Sharky, helping the Russian free of his fiery prison.

"Dad!" the boy called and, somehow above the tumult, Thomas Darkin heard him.

"No, Joe!" shouted his father as he helped the bearded man to his feet. "To the treehouse."

Looking down Joe was shocked to see that the seawater had already reached the tops of the doorframes, and it was still rising. Below the Ghûl were scattering, retreating for higher ground. Joe's fight was over, but the bigger battle was to come. The boy rushed to the edge of the temple and threw himself onto the roof of the next building. He didn't look back. By the time he reached the rope ladder the temple complex had vanished under the waves. Hauling himself hand over hand, Joe was forced endlessly up, hounded by the ever-advancing water. Now only the highest trees were visible, and still the tide was continuing to advance.

Will it ever stop? Joe thought.

Then the water reached whatever source had been powering the lights and the entire world was plunged into darkness.

Climbing up into the spirit house, Joe saw that candles and incense still burned on the altar, illuminating the seated form of the statue. The face looked peaceful and calm, so different from the growling, angry figure that guarded the four pools. Dog-tired to the point of collapse, the boy crawled towards the flickering lights of the altar. He knew he was trapped in this room without doors, but could think of nothing else to do. The face and the shrine offered light and a sense of safety he could not articulate. He didn't question it. His legs were barely able to hold him up. He'd sit for a minute. Just a minute.

All was silent. After the madness and chaos of the battle and the flood, now all that the boy could hear was the creaking of the tree and the leaves in the wind. Joe placed his hands in his lap and closed his eyes. Serenity washed through him. Joe took a deep breath and felt his body relax.

Here there is no Time, said the tree.

Here there is no Place, said the wind.

And here there is no You, said the statue.

But I have lost so much, he answered the voices. I have no reflection, no shadow and no life. Do I even exist at all?

There is no you. There is only this moment.

And what is this moment?

This is the moment when you discover your secret.

When the vision came it filled his mind exactly as the ocean did in the throat of the hatchway at his back. Brimmed and then spilled onto the wooden floorboards and began to fill the treehouse with dark water.

JOE CROUCHED IN THE TWISTED roots of a long-dead tree. Its monstrous form clung precariously to a pillar of rock that rose from the middle of a lava lake. The boy was inside a volcano, its tangerine-coloured walls domed to a ragged circle of sky far above. Looking down, billowing curtains of smoke obscured his view, but like in the L'Estrange kitchen, the infernal heat did not burn him. Far below a crowd of figures stood upon a wide outcrop of rock, its edge a tall cliff falling away into the lava. Nathaniel Grey was the first he recognised. The reverend was dressed in a black greatcoat and top hat, his hands clasping a strange compass. Beside him were Jonathan D'Ante, then Boann, Jin-Lin and even Pandoro. Each held a different object: a black mirror, a tea cup, a flask… They were holding the oracles!

Within the wider ring was a second circle. Here four more people stood with another at the centre. These five held two objects, an oracle and one of the talismans. Nirromelhe was there, with Balthazard and Megquier, plus an older woman with silver hair that Joe didn't recognise. The figure in the middle was Hrishikeshr, Guardian of the Tree of Life and the one who was not Maje or Ghûl, but Wych. Whatever that was. Hrishikeshr carried a leather bag and the shadowstone. Upon his head he wore a magnificent plumed helmet in the shape of a bird's head. The boy would have expected there to be thirteen people, but in total they numbered twenty-three.

"Cr-r-ruck!" Joe looked up and his whole world swung giddily. In the leafless branches sat Griswald, his oil-black feathers ruffling in the heat.

"Why are you here?" asked Joe, not unkindly.

"Better perhaps to ask, why are *you*?" the raven shot back.

"I've realised these visions are glimpses into other moments. As if the walls of Time in some places are worn thin or glass."

"And what is this one?"

This moment had already been described to him. Joe remembered the Black King's story of a sacred Inca temple carved inside a volcano. Of how the Maje had used the power of its gemstone talismans to set the last magical places into the walls of an immortal labyrinth.

"It's the creation of Talliston," he said.

"Yes, it is." Griswald hopped from the tree and glided down beside Joe. "It is June 1848 and this is Peru. But that is not why this moment is shown to you."

"What then?"

"Look there." The bird pointed with its curved beak to the figure closest to the cliff edge. Straining to see through the sweltering haze, Joe recognised his father. Thomas Darkin was holding the crystal ball from the Alhambra, and in a woven papoose upon his back he carried a small child. No older than one or two, the blond toddler was sleeping soundly.

"Oh, bloody hell," said Joe, "that's me!"

"Yes, it is." The raven took wing. Immediately his feathers caught in the fierce updraught, and he was gone.

At the centre of the circle, Hrishikeshr raised his arms and voice to address the assembled Maje. "Behold the Twenty-Three Doors!" Around the ledge portals appeared. Some were stone, some wood and glass. Others were iron or shadow-filled arches. "Once long ago when all the land was one, a colossal tree grew that contained all life. It stretched from the depths of the Within to the highest places of the Without, from the deepest parts of the Infinite Ocean to the furthest star of the Immortal Sky. In its destruction, its seeds were sown. Where once one tree grew, then there were hundreds. These doors are the last fragments and I bind them together to hide and protect these last sacred places. My friends, offer up your keys!" As one, the gathered shamans, magicians and witches held out the oracles, and the elemental power of the talismans swirled from the centre of the gemstones, bathing the circle in a myriad of colours. "I bind these objects to these doors," Hrishikeshr continued, "to be the one and only way to open these—"

"Never!"

The cry came from Joe's father. Everyone turned towards Thomas Darkin, a mix of emotions – shock, fear, incredulity – in their faces.

"My fellow," said Hrishikeshr, "what say you?" But then the Wych's body burst into blinding light, as if he'd been hit by a falling star. Joe's eyes were scorched by the sudden brightness. When his sight returned the calmness of the ceremony was over. Now upon the ledge was outright war. Laverna led the attack, with Damfino and his rabid horde in her dark wake.

Joe looked on in horror, knowing now what this vision was and why he was here to witness it. This was the moment of his father's betrayal.

But then Joe forgot all about the fighting, the labyrinth and the implications of the battle. For as he watched, a fiery blast of power slammed into his father and his infant self, and in full view of the assembled Maje and Ghûl, both were swept over the cliff and plunged headlong into the magma below.

THE BOY WHO WAS NO longer a boy except in his own mind woke, screaming, to find seawater lapping against his chin. Thrashing in panic, Joe stood up, cracking his head on a bamboo beam. Then he heard the voice above him and the clatter of feet against tin panels that half-covered the thatched roof. It was his mother, shouting to her slaves and warriors, calling them from the waves. The mistress who ultimately led the Wild Hunt sounded triumphant, knowing that her prey was inside, and knowing it was weak, trapped and completely alone. The boy had only one way to go. Ducking beneath the icy water, Joe surfaced with the field telescope on its wooden tripod and forced it into the thatched ceiling. Once he had punctured a hole, the boy climbed one of the trunks and pushed himself through the bamboo framework. The rain had passed, the clouds gone. Now there was just an open sea beneath an endless starry sky.

The Black Queen of the Ghûl watched as Joe dragged himself up onto the roof. In her hands, Laverna's staff glowed a pale aquamarine, illuminating a face as cold as death. She was dripping wet and looked set to plunge the cruel heel of her staff through his heart.

Joe quailed. His staff and sword were gone, as was their support, their power. The birds too. He did not have the strength to call them again.

Now there was only him. Only Joe. Just ordinary Joe.

"Son!"

His father's voice was faint, but clear as a bell over the water. Joe turned and saw amid the floating debris his father and Mr Sharky in a makeshift boat made from one of the elephant carriages. The relief he felt was almost enough to finish the last of his strength completely.

Thomas Darkin held a lantern on a long pole, his other hand clamped over the wound on his forehead. His face was ashen and he looked as if he would collapse any moment, yet in his eyes there was a fire that Joe had never seen. Mr Sharky was paddling, trying to get to the treehouse. In the waves, dark shapes swam. They were heading for the boat.

"Stop them. Please," Joe begged.

"And why ever would I do that?" Laverna's face was a mask of hate.

"They'll kill them," Joe replied.

"Yes, they may, but I can always get another husband. Or, for that matter, another child."

He wanted to kill her then, to run her through and kick her corpse into the black ocean for the fishes, but even if he still had his sword, he realised he couldn't. She was a part of him and he of her. After everything, she was still his mother. Raising her arms, Laverna moved the water around and around, beginning the creation of a giant whirlpool circling the treehouse. The first of the Ghûl reached the roof, hauling their diseased bodies from the sea. Weaponless and alone, all Joe could do was stare paralysed with terror and indecision. Laverna stood over him and watched them come.

"Dad, help me!" he called.

Out across the water Thomas Darkin raised his staff and called out, "Laverna! He is my son. You will not touch him again."

"Who are you to threaten me?" she laughed.

"I am Thomas Quinn Darkin, White King and Warlock of the Mountain City of Sarkenholm. I am the Air and will not be defied by a stone-hearted harpy." Above the maelstrom a vortex of air formed and from it storms leapt. Blizzards of snow wheeled across the sky. Thunder rolled at the heart of the whirlwind. "You should never have used my son as a pawn in your game." Lightning leaped across the water, spearing the sea and slaying each Ghûl it touched.

"You worthless fool. Do you think I cannot just pull you to the bottom of the ocean with a word?" The Black Queen drew back her hand and the waters boiled. Her power was stronger here, because the magic was stronger.

"Mum, please. Don't—"

The Black Queen whirled upon him and spat, "I am not your mother!"

Joe looked up at the woman before him. Right into the blackness of her eyes. The flaring light from her staff illuminated the grotesque sneer on her face.

Not his mother?

Her words were like a key, unlocking a door in his mind. He roared and leapt at her, but she thrust forward her talisman and a blaze of emerald swept over Joe, engulfing him in its jade heart. Pain lanced through the boy and he screamed – and as he did so he felt a sensation like the Ghûl poison start to swarm through him. Was this the moment they would possess him and through him enter the Thirteenth Door? He would rather die than let that happen.

From somewhere impossibly distant, Joe heard his father scream too. Then Thomas Darkin was there on the roof, summoning a wall of lightning that sprang between his wife and son. The thunderbolts sparked off the tin panels, igniting the thatched roof into flames. The White King and the Black Queen clashed. There was a blinding burst of silver and green that felt like dragon's breath against Joe's chest, then the entire world seemed to be on fire. For one moment the surge of power was uncontrollable and uncontained and then it was gone. Like a candle flame in a hurricane, all the magic of San Phra Phum was consumed and snuffed out. Room XII in the labyrinth was no more.

In that final blast Joe was thrown backwards and into the churning water. His heavy pack instantly pulled him under and he sank into the darkness of the midnight ocean. Struggling and kicking, he tried to free himself of the weight, but his fingers were numbed by the cold water and he could not feel the straps. Filled with panic, he thrashed, twisted and writhed. When his lungs started burning, he could do nothing except suck in salt water. In all that great infinity of ocean, Joe felt a sense of warmth and calm spreading through him and knew he was drowning.

Something touched his shoulder and he whirled. It was Thomas Darkin, his face lit crimson by his talisman's glow. Reaching out, Joe forced himself into his father's arms. Thomas made no attempt to swim for the surface. Instead they continued to descend. Through blurred eyes Joe saw below – or thought he saw, or imagined, or thought he imagined – the painted canvas of the Thirteenth Room. It might as well have been on another planet.

Then his lungs stopped working and a short while later his heart did too.

After that there was no light.

After that, there was just a father and son and the Infinite Ocean.

XIII

THIRTEENTH MOON: OAK MOON (OF TREES)

BAH-HAS-TKIH

MONUMENT VALLEY, ARIZONA, USA

MONDAY 12 OCTOBER 2015 | 00:00:00

WHAT JOE SAW WHEN HE opened his stinging eyes was the face of his father. He was lying in Thomas Darkin's arms upon skins and blankets beside a roaring fire. The air was filled with sweet-scented wood smoke, which was drawn upwards through a lattice of black poles framing a starry night.

"Am I dead?" the boy asked, as soon as his eyes were open.

"Perhaps just a little," his father said, trying to smile.

"Is this the Thirteenth Room? Am I there?"

"Yes, this is the lost room inside the hidden place. You are here. We both are."

"How?"

Thomas touched the talisman at his throat. "The shadowstone is part of the power that created this labyrinth. With it you can move Moons, open all Doors, step into all Rooms."

"You mean I had the power to walk through the doors without all that working out of oracles? All the time?" Griswald had showed him how to travel with the talisman right at the start; he just hadn't realised.

"You do not need talismans and oracles and spells for that. Within you hold more power than all the things you have lost."

Joe felt impossibly tired. For a while he watched the sparks from the fire rise and fade, focusing on the dancing shapes against the canvas of the tent. For a long time there was only the crackle of the logs and the shadows. Then he said, "Is she dead?"

"Yes," his father said.

"I didn't want her to die."

"I know," his father replied. Slowly he stroked his son's hair, the corners of his mouth tight. "I was wrong. That thing I said to you in the woods. I couldn't save you both."

"She said she wasn't my mother."

His father nodded slightly but said nothing.

"Who—?" Joe began, but Thomas stopped him.

"Not now, Joe."

Someone was chanting outside and the boy became aware that the shadows on the canvas were silhouettes of people. A flute was playing an echoing melody. He sat up and gave his surroundings a good look. They were lying in an area of the tipi set aside for sleeping, while in the centre was an iron brazier seated on a metal tripod. The rest of the room was almost bare, with just a pile of wicker baskets as makeshift furniture.

"Why did you leave me?" asked Joe, but he realised he already knew.

"It was to protect you, son. I asked that the assault for control of the

Thirteenth Room was after your birthday. The attack just fast-tracked things a little."

"Where are we?" Joe felt full of questions.

"We are in the heart of the Navajo ancestral lands. In North America, in Arizona. Most call this place Monument Valley, but it has had many names. This camp is at the foot of Agathla Peak. We are guests of the Diné who call this the Valley of the Rocks. Tsé Bii' Ndzisgaii."

"How did we get here?"

"The tipi can travel geographically anywhere, but its home is here."

"What time is it?" Joe asked.

"There is no time here," Thomas replied. "Anyway, the Thirteenth Room can also travel temporally, but that is another matter entirely. We are safe here for a while. At least until you are back to health."

"How long?"

"The shaman is a powerful healer and this is a power-filled place. Not long. Look…" His father indicated a fringed leather pouch that hung around the boy's neck. "He gave you this medicine bag. It is filled with sacred objects. Keep it close to your heart and it will nourish you."

"What objects?"

"Well, get some strength and you can ask him yourself."

Time passed. It could have been minutes. It could have been days. There was no way of telling in the heart of the labyrinth. Perhaps Joe slept, perhaps he just blinked his eyes. During this time he had many dreams of the people and places he had encountered on his journey. Some were beautiful and showed Serene and Evangeline. Others were dark and filled with remorse for all those who had suffered helping him. He also had memories of finishing the map of the labyrinth, but that could have been just a dream, too. When he next focused, he was sitting up in front of the embers of the fire. His father was at the door beckoning him. "Come on," he was saying. "There's someone I want you to meet."

Thomas Darkin led his son to the door flap and then through it. Outside was a starry night in the barren beauty of the Arizona wilderness. It reminded Joe of a hundred Westerns he had devoured as a child. Except so much more real. The tent was one of three set around a roaring fire. Seated here was the Navajo shaman his father had mentioned. The man was red-skinned – or was that just the firelight? – his beaded tunic matching the headband that kept back his long, thick hair. The wise man bade them sit by the fire, and once seated, he pointed at the bag around Joe's neck. The boy went to take it off, but the man shook his head. The shaman said something in his own tongue and his father translated. "You return it to me. When you no longer need it."

Opening the pouch, Joe found inside the shadowstone. The first and last object from his journey. "OK," he said.

"This is Mágí'łizhiní," said his father. The strange name sounded like 'maa-jee-loo-zini'. "He is pleased to meet you."

"Tell him I am too."

And so the conversation went on. With the shaman speaking and Thomas translating.

"See the sacred island mountain?" Mágí'łizhiní pointed up to the stone sentinel that overshadowed their tiny encampment. "I cannot leave the land between the sacred mountains. It is one of four, but only one is true."

"There's a place in Italy just like this," said Joe.

"It is said that climbing to the top we may receive answers from the gods. But this is not so. The climb is the teacher. The same is true of the labyrinth. Look to the little things to see all things."

"What do you mean?" asked the boy.

"Bah-Has-Tkih—" he indicated the painted tent at his back, "—is a little thing, yet it is the mirror for the entire Diné lands." Mágí'łizhiní indicated the valley, the rocks, the starry sky. "The posts represent the sacred mountains, the floor is Mother Earth, and the roof is Father Sky.

The entire structure represents the journey from Earth to the spirit world; the link between man and Wakan-Tanka, the Great Mystery. It is a place of Shadow. A place of belief."

"Belief in what?"

"Belief makes things true. Belief is three things…"

"What things?"

"*Hashniih t'áá nihí,*" said the medicine man. "*Oodlą t'áá nihí. Nilį̇ t'áá nihí.*"

"Know thyself," said his father. "Trust thyself. Be thyself."

The boy looked dazzled. Thomas Darkin ruffled Joe's hair.

"The power of the coyote is in this child," said the shaman. "I am a skinwalker, so I know."

"What's a skinwalker?"

"One who walks as an animal. Seeking knowledge that only the animals know." Joe looked to the two other tents, noticing for the first time the crudely painted emblems on the canvas. The black bird, the white bird and the brown bird.

"So many people gave so much to get me here. Were these real places? Did they really die?"

"This is the labyrinth of you," Thomas translated. "It is an ever-changing domain. Walking within you encounter all the things you need to learn. At its centre is your secret. The journey's shape and structure are entirely dependent on your rules."

"My rules?" said Joe.

"Unquestionably. The rules we make for ourselves are the rules we make for our universe. That is the secret that lies within."

"But my rules are—" started Joe.

"I know." The shaman's words were coming out of his father's mouth. The things his father should have said long ago. "But rules, like entire universes, can be changed."

There was silence then as Joe thought about that. Seated under a canopy of stars, around the fire. In the Deathless Dark, before the Everlasting Flame.

The shaman stood and chanted into the night, and when he was done turned to Joe's father. He said something that made Thomas bow his head in shame.

"Yes," Thomas said. "But I am here now. I renounce my kingship and fealty to the Ghûl. I want to stay. To learn with you." The other man snorted but said nothing. Turning to his son, Joe's father added, "When I was a boy I found the entrance to this house. I followed the times set on the clocks and in the calendars, but I could not do what you have done. I could not reach this place. My path led me through darker doors."

"The Killing Tree told me you wrote *The Stranger's Guide*," Joe said. "We followed the same path."

"No," his father said. "I failed, Joe. You did not."

Suddenly the shaman spoke in Nature's Tongue. "The Thirteenth Door has opened once, but three paths appear. The mother-not-mother has descended into the Infinite Ocean. The father-not-father ascends the mountain to face the Immortal Sky."

"And the son?" Joe asked.

"The son must return to the Eternal Forest and take Balthazard's place as guardian of the labyrinth."

So, here was the secret of Talliston, the purpose of the moments revealed. Thomas Darkin had deciphered the labyrinth's moons, rooms and doors – had written them in *The Stranger's Guide*. Now Joe had followed in his father's footsteps. That was why his moments and the book's were the same.

"From the centre, the path leads out," said Mági'łizhiní. "You must walk the labyrinth. You must return. It is time."

"Dad, I don't want you to go."

"You heard the man. I must. I have to take my medicine."

Joe embraced his father and tried not to cry.

"Do you want this, Joe?"

"Yes, I do."

Joe stood and walked towards the tipi. He pulled the entrance open and stepped inside. He began to walk, and as he did so he passed back through the last magical places on earth. Through all those times and places. All those moons, rooms and doors.

As he walked the Navajo tipi faded as the Thirteenth Room transformed into the bamboo spirit house in the Cambodian treetops, a ghost-place since its magic had been drained in the battle. Then the House of the Spirits became A. R. Kane's smoky office in New York City, before melding into the Moorish tiled sanctuary of the Moon's Nest. For a moment Joe basked in the rich, sweet smell of orange blossom, the sound of fountains and evening insects, and then he was back in the blackness of Master Jack's forgotten bedchamber. Shivering in the coldness, the boy quickened his pace and within moments travelled centuries forward into the Japanese teahouse vivarium, its crystal mountain throbbing within its ancient bookcase. And from there, the monochrome panels slid and transmuted to the rustic wood of the Canadian cabin in the woods, filled as it was with the life of the trapper and his Cree wife. The journey filled Joe with wonder, showing in more than words just how far he had travelled. Then the cabin was gone and he was walking through the courtyard behind the cottage of Tigh Samhraidh, then through the bathroom of the converted Norwegian lighthouse. His mind overspilled with memories of the captain and Evangeline, of the ship and the cave of crystals. How could there be so much magic in the world? So much hidden joy and dear friends, just waiting to be discovered. The humid cream kitchen at Manse L'Estrange came next, where he had met the wilful maid and spoken to the first of the three trees. Wishing, Kissing, Killing, he thought. It's like an entire life in three words. The watchtower came next, the stone room stuffed with all the comforts of the Victorian age, and then even that was gone and he was descending the stone stairs in the Palazzo di Ombre. Saturn looked down upon him with unreadable eyes as if imparting some last shred of knowledge or instruction, and then he emerged from the rectory porch onto the red-brick pathways of the labyrinth garden. He walked towards the arched gate in the tall trimmed hedge, then stopped and pulled *The Stranger's Guide* from his pack. Reluctantly, deferentially, he placed the great scrapbook inside the doorway, to make sure it was found when the next traveller passed that way.

Sighing, he turned and carried on, taking the last steps along the labyrinth back to the exact point where he had begun all those centuries ago. The harvest festival garden, filled with autumn colour and vegetables, was a splendid sight, but then even this faded and, with a lurch, Joe stepped back through the crack in the night and found himself walking out of the tipi that stood in the very centre of the green. It was night and around him stood the ring of ordinary houses. To his left the black car swept slowly along, searching for him. There ahead were the overgrown gardens of the derelict council house. In the darkness he made out the living spider's web of the hedge choked with brambles, his bike and the raven's dark shape on the edge of the pavement. He had returned to the exact moment he had begun. The very second he had entered the house.

For one splinter of time, a sudden wracking pain coursed through him. Like the worst stitch. Like his bones and muscles were being stretched on a rack. Then, with a sudden terrifying feeling, he realised he was aging. Just like the villager at the Cambodian temple. Instantly the raven's words from the palazzo came back into his head.

How old will I be at the end of this journey?

That depends how fast you can run.

Joe ran.

O

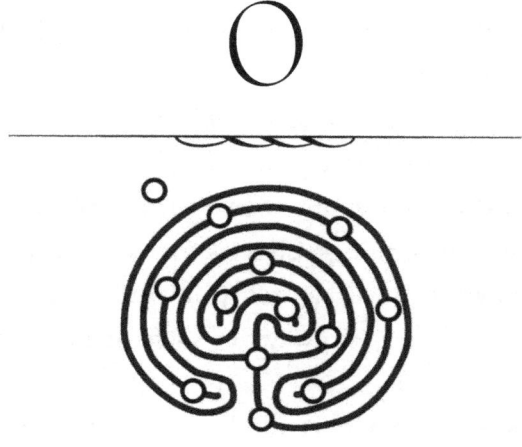

ALL GODS' DAY (MIDNIGHT)
NO. 51 NEWTON GREEN
GREAT DUNMOW, ESSEX, UNITED KINGDOM
NOW

WITH ALL THE STRENGTH IN his aching muscles, Joe bolted for the house. Trying to keep out of the sweeping headlights. Trying to reach it before time caught up with him and he died. Up ahead the car's lights illuminated the raven. Griswald took flight, a swift silhouette against the brightness then vanished. The pain in Joe's arms and legs was excruciating. It was only a short distance – fifty metres, maybe less – but it felt further than the other side of the moon. He began that run as a boy yet by the time he reached the edge of the green, he was a young man. And by the time he reached the gate, he was even older. Joe didn't stop. He careened into the hedge and burst through, almost knocking over the dark figure who hid there. With a cry, the shape leapt from the undergrowth and whirled to confront him. It was Gunner, his hairless face snarling from beneath his dark hoodie.

"Don't move a muscle," Joe said.

The teenage thug leapt out of his skin, then filled the air with curses. "Who in hell are you?"

He doesn't recognise me at all, thought Joe.

"Hello, Scott. I'm a friend of your sister."

"What? How'd you know my name? How'd you know her?"

"Oh, I know a lot of things. Like I know what you did to Lakelyn and why she ran away. But I can tell you, you're wrong. Your sister is not in this house. She's far, far away. She's safe in a place you can never reach her."

"You lying snake!" Suddenly the knife was in Gunner's hand. Joe reached out and took it from him. It was like taking a stick from a dog's mouth. Joe drew back his arm and threw it high into the air. It flashed in the orange street lights, then was gone.

"Fetch, boy," said Joe, and Gunner fled. Bursting from the hedge, the frightened youth ran clean across the road and straight into the path of the black car. Brakes screeched, shrill as a bird's call. The driver tried to stop, but the distance was too short, the runner too slow. Gunner collided with the car, was knocked to the ground. For a moment he lay there, then shock and panic forced him up and he was gone, limping into the inky night.

Joe stood under the arch of ruptured hedge and watched as the bald-headed driver got out and inspected his bonnet. He didn't look like one of the Ghûl, but Joe knew that looks could be deceptive. The man bent down and retrieved something from the road. It was Gunner's bag. He walked around the front of the car to the rear passenger door and opened it. Inside golden light spilled from floor-mounted bulbs, illuminating a plush red leather interior. On the back seat sat a man and a woman, and Joe was shocked to realise he knew them both.

It was Nirromelhe and Jin-Lin. The Black King of the Maje was dressed in an immaculate blue suit, while his queen was all in cream. Seeing Joe, her face broke into the widest smile anyone could ever have. Set within a panel on the seat between them was the last shard of magical crystal.

"My, my," said Nirromelhe, "haven't we grown?"

"Hello, son," said the White Queen of the Maje.

"Jin-Lin?" Joe asked.

"I am now," she said, "but once I was Virginia-Lynne Darkin. Your mother."

In a weird way, at that moment everything made sense to the young man. Not logically, but emotionally. Magically. He saw the shrine maiden holding the message in the salt-caked bottle. Telling him how any mother would want to read those words. Yes, it was her, but that only sparked darker questions.

"Why did you leave me?" Joe asked. "What mother could do that?"

"I thought you were dead. We were in Peru and you were just a baby…" The boy knew this was true. He had seen it. "I saw you swept off the ledge. You fell into the fire…" Jin-Lin faltered, the memories intensely painful. Nirromelhe reached out and took her hands.

"How did you find me?" asked Joe, hating having to question her but needing to know.

Composing herself, she answered, "When I found the message in the bottle, I knew you were alive. I began to search for you. The Medicine obscured your where and when, so I waited for you to be revealed."

"But, the waystation? I met you there?"

His mother's features clouded with remorse. "By then I had long stopped looking. I no more recognised you than I would a stranger."

Joe was hit with a sudden image of figures moving in the trees, through the bushes. Of the word 'Today' written on the calendar page.

"It was you at the barbecue and the roundabout. It wasn't the Ghûl. I didn't take my medicine and you found me."

"Yes," said Jin-Lin, her eyes brimming with tears. "And now I'm here. I came as fast as I could, but you ran into the labyrinth and we lost you again…"

"But now you're back," said Nirromelhe.

"Mum, I'm so, so sorry." Now Joe was crying too, aching to be with her. Numbly, he took a step out from under the hedge and through the gateway.

"Cr-r-ruck!" Griswald was suddenly upon his shoulder, warning him. "You do know that you cannot leave the house now," the raven said sternly.

"Why?" he asked.

"You have walked paths from 1852 to 2282 and back again. You have travelled with the fayre, lost your reflection, shadow and life to gain entrance to the lost room and return here. Those are not the sort of things that human bodies are up to handling." Joe thought of batty old Granny Em in the cottage of Tigh Samhraidh. Of the madness of his stepmother. Of the dead hanging in the branches of the Killing Tree. He realised the raven spoke the truth. He couldn't leave the house now, just as they could not leave the protection of the crystal. If they did all those hundreds upon hundreds of years would be realised in one single moment.

The gulf between the vehicle and the gate was barely three metres. It might as well have been the distance between the stars.

"Father knew," he said. "He sent me to you. In the bus from Whiskey Jack's cabin. He said he was sending me to someone who could save me."

"Did he now?" replied his mother in surprise. "Well, from where I'm sitting, you did that all by yourself." Jin-Lin wiped her eyes. "Remember what you wrote to me: 'it's never too late to have a happy life.'"

Within the car, the crystal shuddered and Griswald let out a heart-stopping cry.

"We have to go," said his mother stiffly.

"But, you can't," Joe stammered. "You only just got here."

"You know where I'll be," the White Queen said as the driver slipped back into his seat and the car's engine roared into life. "You know the way and how to get there. I will be waiting for you, I promise. But here and now you have a far greater task. You need to guard and protect the labyrinth for all those who need to walk its path. Do you understand?"

"Yes," said her son.

"And, son?"

"Yes?"

"The reason you were ordinary, Joe, was because you didn't believe you could be extraordinary. You were extraordinary to me. Always."

Joseph Darkin watched as she bowed to him, then closed the door and the black car pulled away. Joe looked up to stop the tears from rolling down his face. Above the night was clear and though there were stars, the Dead Moon hung invisible in the sky above. Hiding in plain sight.

Joe dragged his bike through the hedge and forced the gate as closed as he could get it. Then he began walking slowly towards the dark shadow of the small house. How can that entire world be in there? he thought to himself. After a dozen steps he trod on something in the dirt, something that cracked and splintered under his feet. Reaching down through the weeds he found it was the Wolverine action figure, lying on a rotten FOR SALE sign.

Who would want to buy this dump? he thought, then smiled a wide smile.

Stepping into the tall grass, he bent down to dig in the wet dirt under the sign. A hand's width below the surface he touched something solid. Clawing at the soil, he revealed the fallen standing stone, brushed aside the grime and dirt to reveal part of the engraved labyrinth. From within the medicine bag around his neck, the shadowstone glowed like a sunrise.

Looking up at the building, he announced, "It's been here all the time. I just couldn't see it until now."

Joe knew what he had to do. It was as clear and obvious as his previous life had been uncertain and meaningless. He should do as his mother had said. His true mother. Embrace all. Follow none. Why couldn't he become Prince of the Eternal Forest? Why couldn't anyone become absolutely anything?

"Because they do not believe they can," said the raven at his ear.

"The secret lies within," said Joe.

"As I live and breathe," said the bird, "I think he's got it."

The boy knew now that true magic existed inside everyone, and that it was by far the greatest power of all. He would live here in this old abandoned house upon the edge of the magical labyrinth of ancient *Tal Istia'on*.

Hiding in plain sight.

Waiting for the next child to find its entrance.

ACKNOWLEDGEMENTS

No hero completes his quest alone, and that's doubly true of authors and books. Writers need others to inspire, to encourage, to go on long walks endlessly discussing character, scene and plot. And, in the case of this tale, there's the twenty-five-year task of building the house and gardens in the first place. To say this is anything short of a life's work is understatement.

Imagining, writing and bringing Talliston into reality has been a long process, and in the thirty-five years since having the idea of taking the house I could afford and building inside the world I wanted to live in, I have been guided and encouraged by some amazing people. So:

To my mother and father, Jean and Ron, who have supported the craziness of their eldest son without question through every day that I've lived. Without your encouragement, I wouldn't have written a word or wired a single plug.

To Bryn Bardsley, Lin Bardsley, Marcus Cotton, Michelle Garrett, Susan Mac Nicol, Linda Stratmann and Sarah Wragg. Your friendship, help and honesty have each had a profound effect on my life and writing, and could not fail to inspire the characters herein.

To Grace James (née Maxwell), my primary school teacher, for her inspiring words of wisdom in my hymn book and in all things Welsh.

To my editors Anna Simpson and Ella Chappell, Justine Taylor, Hugh Davies, Hayley Shepherd, Alex Eccles and Sarah Bance.

To the one hundred and thirty-eight friends, family, artisans, builders and volunteers who helped transform the UK's most ordinary house into Britain's most extraordinary home. And to the many people, most especially Gail Courtney and Kathy Westhead, whose generosity saved the project from being sold to strangers.

To John Tode, who was the Knowing of the Raven, and John Trevillian, who was the Doing of the Eagle. Only through you could there be me, the Being of the Owl.

Embrace All. Follow None. And always remember: Within the labyrinth you do not lose yourself. You find yourself...

ABOUT THE AUTHOR

John Tarrow was born in London and spent his childhood with a Smith-Corona Calypso typewriter and a wild imagination, both of which he still owns. Now a novelist, poet, storyteller and award-winning writer, his fascination with folk and faerie tales has taken him around the world, gathering threads of story and legend to weave into his own mythologies. His extensive studies in Lakota Sioux and Druidic traditions offer readers stories resonant with magic, folklore and the wonders of the natural world.

As creative lead at Talliston House & Gardens, John's transformation of the house and gardens showcases his ability to design extraordinary locations in the most ordinary of places. Using objects sourced from around the world, these spaces tell incredibly powerful and timeless stories.

The author wishes when he was thirteen he could have discovered Talliston and read this book – because at its heart is the idea that built the entire house: that with inner belief, we can all achieve extraordinary things.

Visit www.talliston.com for related material and the latest information about the author and his other adventures.

ABOUT THE
HOUSE & GARDENS

Did you realise the locations of this book exist within a quite remarkable real house and gardens?

Welcome to Talliston, a twenty-five-year project that took the UK's most ordinary house and transformed it, room by room, by ordinary people on an ordinary budget, into Britain's Most Extraordinary Home.

Starting as a three-bedroomed, semi-detached, ex-council house in Essex, today not a single square centimetre of the original house remains. In its place is an extraordinary labyrinth of locations, each set in different times and places.

This incredible and inspirational journey began when John realised the house that he wanted to live in and the house he could afford were very far apart. The project was his way of putting those two things together.

Each room was deconstructed back to the brickwork and rebuilt from scratch, and now completed not one square centimetre of the original house remains, neither inside nor out. By walking from room to room, you find yourself leaving the present, and entering the past (and even at one point entering the future). So you too can follow Joe Darkin's journey through the labyrinth – all just by opening the house's many doors and seeing what lies behind them.

To find out more about this incredible project or to visit the house and gardens, go to www.talliston.com